Betty Walker lives in Cornwall with her large family, where she enjoys gardening and coastal walks. She loves discovering curious historical facts, and devotes much time to investigating her family tree. She also writes bestselling contemporary thrillers as Jane Holland.

Brighter Days for the Cornish Girls is the eighth novel in Betty Walker's heart-warming series.

Readers have fallen for the Cornish Girls

'A fascinating story, beautifully written, with interesting characters I really liked. A most enjoyable read!'
Kitty Neale

'A warm-hearted story – at times I laughed and at others I held my breath . . . I loved the characters and I'm delighted it is the first in a series'
Pam Weaver

'Much loved characters that will stay with you, due to their courage, determination and patriotic spirit'
******* Reader Review**

'Beautifully written and totally draws you in from the beginning'
******* Reader Review**

'A poignant and all-round heart-warming saga'
******* Reader Review**

'Truly beautiful historical fiction. What a wonderful cast of characters to meet!'
******* Reader Review**

The Cornish Girls series:

Wartime with the Cornish Girls
Christmas with the Cornish Girls
Courage for the Cornish Girls
A Mother's Hope for the Cornish Girls
A Wedding for the Cornish Girls
Victory for the Cornish Girls
A New Hope for the Cornish Girls

Brighter Days for the Cornish Girls

BETTY WALKER

avon.

Published by AVON
A division of HarperCollins*Publishers*
1 London Bridge Street
London SE1 9GF

www.harpercollins.co.uk

HarperCollins*Publishers*
Macken House, 39/40 Mayor Street Upper
Dublin 1
D01 C9W8

A Paperback Original 2025
2
First published in Great Britain by HarperCollins*Publishers* 2025

A catalogue copy of this book is available from the British Library.

ISBN: 978-0-00-871514-4

This novel is entirely a work of fiction. The names, characters and incidents portrayed in it are the work of the author's imagination. Any resemblance to actual persons, living or dead, events or localities is entirely coincidental.

Typeset in Minion Pro by Palimpsest Book Production Limited, Falkirk, Stirlingshire

Printed and bound in the United States

Dedicated with grateful admiration to the real-life Cornish Girls – those 1940s women, young and old, whose courage and resilience inspired these stories

CHAPTER ONE

September 1946, Porthcurno, South Cornwall

Sheila was working up a sweat in the warm sunshine, vigorously cleaning the windows of her shop, when the bus from Penzance lumbered into view and stopped just opposite. A young woman jumped down and stood blinking about herself at the tiny Cornish village of Porthcurno as the bus trundled on noisily without her, soon disappearing up the other side of the valley.

Dropping the dirty washcloth back into her bucket of suds, Sheila looked this stranger up and down, and then grinned. She couldn't recall seeing someone from the Caribbean since she'd left Dagenham, where some of her regulars at the caff had come from big, lively Jamaican families.

As the young woman turned towards her, Sheila gave her a friendly nod. 'Hello, Miss, you here on your holidays? Bit late in the season for dipping your toes, but the beach is that way.' Helpfully, she pointed down the track that ran past Eastern House towards the beach. Most of the ugly great sea defences had been dismantled since the war, so it was no longer impossible to get onto the white sands for a bathe. But the path was still cluttered with posts and barbed wire from the soldiers' encampment, making it hazardous. 'Best watch your step, though.'

The young woman wore her shoulder-length hair tied back tightly, a huge smile dominating her striking face. Under her coat, a smart cream and beige dress fell to her knees, and she wore sturdy boots on her feet that looked clean and never worn before. She was carrying a small, battered suitcase and a handbag that bulged.

As she stopped in front of Sheila, she replied without any sign of shyness, 'Good morning. I wish I *was* here for the beach. Sounds lovely. But I'm looking for Postbridge Farm. Do you know it?' Her accent was unusual, a mixture of a faint Caribbean lilt with a distinctly northern twang. Liverpudlian?

'Do I know it? I live there, love.' Sheila studied her closely and then laughed in surprise. 'Gawd, I know who you are. You'll be the new girl they've sent from the Women's Land Army to replace Joan.'

'That's right.' The young woman put down her case. 'Are you Mrs Postbridge, then?'

'No, she's my daughter. The farmer – Joe Postbridge – is my son-in-law. But what's your name?'

The young woman smiled, putting out a hand. 'Grace Morgan.'

'Grace? What a lovely name. Welcome to Porthcurno, Miss Morgan.' Sheila wiped wet palms on her pinny before shaking the girl's hand. 'Sorry, I've been washing the windows . . . I'm Mrs Newton. I run the village shop.'

'So this is your place? Yours and Mr Newton's?'

'Lord bless you, my Arnie's been dead and buried this past year. It's my name above the door now.' Sheila nodded to the sign above the village shop which read, *Mrs S. Newton, Proprietor*. 'Though you're right, this *was* his shop. But I felt Arnie would have wanted me to carry on running it for the sake of the village.' She grinned. 'So here I am, doling out veg and Cornish pasties to all comers. Plus a pinch of baccy for those partial to it.'

'Well, I'm glad Porthcurno has a little shop.' The new Land Girl looked surprised but pleased by this information, peering past her through the soapy windows. 'I was worried I'd need to take the bus to Penzance to go shopping. And that rickety old bus nearly shook all me bones to pieces on the way here, so I wasn't keen to repeat the experience.'

The girl had an odd turn of phrase, which suited the striking accent, and Sheila liked it. 'If there's anything we don't have in stock, I can put in a special order,' she told her proudly. 'You might have to wait a few days, but I can get most things. Even nylons, now the war's over.'

'I don't bother much with nylons, to be honest,' Grace said conspiratorially, lowering her voice, even though there was hardly anybody around on the main village street. 'Not much call for them on a farm, is there? I've three pairs of socks in my suitcase. That'll do me just fine.' She paused. 'Do you sell yarn for darning, though? Between you and me, one of them socks is on its way out. Got a ruddy big hole in the toe, if you'll pardon me French. I keep getting my toe stuck in it, and that's not funny when you're digging a ditch and there's still five hours of daylight before you can go home and change your socks.'

'Yes, love,' Sheila said, chuckling at this comical rush of words, 'I can sell you a card of yarn right now, if you like.'

'Maybe next time.' Grace pulled a face, glancing at her luggage. 'I'm already laden down as it is. If I was to add any more to this lot, it'd likely prove the yarn that broke the camel's back. How far a walk is this farm, then?'

'Ten to fifteen minutes, depending how often you need to stop for a breather. It's quite a steep hill, you see.'

Grace followed her pointing arm out of the village, her eyes widening. 'All the way up there? Saints alive . . . I'll be lucky if I reach the farm by next week, let alone fifteen minutes.'

Old Mr Faragher, who usually popped into the shop about that time, came ambling down from his cottage during this lively conversation and stopped dead in astonishment, staring at the young black woman standing in the middle of Porthcurno village. His eyes bulged as though he'd never seen such a sight in his life, which perhaps he hadn't, and then he whipped off his cap in hurried respect.

'Well, I never,' he croaked in his rusty old voice, looking Grace up and down, 'you're not from hereabouts.' He glanced slyly at Sheila. 'Morning, Mrs Newton. Lovely day, isn't it?' He paused. 'Friend of yours?'

'She's from the Land Army, Mr Faragher,' Sheila said, raising her voice as she knew he had trouble with his hearing. 'She's come to work at the farm with Joe and the other girls.'

'Ah . . . Replacing that Joan girl who up and married Arthur Green out of the blue? Bit of a rush job, that wedding.' He waited with interest, but Sheila didn't rise to the bait. 'I hope she can sort out that young man's problems.'

'I'm sure Joan can.'

He turned his cap in his hands, still staring at Grace. 'Well, this is a turn-up.' But he nodded to her in a cheerful enough manner. 'Welcome to Porthcurno, Miss. Where are you from, then?'

'Liverpool.'

This silenced him.

Picking up her suitcase again, Grace turned to Sheila with a wink and another of her beaming smiles. 'I'd best be on my way or my arms are going to drop off. You say you live up there at Postbridge Farm? And your daughter's the farmer's wife? I'll see you later, then?'

'For supper, yes. Though you can remind my daughter not to wait for me but to leave my supper on the range if I'm late. I've a council meeting first, you see.'

Sheila gave her clear directions to the farm, and she and Mr Faragher watched as Grace trudged off up the sunny hill in her sturdy, new-looking boots. *She'll be getting blisters in those*, Sheila thought wisely.

The old man cleared his throat, catching her eye. 'Did you happen to get that new delivery of baccy in yet, Mrs Newton? That nice leaf I like?'

'I did, Mr Faragher,' Sheila agreed, and led him into the shop.

As Sheila was closing up, half an hour earlier than usual, she turned to her sister Margaret, who now lived above the shop and helped her run the place. 'I hope that new Land Girl will fit in all right.' She had already told Margaret about the young woman with the strong Liverpudlian accent. 'You should have seen old Mr Faragher's face . . . He won't keep it to himself, of course. The whole village will be talking about her by tomorrow, you mark my words.' She flipped the hanging shop sign from OPEN to CLOSED. 'Thing is, he didn't mean any harm by staring. We don't see much excitement down here, do we? And Porthcurno's been bloomin' quiet this year.' She grinned, remembering the chaos of her first few months in Cornwall, keeping house for her daughter Violet and her orphaned nieces Lily and Alice, the three of them somehow always getting into trouble. 'Though we had our hands full during the war, didn't we?'

'It must be a year at least since the soldiers left who were guarding Eastern House.' Margaret put away her broom. Her face was wistful. 'I don't miss the war. Who could? A government listening post on our doorstep, Germans bombing us nightly, and never knowing if we were about to be invaded and rounded up by men in jackboots . . . But it was *exciting*, I'll say that for it. These days,' she added defiantly, 'the most excitement I get is when that nice Mr Lister comes in for a few rashers of streaky bacon.'

Sheila flashed her a look but didn't pass comment. Her sister was in the middle of seeking a divorce from an abusive husband, but she wouldn't be free to look elsewhere for some years if Stanley Chellew continued to ignore her solicitor's letters.

'When I was running that caff in Dagenham,' she recalled, 'we had a Jamaican family just down the street from us. They were always coming in for a nice cuppa and a slice of my home-made ginger cake. Oh, they were lovely people. In fact, the grandma, Judith, used to share family recipes with me. I've still got 'em somewhere. Spicy, mind you. But tasty with it.' She smacked her lips with nostalgia. 'Gawd, it must be years since I made a proper Jamaican dish.'

'You said she was from Liverpool.' Maggie looked mystified.

'Yes,' Sheila said patiently, 'but her looks are Caribbean, by my reckoning. I could be wrong. But I'm sure Grace will tell us all about herself and her family once she's settled in at the farm.'

Unfastening her work apron, her sister nudged her. 'Hullo, look at that.' A car had just pulled up outside the shop. 'That'll be your fancy man, come to whisk you away for another evening of pleasure.'

Sure enough, Bernie had arrived in his swish Daimler and was parking opposite. Hurriedly, Sheila patted her wayward greying hair and reapplied her lippy in the mirror. 'Hardly pleasure, Mags,' she hissed. 'He's taking me to the council meeting tonight, then driving me home afterwards. He's a gent though, ain't he? I don't mind a good walk, as you know, but it's been getting too bloomin' cold lately, and we likely won't be finished before it's dark.'

'What on earth do you councillors find to jar on about for so many hours? Sounds like a dead bore to me.'

'The posh ones do love to talk,' Sheila admitted. 'La-di-da this, la-di-da that. Sometimes I have to pinch meself so I don't nod off. Still, we get a few good things done for the community, despite all the airs and graces,' she added, dropping her lipstick back into her handbag as her suitor came strolling across to the shop. 'And that's why I'm there, ain't it? To help all of us villagers. Not for the bleedin' cake.'

With a shy smile, Sheila opened the door to Bernie. She still wasn't sure if their courtship was serious or not. Both widowed, both past sixty, they ought not to be messing about like a couple of kids. But even at school she'd liked Bernie – before her parents had dragged her away to Dagenham, leaving her older sister behind to get married – and he still had the same gentle way about him. Besides which, he was always punctual – a strong point in his favour. But then, the old boy was retired, unlike her. If he had a village shop to run, he'd probably look a sight more flustered . . . Like she did, in fact.

'Nice to see you again, Bernie. This is very kind of you. Though I haven't had time to do my hair properly,' she added awkwardly.

'You look marvellous, as always,' Bernie assured her. 'Just the thing.'

Margaret rolled her eyes but said nothing.

Sheila pulled on her coat, said a prim goodbye to her sister, and followed him out to the car, knotting a headscarf under her chin.

Bernie was looking his usual smart and dapper self in a charcoal-grey, double-breasted suit, though it wouldn't do to tell him so. They might be courting, but she didn't want him taking liberties. Or getting the idea she was sweet on him. She was, of course. But that was *her* business.

At the council meeting, Sheila and Bernie walked in together but sat a few seats apart from each other. This was a policy she'd insisted on after being co-opted onto the council earlier that year. It wasn't a secret that they were stepping out together. But she didn't feel they ought to be rubbing people's faces in it by sitting next to each other at council meetings. Bernie was Chair of the Parish Council, and she herself was now chairing the newly formed Community Committee, tasked with administering a fund for the poor and needy thereabouts.

The local fund was her own idea, and she was bloomin' proud of it. But she didn't want folk getting the wrong end of the stick. It would be too easy to assume she'd wheedled her way onto the council because Bernie was her beau. And her daughter Violet, a stickler for 'respectable' behaviour, would be livid if she thought villagers were gossiping behind their backs . . .

'Mrs Newton, how are plans coming along for your charity event?' Mrs Brewer asked when the agenda turned towards the ongoing work of Sheila's special Community Committee.

The 'charity event' in question was due to be held in December, though the date was still a bit woolly.

'Erm, not too bad, thanks,' Sheila replied croakily, conscious of all eyes turning to her, and cleared her throat.

To her embarrassment, she'd caught herself using a less Dagenham accent when at council meetings, overawed by the posher ladies with their big hats and flashy jewellery. But Bernie had assured her it was perfectly reasonable to want to fit in, confiding that he'd been doing the same for years, concealing humble origins with a smart suit and a cut-glass voice like one of them BBC presenters off the wireless.

'It's meant to bring people together,' she went on, 'and a chance for us to talk to them in need . . . I mean, *those* in need without intruding by going to their homes. We ain't . . . That is, we *haven't* managed to find a suitable venue yet,' she said, straining to sound her 'h' properly, like the others did. 'But we're still asking around.'

'And what will the event entail?' Mrs Brewer asked.

Sheila said awkwardly, 'Well, we ain't exactly sure . . . I mean to say, we *haven't* made a decision on that yet.'

'I believe you need more volunteers to sit on the committee,' Bernie put in, his smile encouraging. 'Isn't that right?'

'Yes.' Sheila looked pleadingly around at the other councillors. 'There's only three of us at the moment. And we're stretched thin. So if anyone would like to join us . . .'

Nobody said anything. Several people shuffled their papers. One gentleman produced a hanky and blew his nose.

'Perhaps you could ask customers at the shop,' Bernie suggested. 'There might be villagers willing to come on board. I'm on several committees already, otherwise I'd gladly lend a hand.'

Sheila threw him a grateful look. It was as plain as the nose on her face that the other councillors wanted nothing to do with her fund to help the needy. She'd have to look further afield for people to help with the committee work, that was all.

But her heart sank. If she couldn't persuade a single one of these councillors to muck in with the arrangements, how on earth was she to recruit anyone else?

Bernie drove her back to Postbridge Farm once the council meeting had ended. Sheila was dog-tired after a long day on her feet in the shop, but at least the meeting had not run on like so many of them did, which meant she was still in time to sit down for supper with the others.

'Thanks for the lift, Bernie,' she said, peering out at the farmyard, where a few hens were still pecking interestedly at the cobbles, not yet having been encouraged into the coop for the night. 'Have you bought a ticket to the Harvest

Supper? Violet and the girls are helping out with the food. So it should be a nice spread this year.'

'Wild horses couldn't drag me away.' His eyes paused on her face, softening. 'Sheila, I've been meaning to ask . . . Where do you think all this is going, for you and I? We've been courting a good few months now, but I'm still not sure where I stand.'

'You're not standing anywhere. You're sitting.'

He chuckled. 'You can always make me laugh. I love that about you. But, seriously, if I was to give you a goodnight kiss right now, would I be risking a slap? I don't want to overstep the mark.'

Sheila felt her cheeks warm. 'Well, I never . . .' She gripped her handbag tightly in her lap. 'You won't get a slap. Bit silly if you can't give me a kiss when we've been walking out together all this time.' But her voice wavered.

She was nervous, that's what it was. Which was ridiculous, given that she'd been married and widowed twice now. She was hardly a spring chicken. And a kiss goodnight after a council meeting was surely not too much to ask for her own beau.

'I'm glad to hear that.' Bernie hesitated, and then leant forward. She tilted her face to his, and their lips met and lingered. Sheila felt a thrill run through her, quite as though she were sixteen, not gone sixty. When he drew back, he was smiling. Getting out, he came around to open the car door for her with a gallant bow, as he always did. 'Goodnight, Sheila.'

'Goodnight then,' she replied unsteadily. 'I'll see you at the Harvest Supper.'

He had already turned his car in the muddy farmyard and was motoring down the hill when she removed her headscarf and coat in the porch and let herself into the warm kitchen. The range was steamy with bubbling pans, kitchen windows misted up. The residents of Postbridge Farm were mostly gathered about the table, chattering noisily as Violet stamped back and forth, grumbling to herself as she prepared their supper.

Sarah Jane, Violet's lively little daughter, was nowhere to be seen, so Sheila guessed she must have already had her tea and gone up to bed.

But Tilly and Caroline, the two Land Girls, were seated at the table, along with her widowed son-in-law Ernest, chatting about the weather. An unusually humdrum conversation for him. Ernest had spied for Britain during the war, mostly behind enemy lines, and had a funny, almost daft way of talking that often left people baffled. Still, her late daughter Betsy had adored him, as did his grown-up daughters, Lily and Alice, so that was enough for her. And since Ernest still worked for the government down in the valley at Eastern House – the wartime listening post – he was welcome to live here with them as long as he liked.

Joe emerged from the snug as Sheila bustled across to grab an apron and help her daughter serve dinner. Surprised, he raised his gaze from the newspaper he'd been reading. 'I thought you were eating supper late tonight, Sheila,' he rumbled, and then cleared his throat. 'It's good to see you back early. But there's not been a place laid for you.'

'I'll sort that out for you, Mrs Newton,' Caroline said promptly. A tall, bouncing, fair-haired girl, she'd been among the first Land Girls to come to Postbridge Farm early in the war, and had been living with them ever since, barring a few trips home to see her folks in Ealing. Other Land Girls had come and gone, but Caroline was almost one of the family now. She fetched a plate and cutlery from the crowded dresser and set them out for Sheila. 'We've had a new Land Girl arrive,' she added, her voice high-pitched with excitement. 'Did you know? I was just about to call her down for supper.'

'Yes, I met her when she was getting off the bus,' Sheila admitted, helping Violet with the heavy oven door. 'You'll be glad to have another pair of hands about the farm, Joe.'

'That I am,' Joe agreed, sharpening the carving knife.

Caroline sniffed the air. Violet had roasted a chicken for dinner, the delicious smell now wafting through the kitchen.

'What did you think of the new girl, Mrs Postbridge?' Caroline asked.

Handling the chicken pan cautiously, Violet glanced round at her, thin brows arched. 'She wasn't what we were expecting, that's for sure. Joe had a letter yesterday, telling us she was due today. Miss Grace Morgan was the name on the paperwork. *Morgan*.' Violet pursed her lips. 'We thought she was Welsh.'

'She's a Liverpudlian,' Tilly said loudly.

'Vi, do you remember a Welshman who used to come into the caff in Dagenham?' Sheila threw in swiftly. She'd heard the creak of the stairs and guessed the new girl must be on her way down to supper. It wouldn't do for the poor girl to hear them gossiping about her. 'Dai, his name was, and he had a dog so small, he carried it around in his pocket.' Sheila strained boiled greens into a colander while Violet carried the rather meagre-looking chicken to the table for Joe to carve, still sizzling in its roasting pan. 'Though it was bigger than that bloomin' bird. My goodness, Violet . . . Where's the rest of that chicken?'

'Just be grateful it's not ox tongue again, Mum,' her daughter muttered, and then everyone fell silent as the door opened and Grace Morgan stood on the threshold.

Joe gave his new Land Girl a welcoming nod, and then returned to his task of carving the chicken.

'Hello again, love,' Sheila said cheerfully and pointed to the empty space between Caroline and Tilly. 'You must be exhausted, poor lamb. Did you come all the way from Liverpool today?'

'Goodness, no. That would have wore me out, and no mistake.' Giving her a nervous smile, Grace climbed over the bench to sit between the other two Land Girls, apparently oblivious to their fascinated stares, and poured herself a glass of water from the jug on the table. 'I got a transfer from a farm upcountry. Just fancied a change of scenery, I suppose.' She glanced at Caroline, jug still poised. 'Care for some water? And you, Tilly?'

'Yes, please,' they both chorused.

Sheila smiled to herself, spooning stewed greens onto her plate and passing the bowl. She needn't have worried earlier. The new girl was already settling in just fine. 'Veg, Joe?'

Joe had finished carving the chicken and was now reading the newspaper. 'Eh?'

Violet clucked her tongue in disapproval. 'No reading at the table, Joe Postbridge.'

'Sorry, love.' Joe folded the newspaper he'd been studying and laid it aside, his look sheepish. 'Football league's started up again. I was just catching up on the latest results.'

Sheila paused, her forkful of chicken almost at her mouth. Her attention had been caught by a story in the local paper, just visible where Joe had folded it over.

FORMER MP TO SET UP PENZANCE HARDSHIP FUND

'I'd like a quick read of that newspaper once you're done,' she told her son-in-law, resisting the urge to grab it up and risk her daughter's ire.

'You keen on football too, Mrs Newton?' Grace asked innocently, and everyone at the table fell about laughing.

'There's your answer, I'd say,' Sheila told her with a wink. But as she was eating, her gaze slid back to the newspaper.

The grainy black-and-white photograph accompanying the story was of a tall, angular woman in a fashionable twinset and pearls, smiling for the camera. A woman who was a former Member of Parliament. In other words, someone as rare as hen's teeth. And she was setting up a hardship fund in Penzance.

If anyone would know how to go about helping the poor and needy of Porthcurno, it would be that woman. But how could Mrs Newton, a nobody from the middle of nowhere, ask for a meeting with someone as lofty as a former Member of Parliament? She'd be sent on her way with a flea in her ear. Wouldn't she?

CHAPTER TWO

Grace, the new Land Girl, was sitting down to eat supper with them for the first time, and it seemed to Caroline, stealing fascinated peeks at her between mouthfuls, that everything had changed in the space of a few hours. Even the cluttered farmhouse kitchen, littered with shepherd's crooks and muddy dogs, looked different and more interesting now that Grace was sitting among them. Her laughter trilled out, so quick and infectious that Caroline found herself grinning every time she heard it. And she wasn't alone in being mesmerised. Her fellow Land Girl, Tilly, seemed enchanted too, twining her red hair round her finger and staring as they listened to the new Land Girl holding forth on every topic, from the weather to her previous work on farms . . .

Back in 1942, when she'd first come to Postbridge Farm, perched precariously on the cliffs above Porthcurno, Caroline had found it difficult to fit in with the other Land Girls. Selina – an elegant blonde, far posher than the rest of them – had been quite mean at times, lording it over them. Unsure how to deal with this, Caroline had developed a thick skin, and even tried to outdo Selina with sarcastic comments and cruel digs, though this had made her uncomfortable. But her ploy had worked faster than even she had expected, and, for a time, she and Selina had become an unstoppable duo. Both pretty and fair-haired, they'd been the golden girls, rulers of the roost.

As the war had dragged on, though, things had begun to fall apart. Penny, the other Land Girl who'd originally been drafted to the farm with them, had grown tired of their well-aimed barbs, and moved away to Bude with Alice, the youngest niece of the farmer's wife, who'd been offered war work there. Then Penny, with her homely charms, had married a rugged Bude fisherman, and Alice had gone away to London on some hush-hush business. The old gang had broken up for good.

For a spell, she and Selina had worked the land alone together, growing closer than ever. But that very closeness had worked against them in the end. Over time, Caroline had developed feelings for her best friend, and they had not been reciprocated. It had all become rather hurtful and embarrassing, and also difficult to hide from Joan and Tilly, the other two Land Girls who'd eventually joined them at Postbridge Farm. Then Caroline's heart had been shattered to pieces when Selina left the farm for the wilds of Bodmin Moor to care for her dying sister.

It had been months since Selina had left. After her sister Bella had sadly died, Selina had resolved to stay on and look after her nephew and two young nieces. Caroline had visited, but had found Selina much changed since her sister's death, more mature and focused on her new family.

It had been hard at first, but Caroline had gradually made peace with the idea that there would never be anything between them now but friendship.

She was trying to stay happy and busy all the same, and to be a reliable member of the farming team. She wrote to Selina weekly, to tell her what they were doing on the farm, about the weather and the pigs, and all the goings-on in Porthcurno. And although Joan had now left the farm to get married, there was still fun, lively Tilly to keep her company and make her laugh.

But inside her heart was broken.

One day, she would be over Selina and able to move on with her life. That day had not yet arrived. Until it did, though, she would keep smiling and carrying on with her duties as though everything was fine.

The list of her tasks was long and included mucking out the pigsty and the chicken coop, brushing down old Barney, the sturdy shire horse who did the work of Joe's old tractor when it was off the road, digging muddy trenches and mending fences, chitting potatoes and harvesting cabbages, and sometimes even helping with the sheep shearing, though Joe usually did that himself with the help of a few stout boys from the village, as it demanded great physical strength.

But she knew her job inside out, and could almost have dug a ditch in the dark. Indeed, Caroline could scarcely remember a time when she hadn't been a Land Girl.

Of course, it was only about four years since she'd first enlisted in the Women's Land Army and received her draft papers, sending her to Postbridge Farm, here on the wild and rural south-west coast of Cornwall. Yet it felt more like a lifetime. Her happy childhood, spent at the family home in Ealing, West London, seemed far-off and dreamlike now.

Then the war had miraculously ended in 1945. Everyone had been so overjoyed. She and the other Land Girls had danced in the fields and drunk wine out of wellington boots, foolishly expecting their lives to revert overnight to how they'd been before war broke out.

But nothing had changed, not essentially. The soldiers had mostly stayed abroad to clean up the mess from the carnage left behind by the war machine, while here at home, their work on the farm had continued just the same. Except now they weren't digging for victory, they were digging for the survivors.

She'd begun to think her life would be one long, dreary round of early mornings and digging for potatoes. So it had been a strange shock to hear Violet Postbridge, the farmer's wife, talking to someone on the landing outside her attic-room door, and to poke her head round the door, expecting to see Tilly there, only to be confronted with a girl she had never seen before in her life.

And what an unusual girl! Dark-skinned, dark-haired, with eyes that sparkled with friendly humour when Caroline stopped dead on the threshold, staring.

'Hullo,' the young woman had said.

'Oh, erm, goodness, hullo!' Caroline had heard herself stutter. 'I'm sorry . . . I thought you were Tilly. She went out to feed the pigs and she's been gone ever so long. I thought she must've fallen over in the mud again . . .'

She'd blushed, seeing Mrs Postbridge stare at her in astonishment, but the girl had merely grinned at this stammering nonsense, seeming unfazed by it.

'Sorry,' Caroline had repeated breathlessly. 'I don't usually lollygag about the farmhouse like this in the middle of the day. It's just I'd finished my chores for the morning and Mr Postbridge – that's the farmer – said I could come back to write a letter to my friend Selina before lunch.' Then she'd blinked, realising she ought to introduce herself. 'I'm Caroline Ponsby.'

'Grace Morgan, pleased to meet you.' The young woman's handshake was bold and confident, her grin widening. 'I know, I've got a strong accent. It's not my fault, though. I come from a village near Liverpool. There must be something in the water there, because we all talk like this thereabouts. Well, my dad does, because he was born on the banks of the Mersey, or so he's always saying, and I suppose I got the accent from him. You get used to it after a bit. At least, I hope you will . . . Otherwise, we'll be having some very short conversations.'

Taken aback by that flood of information, Caroline had laughed, and then had stood and listened intently as Mrs Postbridge showed the new Land Girl into her room next door. It was the room that Joan had occupied before she'd left to get married. Now a new girl would be living there . . .

None of them had wanted Joan to leave the farm, though she'd been quieter than a mouse and rarely joined in with their expeditions to the picture house in Penzance or to any local dances. But she'd always pulled her weight and never said a mean word to any of them.

But Joan's young man, Arthur Green, had needed her more than they did. Not to grow crops or muck out pigs, but to be his 'friend and helpmate', as Joan herself had described it a few days before their wedding, while poor

Arthur struggled to get past his awful experiences in the war.

After Mrs Postbridge had shown Grace her room, and discussed rent, uniforms and the rules of the house, she'd left Caroline to show her about the rest of the farm.

They'd walked across the farmyard, Grace telling a funny anecdote about her train journey to Penzance, and met young Tilly leaving the pigsty, empty swill bucket in hand.

'Who's this?' Tilly had asked in blank astonishment, and then beamed when she discovered who she was. 'Gosh, how marvellous . . .' She'd pumped Grace's hand enthusiastically before realising her glove was filthy. 'Oops, sorry.'

'That's all right,' Grace had insisted, wrinkling her nose while producing a hanky to wipe her dirty palm. 'Farms are all about muck, aren't they? Can't have one without the other.'

'I suppose not.' Tilly had bitten her lip, looking contrite. 'I say, why don't you come and meet the pigs? They do smell dreadful, but they're awfully good fun.' As they'd hung on the iron gate, gazing down into the pigsty at the young pigs grunting and snuffling, she'd added joyfully, 'Oh, I'm *so* glad you're here. Caro and I have been doing the work of three for absolutely yonks. Now the time will just fly by.'

To Caroline, though, it seemed as though time were standing still. At least, that first evening meal with Grace went on far longer than usual, with everyone reluctant to leave the table even after they'd finished their dessert of bread and butter pudding, too entertained by lurid tales of her previous experience as a Land Girl to stop listening and head up to bed for the night.

'It's quite rural where I was brought up,' Grace explained, leaning both elbows on the table, without Mrs Postbridge telling her off even once for bad manners, 'so it wasn't too much of a shock to find myself on a farm for the first time ever. But I was only just out of school, and I swear, I had no idea how to milk a cow.' She looked round at them all. 'Now don't laugh. But, to be honest, I didn't even know that's where milk came from.'

'Eh?' Joe scratched his head, clearly perplexed. 'Where did you think it came from, then?'

'A bottle,' Grace told him, chuckling at her own naivety. 'Well, you can imagine my surprise when the farmer handed me a bucket and a three-legged stool and pointed me towards a ruddy great cow, saying, "Milk her!" I was that confused, I was tugging on the poor animal's tail for the first half-hour.' And everyone roared with laughter.

The clock chimed ten, yet nobody moved towards the stairs, except Mrs Postbridge, who went up briefly to check on her little girl. Mr Fisher, Alice's dad, produced a deck of cards, and Joe brought out a book of matches, and they played a lively game of three-card brag for matchsticks.

Halfway through this epic game, Mrs Newton announced that she would open a bottle of her home-made sloe wine, since it was such a special occasion, and soon everyone had a small glass of the near-lethal concoction at their elbow.

Grace gasped and choked at her first mouthful of Mrs Newton's famously potent sloe wine, while they all watched in expectant silence.

But the new Land Girl soon rallied, and even asked for a second helping, adding in a faint voice, 'Only, make it a thimbleful this time, please,' so that Joe gave a guffaw and Mr Fisher rocked back and forth, thumping the table in his mirth.

Eventually, this impromptu party was broken up by the overhead light going out abruptly. Everyone groaned. But Mrs Newton said it was for the best, as they would need to be up early as usual in the morning.

'Is it a power cut?' Grace asked in surprise as Mrs Postbridge brought out a handful of old candle stumps to light them to bed. 'I thought it was only big towns that were getting blackouts.'

'Bless you, no,' Mrs Newton exclaimed, a shadowy figure at the foot of the stairs. 'They're worse out here in the sticks, love.'

'They certainly are,' Tilly agreed gloomily, pulling her cardigan close about her narrow shoulders. 'Better get used to it, Grace. The cuts started off being once or twice a week, and only for an hour or two. Now they seem to be switching the power off after ten o'clock most evenings. So if you're not done reading by then, it's lights out, like it or not.'

'Yes, like a curfew,' Caroline added.

'Saints alive!' Grace had groped for all the glasses, crowding them together on a tray, and now carried this carefully to the draining board. 'I don't like the sound of that.'

'It's this new Labour government. Power cuts, fuel shortages . . . They need to get their act together,' Mr Fisher muttered.

'Is there any hot water left?' Grace asked.

'Yes, but leave 'em, love. I'll wash those glasses up in the morning,' Violet insisted, steering Grace towards the stairs. 'That's not your job.'

They all traipsed up to bed in the dark, clutching their candle stumps and trying not to get hot wax on their fingers.

Tilly and Caroline, who'd been sharing a room since Joan

left to save on heating, reminded Grace where the washroom was, made sure the new girl had clean towels and matches to relight her candle if need be, and said goodnight.

'I never thought Joe would manage to recruit another Land Girl. Not all the way out here,' Caroline whispered through the dark as they huddled under the blankets, trying to get warm. 'And Grace is very unusual.' She could feel her heart thump loudly in the quiet, as though she'd been running. Too much sloe wine, she thought. 'Did you like her, by the way? What do you think of her?'

'I think she's smashing,' Tilly whispered back. 'You?'

Caroline, who for some time had been listening to the new girl tiptoeing cautiously about the attic room next door, no doubt hunting for slippers and nightclothes in an unfamiliar space, finally caught the creak of the mattress as she too got into bed.

'Smashing,' she agreed with a sigh, and turned over to face the wall. 'Absolutely first-rate.'

Next day, the three Land Girls marched out into the cobbled farmyard where Joe was harnessing Barney, the shire horse, ready for turning the soil in one of the top fields.

Grace shocked them on first rising, emerging with her vast halo of hair puffed. She had now ruthlessly tied back her locks and jammed her beret down on top. Her uniform wasn't new, as she had previously worked as a Land Girl in Devon, as she'd told them at dinner last night. But the breeches and jersey were both clean and neatly ironed, and the only tear had been meticulously repaired.

Caroline thought she looked very smart indeed in her standard Land Army uniform of mustard breeches teamed with a green jersey, even the bulky taupe jacket suiting her height.

'Not exactly warm today, is it?' Grace remarked, peering up into partly cloudy skies, a faint sunshine filtering through occasionally. 'I was told you don't get snow in Cornwall. I hope that wasn't a daydream.'

Caroline laughed. 'Oh, we've had snow here in the winter. But it doesn't tend to stick, not this close to the sea. At least, that's what Joe says.' She saw the farmer straighten from his work, frowning at the sound of his Christian name, and blushed. 'Mr Postbridge, I mean.' Joe was quite relaxed about most things, but he preferred the Land Girls to refer to him as Mr Postbridge. Though she recalled it had been *Mrs* Postbridge, not the farmer, who'd instigated that rule after she and Joe had got married. But no doubt she'd wanted to put as much distance as possible between her new husband and his young Land Girls. 'Grace was just wondering whether it snows in Cornwall.'

Joe cracked a rare smile. 'Not often enough to worry about.' He banged his gloved hands together. 'Still, it's chilly today, I'll grant you that. So you'd best get ploughing on the double. That'll keep you warm.'

Grace had made a beeline for the horse and was stroking his soft, downy muzzle. She beamed when he nudged into her palm, snuffling noisily. 'I love horses. So huge and yet so gentle.'

'He's just hoping you've brought him an apple or a bit o' carrot,' Joe told her with a wink and turned to shut the gate into Barney's enclosure. 'Never stops eating, that one.'

Tilly, buttoning up her jacket, muttered, '*Gentle*? Don't stand behind him, that's all I'm saying.'

'Oh, Barney doesn't kick. He's a sweetheart.' With an expert hand, Caroline slipped the halter over his head and checked it was secure, and caught Grace watching her with interest.

'Do you ride?' Grace asked promptly.

'I used to ride,' Caroline admitted shyly, 'when I was much younger. My granddad had a pony on a bit of land behind his house in Ealing. But then he died and the pony was sold. It's all built up around there now.' She paused, a wave of sadness crashing over her. 'Goodness, I've not thought about Grandad in years. I expect his house was bombed to smithereens in the Blitz. It'll be all rubble down that street now.'

Nobody said anything for a moment, then Joe passed the lead rope to Caroline, instructing her gruffly to walk Barney up to the top field. 'Plough's already up there, harness too, and the guideposts are in place, to show you where to start and finish. Caroline, you're the most experienced, so I'm putting you in charge. You remember how to harness him up and couple the plough to the harness?'

'Yes, Mr Postbridge,' Caroline assured him.

'I'll be working on the tractor if you need me. Oh, and my wife would like a word when you get back. She's looking for volunteers for a sing-song at the Harvest Supper.'

Tilly and Caroline looked at each other, silent and aghast.

'I can sing,' Grace announced, surprising them all.

'Thank you, Grace. I'll let Mrs Postbridge know when I see her.' Pushing up the brim of his cloth cap, the farmer peered at them from under dark bushy brows. 'Straight lines this time, ladies. No more of your wonky ones.'

Caroline and Tilly laughed nervously. Last time they'd been left to plough a field on their own, the lines had indeed ended up crooked, and Joe had nearly burst a gasket.

'I'll keep these girls on the straight and narrow, never you fear,' Grace told him airily in her distinctive Liverpudlian accent, and linked arms with Tilly. 'Eh, can you whistle? Do you know this one?'

They trudged up the narrow track that led to the top field, Tilly and Grace whistling an old sea shanty very imperfectly.

Once Joe had disappeared back into the barn, Caroline slowed her pace. She always enjoying walking with the horse through green, rolling countryside, even uphill. Although it was nippy, she'd stuffed her beret in one of her pockets, and a light breeze was lifting her blonde hair as they grew closer to the cliffs.

It was at times like these that she remembered why she'd chosen to join the Women's Land Army in the first place. For all the fresh air and sense of freedom that came from being in the open countryside. It was so different from the town life she'd led in Ealing. And although she missed her family from time to time, she didn't regret coming to Cornwall, so far from London. Not one little bit.

'Now, girls, isn't this just the life?' Grace declared, throwing Caroline a smile over her shoulder as though she had read her mind. 'Look at the view . . . Aren't we the luckiest creatures alive?'

'Oh yes,' Tilly agreed sarcastically. 'But what a pity you missed the harvest a few weeks back. We had a wonderful time, to be sure. My hands are still sore from hours of bundling wheat into stacks. Then all that dust from the great noisy threshing machines kept getting under my eyelids, and Mrs Newton had to give me an eye bath, and it stung like billy-o. Oh, and we had to tie string around the bottoms of our trouser legs, to stop rats and mice climbing up them.'

She gave a melodramatic shudder. 'Yes, sometimes I'm *so glad* to be a Land Girl.'

'It was quite dusty in the threshing barn,' Caroline admitted, chuckling. 'Even after I'd washed and washed, there was still dust on my bed sheets every morning. And you're right about the eyes . . . They were so itchy, I hated it. Joe ought to give us goggles at harvest time.'

'Goggles? Like the ones Spitfire pilots wear, you mean?' Grace chuckled. 'I can see it now . . . All us Land Girls stumbling about in goggles, unable to see a bleedin' thing, grabbing men instead of wheat stalks and throwing *them* in the thresher.' She tutted and rolled her eyes. 'What a shame that would be, eh? Those poor men.'

The three girls fell about, snorting with laughter.

Life on the farm was going to be very different with Grace there, Caroline decided, and then felt guilty. She realised she hadn't thought about Selina that morning. Not once. Worse, the letter she'd started writing to her absent friend still lay unfinished. But now she would have so many funny new anecdotes to tell Selina, wouldn't she?

The letter would be worth the wait.

CHAPTER THREE

High on the sunlit moors above Bodmin, Selina gripped the steering wheel and stared out over the gleaming black bonnet, frozen in panic. 'I . . . I don't know what to do next,' she admitted.

'Well, let's take it step by step.' William MacGregor smiled at her encouragingly. 'You've pressed the starter button, so now you just need to select first gear, release the clutch slowly, *very* slowly, while pressing down on the accelerator at the same time. And don't look so worried, Miss Tiptree. This Wolseley is one of the safest, most reliable cars on the road today, and I have complete faith that you can drive it.'

The gear lever juddered under her gloved hand as Selina replied, a little caustically, 'That's the triumph of hope over experience, Mr MacGregor. We've been through this at least five times already . . . And every time I've managed to stall the blasted engine.'

William MacGregor's stately black Wolseley was parked in a deserted Cornish lane several miles above Thornton Hall. In fact, peering down the long bonnet with its silver mascot, she could just see the hall chimneys rising above the trees below them, the wild moors their backdrop.

Thornton Hall had been her sister's home, but Selina had lived there ever since Bella's tragic death that summer, caring for her orphaned nieces and nephew. And it was because of them that she was here today. She'd never before felt the urge to drive, though once or twice had got the farmer's tractor chugging up and down the muddy tracks at Postbridge Farm, back in Porthcurno where she'd been working as a Land Girl. But not being able to drive herself or her charges about had become a severe restriction, given how isolated they were at Thornton Hall. So here she was, determined to add driving to her short list of accomplishments.

William MacGregor – a handsome man in his early forties, with a distinguished streak of silvering hair at his temple – had been her late sister's solicitor, and was executor of her large estate now. He lived in the nearby town of Bodmin but visited the hall at least once a week to make sure everything was running smoothly. She'd resented his visits as interference at first, but Selina had come to value his advice, as the complications of overseeing such a large and expensive household had become clearer to her.

'Gently does it, remember.' Mr MacGregor gave her a nod. 'All right, clutch in. First gear. That's the way. Now, slowly ease off the—' The car shook violently and then died to silence. '*Slowly*, Miss Tiptree,' he repeated with a sigh. 'You can't rush it.'

'Oh blow.' Selina buried her face in her gloved hands. She could have wept with frustration. 'Perhaps the doctor's right.'

'I've very rarely found that to be the case. But go on . . . What has Dr Ford said now?'

'When he dropped in the other day, I mentioned that you were teaching me to drive, and he said "females are not meant to drive". Apparently, it was all very well during the war, when women had no choice but to drive ambulances and so on. But "the female brain is simply not capable of motoring".'

'Surely he didn't say that?'

'I'm afraid he did. Indeed, he insisted that whenever women *do* try to drive, we inevitably murder some hapless pedestrian or end up in a ditch. He was quite forthright on the matter.'

William MacGregor chuckled. 'A chauvinist, eh? But a damn good doctor. So I suppose we must forgive his outdated views.'

'And he looked after my sister with touching devotion,' Selina conceded, and forced a reluctant smile to her lips. 'How Bella would have laughed to see me behind the wheel of a car. She hated cars. Horrid, noisy things, she used to say.' She swallowed down a sob, assailed by unexpected grief. 'Goodness, I miss her.'

The solicitor waited discreetly before saying, 'Look, don't despair . . . I suspect it's your footwear rather than your female brain that's the cause of your problems.' At her puzzled look, he nodded to her feet. 'Those are very fetching, but I doubt the Wolseley clutch pedal was intended to be operated in high heels.'

Feeling foolish, Selina made a mental note to wear flats for her next driving lesson.

'Now, shall we try it one more time? Clutch in, hit the starter button, and then . . .' As the engine rattled back into life, he moved to select first gear at exactly the same time as her, and their gloved hands tangled. His gaze shot to hers, and there was a brief, embarrassed hesitation before he withdrew his hand. 'I'm ever so sorry. The car is yours to drive, Miss Tiptree.'

'Oh, please call me Selina,' she said, raising a shy gaze to his. 'The housekeeper calls me Miss Tiptree. My nieces and nephew call me Aunt Selly. All my closest friends are miles away in Porthcurno. There's nobody left in my life who calls me by my first name, and it's too dreary for words.'

'I suppose old habits die hard. Besides, I am a great deal older than you.' Though his eyes twinkled as he said that.

'That's true. Any day now, I expect you to turn up at the hall with a long, white beard.' Selina was joking, of course. Holding her breath, she selected first gear again, then let the clutch out as slowly as she could, while also pressing the accelerator pedal. To her relief, there was a sort of catch, and then the car started rolling forward, faster and faster. 'Oh my gosh, I've done it!'

'Don't forget to steer,' William exclaimed in alarm.

'Oops.' About to crash into the hedgerow, Selina wrenched the large steering wheel to the left with a grunt of effort, and promptly found herself heading for a gnarled tree on the other side of the lane. With another tremendous heave, she corrected her course again. 'For goodness' sake . . . It's like wrestling with an elephant.'

'You're doing fine.'

She was only somewhat reassured by his calmness. Steering the big, heavy car took all her strength. Still, she managed to navigate a respectable middle course along the road for a good minute or so. But, as the car sped up, the engine was soon roaring like a beast.

'What's that noise?' She stared down at the elegant dashboard, studying the row of gauges and dials in consternation. 'What have I done wrong?'

'You need to move up a gear,' he reminded her.

'How do I do that?'

'Same as before. Clutch in, select second gear, slowly release . . . *Slowly*!' As the car juddered to an embarrassing halt again, William MacGregor laughed. 'Well, it's a start. A good start. Lose those heels, and a few more lessons, you'll be whizzing along like a regular roadster.'

'I think that's enough for today.' Selina got out of the driver's seat and walked around to the passenger side. 'You should drive us back to the hall. I'm worried about scratching your paintwork.'

Without argument, William jumped across into the driver's seat. 'I saw Jemima and Faith waving out of the window as we left,' he remarked conversationally, starting the engine and driving off with expertise. 'They looked chipper as always. But how's your nephew getting along? Last time we spoke, he had influenza. A nasty illness even for the young.' He frowned, focused on the road ahead. 'How old is Peter now?'

She smiled, thinking of young Peter, who had sprouted since the summer. 'Fourteen. And his health is much improved. I have to admit, he was quite unwell at one point. I called Dr Ford to the house twice, and Mrs Hawley and I took turns to sit up with him last week. He was so hot and restless, he barely got a wink of sleep.'

Selina glanced out of the car window. She was not used to caring for her sister's children and it was a relief to be able to confide in someone about her fears. Also, she realised with a pang of guilt, she felt much more comfortable with William MacGregor behind the wheel than trying to drive herself. She still wanted to be more independent, though, with her own car. These past few months she'd been entirely reliant on Mrs Hawley, the housekeeper, to drive her into Bodmin, the nearest town, if she wanted to go shopping, and that could not continue. Mrs Hawley had other duties, and Selina relished the idea of being able to drive into Bodmin whenever she wished, as there wasn't a reliable bus service across the moors.

Mr MacGregor was looking concerned. 'Poor boy. Wasn't he due to start at a Devon boarding school last month?'

She nodded. 'I wrote to the headmaster and explained why Peter would be late taking up his place. He was perfectly reasonable about it, though I'm afraid he insisted that we still pay the fees for the whole term.'

'I bet he did. But Peter will be going eventually, I take it?'

'Yes, of course,' Selina agreed, flushing. 'The only thing is, I'd been rather hoping I could buy a car and drive him there myself.'

William MacGregor looked at her, startled. '*You*? It'll take a few more weeks for you to get the hang of this driving lark, I'm afraid. You'd never pass the test, for starters.'

'But when I applied for my provisional licence, they told me I wouldn't need to take a test. That I can legally drive for up to a year on the provisional alone.'

'That's true,' he agreed grudgingly. 'The government suspended driving tests during the war. But they're bringing them back in soon.'

'Soon . . . but not yet,' she pointed out, and saw him smile.

'All the same, I wouldn't feel comfortable at the thought

of you driving into Devon on the strength of a few lessons with me.'

'I suppose you're right. Running before I can walk, and all that. Though, in that case, I wonder if I might impose on you further . . .' Selina broke off, embarrassed by what she'd been about to ask.

'You want me to drive Peter there for you?'

'I'm sorry, I shouldn't have asked. But I honestly did hope to have a car of my own by now and to be more independent.'

He was silent for a moment, then said gently, 'You know, your sister wasn't simply another client of mine. Bella and Sebastian were friends of mine for many years. It broke my heart when we lost him. But I consoled myself that Bella would be with us for many more years. Her illness took us all by surprise . . .' He hesitated. 'You promised Bella you'd care for her children after her passing. Well, I promised her husband years ago that I'd take care of his family if he ever . . .' He pulled a face, his hands tightening on the wheel. 'In a nutshell, I'm happy to drive Peter to school any time he's ready to go.'

'That's awfully kind of you, Mr MacGregor.'

'William, please.' Concentrating on the tight bend ahead, William added with a wry grin, 'If I'm allowed to call you Selina, I'll be damned if you're going to call me Mr MacGregor.'

Selina smiled and thanked him, though she still felt uncomfortable. She'd happily accepted his help with driving lessons. But expecting him to drive such a long distance in order to deliver her nephew to boarding school was a more serious imposition. 'If you're sure I'm not taking you away from your work?'

'All work and no play makes William a very dull boy.'

Soon, they turned through the gates towards Thornton Hall, where her widowed sister Bella had lived, and where she had died that summer, inoperable tumours in her lungs. Bella had been so young when she died, only in her mid-thirties, with three wonderful, lively children. Her loss still hurt Selina deeply. And the children were suffering too.

Going back to school for the first time since his mother's passing would be a difficult and important moment for Peter, Bella's eldest, and Selina wanted it to go as smoothly as possible. Especially as this was a new school where he had no friends yet and might find being away from home a struggle. But she feared harming his chances of a future university place if she kept him at home for another year.

'Thank you so much,' she told William at the hall, when he came round to open the passenger door for her. 'For the driving lesson . . . and for everything else. You've been a brick. I won't forget it.'

'You're welcome.' He glanced round as Peter himself emerged from the front entrance, his dark blond hair almost brushing his collar again. It would need cutting before he went back to school, Selina noted. 'Hullo, Peter. Should you be out of bed?'

'I've been stuck indoors for weeks, it's a dead bore. And I'm definitely on the mend, the doctor says . . . Barely any sniffles left.' Peter, who had grown at least another inch since the summer, shook hands politely with William MacGregor. 'I say, your car is absolutely spiffing. A Wolseley Super Six, isn't she?'

'That's right. Care to see under the bonnet?' With a smile,

he began to show the boy around the car, giving Selina a nod. 'I'll call in a few days, shall I?'

'Thank you.'

Smiling, she went inside the house, stripping off her driving gloves, and found her two nieces in the hall, hearing their angry squeals and cries before she saw them. Four-year-old Faith was in a tug-of-war with Jemima, her eleven-year-old sister.

Horrified, she stepped between the two fair-haired girls. 'Jemima? Why aren't you with your tutor? And it's not very nice to be fighting with Faith. She's only small, for goodness' sake.'

'Sorry, Aunt Selly.' With a muffled sob, Jemima let go of the rag doll they'd been squabbling over and stepped back, flushed and guilty. 'Mr Harrington went home early with a bad head cold. And I didn't mean to fight with Faith,' she added unhappily. 'But Tabitha is mine and she won't give her back.'

'Mine, mine!' Faith insisted with a shake of her head, clutching her trophy to her chest.

'Tabitha? Is that the name of the doll?' Selina asked.

Jemima nodded solemnly.

With a sigh, Selina crouched. 'May I see her, Faith?' Reluctantly, the little girl relinquished the rag doll. It was worn and tatty, and had clearly seen better days. She glanced around at Jemima, and was surprised to see a tear rolling down the older girl's cheek. 'This was your doll once?'

Jemima gave a jerky nod. 'Mummy gave it to me when Faith was born. She helped me choose the name. Only Faith found the doll under my bed today and stole it. It's not fair.'

'You're a bit old now for rag dolls, Jemima.' Selina studied her averted profile sympathetically. The older girl had rallied surprisingly well after her mother's death. But now that Peter was due to leave for boarding school, she was showing signs of nervous strain. 'Shall we let Faith have Tabitha for now, and see about getting you something more fitting for a girl your age?' She hesitated. 'Didn't you say you'd like a pony one day?'

Jemima turned astonished eyes on her. '*A pony*? Oh, Aunt Selly, you're simply the best. Do you really mean it?'

'Of course I do.' Selina smiled. 'When I was your age, I was horse-mad. There are riding stables in Bodmin. I'll write and ask if they have any suitable animals for sale. Anyway, a pony would be good company for your mother's horse. I don't ride her as often as I should, and I expect she gets lonely on her own, poor thing.'

Jemima threw her arms about Selina's neck, hugging her tight. 'Thank you, thank you. I'm sorry I was such a prig over the doll. Of course Faith can have it.'

'Excellent. Now, go and put Tabitha back in the nursery, and wash your hands and face before lunch.'

Selina straightened, watching with relief as both girls hurried back up to the nursery together, holding hands now.

She was just hanging up her hat and coat in the cloakroom when she heard Mrs Hawley come hurrying down the hall towards her, her heels clacking on the polished floor.

'Ah, Miss Tiptree. I heard the car come back. The girls have got some bee in their bonnet over a rag doll,' the housekeeper told her, exasperation in her voice. She wore her silvery hair in an austere bun, her lips garishly scarlet, often pursed in disapproving lines, but Selina knew Mrs

Hawley to be a kindly woman at heart, who had supported her every step of the way since her sister's death.

'It's all sorted out.' Selina gave her a weary smile. 'Though I had to offer Jemima a pony to do it.'

The older woman looked aghast. '*A pony*, Miss? I don't know how you'll manage to feed it as well as Mrs March's old horse. Everything's in such short supply at the moment, and the weather's getting colder every day. We'd have to order in some extra feed and bales of hay, and I don't know if the housekeeping would stretch to that.'

Selina looked at her, stricken. She hadn't fully considered the ramifications of her impulsive offer. Mr MacGregor handled the estate finances and was always very generous. But she knew that funds were not limitless. And an extra animal to feed over the winter might indeed prove a strain on the household budget. 'I could put Jemima off until the spring, I suppose,' she admitted. 'Ask her to wait until her twelfth birthday. Though she won't be very happy. Not now I've promised.'

'We all have to make sacrifices in times of need,' Mrs Hawley said shortly, and handed over an envelope. 'This came in the post for you, Miss. Shall I bring the tea tray now you're back or will you wait until after lunch?'

'Mrs Hawley, you are a treasure. I would *love* a cup of tea now, if you don't mind. Learning to drive is terrifying . . . I don't suppose you'd care to give me lessons, would you?'

Mrs Hawley drove a battered old vehicle that was always covered in mud, and while Selina wasn't keen on learning to drive in such a wreck, it would certainly be less worrying than the thought of denting Mr MacGregor's elegant Wolseley.

'Sorry, Miss, but I'm run off my feet at the moment. Talking of which, have you advertised for a new nanny yet?'

'You know I promised my sister I'd look after the children myself. Besides, their last nanny was *awful*.' Selina pulled a face, remembering the ordeal of having to sack her. 'She made the children cry. Or have you forgotten?'

'I haven't forgotten Martha,' Mrs Hawley assured her. 'We were all glad when you dismissed that good-for-nothing girl, and no mistake. But I've only one pair of hands, and no time to be giving driving lessons. Now, I'll see about that tea tray.'

With a sigh, Selina changed into her slippers and housecoat and headed for the drawing room. There, she sat down in a comfortable armchair to read her letter. Mrs Hawley soon came in with the tea tray before hurrying away.

She'd recognised the handwriting on the envelope at once. It was from her dear friend Caroline Ponsby, who was still working as a Land Girl in Porthcurno, just as she herself had been before her sister had written earlier that year, asking for help.

Her own life as a Land Girl seemed such a long time ago. So much had happened since leaving Postbridge Farm for the intimidating moorland grandeur of Thornton Hall, and much of her time here had been spent in mourning, grief-stricken. But she enjoyed hearing from Caroline, who wrote to her every week, so that her memories of those days never faded.

Caro's letters were always crammed with amusing anecdotes and tales of other residents at the farm, so that it felt as though she were still there.

* * *

After she'd finished reading the letter for the second time, Selina got up and walked to the window. She stared out across the autumnal grounds, lost in thought. It seemed to have been a busy and momentous week at the farm. A third Land Girl had come to live with the Postbridges, and it sounded as though Caroline had made herself a new best friend . . .

Her name is Miss Grace Morgan, and she's from Liverpool, though her mother is Trinidadian. She's wonderfully striking, and she's quite a chatterbox, more talkative even than old Mrs Newton.

I know you wrote in your last letter that it was unlikely you could visit us again for a long while, fuel rationing being what it is. But I hope you will reconsider so you can meet Grace. She's already made such an impact at the farm. She's experienced as a Land Girl and knows a few tricks of the trade that even Tilly and I had never thought of.

Oh, and she can sing too. At dinner on her first night, Mrs Newton mentioned the vicar's wife was looking for volunteers to help with the meal and entertainment at the Harvest Supper, and Grace told us she can sing and would gladly stand up and entertain everyone with a song. She really is the most smashing girl.

Taken aback by her friend's bubbling enthusiasm for this newcomer, Selina was tempted to make a visit to Porthcurno one of her top priorities once she had learned to drive a car. But then she recalled her responsibilities here, which made it unlikely she would be able to visit the farm until next year at least. Bad enough she had already gone back once for her fellow Land Girl Joan's wedding to Arthur Green. She couldn't ask poor Mrs Hawley to look after the two girls again, along with her other duties, while she went on another visit to Porthcurno . . .

Nonetheless, she could at least write back to her friend and let her know everything that had been going on at Thornton Hall. She didn't write as often as Caroline, but her letters tended to be longer. There was always so much to say about the girls and Peter. And now she would be able to share the news that she was finally learning to drive. Though she didn't own a car yet, an additional problem she would have to rectify once she had her licence. How she would afford it, she had no idea. But one step at a time, as William MacGregor would say.

Selina sat down at the elegant writing desk, drew out paper and pen, and began to compose a reply to Caroline's letter.

Grace sounds amazing, she wrote carefully. *I can't wait to meet her. But you're right, it may be hard for me to get away until after Christmas.*

Do you remember Mr MacGregor, the solicitor? He called once while you were visiting in the summer. He's been very kindly teaching me to drive.

She was just hesitating over those lines when Peter peered around the door. 'Aunt Selly?'

Quickly, she laid aside her pen, turning with a smile. 'Yes, Peter, dear?'

'Mr MacGregor says he'll be driving me to boarding school.' He looked oddly sullen, no sign now of the impish smile with which he'd greeted her outside. 'I don't understand. I thought, since I'd been ill, that I wouldn't be starting school until next term now.'

'But you've been feeling much better, haven't you?' Selina got up and checked his forehead, which was cool. He certainly didn't seem unwell. Frowning, she studied her nephew's averted face. 'What's this about, Peter? You know I can't let you miss any more school days without good reason.'

'But Mr Harrington—'

'Mr Harrington is an excellent home tutor for Jemima,' she pointed out, 'but you're fourteen and you need proper tuition at a good public school if you're to achieve top grades in your examinations. Your mother wanted you to have the best possible chance of a university place, and it would be wrong of me not to heed her wishes.'

'Yes, I see that.' He stuck his hands in his trouser pockets, his chin jutting. 'Only I d-don't want to go to school,' he stammered, 'or to university, if it comes to that. I want to stay here with you and Jemima and Faith forever.'

'Oh, Peter, you know that's not possible.'

Selina put a hand on the boy's shoulder, meaning to be reassuring, but he ducked away with an angry scowl, and ran from the room, shouting, 'Don't touch me!'

She started after him in dismay, but then stopped herself, deciding to let it go for now. Her nephew was clearly not ready to face the world again yet. And she could hardly blame him after the horrors he'd endured that summer. Losing his mother had hit him hard, as it had hit all of them. But Peter was a boy, and boys were often expected to grit their teeth and show no emotion, which was impossible, not to mention unfair.

She would have to take this slowly. And perhaps ask William for advice. She didn't know much about dealing with boys his age, and the friendly solicitor might know better than her how to encourage Peter back to school without upsetting the poor child further.

CHAPTER FOUR

Sheila couldn't believe how her life had changed since she'd taken over running her late husband's village shop. It wasn't just how busy she always was, nor the new skills she'd acquired in terms of ordering stock, dealing with suppliers, and making sure her customers always went away happy. No, it was how the shop had become a focal point for the village in ways she didn't recall from when her dearest Arnie had run it. Everyone had respected Arnold Newton, but he'd had a sharp tongue and it had made him a few enemies over the years. When she had to be sharp, she tried to be funny too, finding people preferred a smile over a scowl.

That Saturday morning, Sheila was not only selling fruit and veg to the villagers and overseeing Margaret's dusting and rearranging of the magazine shelves, but also teaching Jack Treedy to read and write. A task which required her to smile more than usual, coaxing the reluctant lad to learn his letters.

Jack was one of the village youngsters, a boy who'd left school early to help out at home. About to turn sixteen, he was the eldest son of Mrs Treedy, a doughty, reed-thin woman with a parcel of hungry-looking kids, all ginger-haired like herself, who'd come round asking for a job when the shop had reopened. Unable to give her work, Sheila had found Mrs Treedy a position at Eastern House instead. The listening post was not as busy as it had been during the war, but they always needed cleaning staff. Sheila's own daughter Violet had worked there as a cleaner when they'd first come to Cornwall in the early forties, and later as housekeeper too. That had been before her marriage to Joe Postbridge though, and Sheila had to admit that Violet suited being a farmer's wife much better than being a housekeeper.

Now she was trying to help the woman's son as well.

'I can't do it, Mrs Newton,' Jack complained, shoving his hands in his pockets and turning away from the book she had been showing him. He stared moodily through the shop window at the sunlit village street. 'I couldn't learn me letters in school and I can't learn 'em now. I don't have that kind of brain.'

'Now you listen to me, young man,' she told the boy firmly. 'There ain't nothing wrong with your brain, even under that mop of hair which you could have done with combing this morning.' She nodded to his unruly ginger curls, cut pudding-basin style above pale brows. 'If you hadn't left school early to help your mum, you'd have learned to read and write like everyone else. It ain't hard, you just need a little confidence in yourself.'

Sheila tapped the simple alphabet book again, refusing to let him give up. She couldn't stand idly by when a lad in her own village was being held back simply as a result of not knowing his letters. He had left school far too early and never been chased up for it, on account of the war.

'Come on, let's start again at the letter A.'

Reluctantly, Jack returned to the shop counter, where they'd been poring over the book for almost an hour now, and peered down at the page. 'A is for apple,' he recited, looking bored, so that she wondered if he'd be more interested by something less obviously for children. He often talked enthusiastically about news he'd heard on the wireless, so maybe she could help him spell out a few newspaper headlines once he knew his alphabet, and show him how useful reading could be.

'Good lad,' she said encouragingly. 'Now, pick up the pencil and write me the letter A in a capital and lower case.'

Gritting his teeth, Jack obeyed, holding the pencil like a fork in his left hand. The squiggly effort looked more like a doodle than any letter she could recognise, but at least he was trying.

'Hmm, well, it's more important that you can read than write,' she said, seeing him glare down at his handiwork in frustration. 'Did you never try to write with your right hand?'

'The teacher used to smack me with the ruler when I didn't use my right,' he admitted, 'but I still couldn't get the hang of it. Everything's just easier with my left.'

'Gawd,' she muttered, furious at the idea of this boy being punished simply for being left-handed. But she gave him a strained smile. 'Well, practice makes perfect. Read through the alphabet every day, and you'll get there in the end.'

'*Every day*?' Jack sounded horrified. 'I've got the little 'uns to look after while Mum's at work. She's even got me cooking and cleaning now too. I've no time for lessons.'

Folding her arms, Sheila stared at him in exasperation.

'You don't want to be stuck here for years, looking after your brothers and sisters, do you?'

His mother had struggled to feed her large family since losing her husband in the war. Not having a job himself, Jack had been lumped with caring for his youngest brothers and sisters who weren't in school yet and had brought the whole family with him for his reading lesson that Saturday morning.

Thankfully, the youngest child went to work with Mrs Treedy, lying in a pram at Eastern House while she mopped and dusted, as the poor thing wasn't fully weaned yet. But the rest were left to entertain themselves when she had work on a Saturday. Two ginger-haired girls were perched on the wall opposite the shop, kicking their legs as they chattered and giggled in the sunshine, their older sister looking after a toddler. And the three younger boys were inexpertly kicking a ball back and forth out there, and occasionally falling into fisticuffs, at which point Jack would stride outside to break them apart.

'I suppose not,' he admitted, his look sullen.

'Right, then let's try B for ball.' She pointed to the next page. 'Which you'd rather be kicking down the road with your brothers out there than reading about in this book, I daresay.' She chuckled at his embarrassment, and he laughed reluctantly too. 'At least they're behaving themselves nicely now, though.' She nodded across at the oldest girl, who had a toddler with flushed cheeks balanced precariously on her hip and was trying to quieten its whimpers by crooning a song. 'Looks like that little one is teething again. I've a bottle of gripe water you could have on tick if you like.'

'That's very kind of you, Mrs Newton,' he said gruffly, 'but we'll be fine.'

It was clear that Jack loved his siblings very much, and he had his mother's pride in not asking for handouts. But Sheila's heart ached for the boy. He was lively and quick-witted, despite a lack of education, and not cut out for a job as a labourer or farmhand. Yet he was unlikely to make something of his life if he couldn't even read, not here in rural Cornwall.

The door jangled, heralding a new customer. Margaret turned, duster in hand, to see who it was. Sheila herself looked up and smiled, recognising the new Land Girl who had come to work for her son-in-law Joe.

'Good morning, Grace,' she said cheerily.

Behind Grace Morgan came the other two Land Girls, young Tilly Coombes with her sweet smile and shining red hair, and Caroline Ponsby in sturdy boots and taupe uniform jacket, looking happier than she'd done in a long while, poor girl. She'd been at a loss since her best friend had left the farm. Still, Caroline was clearly making friends with Grace instead, who seemed a nice girl and funny too. Sheila much preferred people with a strong sense of humour to dour types who never got a joke . . .

'Good morning, Caroline . . . Tilly.' Sheila nodded. 'What can I do for you young ladies?'

'Morning, Mrs Newton. I've come for my weekly sweet ration.' Grace produced a folded ration book from her pocket, and the other two girls followed suit.

'Of course, love.' Sheila turned for her sweet scoop, beaming round at them. Grace having recited her order, Sheila unscrewed the jars and set about weighing out the sugary treats. 'No picture house today?' The Land Girls often caught the bus into Penzance for their Saturday entertainment, visiting the shops as well as the cinema, especially when there was a good matinee showing.

'We decided to have a quiet Saturday instead,' Tilly said, looking unimpressed.

'Only because it'll be the Harvest Supper soon,' Grace added with a wink, 'and we're saving our pennies in case there's some exciting vegetables for sale there.'

Sheila chuckled, enjoying the new Land Girl's sense of humour.

Jack had been gawping at Grace ever since she'd walked into the shop. Now Grace turned her gaze on the boy, asking casually, 'Is there something on my face?'

'N-no,' Jack stammered, blushing fierily. 'I'm sorry if I was staring. But I've never seen you before. We don't get many new people in Porthcurno.'

'You mean, people who look like me?' But Grace was smiling. 'I'm Grace Morgan, from Liverpool.' She held out a hand, which he shook, muttering his name. 'Jack Treedy? Mrs Newton said she's been teaching you to read. Is that right?'

Jack looked mortified. 'I can read, it's just—'

'Nothing to be ashamed of,' Grace said hurriedly. 'It took me ages to learn anything at school. Teacher used to say, in one ear, out the other. That's why I took up as a Land Girl when the war started. Not much use for reading and writing when you're digging a hole, is there?'

'Here's your sweet ration, love,' Sheila interrupted, passing the bulging paper bag to Grace. 'Now, what's your fancy?' She turned to Caroline and Tilly and took their orders, measuring out the sugary sweets with her scoop and pouring them into paper bags, sealed with a practised twist of her wrist. 'There you go, my lovelies. Now if I could just have your ration coupons.' While she was tearing out each coupon, she noticed Grace slip outside and dole out her sweets among the playing children. 'Well, I never . . .'

When Grace returned, Jack asked, 'Are you sure you've left enough for yourself, Miss Morgan? You can have my sweet ration if you like.'

'That's kind of you, Jack. But no thanks . . . And I'm Grace, that's what everyone calls me. Are those *all* your brothers and sisters out there?' She was looking at his ginger hair, which the others shared. When he nodded, she smiled. 'I was happy to let them have my ration. I'm looking after my figure, see?'

Jack blinked. 'I wouldn't say you had to do that, Miss . . . I mean, Grace.' He swallowed hard, playing with the cloth cap he'd whipped off his head as soon as she walked in. 'Erm, you must need someone to show you about the village, seeing as you're new to Porthcurno. I'd be happy to do that. Right now, in fact.'

Sheila pursed her lips, slipping the alphabet book back under the counter. It seemed his reading lessons had been eclipsed by Joe's new Land Girl. Next time though, she would show Jack some newspaper headlines and let him spell out a few simple words. That ought to prove more interesting for him.

Grace hesitated. 'Sorry. Me and my friends are planning to walk around the village, and . . . Not wanting to hurt your feelings, but you know what girls are like. We prefer a good natter without any boys earwigging.'

His blush extending right to his hairline, Jack backed away. 'Of course. Maybe I'll see you around sometime.'

Once the three Land Girls had left the shop, Margaret turned from the shelves she'd been dusting, and told the boy firmly, 'Never you mind about her, Jack Treedy. Plenty more fish in the sea. Besides, what are you now, sixteen or thereabouts? She may be a looker, but she's a bit old for you . . . Twenty at least.'

'Twenty-three,' Sheila informed her. Grace had told them all about herself at dinner that first night. 'The only child of doting parents, by the sounds of it.'

Margaret's eyebrows shot up. 'I'm surprised they don't mind her working so far from home. Now the war's over, I mean.'

'Miss Morgan is a young lady with a mind of her own,' Sheila told her approvingly, 'and good luck to her, that's what I say.'

'I'd better take the kids home now,' was all Jack said, looking defeated, and shuffled out to collect his siblings and herd them back to the tiny dwelling they shared with his widowed mother.

With quiet sympathy, Sheila watched him go. 'Poor lad, he ain't got a bloomin' chance with Grace,' she sighed. 'I like his ambition, though,' she added with a wink, and the two sisters had a good chuckle before settling back to work.

Soon, autumn banished the last of the warm days with a series of chilly starts and murky afternoons, and Sheila found herself walking more briskly to and from work, swinging her arms to keep warm. But the new season also brought one of her favourite village celebrations, the Harvest Supper, which always fell on the Sunday closest to the first full moon of autumn. That evening, with clouds obscuring the silver moon, the ground was frosty underfoot as Sheila and Violet headed down the steep farm track into Porthcurno, carrying goodies for the communal supper and taking care not to slip.

The three Land Girls walked ahead of them, chattering and waving their torches to light the way. Joe brought up the rear, leaning heavily on his stick. His false leg had been chafing him in recent days, she knew. Probably the change in the weather, Sheila had told him earlier, since her arthritis always troubled her more once summer was over. Seeing his discomfort, she had tactfully suggested they take the farm van instead. But Joe had grumbled about a waste of fuel when the Harvest Supper was within walking distance.

Thankfully, her other son-in-law Ernest had opted to walk with Joe, despite his slower pace, and Sheila could hear them discussing a letter from Alice, her granddaughter. Alice was still working in London with British Intelligence, despite having married recently, and enjoying herself thoroughly by all accounts. Though heaven knows how long that would continue, Sheila thought secretly. Alice had confided that she and Patrick hoped to start a family as soon as possible.

Violet had brought Sarah Jane in her old pram, the little girl cosily wrapped up in a blanket, as it meant she could load the wire basket underneath with produce for the Harvest Supper. Sheila herself was carrying a wicker basket filled with the last of the sweet, wrinkly apples from their orchard that she'd kept under paper in the attic, especially for this occasion.

'It's lovely to hear of our Alice doing so well back in London,' she told Violet. 'She and Lily are such lovely girls. They've turned out beautiful, don't you think?'

'Yes, Betsy would have been proud of them both. And thrilled to have been a grandmother. Lily's Morris is a little darling, if a bit noisy at times.' Her daughter leant forward to peer into the pram. 'Ah, Sarah Jane's asleep at last,' she said softly. 'That's a mercy, you know how she gets fidgety when she's tired.'

Sheila hesitated, wondering if the time was right to broach her plan. 'You know, talking of Lily, I think I'll pay her and Tristan a visit next month. Not just a day trip but stay over for a while.'

'Excuse me?' The clouds over the moon shifted, and Violet stared round at her, her pretty, oval face lit up by its pale light. 'You're going to Penzance?'

'Only for a week or two,' Sheila assured her hurriedly. 'I can take Christmas presents for her and the kiddy. You've nearly finished knitting them socks for Tristan, haven't you? It would save on the postage.'

Violet was frowning. 'Yes, but . . . Who's going to mind the shop while you're gone? And don't say Aunt Margaret, because she couldn't mind a biscuit tin. Anyway, it's too much work for one person.'

'I've thought about that.' Sheila felt her way cautiously. Violet had a trigger temper, whereas her sister Betsy, God rest her soul, had always been such a sweetheart. 'I'm planning to ask Jack Treedy to help her out.'

'Jack Treedy?' Her steps slowing, Violet looked scandalised now. 'The lad who stole that pork pie right off the shop counter? Have you lost your senses, Mum? The boy's a thief.'

Sheila gritted her teeth but kept her tone civil. 'He made a mistake, owned up to it and gave me back the pie.' She paused, aware of her daughter's glare on her face. 'Which I then allowed him to keep, all right. I couldn't let those little kiddies go hungry. I'm not a monster.'

'Neither am I,' Violet snapped, 'but I'm no idiot either. If you give work to a boy who's proven himself a thief, you'll only have yourself to blame when he pinches something.'

Sheila sighed. 'But we have to give him a chance first, to show that he can be trusted. Oh Vi, he's not a bad lad.'

'And how would you know?"

Feeling cornered, she admitted, 'I've been teaching him to read.'

While they'd been arguing, Joe and Ernest had caught up with them. Ernest sounded interested. 'Who have you been teaching to read, Sheila?'

'Only that little scoundrel who nicked her pie,' Violet answered for her.

'Why have you been doing that?' Joe chimed in, clearly bemused.

'Because the poor boy's barely literate.' Sheila heaved a deep breath, gripping her heavy basket of apples with both hands. 'I taught Lily and Alice to read when they were little, so I know how. Besides, I enjoy it. It's good to see a boy learning.'

'Quite right, Sheila,' Ernest agreed, and lifted the basket of apples away from her. 'Here, let me carry that.'

Sheila thanked him, but was quite thrown by Violet's attitude. Young Jack wasn't a bad sort. And if the odd sweetie went missing, what was that to her? She herself was forever scrumping an apple or grabbing a handful of lemon sherbets when nobody was about. That was one of the perks of running a shop, wasn't it? Anyway, she couldn't abide penny pinchers.

But she knew Violet meant well under all the bluster. Her daughter was just trying to protect her.

The clouds blew away from the full moon, lighting their path ahead. 'Ah now,' Joe said with one of his rare smiles, halting to point upwards with his stick. 'There's the Harvest Moon. Beautiful, ain't she?'

Down in the village, Sheila spotted Maggie waiting outside the shop, its windows dark and shut up for the night. Maggie lived above the shop now, in what had once been Arnie's old rooms before he and Sheila were married. It was dark and cramped up there, but her sister seemed to enjoy living independently. As well she might, given how awful her marriage had been. Still was, truth be told. Although Maggie had decided to divorce Stanley, the lawyers had told her she was unlikely to be granted a divorce unless she could prove sufficient grounds, such as cruelty or adultery.

Stanley wasn't happy about their separation, and could have cited desertion himself to get a divorce. But the truth was, he was a mean man who wanted his wife back home, where he could treat her as badly as he liked behind closed doors. He'd even been round to the shop several times, demanding her back. The last time, Sheila and Violet had given him what for while Maggie laid about his head with a rolling pin. But Stanley was a persistent beggar, so they always kept an eye out for him.

'There's Aunt Margaret . . . Is she coming with us to the Harvest Supper, then?' Violet looked annoyed.

Her daughter didn't like Maggie much, and for good reason. Stanley had behaved shockingly towards young Lily when Violet and the two girls had stayed with them on first coming to Cornwall. Despite the two women making peace since then, it was clear that Violet had still not forgiven her aunt for turning a blind eye to her husband's abusive ways. She hadn't even wanted Margaret working at the shop. But Sheila had paid little attention, giving her sister a second chance.

'Yes, so keep your thoughts to yourself.' Sheila waved to her sister. 'Sorry to have kept you waiting, Maggie, love.'

'Evening, all.' Her sister came out of the shop doorway, a basket of vegetables hooked over her arm and carrying a bag of spuds. 'I hope this will be enough for the harvest raffle.'

Maggie was wearing make-up and dressed smartly, with a navy-blue jacket buttoned up against the cold and a headscarf knotted under her chin. But when Sheila complimented her on her outfit, her sister didn't reply. She was unsmiling and agitated, in fact.

''Ere, what's up, Maggie love?' Sheila put a hand on her arm. 'Not sickening for something, are you?'

Maggie shook her head. 'He's here,' she hissed in Sheila's ear, peering up and down the street. 'I think he's going to the Harvest Supper.'

Sheila felt cold creep down her spine. 'Stanley?'

Ernest had helpfully lifted the bag of spuds out of Maggie's hands. Now he took one look at her face and asked swiftly, 'What is it, Margaret? Your husband causing trouble again?' he guessed, being no fool. 'Walk with us. He won't come near you, I swear it.'

'Thank you,' Maggie said breathlessly, and fell in beside Sheila. But she still looked worried. 'He banged on the shop door earlier and shouted at me through the letterbox. Slurring his words and weaving all over the place.'

'They won't let him in at the Harvest Supper,' Violet said shortly. 'Not if he's been drinking.'

'That's right,' Sheila agreed, though her heart sank. Stanley could cause trouble for them in the village, where he still had friends. She hated the thought of people gossiping about their family. 'Plus, you've got me and Violet, Joe and Ernest, all willing to send that wicked beggar on his way. So there's no need to fret.'

Maggie smiled tremulously around at them. 'I'm sorry to be such a nuisance. And I know he's been rude to you, Ernest, just because you're half German. There's no call for that sort of thing, not now the war's over. And he knows it.'

Ernest cleared his throat. 'I don't mind. Besides, he won't be able to play that game for much longer.'

Puzzled, Sheila glanced at her son-in-law. 'Whatever do you mean, Ernest?'

'I've had a letter from London. I'm needed there urgently for some . . . translation work, let's say. I'll be leaving in a day or so, and I don't know when I'll be back.'

They had all stopped, staring at him.

'You don't mean it, Ernest?' Joe rubbed his chin, perplexed. 'Going back to London? With so little warning?'

Ernest shrugged, his smile apologetic. 'That's the way it goes sometimes in my business. Anyway, I'll be staying with Alice, at least initially. So I'll be able to write and tell you how she and Patrick are getting along. I know you worry about your granddaughter, Sheila, so I hope this will sweeten the blow.'

Mulling it over, Sheila didn't know what to say at first. Over the past year, Ernest had become one of the family again after being missing, presumed dead for most of the war. But she knew his work was vitally important to the security of their country, and there weren't many folk who could say that and mean it.

'Well, that's hard news, and we'll miss you, Ernest,' she said, linking arms with him as they trudged after the Land Girls. 'But whatever you've been asked to do by our government,' she added in a lower tone, 'I know you'll do your best for Britain, just as you done in the war.'

'Thank you, Sheila. That means a great deal.' He paused. 'I shall try to visit you all in the spring, if Violet and Joe don't mind.'

'You'll always be welcome at Postbridge Farm,' Joe told him, and Violet nodded.

Ernest smiled. 'That's very kind of you both. No promises, mind you. I may be required to stay in London for some time. Regardless of the cheerful propaganda in the newspapers, I'm afraid Britain is in a fragile state,' he added, his tone turning sombre, 'and we are all skating on very thin ice, indeed.'

CHAPTER FIVE

Caroline swung through the kitchen door of the parish hall, bearing a tray of stew for Table 3, and almost bumped into Grace hurrying in the opposite direction, coming back for more. 'Oops, sorry,' she exclaimed, dancing out of her way. 'That was close.'

'Goodness, I nearly ended up with stew all over me best togs.' Grace gave her a cheeky wink. She was wearing her hair up in a high, elaborate bun, her dress a glorious bright orange with brown bands at the hem and cuffs. She looked about as far from a Land Girl as it was possible to get, in Caroline's opinion. It was hard not to stare. 'By the way, have you seen old Mrs Newton with her boyfriend?' she went on cheerily. 'Both of them old enough to remember when Queen Vic was on the throne. I just saw them holding hands under the table . . . Young love, eh?'

'Poor lady. She deserves a little happiness though,' Caroline told her, hanging back in the doorway, the bowls of stew on her tray steaming deliciously in her face. 'Mrs Newton only remarried a couple of years back, and her husband died not long after. Her second time being widowed. It was very sad. And Mr Bailey's a widower too. Only, fancy, they knew each other as kids in school, Mrs Postbridge says,' she added in a discreet whisper. 'Her mum was born in Cornwall, you see, before the family moved to East London. So it's like their second chance at love.'

Grace's eyes softened. 'I didn't realise . . . In that case, good luck to them both.' She nodded to the stew. 'Smells amazing, doesn't it? I can't wait to tuck in. Only we've at least another twenty bowls to dish out, and then there's puddin' after.' She rolled her eyes. 'If I'd known how many people come to this Harvest Supper lark, I'd never have volunteered to help out. We're rushed off our feet here.'

And with that, she dashed on.

Caroline carried her tray to Table 3 and carefully handed out the bowls to the large family of villagers sitting there. The lady of the family was looking harassed. 'Do you have any more paper napkins?' she asked Caroline, jiggling a restless baby on her knee. 'My little boy spilt his orange squash, and I had to mop it up. Now we've no napkins left for the meal.'

'Of course.' Caroline returned to the kitchen, and once again almost collided with Grace coming out. 'Where's Tilly gone? I thought she was helping too.'

Grace nodded across the crowded parish hall, and Caroline spotted Tilly deep in conversation with a young lad she recognised as Benny, a local farmer's son. They were probably about the same age, she realised, and Tilly seemed flushed and happy, the empty tray under her arm quite forgotten. 'Talking of young love . . .' Grace murmured.

Caroline blinked, not having realised her fellow Land Girl was sweet on any of the local boys. 'Oh golly.'

'So it looks like we're on our own back here, eh?'

Meeting the other girl's amused gaze, Caroline felt herself suddenly tongue-tied. She tried to smile and only managed an odd, twitching grimace.

Embarrassment swept through her at Grace's surprised look. What on earth was wrong with her? If she couldn't sort herself out and be more careful, she would end up causing yet another awkward situation like the one she'd failed to avoid with Selina. Yes, she liked the new Land Girl – rather more, now she realised, than she ought. But she dared not let Grace see that. The thought of being rebuffed by another girl was almost too much to bear . . . Worse, if Grace were to become angry about it, maybe even to denounce her publicly, she would have to leave Porthcurno. And Postbridge Farm had become her whole life.

'We'd best get on with it, then,' Caroline muttered, and hurried into the kitchen for more bowls of stew, entirely forgetting the napkins she'd promised to fetch and had to dash back for them a moment later.

At last, the Land Girls were able to sit down at a table together and hurriedly eat the last of the stew before there was pudding still to serve. As soon as they'd eaten, they rushed around the parish hall, collecting up dirty bowls and doling out stewed apple and custard for pudding. Thankfully, they were not expected to do the washing-up themselves. The vicar and his wife had dragooned other volunteers into that job.

'Goodness, this feels never-ending,' Caroline groaned, passing Tilly on their way into the kitchen, their arms stacked with dirty bowls and cutlery. 'Remind me why we volunteered for this?'

'Technically, I never volunteered,' Tilly said, tipping used cutlery into the steel tray next to the sink. 'Mrs Newton asked, wouldn't you like to help out in a good cause? And I had a mouthful of food so couldn't reply. Next thing I knew, my name was on the list.'

Grace, mopping up spilt water beside the cutlery washers, grinned. 'She's a canny old bird, Mrs Newton. But I have to admit, I put my hand up to sing. So I can't blame that on anyone else.'

'Yes, and you should stop cleaning up now,' Tilly told her, snatching away the mop, 'and get out there, ready to do your bit.'

'I'd forgotten you'd volunteered for the entertainment too,' Caroline admitted, looking round at her with awe. 'You don't look nervous. Are you?'

'Not a bit, bless you.' Grace laughed at them both. 'I was always picked to do the solos in church when I was younger, so it's second nature to me now. And it's not difficult, singing. My old teacher used to say, all you have to do is open your gob and let the song come out.'

Caroline followed the other two girls out into the hall. The hubbub was deafening, everyone chattering merrily as they scraped away at their stewed apple and custard. Eventually, all the pudding dishes were gathered in for washing, and cups of tea handed out to everyone, with more squash for the kiddies.

There was a slight commotion at the door, and everyone turned to stare. Caroline saw Mrs Newton and her sister Mrs Chellew jump to their feet. She realised the man swaying towards Mrs Chellew must be her estranged husband. He looked drunk and quite unpleasant.

'Go home, Stanley,' Mrs Newton exclaimed, shooing him away.

'I want my wife,' he growled, reaching for Mrs Chellew. 'Come on with me, Maggie.'

'I ain't going anywhere with you, Stanley,' Mrs Chellew said loudly into the silence. 'You're a brute and a drunk, and I don't want anything more to do with you.'

In a matter of seconds, it was over. Mr Bailey and Ernest Fisher got to their feet and escorted Stanley unceremoniously out of the hall. Well, *dragged* more than escorted. There was a quiet ripple of applause, and then everyone hurriedly returned to their conversations as though nothing had happened. Caroline watched the door for some time, and eventually the two men returned, bending to reassure Mrs Chellew with a few words.

After the vicar had stood to give his annual speech of thanksgiving for the harvest, the raffle was called. One of the parish councillors, a thin gentleman with spectacles and tweed jacket, drew the winning tickets, and everyone dutifully applauded as bags of potatoes, carrots and apples were won, along with the odd bottle of home-made wine. 'The proceeds from the raffle go towards our community fund for the poor and needy,' the vicar reminded them all, 'kindly administered by Mrs Newton and her committee.' After much lengthy applause, he nodded to his wife, and Mrs Clewson rose to take her seat at the piano. 'Now, how about a sing-song to round off the evening? I believe we also have two new soloists this year, so please show them your appreciation.'

They all sang a few old country favourites together, everyone joining in with gusto. Then a farmer's wife, Mrs Hayle, gave a solo rendition of a haunting sea shanty while Mrs Clewson accompanied her on the piano. She had a good voice but was slightly off tune in places. Still, Caroline couldn't sing to save her life, so thought it awfully brave of the lady to stand up and give it a try in front of all these people. Then it was Grace's turn.

'Now for Miss Grace Morgan,' the vicar announced, smiling at her, 'a member of the Women's Land Army currently based up at Postbridge Farm.'

As Grace went forward, the room hushed in expectation. Several people whispered behind their hands, others stared in fascination at the new Land Girl who had been the talk of the village ever since she arrived.

Caroline knew she would have cringed and sunk through the floorboards to have so many people gaping at her. But Grace paid no attention to the crowd, bending to murmur something to Mrs Clewson as she took her place beside the piano.

'What are you going to sing?' one young man called out daringly.

Grace turned his way, smiling. 'One of our lovely Vera Lynn's most popular tunes,' she told him in her clear voice. '"We'll Meet Again." I'm sure you all know the words, so do join in at the chorus if you like.' And with that, she nodded to the vicar's wife to begin playing.

The room fell silent, the crowd mesmerised as her voice soared in the opening lines of the well-known song. Caroline too gave a little exclamation of surprise, quickly hushing it with a hand at her mouth. Although Grace had said she was a good singer, Caroline hadn't expected such a beautiful voice.

'Oh my,' Tilly whispered beside her.

Caroline glanced at her friend. 'Awfully good, isn't she?'

'*Good*? I'll say so.'

As the chorus came along, many villagers joined in with the familiar words, but quietly and respectfully, not wanting to drown out such a glorious voice.

When Grace finished, the applause nearly raised the rafters. She smiled around at them all and gave a little curtsey before returning to her seat. Some called out for her to sing again, shouting, 'Bravo! Encore, encore!' but Grace merely shook her head, still smiling, and took a sip of her tea, though it must have been lukewarm by then.

'Blimey, talk about amazing, Grace,' Mrs Newton exclaimed, stopping beside their table to congratulate the Land Girl on her singing ability. 'You should be singing professionally, my girl. That was bloomin' marvellous.'

Mr Bailey had followed her, and he also stopped to smile at Grace. 'Thank you for that, young lady. What a lovely voice you have. It brought tears to my eyes.' He reached across to shake the girl's hand in a friendly manner. 'Hope you're settling in well here in Porthcurno.'

After that, everyone wanted to stop at their table and shake Grace's hand, or ask questions about where she'd come from and if she'd ever sung professionally, or simply stare at the newcomer, silent and bolt-eyed, too overawed to say a word.

'I had no idea what a talented singer you were,' Caroline whispered shyly in her ear when at last the hall started to empty and the wave of hand-shakers and well-wishers were filing out into the cold October night with their raffle prizes. 'That took my breath away.'

Grace nudged her in the ribs, grinning. 'Oh, not you too.'

'Sorry, I didn't mean to embarrass you.'

'Don't worry about it. It's just I spent my childhood being asked to sing for relatives or the neighbours, and then in the church choir,' Grace went on. 'I love singing, but it's always so painful afterwards, people coming up and telling me how good I am. Honestly, I love singing, but I hate all that attention.' Abruptly, she stood up. 'Never mind . . . Shall we get going? Looks like it's kick-out time.' She collected the last cups and saucers on their table and bore them away to be washed up, Caroline hurrying after her with milk jugs and a sugar bowl.

'I never thought of it like that. But I perfectly understand. It makes me queasy when everyone turns to look at me . . . People call me shy, but that's not true. It's just much easier to say nothing and keep your head down.' Caroline rummaged in the kitchen for the containers they'd brought down from the farm; Mrs Postbridge would be on the warpath if they failed to take them back home. 'I won't say another word on the subject, I promise.'

They walked outside to join the others but found Tilly squeezing into the back of Mr Bailey's big car beside Violet and Joe Postbridge. Mrs Newton was seated in the front with Bernie at the wheel.

Tilly bit her lip on seeing them emerge from the hall, hesitating. 'Oh, I'm sorry . . . Mr Bailey offered me a lift up to the farm. But shall I walk back with you instead? There's not enough room for two more.'

'My apologies too, girls,' Mr Bailey called out, laboriously winding down his window. 'I can come back for you if you'd care to wait fifteen or twenty minutes. I already drove Margaret home to make sure she was safe. Besides, it's quite a cold night for walking.'

'Goodness, no, we'll be fine,' Grace insisted with a merry laugh. 'You go ahead. I need a good long walk after that enormous supper anyway. So much food!' She hesitated, glancing at Caroline. 'Unless *you'd* prefer to wait?'

'Tilly, can you hold this on your lap?' Smiling, Caroline passed the empty containers to Tilly. 'No, you're right, we can walk up the hill together,' she told her new friend, secretly thrilled to have the chance of a proper chat without half a dozen others listening in. 'It won't take long.'

Once the big car had pulled away, its engine throbbing deeply in the quiet evening, the two girls were left standing alone outside the parish hall, which was being locked up by the vicar and his church warden. There were a few lads hanging about further along the lane to the village centre, but Caroline and Grace linked arms and strode out together, their breath steaming on the cold night air.

The ground was white with a touch of frost, and now the obscuring clouds had rolled back, the Cornish landscape lay eerily bright under the full moon.

'I wonder what happened to that fella who got dragged out of the hall,' Grace mused. 'Who was he?'

Caroline explained briefly about Mrs Chellew and her estranged husband.

'They should make it easier for folk like that to get a divorce,' Grace said, shaking her head. 'My aunt and uncle, for instance. I've never known two happily married people hate each other as much as those two.'

Caroline chuckled. 'Or maybe they should make it harder for people to get married in the first place,' she began, only half joking, but was interrupted by a shout from the lads ahead of them.

'Hey, darky!' one of them yelled, followed by snorts of laughter from the others.

'*What* did you say?' Caroline's steps faltered.

She threw a horrified glance at Grace, expecting to see a similar shock on her face. But her new friend, apart from briefly compressing her lips, seemed almost not to have heard the boy. Her smile had vanished though, replaced by a mask of calm, her head held high.

Fury fizzed through Caroline's veins on her behalf and she choked out, 'How . . . How dare you? Apologise to my friend right this minute.'

The boy who'd spoken jeered at them, taller than the others and wearing a leather-patched flat cap. 'Not a bloody chance,' he spat back at her, adding another coarse slur that left Caroline shuddering.

'Then I'll march you home to your parents,' she said crossly, 'and tell them exactly what you just said to me and my friend.'

'My dad wouldn't give a stuff,' the lad told Caroline, still grinning as he stepped clear of the shadows. He only looked about twelve or thirteen, but his manner was swaggering, like a much older boy. Clearly the ringleader, she decided.

'What's your name?' Caroline peered at the gaggle of lads behind him, trying to see if she recognised any of them. One boy looked vaguely familiar. 'And yours?'

'No, what's *your* name?' the ringleader demanded, his tone belligerent. He hooked his fingers in his belt, staring at her. 'Perhaps you should walk with us instead. We'll make sure you get home safe,' he added, and again the boys snorted and giggled.

Caroline was alarmed. 'I beg your pardon?'

'You heard me.' He came menacingly towards them, the other lads at his back. 'A pretty girl like you shouldn't be walking about the village after dark. Especially not with *her*. You'll get yourself a reputation.'

The lad reached for her, and Caroline stumbled backwards with a cry.

'Careful . . . You all right?' Grace helped her back to her feet. Then she turned to glare at the boys. 'Get lost, do you hear me? Go home and stop making idiots of yourselves.'

The ringleader snarled something under his breath, eyes narrowed dangerously on Grace. But before he could do anything worse, someone came quickly along the lane behind them. A young male voice called out roughly, 'Hullo, who's there? What's going on?'

With muttered oaths, the boys scattered, disappearing over walls and through gates into the dark, frosty fields beyond the lane.

Caroline turned to see the eldest Treedy boy appear behind them at a trot, his face lit up in the moonlight.

'Oh, thank goodness,' she muttered, sagging with relief. 'It's Jack, isn't it?'

'Yes, Miss.' Jack Treedy swiped off his cap and smoothed back his unruly hair. 'I saw them village boys crowding you and heard a shout. Were they bothering you?'

'They were rather,' Caroline admitted, a little shakily. 'Thank you for coming to our rescue.'

'It weren't nothing. And you, Miss? Are you all right?' Jack asked Grace, his admiring gaze fixed on her face. 'I know that lad with the cap . . . Tommy Skellin. He's a bad sort. Aye, and his dad too. Got no respect for anyone, them two.' He pulled a disgusted face. 'I can go after Tommy if you like, bring him back to say sorry for scaring you.'

'Oh, I was never scared,' Grace told him airily, though Caroline thought she detected a note of strain in her voice. She threw one last scathing look across the field, where shadowy figures could still be seen moving as the village boys tried to make their way home without being caught. 'Just a parcel of brats with big gobs, aren't they? Not worth the shoe leather.'

With a shrug, Jack replaced his cap. 'Let me walk you home, at least,' he insisted. 'In case them little beggars come back, eh?'

'Thank you,' Caroline said, with a quick glance at Grace, who looked away but did not protest. 'We'd be very grateful.'

There seemed little point in refusing the lad's company. Caroline would have preferred a cosy chat with Grace on the walk home, as it was rare at the farm to get anyone on their own for long. But the run-in with those horrid boys had rattled her, there was no denying it.

The three of them set off up the frosty lane towards Postbridge Farm, the moon glowing high above them.

With a murmured, 'Brr,' Grace threaded her arm through Caroline's and drew her jacket closer for warmth. 'Nippy, isn't it?'

Caroline had tilted her face to the silvery moon, which she'd thought so beautiful and magical when they'd left the Harvest Supper. But her earlier happiness had evaporated. The moonlight seemed colder now, its beauty at odds with the nastiness Grace had just faced. She glanced at her new friend and, with a feeling of unease, guessed it could not be the first time Grace had faced such comments. It was all so unfair. Yet Grace had stood up so bravely to those boys, brushing off their vile insults and menacing looks as though they were unimportant. She really was an amazing girl, Caroline decided.

'Yes, but we'll soon be home,' she pointed out.

'Mmm.' Grace grinned, one eye on Jack as he strode manfully ahead, scouting out the fields on either side of the lane for any signs of the gang of boys. 'Shame,' she whispered in Caroline's ear. 'I was rather enjoying our night out.'

Caroline sucked in a breath, a flutter in her chest. 'Me too,' she whispered back.

CHAPTER SIX

'Oh dear, what now?' Hearing the sound of a car horn outside Thornton Hall, Selina folded the last pile of neatly laundered school uniform into Peter's large trunk. Beyond the window, she could see golden sunshine over the moors towards Bodmin, another lovely autumn day. There were half a dozen miscellaneous items laid out on the bed, reading for packing, and several cases to fasten and properly label. Yet already she could hear children shrieking and the crunch of tyres over gravel.

'That'll be Mr MacGregor arriving, ma'am,' Mrs Hawley replied without looking up, busily writing a label for the trunk.

Selina pulled a face. 'But he's nearly an hour early. I hope he doesn't mind waiting around. There's still so much to pack. What about Peter's sports gear?'

With an indulgent smile, the housekeeper attached the label to the lid of the trunk and closed it. 'You go downstairs and meet the solicitor, ma'am. I can finish packing these cases for you.'

'Are you sure?'

'Of course.' The older woman bent to fasten the leather straps on the trunk. 'It's nearly all done, anyhow.'

'Thank you, Mrs Hawley, you're a dear.'

Selina hurried downstairs, though she felt guilty lumping the housekeeper with extra work. Once they'd set off for Peter's school in Devon, the poor woman would be forced to look after the two girls today, as well as attend to her daily duties. She had a new helper from the village who'd just started at the hall, but Peggy was young and not fully trained up yet. Still, it couldn't be helped. Peter needed to go to school, and there simply wasn't room to take the girls with them as well. Especially given how queasy Faith was prone to become on car journeys.

William was standing outside in the sunshine, leaning on his sleek, black Wolseley Super Six. The children were jumping around him, with Peter exclaiming animatedly over his car, with which the boy had become obsessed. William removed his hat on seeing her at the door and came up the steps. They shook hands.

'I know, I'm early,' he said apologetically, perhaps seeing the frustration in her face. 'I was visiting a client a few miles away and the meeting finished early. I hope you don't mind.'

'Not at all,' Selina fibbed, crossing her fingers behind her back.

'Peter looks smart in his new uniform.'

'Doesn't he just? I only hope he can keep it clean on the journey.' She hesitated, embarrassed. 'I'm afraid we're not ready to leave yet. Peter's trunk and cases need to be double-checked before they're packed into the car. Why don't you come inside and have a cup of tea while you wait?'

Not looking at all put out by the delay, he followed her

into the house. The dogs ran towards him, panting and wagging their tails. William MacGregor crouched to pet them, grinning up at her. 'I love dogs. But my mother won't allow them in the house.' He gave her a crooked smile. 'Yes, for my sins, I still live with my mother. Or, rather, she lives with me now. I insisted on it after my father's death. Someone has to look after her and I'm an only child.'

'I think it's marvellous that she's got such a loving son.' Selina tugged on the bell pull that connected to the kitchen, adding in a confidential voice, 'Young Peggy is here today, helping out around the house. She's very new, but I daresay her skills extend to making tea.' She paused, checking her watch. 'I'm sorry, but I may have to desert you, to see how Mrs Hawley is getting on with the packing.'

'Not at all,' he said politely.

But the girl arrived promptly, and Selina decided on a whim to ask for tea for two, and accompanying cake, even though it might mean delaying their departure by half an hour. After all, it would be rude not to sit and take tea with the solicitor first, given that she'd roped the unfortunate man into driving them all the way to Devon.

The new maid, Peggy, a sixteen-year-old with fair braided hair and prominent teeth, seemed thrilled to be given the responsibility of providing a tea tray with a slice of cake each.

'Yes, ma'am,' Peggy lisped, darting awed glances at William MacGregor, who was looking fearfully smart in his charcoal-grey striped suit and polished shoes. 'Right away, ma'am.'

Once Peggy had dashed away, the solicitor sat down on the sofa, crossed his legs and balanced his hat on his knee. He already knew about the new girl, of course, given he handled the finances for the estate of Selina's late sister. But this was his first time meeting her.

'What do you think of the new maid?' she asked, smiling.

'I'm glad Mrs Hawley has got herself proper help at last. I approved the extra expense gladly. She does sterling work, your housekeeper. In fact, I should probably give her a raise.'

'Oh, please do,' Selina agreed at once. 'I couldn't cope without her, and that's the truth.'

He made some comment in response, but Selina found she had no idea what. The children had all run up to the first floor and were now whooping and galloping about upstairs, making the ceiling shake. She should really go and see what they were up to.

He grinned. 'They sound rather excitable.'

'Yes, it's a big day, what with Peter leaving . . .' There was a loud crash from upstairs and she fell silent, staring upwards.

'Go on,' he told her, leaning back against the cushions. 'I'll keep the tea warm until you return. And I won't eat your slice of cake, I promise. I can see you're eager to get upstairs and sort those rascals out.'

Laughing, Selina whisked upstairs to calm the girls down, tidy up a tumbled plant pot on the landing, and usher Peter back to his bedroom, where his trunk and bags were now packed to bursting point.

'Golly, well done,' she told the housekeeper, now sweating and red-faced from her exertions. 'Thank you so much. Though Peter really ought to have been packing his own cases.'

She turned to her nephew to find he was upside down, engaged in fishing a lost tennis ball out from under his bed.

'Peter, apologise to Mrs Hawley for dashing off earlier when you ought to have been helping.'

The boy apologised, his voice muffled.

'And you're not taking that ball. Or your tennis racket. Your school doesn't play tennis in the winter terms. Mrs Hawley has packed your rugby gear instead.'

'I hate rugby,' Peter mumbled, turning himself upright.

'Only because you've barely played it.' She seized the tennis ball before he could stuff it into his blazer pocket. 'Look, I expect Mr MacGregor is a rugby man. It's a long journey into Devon. Maybe you can talk to him about it on the way?'

'I don't know about that, but his car is smashing,' Peter burst out, his face lighting up. 'Do you think he'll let me drive it one day?'

Mrs Hawley gave a shriek. '*You*? Drive a car?' She shook her head. 'You'd never reach the pedals, Master Peter. Especially not in a big beast like that.'

'I might,' he told her, looking sullen again.

'Peter, would you give me a hand taking these cases down to the car?' Selina asked diplomatically, picking up a bag of plimsolls and rugby boots. 'I expect Mrs Hawley can ask Mr Underhill to carry the trunk downstairs for us. But then you must say your goodbyes to your sisters. We'll be leaving within the hour. You won't be back until Christmas, remember.'

Dutifully, Peter took a case in each hand. But his smile had faded at this reminder, the sparkle gone from his eyes. 'Must I go away to boarding school, Aunt Selly?' he pleaded, not for the first time. 'Must I really?'

Selina bit her lip, overwhelmed by guilt at his forlorn expression. She hated parting him from his family like this but was unsure what to do.

This was what Bella had wanted for her son, after all, for Peter to get a good education at a fee-paying school and then gain a place at university, just like his father Sebastian. She was only following her late sister's instructions in sending him away. But it broke her heart to hear that despairing note in his voice.

'Oh, Peter,' she groaned. 'I know you're going to miss everyone madly. But you'll make so many new friends at school. You'll have forgotten all about us by this time next week, I promise.'

Deep down, however, Selina suspected the poor boy would be homesick for a good while longer than that. Peter was a sensitive soul, and she was fiercely glad that he'd been just a child during the war and couldn't be drafted to fight. Being forced to kill or be killed, and to witness the atrocities of war, would have destroyed the sweet, loving child she sensed behind her nephew's boyish bravado.

Boarding school, however, was a rite of passage for young men of his class, and one she could not in all conscience deny him. Not when her late sister had so particularly stressed her wishes for Peter's future.

There was much sobbing and hugging when the time came for the siblings to part. Jemima's lip trembled, and a tear rolled down her cheek as she embraced her older brother on the steps to Thornton Hall. 'Have a good time at school,' she told him, her voice shaking. 'You . . . You must write to us. If you don't, I'll be ever so cross. And we shall write too, every day.'

'You'll make me look ridiculous if you do that,' Peter muttered, but hugged her back. 'One letter a week is enough.'

He bent to kiss his baby sister on the cheek. 'Jemmy will look after you while I'm gone, Faith. Be a good girl, won't you?'

Faith clung to him, sobbing her heart out, wordless.

Pulling on her gloves, Selina stood watching this touching farewell with an unhappy heart. She wished again that it wasn't necessary. But what could she do?

Thankfully, Mrs Hawley swept Faith into her arms, drying the little girl's tears and saying comfortably, 'There, there . . . Master Peter will be back with us come Christmastime. And we'll have fun and games until then. You can help me with cooking, and Jemima will take lessons with Mr Harrington. Besides, you've letters to learn, young miss, if you want to write a letter to Master Peter yourself.'

Faith looked much happier at this suggestion. 'Yes, yes!'

'We really should go,' William MacGregor told Selina discreetly, opening the passenger door for her. 'We need to get to Devon and back, and I'd much rather not be driving home in the dark. Not over the moors.'

'Come along, Peter,' Selina told her nephew, and guided him gently to the car. Behind her, the groundsman came out with the heavy school trunk. 'Yes please, in the boot, Mr Underhill. That's very good of you.' Turning to the two girls, she told them, 'Be good for Mrs Hawley,' and gave them both a quick hug. 'Don't worry, I'll be back this evening.'

Once they had driven away, Peter waving forlornly out of the back window to his sisters, the boy's mood improved. He spent the first hour of their drive exclaiming over the 'spiffing' interior of the Wolseley, which he declared to be his 'favourite car in all the world'. He found a secret cubbyhole beside his seat where he could hide his sweets, and later peered over William's shoulder, asking curiously about the instruments on the dashboard, and how the Super Six engine worked. Selina was relieved that he seemed more cheerful now he was finally on his way to school. Maybe, she thought warily, everything would be fine. But then she caught a sad, wistful look in the boy's eyes as he glanced out at the rolling, sunlit moors, and guessed that he was merely putting on a brave face.

Peter's private school was not as grand as she'd expected, but William assured her it had a solid academic reputation and was worth its hefty fees. There were boys playing rugby on the school fields as they pulled up the long drive, and the few teachers they saw in the entrance courtyard seemed friendly enough, touching their tasselled caps to her before hurrying on.

Meeting the headmaster in his study, they shook hands and sat to wait while he spoke with Peter about joining the school and asked a few questions about his previous schooling. Mr Beeton was a smiling, rotund little man with an unfortunate moustache. But his friendliness seemed genuine enough. 'Trust me, your nephew will soon be perfectly at home here,' he told her, with such an air of authority and confidence that her fears were put to rest.

Finally, the time came for them to say goodbye.

Peter was pale and tight-lipped, but gave an abrupt nod, refusing to hug her. 'I'll write next week and let you know how I'm getting along, Aunt Selly,' he muttered, adding with stilted formality, 'Thank you for driving me here, Mr MacGregor.'

As they drove away, heading back towards Cornwall in the late sunshine, Selina found herself crying. 'How I hate this.' She dabbed at her eyes with a hanky. 'Poor boy . . . I wish I could have kept him at Thornton Hall forever. But this is what Bella wanted.'

William glanced at her, concern in his eyes. 'Please don't feel bad. I went to boarding school myself. It's not always wonderful, agreed. But it hardens you up. Makes you more independent too. That's what Peter needs right now. He's a good-hearted young fellow, but he still behaves like a child at times.' His hands tightened on the wheel as he stared at the misty road ahead. 'Boys his age had to grow up more quickly during the war.'

'Yes, and thank goodness that's all over. But you're right, I'm just being silly. Peter will be fine, I'm sure.'

But she still felt unhappy, imagining the boy alone and friendless in that great big school.

By the time they stopped for a rest at a moorland inn with a roaring fire, dusk had fallen and the autumn air was nippy. William bought her a glass of brandy. 'Here, this will warm your cockles.'

She wasn't used to drinking brandy, but accepted thankfully, feeling chilled. Climbing back into the car, Selina found herself relaxed and a little giggly. It was good to have a man around, she realised. She had grown accustomed to mainly female company at the house, with young Peter the only male under the roof.

With another man, she might have felt wary being alone in a car with him, especially after a brandy. Her first boyfriend Johnny would have taken advantage of the situation, she felt sure. He had certainly taken advantage of that Frenchwoman he'd been forced to marry, writing to break off their engagement after he got the girl pregnant.

And then there had been Cameron Bourne, her closest neighbour on the moors, whom she'd grown close to after Bella's death. Cameron had turned out to be a rotter, a highly duplicitous man indeed, and she felt lucky to have escaped his clutches with nothing more than the memory of a few awkward kisses.

William MacGregor, on the other hand, was a real gentleman and would never pounce on her, however much brandy she'd drunk. Not that she could ever think of him like *that*. He was far older than her, for a start, and had never shown her any untoward attention. He was a good man, though, and Bella had trusted him with all her affairs. So Selina felt quite safe in his company.

'Thank you for doing this, William,' she told him when they reached Thornton Hall a little after dark, and he got out to open her passenger door in his usual gallant manner. 'You're an absolute brick. I'm really very grateful.'

'There's no need,' he said softly.

She studied the lit windows of the hall with relief. 'No power cut tonight, I see. Though no doubt we'll have another one soon enough. I do wish the government would get their act together.' She hesitated. 'Can I offer you something before you go home? A cup of tea? A hot toddy?'

William shook his head, smiling faintly. 'I'm bushed, to be honest. But thank you for the offer. I'll drop in next week, if I may?'

'Our door is always open to you,' she said gratefully, and shook his hand. 'Goodnight.'

Trudging wearily into the entrance hall, Selina was stripping off her gloves and hat when the two girls came thumping down the stairs, both shouting at once, their excitable words making no sense whatsoever.

'Calm down, you two,' she told them, laughing as she crouched to give Faith a hug. 'What on earth is it? What's happened now?'

'There's a lady waiting for you in the parlour,' Jemima whispered, and Faith nodded urgently, her eyes wide with apprehension.

Puzzled, Selina straightened. 'I beg your pardon?'

'She's been here for hours. Mrs Hawley didn't know what to do with her. We were beginning to think you'd *never* come home. But now you're back, it will all be sorted out, won't it?'

'What will be sorted out? I don't understand.'

'Well, I never saw her before in my entire life,' Jemima hissed. 'But her name's Nancy, and she claims she's our *cousin*.'

Astonished, Selina stalked to the parlour, and sure enough, a young woman perched on the edge of the sofa jumped up at her approach. She had chestnut hair worn short, a strikingly handsome face, and her scarlet lipstick was a shade too strong for her pale complexion. Her huge blue eyes studied Selina warily, and then she gave a strained smile.

'Miss Tiptree?' The young woman held out a shapely hand marred by nails bitten short, pointing to a nervous disposition. Or possibly manual labour. Selina's own nails had only recently grown back since her long years working in the fields as a Land Girl. 'I'm Nancy Furniss. How do you do?' She had a breathy voice that matched the uncertainty in her eyes as they shook hands. 'I'm awfully sorry to impose on you like this, but . . .' Her voice broke off, and she choked, pulling away.

With a growing sense of amazement, Selina realised that the young woman was crying. What on earth . . . ?

Hurriedly, she chased the two fascinated girls out of the room, instructing them to wash their hands and face before supper, and then closed the door.

'Do sit down again,' she insisted, pulling on the bell for Mrs Hawley. 'My niece tells me you've been waiting for hours to see me. I'm sorry I was gone so long, but I had to escort my nephew to his new boarding school in Devon.' The girl said nothing but gave a jerky nod, dabbing at her eyes with a handkerchief. 'Have you eaten?'

'Yes, your housekeeper was most kind. She brought me tea and biscuits. I don't want to be any bother.'

'Nonsense.' Selina sat next to her on the sofa, studying her tear-stained face. 'Jemima tells me you may be a cousin of hers. On Sebastian's side, I assume?' She had certainly never heard of a Cousin Nancy on her and Bella's side of the family.

'That's right. I was Sebastian's second cousin, once removed.'

Selina frowned, trying to work that out. 'I'm sorry, but—'

'I'm not surprised you've never heard of me,' the girl went on, sniffing. 'My grandfather was estranged from his own parents, and my mother promised him never to speak to that branch of the family again. Bad blood or something.' Nancy shrugged, putting away her hanky. 'If you ask me, I think they argued over money.'

'I see.' Selina began to feel suspicious about this unexpected visit. 'You know that Sebastian's widow passed away this summer, I take it?'

'Yes, I'm ever so sorry for your loss,' Nancy told her

earnestly, sitting up straight. 'In fact, that's why I'm here. My parents live in Truro, and that's where we saw her obituary in the newspaper. Of course, Mother is such a stickler, she refused to come to the funeral. She promised Grandpapa, you see. But I didn't make any such promise. I barely knew my grandfather.' She lifted her chin, the look in her blue eyes almost mutinous. 'So I decided to come and pay my poor orphaned cousins a visit. Dear little souls, they're all alone in the world now.' She flushed, seeing Selina's face harden, and stuttered, 'Oh no . . . Please don't think I've come here looking for a handout.'

'Haven't you?' Selina asked bluntly.

Maybe she was being rude, but she refused to see her nieces taken advantage of by this young woman, for she suspected Nancy of being a poor relation, or at least someone short of money. Her cream blouse and knee-length brown skirt were decidedly shabby, and there was a run in her nylons. Yes, maybe she herself had looked just as shabby on her arrival at Thornton Hall, but Bella had invited her there to look after the children. She hadn't turned up in the hope of financial support.

'Goodness, no!' Nancy chewed on her lip. 'Though I must admit . . . I am somewhat down on my luck. During the war, I volunteered as soon as I was old enough, making bandages for wounded soldiers. But now . . . Well, I worked in Truro Hospital for a short while, training as a nurse. Only that fell through.' She looked away awkwardly.

There was something the girl wasn't telling her, Selina guessed, but decided not to probe her explanation further. She didn't want more tears.

'And now you're here.'

'But not for money,' Nancy said quickly, and that seemed truthful at least. 'Though I did see an advertisement in the newspaper last week . . . That's what prompted me to come, you see.' Her gaze searched Selina's face. 'Nanny required at Thornton Hall, Bodmin?'

'I'm sorry, I have no idea what—' With a shock, Selina stopped. She blinked, and then took a deep breath. 'Who placed the advertisement? Not a Mr William MacGregor, Solicitor, by any chance?'

'That's right.' Nancy produced a folded scrap of newspaper from her bag and handed it over. 'I went to his offices in Bodmin, as instructed by the advertisement. But it was closed. So I managed to find a bus that stopped five miles from the house, and walked the rest of the way.'

'No wonder you look so tired!' Selina exclaimed, and shook her head. 'Mr MacGregor means well, but he had no right to advertise for the post of nanny. We don't need one, I'm afraid. So if you were hoping to find employment here, you've had a wasted trip.'

Nancy said nothing, but tears welled up in her eyes again, and she groped for her handkerchief.

'But,' Selina carried on quickly, 'I'm sure the girls will be thrilled to spend some time with you tomorrow. They have so little family left.' Mrs Hawley had come into the room and was waiting for her orders, her distrustful gaze fixed on the young woman's face. 'Mrs Hawley, this is Cousin Nancy. She'll be staying for a day or two. Could you possibly prepare a guest room for her and set an extra place at the dinner table?'

'Very good, ma'am,' the housekeeper said, but as she turned to go, her eyes met Selina's with a look of disapproval.

'Thank you, that's so kind of you,' Nancy gushed, getting to her feet.

'Nonsense,' Selina said briskly. 'If you were Sebastian's cousin, that makes us cousins-in-law, doesn't it? So, please, sit down again and let's get to know each other.' Selina smiled and patted the sofa, determined to find out more about this mysterious newcomer. 'You can start by telling me all about yourself.'

CHAPTER SEVEN

Violet turned to stare as Sheila came into the kitchen, smoothing down her best frock and stepping cautiously in posh shoes she hadn't worn in months. The heels were quite low, but having been clad in wellies since summer's end, she was still finding it hard to balance.

'Mum, what on earth's that you're wearing? Is that your Sunday best?' Her daughter was clutching a stewpot straight out of the range and cursed as the heat burned through the oven cloth she was using. 'Ouch . . . Hang on a tick.' She turned to place the pot on a trivet. 'I thought you didn't have a council meeting tonight. You're not going out *again*, are you?'

Deciding it was wiser not to answer that, Sheila tried to make good her escape before Violet could interrogate her further. But the slate kitchen floor had just been mopped and was shining with soapy water, so she had to take baby steps to avoid slipping over.

'Oh blimey,' she muttered, exhaling in exasperation when car lights swept the farmyard. She'd hoped to find the kitchen empty, knowing that her daughter would no doubt have something to say about her and Bernie seeing each other again. And nothing complimentary.

'Who's that?' Violet peered out of the window.

'Erm, Bernard Bailey,' Sheila admitted, hurriedly pulling on her winter coat and hat. 'It's his birthday, so he suggested we have dinner together to celebrate.'

Violet's mouth compressed. 'You're going to his house for dinner? Just the two of you alone?'

'Oh, for Gawd's sake . . .' Sheila had trouble containing her temper. 'I'm your mother, Violet, not your daughter. Not to mention I've been widowed twice. At my age, if I want to go to a man's house, I certainly won't be asking your permission.'

The door opened with a brusque knock and Bernie stood on the threshold in a double-breasted pinstriped suit and raincoat, looking smart and handsome. 'Ready, Sheila?'

'Ready, Bernie.'

And with that, she strode boldly from the farmhouse, head high. Or would have done, if one of her heels hadn't caught on a loose slate in the porch and sent her flying.

Thankfully, Bernie caught her, grinning as he set her upright again. 'Falling into my arms before you've even left the house?' He gave her a wink. 'That bodes well for the rest of my evening.'

'Don't count your chickens, my lad,' she snapped back, flustered, and set her hat straight again.

Bernie owned a house on the outskirts of Porthcurno, only a short drive away. Yet she'd never been there before, despite his repeated invitations. Truth was, she felt awkward about her growing friendship with a man she knew to be of a higher social class, and so had resisted seeing his house in case it was too grand for her. She didn't want to sit down to dinner with him, secretly embarrassed by Joe's ramshackle farm and her own modest village shop.

'Here we are,' he murmured, turning off the engine outside a pretty whitewashed house with a thatched roof. It stood detached, overlooking the village, with a well-kept front garden still boasting a few late blooms. 'This is my home, Three Chimneys. I asked my housekeeper to leave dinner for us warming on the range. I believe it's a meat pie with gravy and vegetables.' He opened the front gate for her. 'Don't worry, she doesn't live in.'

'I can serve the pie. Just show me where she keeps her pinny, and I'll have dinner on the table in a brace of shakes.'

'Nonsense. You're my guest tonight, Sheila, and I'll be serving the dinner.'

In the dark, wood-panelled hallway, Bernie took her hat and coat before ushering her into a cosy front room. It was set about with armchairs and a handsome sofa, the curtains already drawn and an elegant standard lamp glowing in the corner.

'How about a drink before dinner?' He began rattling bottles on the sideboard, where two glasses sat waiting. 'Maybe a small sherry?'

'Better make it a big 'un,' she muttered, sinking into a deep armchair with green silk covers. Her heart was thumping, though she was determined not to show it. It would never do to show how overwhelmed she felt. It was all so posh. 'I mean, yes, thank you very much.'

With a grin, Bernie poured them both a sherry and brought the glass over. 'Cheers,' he said, and they clinked glasses.

Sheila choked on the strong, sweet sherry, and managed to spill some. 'Sorry.' Embarrassed, she rummaged in her handbag for a hanky. 'Meant to sip it and took a bloomin' great gulp instead.' She dabbed at her lips, hoping her face powder wasn't ruined. 'This is a nice room,' she ended lamely.

'Thank you.' He sat back on the sofa, smiling at her. 'It's a lovely house. But I get lonely here. Especially now the evenings are drawing in.' He took a sip of sherry and gazed thoughtfully about the room. A clock ticked loudly on the mantelpiece in the silence. 'I have to admit, I envy you.'

'Eh?' She wrinkled her brow, baffled.

'Living at Postbridge Farm with your daughter and son-in-law. It's such a busy place, with all the Land Girls too, people constantly coming and going . . . You're never alone up there, are you?'

'Well, you could put it like that, I suppose.' Sheila turned her glass in her hands, not daring to drink any more in case she choked again. 'Still, it was wonderful during the war . . . One big happy family. Whatever 'appened, however bad it was, you always knew you had each other.' Sheila smiled mistily at the memory of those tumultuous days, though the war had been awful too at times. Such as when the German bombers had flown along the Cornish coast, hunting for key targets like Eastern House, which had thankfully been well hidden under camouflage. Before she herself had come to Cornwall, before Joe and Violet had even married, one bomb had hit Postbridge Farm, killing Joe's mother and leaving a crater where the new barn now stood. Yet what she chiefly remembered were the good times . . . The knees-ups and the silly practical jokes they'd played to make life seem less dire. 'When times got tough, we had a good laugh and kept each other going.'

'It must have been a comfort when Arnold died too, having your family around you for support.'

'I would have been lost without them. Especially my lovely granddaughters, Lily and Alice . . . It's wonderful knowing they got through the war unscathed.' She pulled a face. 'Not entirely unscathed. We lost their mum, Betsy, my eldest daughter, to the Blitz. And we thought they'd lost their dad too, Ernest. He was missing, presumed dead, for most of the war. Only then he turned up on the doorstep one day, right as rain.'

'Incredible,' he murmured.

'That's a story for another day,' she told him, grinning. 'He's a wily one, Ernest. And he's left us again now. Gone back to London to live with his daughter Alice. Oh, I do miss her. She has some funny ideas at times, but I love her to bits.'

'You seem to love all your family,' Bernie remarked. 'It's a wonderful quality, that capacity for love.'

'I don't know about that,' she admitted with a chuckle. 'I was never fond of my sister's second husband. I'd gladly see Stanley Chellew fall down a hole and never come out. I do have my favourites though. And my granddaughters are top of the list. I mean, I'm getting on a bit now, but my children and my grandchildren . . . They're the future, aren't they? They're the ones our brave boys fought and died for, the ones we all sacrificed so much for, and they're the ones who'll need to put this country back together again, now it's all over. And my Lily and my Alice . . . Them two girls will do a bang-up job of it.'

She came to a halt, realising belatedly that he and his wife had never had children, and therefore had no grandchildren to be proud of.

Taking another sip of sherry, his gaze moved to a framed photograph on a side table. It was a snap of him and his wife, presumably on their wedding day, the couple posed outside a church door. Clutching a bouquet, the bride looked pretty and vivacious, and a young, handsome Bernie had an arm about her waist, smiling proudly as he held her close.

'Was that snap taken on your wedding day?' she asked, changing the subject. 'Your wife looks lovely. Eugenie, you said her name was?' Sheila had tears in her eyes, and didn't know why. Or perhaps she knew but didn't want to admit why her heart was aching. 'It never gets easier, does it? Losing someone you love, I mean. You just learn to rub along with the pain. Because if you didn't, you'd get nothing done.'

'True enough.' Bernie rose, putting down his glass. 'Now, I'd better see about dinner. No, you stay there.' He shook his head, overriding her protest with a good-humoured smile. 'I may not be much of a cook, it's true, but I've been fending for myself the past few years. I can don a pinny and wield a ladle when necessary.'

'Wait, I'd like to give you this before I forget.' Shyly, she reached into her bag and produced his birthday present. It was a small book on river fishing that she'd been offered by her supplier for sale in the shop and had instantly known would interest him, a keen fisherman. 'Happy birthday, Bernie.'

Surprised, he took the book and turned it over in his hand. 'How clever of you. This looks very interesting. I enjoy fishing.'

'I know you do. You mention it often enough.' She laughed at his chagrined expression. 'No, it's good for a man to have a hobby, especially one that takes him out of the house. I was always on at Arnie to take up fishing. But he wasn't one for going out into nature much.'

'I look forward to reading it, thank you.'

The beef and potato pie provided by his housekeeper turned out to be excellent. The pastry was light and flaky, even better than her own, and although there was more gravy than meat and potato, it was still tasty and filling. Better yet, the vegetables were not stewed to mush, the way Violet preferred to serve them, and the pie was followed by a bowl of tinned fruit with condensed cream, one of her favourite sweet dishes. Along with this feast, Bernie served a French red wine, from a crate of bottles he sheepishly admitted to having acquired on the black market during the war.

After she'd finished her fruit and cream, she pushed the bowl aside with a contented sigh. 'That was lovely, Bernie, thank you. My compliments to the chef.'

'I'll tell Susan tomorrow that you enjoyed it.'

Sheila eyed him suspiciously. 'How old is Susan?'

He grinned. 'Half my age and happily married. So no need to look daggers at me.'

'I never said a bloomin' word.' She lifted her glass of wine. 'Happy birthday, Bernie. I hope it's been a good one.'

He lifted his own glass for the toast, a twinkle in his eyes. 'It's a good birthday now you're here with me, Sheila. Thank you for the fishing book, and for saying yes.'

'I never turn down a free dinner,' she told him, with more humour than truth.

She had in fact dithered over his invitation at first. It had felt like a big step to agree to an intimate dinner at his house, birthday or no birthday. He had led her into the dining room, also wood-panelled, and furnished with a large, highly polished table and chairs. He was playing classical music on the gramophone, while a fire crackled away merrily in the fireplace. He had brought in the hot dishes himself and served her at the table. It all felt rather domestic, perhaps even romantic. But it was a far cry from her life at the farm.

To her surprise, however, she didn't feel uncomfortable here. Yes, the house was grand compared to Postbridge Farm, or where she'd lived in Dagenham, a narrow two-up, two-down terraced house that had probably been blown to kingdom come in the war. But with Bernie sitting opposite her with that smile in his eyes, it was easier than she'd expected to forget *where* she was and focus on *who* she was with instead. This man certainly had a knack for putting her at her ease.

Perhaps sensing her softening mood, Bernie set down his glass and reached for her hand instead. 'Sheila,' he began hesitantly, 'there's something I've been meaning to ask. I'm not usually a coward. But this thing has me on the back foot, so I've been putting it off. But tonight's as good a time as any to take the plunge.'

Sheila narrowed her eyes at him suspiciously. 'I hope you're not about to say something that will give me indigestion, Bernard Bailey. Because I'd rather not be upset.'

He was silent for so long that she thought she'd upset *him*. Then he said, with obvious difficulty, 'I don't want to upset you. Quite the opposite, in fact. I want you to marry me.'

As she stared, thrown by the question, he added softly, 'Will you, Sheila?'

'Oh my Gawd.' Sheila felt her heart begin to thump heavily. 'I . . . I don't know what to say.'

'You could say yes.'

She withdrew her hand, feeling awkward and knocked off balance. 'Or I could say no.'

He blinked at this, and stammered, 'Of course, you don't have to give me an answer immediately.'

'I'm glad to hear it,' she said, perhaps a little tartly.

With a dull clunk, the lights in the dining room went out and the gramophone in its smart wooden cabinet died too, the lively big band music slowing to silence. Exasperated, Sheila muttered something unladylike. As her eyes adjusted to the darkness, she found herself staring across at her would-be next husband by the glow of firelight.

'Damn government,' he said, annoyance in his voice. 'Another power cut.'

'And there was me thinking you'd arranged for the lights to go out, to make your proposal more romantic.'

He gave a bark of laughter. 'I've got a lamp in the hall. Hang on a tick.'

While he was gone, Sheila dropped her head into her hands and groaned. They'd barely even exchanged a kiss, and here he was, proposing marriage already. She'd seen it coming. But not so soon. She liked Bernie. No, it was more than just friendship. But was it love? And did that even matter at her age? The truth was, he was good company, and she wasn't expecting a grand passion. It might even be dangerous. But someone to laugh with, and chat about the old days, someone to hold her hand,

and to share the long, lonely nights of winter . . . That wasn't such a bad deal.

All the same, she couldn't see herself saying yes to his proposal. Not yet, at any rate. She could only hope he wouldn't be offended by a refusal.

He came back with a hurricane lamp that smelt of oil, its soft flame glowing through the glass. 'That's better.' He placed the lamp on the table, and glanced at her hesitantly. 'Can I pour you an after-dinner brandy? Or we could move next door and sit on the sofa.'

'The sofa sounds more comfortable. Though I'd prefer a cup of tea. How about I put the kettle on the range? It doesn't seem right, you doing *all* the work tonight.'

'I could murder a cup of tea.' He smiled, lifting the lamp to light their way. 'But don't think I haven't noticed what you're up to, Sheila.'

'Eh?' She followed him into the kitchen. 'I don't know what you mean.' But she knew perfectly well.

'You still haven't answered my question.' Bernie sat down at the kitchen table, watching as she bustled about the room, busily filling the kettle and setting it on the range to boil. 'I'm going to take it the answer's no. Because if it was yes, you'd have told me by now.'

Embarrassed, Sheila hunted for teacups, finding them displayed on the dresser, and set them on the table next to the milk jug. 'It's not a no,' she told him cautiously, 'but it's not a yes neither.'

'That sounds cryptic.'

She spooned tea leaves into the pot, perhaps a shade too generously, given rationing. 'Thing is, Bernie, it's a no for now. I ain't quite ready to get married again.'

'I see.'

His voice was steady, but she sensed a churning emotion behind it. The kettle began to build to a whistle on the range.

'With Arnie,' she explained gently, 'I was ready. I had nothing better to do than get married, frankly. He asked, and I said yes. There weren't much more to it.'

'And now?'

She fiddled with the teaspoons. 'Now I've a bloomin' load on my plate. I'm a parish councillor, for Gawd's sake. I'm running this charity fund for the poor, and organising hand-me-down clothing for them as need it. Plus, I'm dashing about all day in the shop, trying to keep on top of the paperwork. Ration coupons, the tick slate, ordering in new stock, paying invoices to the suppliers . . . It's never-ending.'

'You could give up the shop,' he suggested.

The kettle was now whistling madly. Snatching it off the range, Sheila glared round at him. 'I beg your pardon?'

'Sorry, that was a stupid thing to say.' While she made the tea, he sat studying his hands, not looking at her. 'So, what are you saying? You want to break things off? Is this birthday dinner our last hurrah?'

'Now you're being daft,' Sheila told him. 'I enjoy our drives about the countryside, and seeing you down the shop. But I also like being a councillor and running my own shop. I'm not ready to give those things up so we can get hitched.'

His troubled look had disappeared. 'But you're not ruling marriage out altogether?'

'I'm making no promises.' Pouring the tea, Sheila went on, 'Why can't we just carry on as we are? Two old friends, enjoying each other's company and not worrying about the future.' She added a splash of milk to each cup. 'Ain't that enough for you, Bernie?'

'I suppose it'll have to be,' he said with a grimace. 'For now.'

'Good.' Sheila spotted a crocheted cosy on the sideboard and covered the teapot to keep it warm. 'I'm glad that's sorted.'

After her first husband had passed, she'd taken on running a busy caff in Dagenham to help make ends meet, and had loved every hectic minute of it. When Arnie had died, leaving her his shop, she'd taken the risky decision to reopen it as sole proprietor, despite Violet's misgivings about her age, and was now enjoying herself immensely as a village shopkeeper. Bernie himself had cajoled her into becoming a parish councillor earlier that year, and helped launch her village fund for the needy too. He was too mild-mannered to demand she give up those pursuits if they married, she felt sure. But she might come under pressure to do so anyway, knowing what other villagers might say behind her back if she didn't.

Despite the recent war, when women had pitched in to do even the toughest jobs, she knew the villagers could still be judgemental when it came to married women daring to have a life of their own. Sitting on the council might be considered acceptable once she was Mrs Bernard Bailey, but running her own shop too?

She pushed his cup of tea towards him. 'By the way, I'll be going away soon.'

He stared at her. 'How's that?'

'November is one of the quieter months up at the farm, so I've decided to take a break and visit my granddaughter

Lily in Penzance. We got a letter from her the other day, saying she'd be happy to put me up for a week or two. I'll be taking the bus next Saturday, most likely, and can't be sure when I'll be back.'

The lights snapped back on at that moment, and from the other room she heard the gramophone begin playing again by itself, though not quite at the right speed yet.

Bernie gave a short laugh. 'I suppose we should be grateful we've any power at all, the way things have been going since the war ended. This country's in ruins and Lord knows how long it will take to rebuild.' He picked up his cup and saucer. 'I'd better turn off the gramophone. Then shall we move into the front room?'

They went through and sat on the sofa together. The fire was glowing embers now but the room was still pleasantly warm. It was also over-tidy compared to the messy farmhouse snug where she and her family sat and chatted until bedtime most evenings, while Joe's two working dogs stretched out happily in front of the fire, damp fur stinking out the place.

Sheila tried to imagine this posh house being her home instead, and had to hide a grin. She'd soon have this room looking more homely, for starters, cluttered with balls of wool and knitting patterns and discarded cardigans everywhere, not to mention Sarah Jane's toys strewn across the floor whenever her youngest granddaughter came to visit. She wondered if Bernie realised how much his life would change if she accepted his proposal, and doubted it.

Bernie said abruptly, 'Let me drive you to Penzance, Sheila. I have a cousin there. Friends too. People I haven't seen in some years. I could stay in the area and drive you back too.' He hesitated. 'We'd be able to have lunch occasionally.

Perhaps walk along the front together or go to the picture house. I haven't seen a film in ages.'

'Me neither,' she murmured, enchanted by the idea.

'You said you enjoy my company,' he pointed out. 'And that you'd like us to keep on courting. So how about it?'

'Violet would have fifty fits if you was to turn up in your car and take me to Penzance for two weeks.' She chuckled, imagining her daughter's outrage. 'She'd think we was running away together.'

'I'd like to run away with you, Sheila.'

Sheila decided to ignore that comment. 'Saying yes doesn't mean I've changed my mind about marrying you.'

'Understood.'

'Well, then,' she said, smiling at him. 'In that case, you may take me to Penzance, Mr Bailey. But no funny business.'

Bernie gave her a wry smile. 'As if I'd dare . . .'

CHAPTER EIGHT

Caroline trudged through muddy slurry after the other Land Girls, barely able to see their shadows ahead of her on the track. It was early November, almost what Joe called 'the dead season' when nothing needed sowing or harvesting, and only their small number of heifers needed attention, two being in calf that year. The lane was thick with dead leaves from the overhanging trees, turned almost to mush by prolonged rain the week before. A dry spell having set in at last, they and Joe had been hedge cutting up in the top fields since mid-morning. But Joe had ferried the heavy equipment back down in the van an hour since, leaving the girls to tidy the trimmings into a stack ready for burning.

'Hang on, girls, wait for me,' Caroline called after the other two, and then wearily stumbled over a loose stone in the mud. 'Oh, why does it have to get dark so early? It's not even teatime yet, and I can barely see my hand in front of my face.'

'Don't exaggerate, it's only dusk,' Grace exclaimed, but fell back and linked her arm with Caroline's. 'It's November . . . What do you expect?' Tilly also slowed her steps, waiting for them to catch up. Grace gave Caroline a playful nudge in the ribs. 'Anyway, does this mean you're too bushed to go into the village tonight for Guy Fawkes? Because, if so, can I have your toffee apple?'

Caroline laughed reluctantly. 'I'm not in the mood for standing around a bonfire for hours in the dark,' she began, but stopped when the other two girls began to chuckle. 'It's not funny. All that work we did today, cutting and clipping back those huge, thorny hedges . . . I swear, I'm exhausted.'

'That's only because you're old,' Tilly told her airily, taking her other arm, though there was scarcely enough room on the narrow track for them to walk three abreast. 'You're a poor old lady, and it's clear we girls need to look after you in your ancientness.'

'I'm not old,' Caroline protested, astonished, 'I'm twenty-six.'

'That's a lot older than me,' Tilly pointed out.

'But you've only just turned nineteen.'

'Dearie me, she sounds jealous.' Grace arched her eyebrows at Tilly. 'If you ask me, I don't think she likes your extreme youth. Eh, what do you say to us getting the old dear a walking stick for Christmas? One of them knobbly ones that only octogenarians use.'

'Why, you . . .' Caroline stared at them both, a little hurt, and the girls dissolved into helpless laughter. 'You're teasing, aren't you? I'm being roasted.'

'It's not our fault, Caro . . . Not when you make it so easy for us,' Tilly told her between snorts. With a grin, she stopped to sniff the air as they entered the farmyard. 'My, that smells delicious. Mrs Postbridge must have made one of her epic stews. I can't wait for supper, I'm absolutely starving.' And with that, she skipped ahead to the farmhouse.

Caroline was hungry too and followed on. She didn't have the energy to hurry, but she didn't want to miss out on Bonfire Night in the village. All through the war, nobody had been allowed to celebrate Guy Fawkes Day, due to strict regulations on the lighting of fires after dark. Since the rules had been relaxed, the village had organised a small celebration for the fifth of November, with the traditional burning of the 'guy' on a bonfire and, it was rumoured, a brazier of hot chestnuts to keep everyone warm.

She was concerned about her friend, though, and couldn't help wondering if Grace would still want to go into the village again at night. They hadn't spoken about what had happened after the Harvest Supper. But Caroline had thought about it often, and now felt uneasy.

'Will you be all right going out tonight?' she asked as they removed their muddy boots before heading into the farmhouse.

Grace looked round at her, surprised. 'What do you mean?'

'Those boys, the ones who were so horrible to you down in the village . . . What will you do if they're there again tonight?'

'Exactly what I did last time. I'll ignore them, won't I?' Grace removed her uniform hat, and her soft curls spilled out, glorious and free.

'You're awfully brave,' Caroline murmured, following Grace into the kitchen.

Joe was talking to his wife by the range, but their voices died away as the two girls came inside. Tilly was nowhere to be seen, presumably having dashed upstairs to get into the washroom first. It seemed to Caroline that the Postbridges must have been arguing again; Violet was looking flushed and Joe was frowning fiercely. But hearing her words, Joe came towards them with a puzzled smile, leaning heavily on his stick.

'Brave?' The farmer's gaze shifted to her companion. 'Is there a problem, Grace?'

'Yes,' Caroline replied for her when Grace said nothing. 'Some boys in the village weren't very nice to Grace after the Harvest Supper. They called her . . . Well, a rude name. Luckily, Jack Treedy was there, and he chased them away, then walked us home.'

Joe's frown had returned. 'What boys? You never said a word about this.'

'Because it wasn't important,' Grace assured him, going to the sink and washing her hands. 'Just stupid lads with nothing better to do.'

Violet, who had been kneading dough, wiped floury hands on her apron, her expression perplexed. 'But who were they?'

'Jack Treedy knew them,' Caroline told her. Seeing Grace's quelling look, she wished that she hadn't said anything. But it wasn't right and Caroline knew something ought to be done. 'We're going to the Guy Fawkes celebration tonight, and I was just hoping they wouldn't be there again. Grace shouldn't have to put up with being teased.'

'Teased about what, though?' Joe persisted.

'I told you, it doesn't matter,' Grace muttered, and hurried upstairs without another word.

Caroline stared after her friend in consternation. Was Grace angry with her for having told the farmer and his wife about those boys? She didn't understand. It wasn't as though Grace had done anything wrong.

'Caroline?' Violet put a hand on her shoulder. 'Perhaps

you'd better sit down and tell us all about it, love,' she suggested softly, 'while Grace isn't here.'

When they went down to the village later, Joe walked with them, leaving Violet to give Sarah Jane a bath and put her to bed. They asked Mrs Newton if she'd like to go too, since she'd just trudged up from the village shop, but she'd merely shaken her head and urged them to, 'Enjoy yourselves!' as she prepared a footbath for her aching feet. It was long after dark and bitterly cold by then, and the puddles dotted along the farm track had frozen to shining strips of ice.

They walked slowly, for Joe's sake, and so found the bonfire already well alight by the time they reached the village. People were gathered about the bonfire in hats and scarves, chatting and munching on hot chestnuts, their faces illuminated by the dancing flames.

Tilly soon slipped away to talk to a boy she liked, Joe fell into conversation with a fellow farmer, and Caroline and Grace huddled for warmth near the brazier where the chestnuts were being roasted. The bonfire crackled cheerfully, sparks floating high into the night sky, and someone even let off a series of fireworks, much to the excitement of the local children. A Catherine wheel was pinned to a post and left to spin, spitting out bright sparks in all directions, followed by several noisy rockets that soon had Caroline cringing and covering her ears.

'Goodness, that hurt my ears.'

'Me too . . . I hate loud bangs,' Grace agreed. 'Didn't we get enough of them during the war?'

'I used to love firework displays when I was a kid.' Caroline grimaced as another rocket screamed into the sky and exploded in a torrent of colourful sparks. 'Now they just bring back bad memories.'

Nobody else seemed particularly affected by the bangs of the fireworks. But she reminded herself that Cornwall, and in particular Porthcurno, had not suffered much bombing during the war. Coming from the London area, she still recalled that first terrible year after war was declared, while she was still living at home, not yet having volunteered to join the Women's Land Army. She'd been an impressionable girl, and the bombing raids had scared her out of her wits, especially after a former schoolfriend and her entire family were killed when a bomb destroyed their home only a few streets away.

That had been her main reason for choosing to sign up for working on the land rather than in a factory. She'd figured there must be less chance of being blown to smithereens in the countryside. The isolation of rural life had come as a severe shock to her at first. Raised in the suburbs, she was used to finding a shop or pub on every corner and people everywhere she looked. It hadn't been long before she'd fallen in love with the sweeping Cornish scenery and the bracing fresh air.

'Were you in Liverpool when war broke out?' Caroline asked.

Grace nodded, looking grim. 'My dad thought we'd be safe, so far north . . . Only, the bleedin' Jerries found us in the end, didn't they? They came along and flattened the city the next summer. That first wave of bombers . . . We were all underground, but when we came back up after the all-clear, it was like a scene from hell. Smoke and flames everywhere, and the ground was still hot under our feet.

The Germans bombed us for days until the whole city was ablaze.' She nodded to the bonfire. 'It was like one long Guy Fawkes night.'

'How dreadful.' Caroline slipped a hand through her friend's arm. 'Is that why you enlisted in the Women's Land Army? To get away from the bombing? That's why I left London,' she admitted with a shudder. 'I couldn't stand it any longer.'

'No, that's not why.' Grace gave a long sigh, shaking her head at the bag of hot chestnuts Caroline was offering her. 'I wanted to get away, all right. But not from the bombing.' She shot Caroline a crooked smile. 'I love my parents . . . Ronald and Audrey Morgan. Everyone loves them. They're very nice people. Very nice parents. But, Lord, I couldn't breathe without having one of them ask how deep.'

'They were . . . interfering, you mean?'

'I'm an only child. Everything they did revolved around me. Don't get me wrong, it's lovely, knowing they'll always be there for me, no matter what.' Grace rolled her eyes, looking up as another firework exploded in a brilliant shower of greens and reds. 'But I could never be myself, could I? Because they want me to be one way, and I'm . . . Well, I'm the other way.'

Caroline held her breath, staring at her raised profile. '*The other way*?' She blinked. 'I don't understand.'

'Oh, you know parents.' Grace made a dismissive gesture. 'They're always desperate to get you to be more like them, aren't they? Only I never could be. For a start, I didn't want to stay in Liverpool. I wanted to get away and see the world. Experience life beyond the "pool".' Grace laughed at some private joke, and then shook her head. 'Anyway, I write home every other month. And Mam writes back. We're not big letter writers in our family, to be honest. It was different when I was afraid they might be getting blown up at any minute. But the war's over. So what do you really need to say, except I'm well, how are you?'

Caroline understood. 'I should write home more often too.' Guiltily, she realised she hadn't been in touch with her own parents for months, when she'd finally written to tell them about Selina leaving the farm and moving to Bodmin, and how she'd spent a few wonderful days with her friend there, walking on the moors and playing with Selina's nieces and nephew. 'Though I write to Selina almost every week.' She had mentioned Selina a few times to Grace, explaining how she'd been a Land Girl until that summer and that they still kept in touch. 'But friends are different to family. When it's a friend, I suppose you have more to say.'

'You really liked that girl, Selina, didn't you?' Grace turned to look at her, her dark eyes intense. 'It must have been hard for you when she left the farm.'

Caroline gulped, not knowing how to reply to that. 'Um . . .'

'What's she like?' Grace pressed her.

'Nice, I suppose.'

'That's not what Tilly said when I asked her. She said Selina had a sharp tongue and was always causing arguments, and that you and she had even driven away one of the other Land Girls once. A girl called Penny. Is that true?'

Caroline's face felt it was on fire. She stared helplessly at Grace, hunting for the right thing to say. It wasn't true that she and Selina had driven Penny away. Was it? She knew Penny had left after a spat with Selina, and perhaps she herself hadn't helped matters by being offhand with Penny too, but she certainly hadn't intended to make her so unhappy that she fled the farm. And what did Tilly know about it, anyway? She hadn't even joined them when that happened, so she must have taken her account from someone else. Violet Postbridge, perhaps – though the farmer's wife wasn't usually one to gossip.

Thankfully, as she began to stammer a response, Joe came over to interrupt the conversation, looking agitated. 'Grace, them boys over there . . .' He pointed with his walking stick. 'Are they the ones who spoke rudely to you after the Harvest Supper?'

Grace looked surprised before glancing at Caroline, whose blush deepened. She knew Grace had not wished her to share that story with the farmer and his wife. But Violet had a way of winkling information out of people. 'I really couldn't say, Mr Postbridge.'

Beyond the bonfire, a group of young lads were clustered together, sharing a bag of hot chestnuts. Caroline told Joe quietly, 'The tall one in the middle . . . I'm not sure about the others.'

Joe nodded grimly, but the boys scattered as soon as they saw him coming.

'I wish you hadn't said anything to the Postbridges,' Grace muttered, sinking her hands in her jacket pockets and hunching her shoulders. 'It's my business, nobody else's.'

'But it's not your fault they were horrible to you. They can't be allowed to speak like that,' Caroline told her, but Grace turned and walked away. She didn't understand why her friend seemed so determined not to defend herself. But perhaps she just wanted to forget the whole thing.

* * *

After the 'guy' representing Guy Fawkes, who'd wickedly tried to blow up the King and Parliament back in the seventeenth century, had been thrown on the bonfire, with everyone cheering and applauding as it burned down to ashes, they began the slow walk back home.

'Remember, remember, the fifth of November,' Caroline chanted as they trudged up the steep hill, 'gunpowder, treason and plot.' As she repeated the well-known rhyme, Grace joined in, and then so did Joe, their voices ringing out across the frosty fields. 'I know no reason . . . why gunpowder treason . . . should ever be forgot!'

At the farm, they found Violet spooning hot soup into mugs for them. 'You must be freezing, going out on a night like this,' she grumbled. 'Mum went up to bed early, so I fed the chickens and shut them in the coop for the night, and checked the pigs were secure. Did you find those nasty boys, Joe?' She handed him a mug of soup, which he sniffed appreciatively.

'I did, but they scarpered before I could have a word. However, I've an idea who the ringleader is. And I'll be having a word with his parents.'

Grace was looking uncomfortable. 'It's very kind of you, but I do wish you wouldn't, Mr Postbridge. I know you mean well, but I'd rather drop it.'

Joe eyed her, frowning. 'Are you worried they might do something worse next time?'

Grace shrugged and blew on her hot soup, uncharacteristically silent.

'Come along with me,' Joe told Grace, then nodded at Caroline. 'You too.' They trooped into the snug after him, his two dogs following eagerly too, having been kept locked up all evening on account of the fireworks. He settled into his armchair next to the fire and nodded to Caroline. 'Fetch me that box on the table, would you?'

Given the wooden box, he riffled through the papers inside until he produced what looked like a letter.

'Sit down, and I'll tell you a story. This letter arrived a few years back from the mother of a friend of mine.' He unfolded it with infinite care, like something precious. 'My friend's name was Benjamin Hollis. His father had been Cornish but his mother was Jamaican, so Benji had dark skin – not much different from yours, Grace.' He fingered a small photograph that had been enclosed with the letter. 'This is him. A likely lad, eh?' He held it up, and Caroline saw a cheery young man in a naval uniform, probably in his mid-twenties. 'Benji loved playing tricks on us all, smiling and joking. But he was a kindly lad too. Whenever I was homesick, or scared on account of them German U-boats that were always looking to sink us, Benjamin would soon set me laughing again. He was a good man, and a good sailor too.' His voice cracked with emotion, and he withdrew a handkerchief from his pocket to blow his nose. 'When our ship was hit, I lost my leg, as you see. But Benjamin . . . He was one of them poor souls that was never found.' He sighed, studying the photograph. 'Lost at sea.'

Grace was sitting very still, head down, hands clasped in her lap. But she was listening. Caroline saw a tear tremble on her friend's long eyelashes, and felt herself gulp too, a thick salty knot in her throat.

'I wrote to Benji's mother after I was shipped home to Cornwall, to say how sorry I was for her loss and to tell her a little bit about her son in his last days. What he'd been up to that week, what I remembered him saying, and so on. It was the least I could do. She was a widow, see, and he'd been her only child. She sent me this nice letter in return, and a photograph for me to keep. Sometimes I take it out and look at it, and think about Benjamin Hollis. You have to keep their memory alive, the ones you've lost.'

He leant forward, holding out the photograph, and Grace took it with trembling fingers. She studied it for a long time, and then passed it to Caroline. 'He was a handsome young man,' she said in a stilted voice. 'I'm sorry he died. But I'm glad you were such good friends with him.'

Joe nodded, watching her. 'Them lads taunting you . . . That reminded me of some of our fellow shipmates. Because Benjamin had dark skin, he was often teased for it. Some men did it as a joke. But others didn't. Once or twice, I saw him with bruises on his face and asked how he got them. And he would never say. Just laugh it off. But it made me furious. He was a man like any other, and them wicked, good-for-nothing . . .' He choked on his words, catching Violet's eye, who was knitting by the fire, and stopped to clear his throat. 'I won't use bad language in front of you ladies. But Benji was worth ten of them, and that's God's honest truth.' His gaze shifted to Grace. 'Just as you're worth twenty of them stupid boys in the village. And don't you forget it, Miss Morgan.'

Caroline handed him back the photograph, and Joe wrapped it up painstakingly in the letter before replacing both in his box of papers.

'If any boy cheeks you again,' he went on, 'or dares lay a finger on you . . . You're to come straight to me, and I'll sort it out. Because it ain't right.'

Grace said nothing, perhaps because she was crying softly. Caroline, very daringly, took her hand and gently squeezed it.

'Please don't cry, Grace,' she whispered, her heart aching. 'You've done nothing wrong, remember?'

But Grace pulled her hand away, rising abruptly to leave the room without another word, and Caroline stared after her in fear and confusion. Cold inside, she could barely meet Joe and Violet's eyes as she stumbled to her feet too.

'I'm sorry . . . She's upset. I'd better go after her. Unless you need a hand washing out the soup mugs, Mrs Postbridge?'

'No, love, you go up to bed,' Violet told her kindly, but her smile seemed troubled.

Pausing on the stairs, Caroline stopped with a shudder and closed her eyes, trying to arrange her scattered thoughts.

Violet's smile had worried her. Her own fault, of course. She shouldn't have touched Grace's hand in that intimate way. It had been the wrong thing to do. But the truth was, she liked Grace rather too much and had acted on impulse. Now it was possible that Violet might have spotted her partiality and was busily drawing her own conclusions. She would need to be more careful, she told herself, especially after what had happened with Selina.

She recalled that awful last day at the farm with Selina, when Caroline, no longer able to bear the pain of her dearest friend's impending departure, had blurted out that she was in love with her.

Thankfully, her dangerous confession had gone no further. Friends with Selina for years, she'd known her to be trustworthy, despite her other faults, so the real danger was only ever to her heart. Yet much as she admired Grace, she'd barely known the girl five minutes. It would be the height of madness to let a newcomer see her true feelings.

Feelings which young women like her were supposed to reserve for men . . . Not other women.

CHAPTER NINE

'Your new car is simply marvellous, Aunt Selly,' Jemima gushed, tucking her hand into Selina's. They were standing on the steps of Thornton Hall, watching with fascination as the head groundsman, Mr Underhill, took a bucket of soapy water and a cloth to Selina's car, a recent acquisition that William MacGregor had helped her make.

'Thank you,' Selina told her niece proudly. 'I'm glad you approve.'

The car was second-hand, purchased out of her own savings. It had a few minor bumps and scrapes to the paintwork, having been in an accident. However, William had assured her it was a 'good runner'. It was a Hillman Minx, and she'd fallen in love with it as soon as the car salesman in Bodmin had shown it to her.

Owning her own car gave her a sense of independence. She was no longer reliant on other people driving her about and, thanks to William's regular driving lessons, now felt confident enough to venture forth alone. She didn't yet have a full licence, but due to wartime changes, her provisional licence would allow her to drive on her own, so long as she took her test within a year.

'Shall I take you out in the car once it's been cleaned?' Selina glanced up at the skies, which were gloomy, but not threatening rain. 'We could take a quick run into the village and back.'

Jemima jumped up and down with excitement. 'Yes, please. Can Faith come too?'

'I suppose so. Though only if she agrees to sit still on the back seat and behave herself.' Selina sucked in a breath as the girl dashed away to tell her younger sister, calling after her, 'Careful, don't run! You might have an accident.'

As usual, Jemima paid no attention, shouting for her sister as she raced up the stairs. Still, it was nice to see her eldest niece happy and enjoying life. Her brother Peter had been gone several weeks now, safely installed in his boarding school in Devon, and both girls had been pining for him ever since. But it seemed the arrival of Selina's sleek Hillman Minx had bucked Jemima's spirits up at least.

Selina went back inside to fetch her gloves and hat. But excited shrieking and the sound of running feet on the floor above made her stop.

With a sigh, she hurried upstairs to remonstrate with the girls, fearful of them slipping on the polished wooden flooring. But everything had gone strangely silent by the time she approached the room designated as Jemima's 'schoolroom'. The tutor had been there earlier, teaching Jemima some elementary French, and helping Faith write out the alphabet. But he'd left at lunchtime, as this was his half-day.

Peering around the schoolroom door, she was astonished

to find Jemima seated quietly at her desk, head bent over a book. At her own, far smaller desk, Faith was diligently tracing letters with a pencil, her tongue sticking out as she concentrated fiercely on the task.

Amazed, Selina soon spotted the reason for this good behaviour. The girls' cousin Nancy was in the room with them. She was sitting neatly in the chair that their tutor, Mr Harrington, usually occupied. She too was reading, though her reading material was a ladies' fashion magazine.

'Hullo,' Selina said, raising her brows. 'I didn't expect to find you in here.'

Nancy looked up with a start, her cheeks turning pink. 'Oh, hullo,' she replied awkwardly, setting aside her magazine, 'I hope you don't mind . . . Jemima said you were planning to take the girls out in your car. But I could see from the window that it's still being washed. So I thought it might be better if they did some quiet work in here while they waited, rather than running about the house like a couple of banshees.'

'No, that was good thinking,' Selina said, smiling. 'Thank you.'

Initially, she had only intended Nancy to be their guest at the hall for a few days. But it had soon become apparent that the young woman had nowhere else to go. There'd been a falling out with her parents, it transpired, and although Nancy had been tearful and incoherent when questioned about this, it was plain that she didn't feel able to return to the family home.

Rather than turn the poor creature out onto the street, Selina had made a strategic decision to allow her to stay for the time being. She had not engaged her as a nanny, however, not knowing the first thing about her character yet, and had taken William MacGregor to task for having advertised the position without consulting her first.

He had apologised, withdrawing the advertisement for a nanny immediately. 'I only did it to help you,' he'd told her, looking embarrassed. 'You always seem rushed off your feet these days.' She had told him in return that she still wished to be a mother to the girls, and pointed out that this should be easier now that Peter was away at school, as the girls were far less likely to get into mischief with their older brother absent.

Yet she couldn't deny that Nancy was a soothing presence in the house. And, indeed, here were the girls now, sitting quietly side by side as they worked, apparent paragons of virtue, and Selina had not even needed to raise her voice to achieve this miracle.

'Since you're both occupied with your studies now,' Selina said, hiding her smile, 'I'd better go down and speak to Mrs Hawley about our dinner tonight. But don't worry. As soon as the car's ready, I'll give you a shout and you can all come out with me on a drive.' She hesitated, glancing at Nancy uncertainly. 'You're welcome to come too, Nancy, if you'd like. There's room for one more.'

Nancy looked pleased. 'How kind of you. Thank you, I'd love to come.'

As Selina descended the staircase, she heard the telephone ringing. Selina had made a few calls using the hall telephone during Bella's illness and in the aftermath of her sister's death, but since then had avoided it, except to take a few calls from William. There had never been a telephone at the farm, and besides, she found speaking on the telephone awkward. Who on earth could be calling?

In the hall, Mrs Hawley came hurrying towards her, biting her lip and looking apprehensive.

'Oh, Miss,' she said breathlessly, 'there's a telephone call for you. It's from Master Peter's school.'

Selina felt the blood drain from her face, her body rigid. 'From his school? Are you sure?'

'It's the headmaster himself on the telephone. Says he needs to speak to you urgently.'

'Thank you.' Terrified, Selina picked up the telephone, her voice shaking as she said, 'Hello? Miss Tiptree speaking.'

'This is Mr Beeton,' the headmaster said. 'No need to be alarmed, Miss Tiptree. Your nephew is quite well.'

'Oh thank goodness.'

'I'm sorry to be calling you like this. But I'm afraid you need to come and collect Peter from the school.' Mr Beeton sounded severe and lofty, almost as though accusing her of something. 'Unfortunately, I've been obliged to expel him.'

Selina sagged against the wall, holding the receiver against her ear in disbelief. 'Expel him? But he's barely been at the school a month.'

'I'm sorry to say this of any boy,' the headmaster began, 'but Peter March is never going to fit in at this school. Nor at any school, I would suggest, until such time as his wild behaviour can be curbed. Though, frankly, I'm not sure it ever can be.'

'Wild behaviour?' Selina repeated, blinking. 'What exactly has he done wrong?'

'We can discuss that when you come to remove him,' Mr Beeton told her flatly. 'I have a Board of Governors meeting in five minutes, and this conversation will take considerably longer than that. Will you be able to fetch him today?'

Stunned, Selina glanced at her watch. Leaving now would mean driving back across the moors in the dark, something she had never done before, and in a new car too.

'I'd rather come tomorrow.'

'You should make the effort to come today. Peter is not popular with his fellow pupils at the moment, let me put it like that.'

'Good God.' Selina swallowed. 'In that case, I'll come at once. Will you see that his trunk and cases are packed for when I arrive?'

'Of course. Thank you, Miss Tiptree.'

And the line went dead.

There was snow on the high moors, but thankfully a number of cars had already passed that way, and Selina was able to steer along the tracks left by their tyres. Come nightfall, however, the road was likely to freeze over and become a skating rink. But with fuel still being strictly rationed, she had to be cautious with the number of miles she drove.

It was already dusk by the time she reached the imposing, iron-wrought gates to the school.

The headmaster must have been anxious for her to arrive. He came out onto the steps to welcome her, with Peter beside him. Mr Beeton came forward, hand outstretched. 'I was beginning to worry . . . Good of you to come at such short notice, Miss Tiptree. I'll have our porter load the boy's trunk into the car while we talk inside.'

'Peter? Are you all right?' She put a hand on her nephew's shoulder, but he shrugged it off, looking away, his face pale and stubborn.

Not knowing what to think, she followed Mr Beeton to his office, Peter trailing behind.

She was too nervous and upset to accept his offer of tea, so Mr Beeton launched straight into his explanation instead. 'I didn't want to say anything on the phone that would upset you. But I'm afraid Peter's transgressions are very serious indeed. In fact, I was in half a mind to summon the police.'

Selina jumped to her feet in alarm. '*The police*?' Her horrified gaze shot to Peter's face. 'What on earth have you done?'

When there was no reply to this, the headmaster cleared his throat. 'He attempted to set fire to the sports pavilion.'

'I beg your pardon?' Her heart was hammering and she felt breathless. 'Good God, Peter . . . Whatever am I to do with you?'

'Please, Miss Tiptree, try to stay calm,' Mr Beeton said. 'There's no need for you to do anything. Peter has already been punished.'

She sank back onto the seat, feeling as though she were in a nightmare. 'P-Punished?'

'I was given the cane,' Peter muttered, staring at the floor.

Her sense of shock disappeared, replaced by fury. 'But how barbarous . . . You *beat* him?' she gasped. 'Why on earth was that considered necessary, Headmaster?'

Mr Beeton raised his brows. 'Miss Tiptree, attempted arson is not the kind of behaviour we expect of our pupils. You should be grateful we didn't involve the authorities. Your nephew could have caused a great deal of damage to school property, and even endangered the lives of everyone here.'

Selina wrung her hands, not sure what to do. 'Peter? You

didn't seriously try to burn down the sports pavilion, did you?'

She hoped he would deny it. But Peter gave a brusque nod.

'Yes, I did,' he agreed, still not meeting her eyes. 'So you'd better take me home.'

She searched his face. 'You *want* to be expelled?'

But the headmaster interrupted this line of questioning, getting to his feet. 'Perhaps it's for the best. Peter has been given every chance to fit in with the other pupils here, but he's made enemies rather than friends, and more than once been involved in a brawl. Believe me, Miss Tiptree, he's caused nothing but trouble since he came to us. He's been caned, given detentions and lines, and been spoken to on numerous occasions. None of it has had any impact.'

Selina glared at the headmaster with cold fury. 'If you think punishing a boy with caning and extra work, or a good talking-to, are policies that will ever prosper with a boy who's clearly homesick and grieving for his late mother, then you are a fool, Mr Beeton, and have no business running a school.' She took Peter's hand, squeezing it reassuringly. 'Goodbye, Headmaster. We can see ourselves out.'

And she swept from the room, keeping Peter tight by her side.

It wasn't until they were almost ten miles down the road that she finally found her voice. 'Why did you try to set fire to the sports pavilion?' she queried. 'And please don't tell me it was a prank gone wrong, for I won't believe it.'

When Peter said nothing, she risked taking her eyes off the road to glance at him. That was when she realised that the boy was crying.

'Oh, Peter!' Hurriedly, she pulled onto the verge. 'Come here.' She gave him a hug, and felt him shudder into sobs. 'Poor boy . . . I've let you down badly. None of this would have happened if I'd kept you at Thornton Hall with your sisters. But your mother was so insistent that you should get a good education. And you've been to boarding school before and seemed to enjoy yourself. What went wrong?'

'I . . . I didn't make a single friend,' he stammered. 'They all hated me from the start. The other boys made fun of my accent. Said I was "proper Cornish" and called me a peasant. When I told my housemaster, he said I should harden up and stop being a crybaby. And I tried, Aunt Selly. Only, the other boys were cross that I'd told on them. They called me a weasel, and stole my books, and scribbled rude words over my homework so I'd get in trouble for it. And sports was the worst thing ever . . . You know how rubbish I am at rugby. The others said I was letting the side down. They took turns punching and kicking me to make me tougher.'

'Good God!' Selina trembled with rage at how badly her nephew had been treated. 'I should drive straight back there and explain all this to that awful headmaster.'

'Please don't,' Peter begged her, bursting into fresh tears. 'I never want to go back to that school. I'd rather *die*!'

'It's all right, I won't take you back. There's no need to cry, it's all over.' She started the engine again. 'Let's go home to Thornton Hall.' As she pulled away, she felt the tyres slither and slide under them, and pulled a face. 'Oops . . . That's assuming I can get us home in one piece.'

'I believe in you, Aunt Selly,' Peter insisted, wiping his

damp face with his sleeve. 'By the way, this is a smashing car,' he added, with a touch of his old enthusiasm. 'Not as bang-up as Mr MacGregor's Wolseley, of course. But still smashing.'

It took twice as long to return in the dark, especially with snow on the roads, but Selina felt proud of herself on reaching Thornton Hall by late evening without once crashing into a ditch on the snowy roads. Wearily, they let themselves into the hall, only to find the girls running towards them, with Nancy and Mrs Hawley behind.

'Welcome home, Peter!' Jemima cried, and threw herself into his arms.

Faith danced about them, clapping her hands for joy. 'Peter, Peter,' she chanted until he bent to give her a hug too.

'You're here very late, Mrs Hawley. Nothing wrong, I hope?' Selina asked anxiously.

'No, ma'am. I couldn't go home without knowing whether you'd got back safely with Master Peter,' the housekeeper admitted. She beamed at the lad indulgently. 'It's marvellous to see you home again,' she told him, and Peter grinned, shuffling his feet in embarrassment. 'I've kept supper warm for you both. Shall I serve it in the dining room, ma'am?'

'Yes, please, Mrs Hawley. We're famished.'

'Oh, and this letter came for you.'

'Thank you.'

Jemima was excitedly introducing Peter to his cousin Nancy, so Selina tore open the envelope and quickly read over the contents. It was from Caroline, begging her again to visit Postbridge Farm, and telling her there would be plenty of room if she came straightaway, as Mrs Newton was going to stay with Lily and Tristan in Penzance for at least two weeks. And Violet's permission had already been sought and given, so there would be no trouble from Mrs and Mrs Postbridge.

'Does this mean you're home for good, Peter?' Nancy was asking. 'Or has the school sent you home because you're unwell?'

Selina watched unhappily as a stammering, red-faced Peter tied himself in knots, trying to explain his return without admitting that he'd been expelled. It was clear the boy wasn't ready to talk about it yet, not even with family. But his expulsion could hardly be kept a secret for long.

She dreaded to think what might have happened if Peter had been left in that horrid place even a single day longer. But she could see that bringing him home had only been half the battle. He would not readily get over all the beastly things they'd done to him at that school. The thought of him suffering such torments made her heart ache with guilt, knowing she was partly to blame for having sent him away against his will.

Perhaps a trip to Porthcurno might be just the thing for her nephew. Somewhere new, with people who didn't know him or his history, where he could relax for a week or two before knuckling down to books and learning again with Mr Harrington. And she felt sure his sisters would be perfectly happy here alone for a short while, now their capable cousin Nancy had come to stay. Nancy had originally asked to be their nanny, after all. It could be a trial run for her, to see how the young woman coped with the girls on her own. And if she got into difficulties, Mrs Hawley was usually around, and William was only a telephone call away.

Yes, a few days in Porthcurno sounded like just the ticket. Folding Caroline's letter back into its envelope, Selina smiled, wondering if Violet Postbridge wouldn't mind catering for an extra guest . . .

CHAPTER TEN

Bernie came into the farmhouse kitchen, stamping snow off his boots. 'That's the last of your bags packed in the car, Sheila. And I've put a blanket on the back seat in case you need it.'

'I'm not going to need a blanket,' Sheila told him firmly.

Violet glared. 'It's bloomin' freezing out there, Mum. You can't drive all the way to Penzance without a blanket. What if snow starts falling again and you get stuck?' Violet handed her a hamper. 'Talking of which, I've made paste sarnies for you both. And a tidy slice of pork pie. It's only what we're having for lunch ourselves, so that's your portion and a bit more besides for Bernie.' She drew a sharp breath, glancing at him. 'Erm . . . I mean, Mr Bailey.'

He grinned, shaking his head. 'Bernie's my name and you're welcome to use it, Mrs Postbridge.'

'When you two have stopped playing silly beggars,' Sheila said before Violet could respond, 'perhaps we could get going? I told Lily we'd be there by lunchtime.'

Bernie's grin widened. 'You make it sound like we're

heading for the Outer Hebrides, not Penzance. Goodness, you even suggested taking the bus there the other day.'

'And then I decided your car would be more comfortable,' Sheila said loftily, and handed him the hamper. 'You can put that on the back seat too, thank you very much.'

'Your wish is my command,' he said with a mock bow. 'I'll wait for you in the car, then.'

As soon as he'd gone, Sheila whirled to face Violet, suddenly panicking. 'Thanks for the sarnies . . . I haven't forgotten anything, have I? I've got the Christmas presents, and that Victoria sponge you baked for Lily, and all my bags.' She looked at her daughter, stricken. 'You'll be all right without me, won't you, love? Because if you need help, you can always ask one of the Land Girls to pitch in.'

Caroline, hurrying into the kitchen with a letter in her hand, and still in her dressing gown, said quickly, 'Oh yes, just holler if you need a hand in the kitchen, Mrs P. Not that any of us are much good at cooking. But we can peel vegetables and lay the table, and we're always happy to wash up.'

'That's kind of you, Caroline, but I can manage on my own, thank you.' Violet glanced at the letter she was clutching. 'Is that from Selina? How's she getting along in Bodmin? It must have been quite a shock for her, landed with three children to look after. Poor girl, I expect she's rushed off her feet.'

'Funnily enough, that's what I was coming to tell you,' Caroline said awkwardly. 'Selina's had a bit of trouble with her nephew, Peter. He's been expelled from school. The thing is, she's written to ask if she can bring him with her when she comes to stay.'

‘Eh?’ Sheila was baffled. ‘Selina’s coming to stay?’

Violet shrugged, looking embarrassed now. ‘I said she could visit us while you’re in Penzance. There’ll be a spare room with you gone, after all.’

‘Oh, I see.’ Sheila rolled her eyes. ‘Turn my back for five minutes and someone’s in my bloomin’ bed. Should I leave me slippers behind too?’

‘Don’t be daft, Mum.’ Violet frowned at Caroline. ‘Hang on, if this lad has been expelled from school, why would I want someone like that staying in my house? What did he do to get thrown out?’

Caroline chewed on her lip, studying the letter again. ‘Well, it’s not clear . . . But Selina claims he didn’t do anything wrong. At least, he didn’t *mean* to.’

‘Hmm.’ Violet pursed her lips.

Grace came in from the yard at that moment, unwinding her scarf and shivering. ‘It’s bitter out there. I’m glad you haven’t gone yet, Mrs Newton. I meant to wish you a happy holiday in Penzance.’

‘Thank you, dear.’ Sheila glanced between the two girls, noticing how Caroline’s gaze had fixed on the other girl as soon as she walked in. With a sympathetic pang, she recognised the wistful expression on her face. Caroline had often looked at Selina the same way, especially in those difficult final weeks before her friend had left the farm for good.

Grace gave Caroline a cool look. ‘You not dressed yet? Best hurry up and get your togs on. You were meant to be outside twenty minutes ago. You and me are cutting kale for fodder, and Tilly’s helping Mr Postbridge check over that new litter of pigs.’

'Sorry, I was reading my letter from Selina. I'll come straightaway.' Caroline turned to Violet, her eyes pleading. 'May I write back, then, and say she can bring Peter?'

'It would be uncharitable of me to say no, wouldn't it? But he's not to cause any trouble.'

'Thank you, Mrs Postbridge, that's awfully kind of you. I'll write back this evening when I've finished work.' Caroline beamed at Grace. 'I'll run and get dressed. Wait for me, won't you?'

Grace gave a crooked smile, shoving her hands deep into the pockets of her mustard breeches. 'Do I have a choice?' But she was laughing as she strolled back into the cold sunshine.

Sheila watched her go, and then shook her head at her daughter. 'Oh dear, oh dear. I see Caroline's developed another pash,' she whispered.

Her daughter stared back at her blankly. 'A *what*?'

'A pash. You know . . . A passion. A little crush.'

'Sorry?' Violet glanced at the door, horrified. 'Blimey. You don't mean . . . her and Grace?'

'Of course. Though Caroline will get over it soon enough. She got over Selina, didn't she? It took her a while, but she's smiling again now.'

'Her and *Selina* too?' Arms folded tight, Violet shook her head in abrupt denial. 'Mum,' she burst out, her voice high with outrage, 'you can't go around accusing people of things like that . . . I swear, I was never more shocked.'

Sheila pulled a face, wishing her daughter had not grown up to be such a prude. 'It's not such a big deal.' She paused, adding with a wink, 'Even *I* liked a girl once.'

'Mum!'

'It was just after I moved to Dagenham with your grandparents. Beatrice, that was her name. Oh, I had such a pash for her. I broke my heart that summer, thought I'd never get over it.' With a smile, Sheila recalled Bea, whose long golden hair had mesmerised her for months. 'But it all came to nothing in the end.'

'Hush, for goodness' sake . . . Bernie will hear you.' Violet's eyes were like saucers now.

'So what if he does?' Sheila exhaled noisily. 'Bernie don't give a fig what I was thinking fifty-odd years ago. All he wants to know is what I'm thinking *now*.' She shook her head, recalling her younger self with amusement. 'I saw Bea in the street one day, you know, years after we'd left school. She was walking along with another young woman, arm in arm, smiling like she'd won the pools. And it didn't bother me one jot,' she added. 'But I'd met your father by then, so that was just as well.'

'You never told me any of this before,' Violet said accusingly.

'There's a great deal I haven't told you, my girl. Besides, who cares? People love who they love, don't they? It's nobody's business but their own.'

Violet cast an aggrieved look towards the staircase. Caroline was hurrying down the stairs. 'That's all well and good, but these girls are under our roof,' she hissed. 'In our charge. We should be keeping an eye on them.'

'Now who's being daft? Caroline's about the same age as our Lily,' Sheila pointed out, 'and Lily's a married woman with a kiddie of her own. You can't go around telling grown women what to bloomin' think and feel.'

'I suppose you're right,' Violet grumbled.

Caroline dashed through the kitchen, oblivious to their gossiping, and waved merrily at Sheila before heading into the yard. 'Have a great time in Penzance, Mrs Newton,' she called over her shoulder.

Staring after the girl, Violet whispered, 'But what about Grace? I don't want that girl made uncomfortable by Caroline mooning after her all day. '

'Best leave them to sort it out for themselves, love. Anyway, something tells me it would take a mite more than that to make Grace uncomfortable.'

Bernie beeped his horn outside.

Sheila started guiltily. 'Gawd, I'd forgotten all about him. Well, goodbye, Vi,' she said hurriedly and kissed her daughter on the cheek. 'I'll give your love to Lily and Tristan. And little Morris, bless his heart.'

'I wish you weren't going,' Violet said unhappily. 'Me and Joe . . .' But she stopped, her lips tightening.

'Yes? You and Joe?' Sheila prompted her, but Violet shook her head, looking stubborn.

'Nothing, Mum. Have a good time and come back safe.'

Sheila sighed. 'I'll do my best, love.'

She wished her daughter would open up about the problems in her marriage, since nobody could have missed the signs . . . Arguments that rumbled on for days, cold looks, and a tension in the air that made mealtimes awkward, even for the Land Girls, who were usually too wrapped up in their own little world to notice anyone else. But there was nothing she could do about it, not when she was going to be in Penzance for the next couple of weeks.

She whisked herself out to Bernie's huge Daimler, clutching her handbag and hoping to goodness she hadn't forgotten anything important. 'Oh, blimey . . . Too late to change my mind now,' she groaned, clambering into the passenger seat just as Bernie started the engine.

'Penzance, here we come,' Bernie said with a grin.

Sheila cranked down the window to wave frantically at poor Violet, who'd come out into the yard to see her off and was wafting a white hanky about like she was planning to surrender.

It was a sunny morning in Porthcurno, despite the chilly, whitened hedgerows and paths, but there were dull cloudbanks ahead, suggestive of heavier snow roughly in the direction they would be taking. Bernie had assured her that if the daily bus was getting through without any problems, so could his car. But the best-laid plans, and all that.

Sheila drew on her thick woollen gloves, suddenly glad of the blanket and hamper on the seat behind her.

They reached Penzance a little after lunchtime, due to Bernie taking the corners at a snail's pace, worried about ice on the roads and the possibility of his prized car ending up in a ditch. But they suffered no mishaps, and Sheila felt her spirits lighten as the pretty seaside town came into view below them.

'Feels like we're running away together,' she said to Bernie with a chuckle.

He flashed her a smile. 'Would you like that? Because we could keep driving past Penzance and not stop until we find a cosy little wayside inn . . .'

'Bernie, don't you dare even suggest such a thing!' But she found herself grinning. 'Gawd, I can just imagine Violet's face if we was to elope. I'd never live it down.'

'You're not afraid of your daughter's opinion, surely?'

'Not afraid so much as wary of causing a row. Violet used to know how to have fun with the rest of us. But since she got married she's been a bit of a dry stick.' She paused, remembering that awkward moment in the kitchen before she'd left. 'Her and Joe are having problems, I think. That's probably why she's always in a bad mood.'

'I've noticed that myself,' he agreed, his smile fading. 'Marriage can be hard going sometimes.'

'Funny you're hankering after a second helping, then.'

'Ah, but with you, it would be all smooth sailing.'

'Flatterer,' she accused him, but chuckled again. 'Where are you planning to stay while I'm at Lily and Tristan's?'

'With my cousin Percy. I haven't seen him in a while, so we'll have plenty of catching up to do. And I have a number of old friends I'd like to visit too, if there's time.' He slowed as they descended towards the town. 'Which way?'

Sheila consulted the map that Lily had sent with her last letter. She'd been to Tristan's sheep farm before, but couldn't quite remember the way. 'Looks like you need to turn left up ahead.'

'How soon?'

'Gawd, I don't know. There's a funny sort of squiggle before the turning.' She leant over, holding up Lily's map so he could see it. 'I can't make head nor tail of this. Is that a picture of a tree, do you think?'

'I think I'll be able to see where I'm going a damn sight easier if you stop waving that in my face,' he said amiably.

'Sorry.' Sheila withdrew the map, abashed. Then flung out an arm, pointing urgently. 'There, there! A bloomin' great oak tree on the corner. Turn left there.'

Thankfully, there was nobody behind them. Bernie slammed on the brakes and negotiated the tight left-hand turn beside the oak tree with a muttered, 'Phew.'

From there, it wasn't too hard to navigate their way to the farm that Tristan and his married sister Demelza owned between them. The two couples lived there together with their children, an arrangement that Sheila found odd, though in these tough times she could see why it might be necessary.

The farmhouse was reached by a long, bumpy drive, and when they finally arrived, shaken up by a few dozen potholes despite Bernie's careful driving, they found Lily and Tristan, and Demelza and her husband Robert, standing in the front yard, waiting for them. Her great-grandson Morris was running about in the snow in a thick jacket and a fetching pair of little boots, while Demelza cradled her own infant, who was thickly swaddled in a blanket.

'You made it safely, Gran,' Lily exclaimed happily, embracing her and then shaking Bernie's hand. She looked strong and vital, her face glowing, her fair hair tucked under a woolly hat. 'Thank you so much for driving my grandmother here. It was very kind of you, Mr Bailey.'

'My pleasure,' he replied, also shaking Tristan's hand. 'How are you both? Very pleased to see you again.'

While they also shook hands with Demelza and Robert, Lily called to intrepid young Morris to stop climbing a snow-covered wall five times his height, and then asked Bernie, 'Will you come in for some lunch, Mr Bailey, or must you dash straight off?'

Bernie glanced hesitantly at Sheila.

'Oh well, you'd better come in for lunch, since Lily's offering,' she said brusquely, aware of her granddaughter and grandson-in-law studying them with interest. No doubt they'd read in her letter that Bernie would be driving her to Penzance and had put two and two together and made sixty-four. 'Can't have you turning up hungry on your cousin's doorstep,' she added deliberately, making sure they knew he'd come to Penzance on an errand of his own, not just as her chauffeur.

It was so lovely to see her granddaughter and dear great-grandson again. Sheila didn't know when she had felt so happy. They sat down to lunch in the large farmhouse kitchen, crowded around the table. She and Bernie had munched on Violet's sandwiches and pork pie during their long drive, but she did love a proper sit-down lunch, so didn't refuse the lavish spread Lily had laid on to welcome her.

'Your father has gone to stay with Alice in London,' she told Lily, raising her voice above the hubbub at the lunch table. 'But I expect you already know that, since you and Alice have always been thick as thieves.'

Lily smiled, helping Morris with his lunch. 'Yes, she wrote to tell me. But Dad had already sent a letter explaining his plans. He was worried I might be offended he hadn't paid us a visit before leaving. But he stayed with us last year. Besides, he's working in London, so of course he'd be staying with Alice.'

'Did he happen to tell you where he's working?' Sheila asked curiously. 'Ernest is as closed as an oyster, I couldn't get a word out of him on the subject. But I daresay it's all hush-hush, even though the war's over.'

Lily grinned. 'No, Dad didn't tell me what he was doing in London. But Alice let slip in her letter that they're working together in the same building. And we all know she's working with British Intelligence.'

'It makes me so proud to think of them two working hard to keep this country safe,' Sheila exclaimed. 'How clever they both are.' She gave Tristan a wink, who'd been listening intently to their conversation. 'Alice gets it from me, of course.'

Tristan laughed, and then stopped, seeing her raised brows.

'Of course, Gran,' Lily said tactfully. 'Pass the butter, Tris.'

After lunch, they chatted over a nice cup of tea for an hour, and then Bernie got up. 'I must get off, I'm afraid,' he said in his deep voice. 'Thank you very much for your hospitality, Mrs Minear. You have a lovely home,' he added, including Tristan, Demelza and Robert in his smile.

'You're very welcome, Mr Bailey,' Lily told him, getting up to see him out. 'But I hope you'll come back soon. Gran says you're staying in the area, so you must come for dinner one evening.'

'I hope to be a regular visitor while your grandmother is here, if that's all right with you.'

On the doorstep, Bernie turned to Sheila, who had followed him out.

'Perhaps I could call in a day or so, and take you for a walk along the seafront. How about it?'

'I'd like that,' Sheila agreed shyly.

'Until later, then.' He bent his head to kiss her on the lips, and she froze in shock. He'd never kissed her in front of anyone else before. 'Goodbye.'

When he'd driven away, Lily turned to her, her eyes twinkling with humour, and Sheila wished to goodness that she wasn't blushing so fiercely. But the truth was, she was mightily embarrassed, and a little giddy too. Because she'd enjoyed that unexpected kiss. Though she hadn't enjoyed her granddaughter witnessing it. She'd be having words with Bernie when next they met, that was for sure.

'You've gone pink, Gran,' Lily said, teasing her.

'Oh, get over.' Still hot-cheeked, but giggling now, Sheila stomped back to the kitchen. 'Blimey, it was just a kiss.'

But she knew that had been more than 'just a kiss'. It had been a public declaration of intent on Bernie's part. And she ought to have been annoyed. Instead, she was excited, and wondering what else he might do while they were on their 'holidays' in Penzance.

While the cat's away, the mice will play . . .

But what might the cat get up to when her bloomin' daughter wasn't there to wag a disapproving finger?

CHAPTER ELEVEN

Grace was leaning against the door frame, watching Caroline with interest as she made up Mrs Newton's bed with fresh sheets. She'd pitched in herself earlier, sweeping the floor and even finding a stack of clean towels for their guests, but Caroline had insisted on doing the rest. Selina was *her* friend, after all, and it wasn't fair to expect anyone else to skivvy for her.

The afternoon was already gloomy outside. Thankfully, there had been no power cut that day, so she'd snapped on the electric light and continued working. She probably could have got the work done more quickly on her own, but she appreciated Grace's company. They'd been chatting about the old days before the war, swapping anecdotes about their growing up and their friends when they were younger.

The conversation had turned perilous at one point, when discussing their 'best' friends, and Caroline had carefully steered it back to neutral territory, fearful she might give herself away. She was rather taken by Grace, and it was clear that Grace liked her too. But she wasn't entirely sure whether

Grace truly understood what she was feeling. Caroline didn't want to shock her by suggesting there could ever be anything more than friendship between them. It could ruin things.

When Tilly had come in from brushing down the shire horse she adored, Grace had hurried away to change out of her muddy Land Girl togs and pull on civvies instead; in this case, her favourite denim dungarees over a thick yellow sweater. Now she was back, her curious gaze following Caroline around the room.

'But what's she like, this Selina? And why are you so excited that she's coming to stay?'

'I'm not *excited*, as such,' Caroline told her warily, bending to tuck in a corner of the sheet. She felt herself blush, though really there was no reason to be embarrassed. She shook out a thick woollen blanket and threw it over the bed. 'I'm just pleased. Anyway, I told you before . . . Selina and I were very close.'

'How close?'

Caroline decided to pretend she hadn't heard that. 'Pass me the towels, would you? I'll put them on the bed now it's made.' She hesitated, smoothing out the blanket. 'Thanks for your help. But I think everything's done now.'

'Suit yourself.' Grace handed her the towels. 'Do Mr and Mrs Postbridge know that you and Selina were "very close"?'

Caroline, who had reached up to close the curtains, stiffened in shock. 'They know that . . . that we were good friends,' she replied carefully, emphasising the word *friends*. She turned to face her, adding breathlessly, 'Why all these questions, anyway?'

Now it was Grace's turn to look embarrassed. 'I was just wondering, that's all. Keep your hair on.'

'Well, you won't need to wonder much longer. She should be arriving any minute. In fact, I'm going downstairs to wait for her.' Caroline collected up the dirty linen and went to the door. But the other girl, blocking the doorway, didn't move aside. Taken aback, Caroline said falteringly, 'I need to put these in the laundry basket. Excuse me.'

Grace seemed on the point of saying something, but then shrugged and let her pass.

As she stuffed the sheets into the laundry basket on the landing, Caroline straightened. 'Hang on . . . Do you hear that?' They both listened. 'Is that a car coming up the hill?' Excitement bubbled inside her, and she dashed past Grace and down the stairs. She practically flew out of the back door and into the farmyard, just in time to see an unfamiliar car lurching across the cobbles, with Selina at the wheel. 'Selina!' she cried.

Her friend got out and picked her way carefully towards her, clad in heels that hadn't been designed with farmyards in mind. 'Caroline, darling . . .' Her accent seemed posher than when she'd been a Land Girl, and it wasn't just her voice that had changed. Selina looked mature and sophisticated in a smart tweed twinset, with a pillbox hat perched on her head. Her fair hair had been cut ruthlessly short since they'd seen each other in the summer, and Caroline could see how the short bob framed her face delightfully, with scarlet lipstick that made her look like a Hollywood film star.

Caroline sucked in her breath, staring. 'Goodness, you look amazing. I'm scared to hug you in case I make a mess of your clothes.'

Selina laughed and held out her arms. 'Come and hug me, don't be silly. I'm all creased from driving anyway.'

As they embraced, the passenger door opened and Peter jumped out. Selina's nephew also looked older than Caroline remembered, but boys sprouted so quickly at that age. 'Hello, Miss Ponsby. Do you remember me?'

She hurried to hug the boy too. 'Of course I remember you. How are your sisters, Peter? I hope they won't be climbing that treehouse of yours in your absence. Though I suppose it's too cold at the moment to be playing outside much.'

'Rather! We've had snow drifts on the moors.' The boy glanced about the yard critically, where a few pockets of frosty white had been left over from the recent cold weather. 'Far more snow than here.'

'Bodmin Moor is one of the higher places in the country, Peter,' Selina reminded him, giving Caroline a wink. 'High places always get more snow.' But her gaze had drifted past the boy to the back door of the farmhouse, and her voice trailed away. 'Goodness, I'm guessing that must be the famous Grace,' she whispered, and Caroline looked round sharply.

Grace was indeed standing outside the back door of the farmhouse, her hands dug into the back pockets of her dungarees, her thick black hair pulled back ruthlessly. Her eyes were wide and intent as she returned Selina's curious stare. But there was a strained air about her, almost rebellious, that left Caroline wondering what could have put her in such a fractious mood.

'Yes,' Caroline said softly, 'do come and meet her.' She hesitated. 'First, though, we should bring in your cases.'

'No need.' Peter was looking affronted. 'You go ahead. I can carry them on my own.'

'Smashing, if you're sure you can manage. Then I'll take

you straight upstairs and show you your rooms.' She grinned at Selina. 'I've given you Mrs Newton's room. But I'm afraid Peter has been lumped with Ernest Fisher's.'

'Of course, I'd forgotten that Alice's dad had left the farm. Gosh, though, that's a tiny cupboard of a room.'

'I don't mind a small room,' Peter said stoutly, dragging a heavy case noisily over the cobbles in a way that made Selina turn with a wince. 'I'd be happy sleeping anywhere. Even in the barn.' He grinned, and Caroline got the impression he was putting on a brave face after his expulsion from the boarding school. 'It would be an adventure.'

'You don't need to sleep in the barn. Mr Fisher's room will be perfectly fine for you,' his aunt told him firmly and removed the heavy case from his grasp. 'I'll carry that one before you bash it to bits. It's mine anyway. You go back and bring your own bag in.'

But on reaching the farmhouse, Selina stopped dead, face to face with Grace, and put down the case.

The two young women stared at each other, roughly the same height, and then Selina stuck out her hand. 'Hello, how do you do? I'm Selina Tiptree.'

'Grace Morgan.' They shook hands. 'Nice to put a face to the name. I've heard so much about you since I got here. You're quite a legend, in fact.'

Selina's thin brows arched, and she shot an enquiring look at Caroline. 'I can't imagine why. Unless people have been telling tall tales about me.'

To Caroline's relief, Peter returned at that moment with a case in each hand, clearly struggling. 'Let me carry one of those, Peter,' she said hurriedly. 'Come along, I'll show you to your rooms. It's too dark now for a proper tour, but if you're up early enough in the morning, I'll show you around the farm before work. There's so much you've missed since the summer, Selina . . . We had another litter of pigs – ten piglets this time – and Joe's just built a new coop for the chickens. You remember the roof was forever leaking on the old one?' she rattled on nervously, ushering her guests inside. 'This way.'

Once she'd shown Selina into Mrs Newton's room, and installed Peter in his own cramped bedroom, Caroline hurried downstairs to make tea and cut some cake to sustain them until dinner time.

Tilly had been out with the pigs, whom she loved visiting. She returned just as Selina and Peter came downstairs. 'Hello, stranger,' Tilly said enthusiastically, hugging Selina. 'And you must be Peter,' she added, grinning at the boy beside her. 'I had quite a different idea of what you'd look like. When Caro said Selina was bringing her nephew, I pictured a little boy in short trousers. But you're all grown up. How old are you?'

'Fourteen.' Peter looked pleased.

'Would you like to see the pigs?' Tilly asked him. 'I've just taken off my boots, but I can put them back on.' She looked him up and down, pulling a face. 'Though you might get muddy. Do you mind?'

'Not a bit,' he insisted, and glanced at his aunt.

Selina nodded. 'Go and enjoy the pigs. I remember when Pinky had a litter, and they were gorgeous. Little wriggling piglets everywhere. You'll love them, and they're not as smelly as everyone thinks. Just try not to tramp mud back into the kitchen or Violet will have fifty fits.'

He laughed and followed Tilly out into the yard. Moments

later, as Caroline, Selina and Grace were sitting around the table with tea and cake, another car pulled into the yard.

The door opened to reveal the Postbridges, back from a trip to the village. 'Please don't get up,' Joe said in his jovial way, coming across to shake Selina's hand. 'How are you? Is that your car out there? It's a nice looker.'

'Yes, I just bought her. She runs like a dream too.'

Violet came puffing in, unwinding her scarf. 'It's getting bitter out there again. I think we'll be due more snow soon. How do you do, Selina? We're very glad you've come to stay. But where's this nephew of yours?'

'Tilly's taken him to meet the pigs,' Caroline told her.

'I hope he likes beef stew.' Violet brought a lidded casserole dish to the table in her gloved hands. She lifted the lid slightly to peer inside, and fragrant steam filled the kitchen. 'I had some errands to run in the village, so I put this stew on in the kitchen out the back of the shop. Left it to cook for a few hours, and then collected it on our way back up. I'm sure Mum won't mind.'

'Why are you telling them only half a story, love?' Joe winked at the girls. 'She had to brave her Aunt Margaret to do it, didn't you, love? I was amazed there were no fisticuffs.'

His wife threw him a fulminating look. 'When you've finished saying daft things, maybe you can fetch some firewood and stoke up the range. It's running low.'

Still grinning, Joe did as he was bade.

'I love beef stew, Mrs Postbridge,' Selina assured her politely, 'and Peter does too. Though he'll eat anything you put in front of him. He's got the appetite of a horse.'

'Boys that age always do,' Violet said, chuckling. She bent to slip the casserole dish into the range and closed the door.

'I heard he had trouble at some fancy boarding school,' she went on. 'Got himself in a spot of bother there, didn't he?'

'He had trouble fitting in, yes. But it was only a few months after he'd lost his mother,' Selina pointed out, bristling as she defended her nephew, 'and I believe some of the older boys bullied him.'

Violet hesitated, wiping her hands on her apron. 'I don't like bullies.'

'Me neither,' Selina said shortly.

'Though I don't hold with boarding schools myself. It ain't natural, separating a child from their family. You'll be glad to have him back with you, I daresay.'

'Yes,' Selina agreed, 'and Peter will do much better with a tutor. We could also try one of the local schools if he's missing company his own age. For now though, it's enough that he's home and safe.'

'Amen to that,' Joe rumbled, and stole a slice of cake while his wife's back was turned.

'And now you've, erm, brought him to the farm for some peace and quiet, is that right?' Violet pressed her, unloading vegetables from her shopping basket, clearly still unhappy that a child who'd been expelled from school was being foisted on her well-run farmhouse, even if there had been a good excuse for any bad behaviour.

Caroline saw Selina's gaze narrow suspiciously on Violet's back and worried that she might be planning to snap at her. 'Exactly right, Mrs Postbridge,' she said quickly, forestalling her friend. 'And maybe one day he'll need to know how a farm is run and animals looked after. So it's a kind of education, you could say.'

Peter soon returned from the pigsty with Tilly, the two

of them giggling over some whispered joke, though of course there wasn't much of an age difference between them, only four or five years.

There was a difference between Grace and Selina, though. And not just one of age. The difference, Caroline decided, lay in her own feelings. She'd trailed after Selina for years during the war, admiring her passionately, copying her behaviour and attitudes even when she disagreed with them, too afraid of losing her friendship to rebel. With Grace, however, they were on more of an equal footing. Caroline was fascinated by her striking looks and quick wit, but not overawed. It felt more real than her passion for Selina had ever done. She had always known, deep down, that Selina would never be hers. Yet there was something about Grace that allowed her to hope . . . and that realisation both excited and terrified her.

It felt strange to smile at Selina, knowing she was no longer head over heels in love with her. Had she made a fool of herself over nothing but a silly crush? She wished now that she'd kept quiet and never admitted to her feelings. Not that her friend would betray her confidence, now that it was over.

'I say, cake!' Peter exclaimed, pulling up a chair at the kitchen table, before glancing warily at Mrs Postbridge. 'May I?'

'Help yourself,' Violet told him, though with more restraint than she usually showed to visiting children.

Caroline guessed that she must still be fretting about the boy's recent expulsion from school, perhaps considering him a troublemaker, and felt embarrassed for her friend. She'd encouraged Selina in her letter to feel free to bring her nephew on this visit, but now the farmer's wife was not bothering to hide her disapproval.

Thankfully, Selina seemed oblivious to any atmosphere. She was studying Grace with occasional sidelong glances, while Grace herself looked back at Selina quite openly, as though accustomed to being stared at and not thrown by it.

'Tomorrow,' Caroline said awkwardly, 'I'm going to get up early and show our guests around the farm before work.' She hesitated. 'If that's all right with you, Mr Postbridge?'

'You're welcome to do what you like, outside work hours,' Joe said easily, and threw a few crusts down for the dogs, who came running, wagging their tails. 'You could show them my new chicken coop,' he added with a hint of pride, glancing at Selina. 'I built it meself, and the chickens are very comfortable in there now.'

'Yes,' his wife agreed, beaming, 'and they're laying heavier now than they ever did before. My mother's been selling the surplus down in the village shop, which brings in a few welcome extra shillings.'

'How's the shop getting along these days?' Selina asked politely.

Listening with interest to the adults' conversation, Peter brushed cake crumbs onto the kitchen floor, where the waiting dogs made short work of them too. Abruptly, he asked Joe, 'Sir? Now the war's over, how long before the soldiers come home, do you think, and take over the Land Girls' work again?'

An awkward silence fell in the kitchen, and Peter blushed.

'That is, I know women can do the job,' he went on, stammering a little, 'because Aunt Selly did, and she says it was no big deal. But the thing is, that was during the war, and I would have thought most girls must be ready to jack in the war work by now and get married. And even if they don't want to get married, girls hate getting mucky, don't they? So when the men come back—'

'Peter, for goodness' sake,' Selina began, but Violet interrupted her.

'No,' she said sharply, replying for her husband, 'that's a fair question, let the boy ask it. The truth is, Peter, we don't know when the soldiers will be coming home. Soon, I hope. And some are home already. Like young Arthur Green, who married Joan this summer, one of our Land Girls. But one thing's for sure,' she added, not looking at the three Land Girls in the room. 'Women can't keep working on farms and in factories forever, and I'm sure some of them *do* want to settle down and start a family, now the war's over. And this country needs more children to be born. We lost so many . . .' She stopped, choking on the words.

Caroline swallowed, a lump in her own throat too. She didn't agree with throwing women aside in favour of men now the war was over. But the thought of how many had died during the war – millions upon millions across the globe, a newspaper had claimed recently, almost half a million among them British citizens – left her close to tears. Not only men, but women and children too.

It didn't bear thinking about. And yet they had to, didn't they? If they didn't remember those who'd died, they might go blindly into yet another conflict, forgetting how bloody war was . . .

'Funnily enough,' Joe said slowly, washing his hands at the sink, 'I was speaking to a young lad in the village only this afternoon, while waiting for Violet to finish her business. He was asking about a job on the farm. Of course, we're headed into winter now, and likely a cold one at that, and not much labouring required. So I told him no. But I did say I might take him on early next year, weather depending. And he's not the first to have asked.'

Caroline caught her breath, not quite able to believe what she'd just heard.

Tilly, too, was staring at the farmer, aghast. 'I don't understand . . . Are you saying you'll be letting us go next year, Mr Postbridge, and employing men instead?'

'There's no simple answer to that. But, as you know, farm labour is hard work, and dirty too, the boy's not wrong about that.' Joe frowned, drying his hands. 'I was thankful to have you ladies here during the war. We couldn't have got by without you, and that's the truth of it. But once the men are home . . .' He caught his wife's eye and cleared his throat. 'Well, I don't plan on letting anyone go just yet. But I may take on a few lads come the spring. And that's an end to the matter.' And with that, he collected his newspaper from the table and limped into the snug, closing the door behind him.

Violet, who had turned away to stack clean plates on the sideboard, gave a long sigh but said nothing.

Shocked, Caroline put a hand to her mouth, her heart thumping.

Grace made a noise under her breath. 'That's us told.'

'What's the matter?' Selina asked her softly, a barb in her voice. 'You worried about having young men about the farm?'

'I don't mind young men,' Grace shot back. 'What I mind is losing my job and having to go home again. I love my parents and Liverpool, don't get me wrong, but I'm happy here in Cornwall, doing an honest day's work like any man, and being free and independent. I don't want any of that to end.'

‘I’m sure it won’t,’ Caroline told her earnestly, though Joe’s admission had shaken her to the core. She didn’t want to go home either. This was her life now, here at Postbridge Farm, with Tilly and Grace, and fresh country air in her lungs every morning.

‘I wish I could share your optimism.’ Grace pulled a face and got up from the table. ‘Well, it was nice to meet you, Selina, and you too, Peter. I’ll see you at dinner. Right now, I’m going upstairs to read a magazine and maybe paint my toenails too.’ She quirked an ironic brow. ‘Because that’s what girls do, isn’t it?’

When she’d gone, Selina got up and insisted on helping to clear the table, even though she was a guest. As she bent to collect Caroline’s empty teacup, she whispered in her ear, ‘I must say, I like your new Land Girl. Though she’s no mild-mannered Joan, that’s for certain. Got rather a sharp tongue, hasn’t she?’

‘Look who’s talking,’ Caroline muttered.

CHAPTER TWELVE

The weather in Porthcurno continued cold and snowy all that week, though salt air meant snow fell less heavily along the coast. Selina woke each morning with a sense of déjà vu, listening to the sounds of a busy farm: the Land Girls thumping sleepily down the stairs at an unholy hour, sheep baaing in the distance, and the dogs barking excitedly, no doubt responding to Joe pulling on his boots in the porch. It was only six months since she'd left here, and yet it felt like a world away from her new life at Thornton Hall. Everything had changed since Bella's letter about her sickness had taken Selina to Bodmin, and she still could not quite believe that her sister was gone forever.

If such a thing were possible, would she go back to being a Land Girl, to dawns spent out in the fields, later traipsing home after dark, muddy and exhausted? Definitely not, she thought wryly. Though she missed the camaraderie of the farm, giggling and messing about with her fellow Land Girls. Now that Nancy had come to Thornton Hall, she did at least have a companion nearer her own age. However, she didn't know her cousin well enough yet for her to be a friend. Besides, seeing Caroline again had reminded her of the good times they'd had together, and there was no denying that she missed her.

Before returning to Porthcurno, she'd been secretly worried that Caroline still held a torch for her, which would have been awkward, especially in front of Peter. But, to her relief, Caroline's affections now lay in a new direction. Her partiality for Grace had not been as difficult to spot, but the Liverpudlian girl was as different from Selina as chalk from cheese.

But what did Grace think of Caroline? That was the real question. Selina knew how hard Caroline found it to conceal her feelings, and she didn't want her friend to be left wounded, her private life exposed to the world, by an unwise emotional declaration. That would be too awful. But Selina didn't feel as if she could wade into the matter. She wanted her time at the farm to be as peaceful and content as possible, for everyone's sake, not least her nephew.

At breakfast a few days into their visit, she noticed that Peter kept yawning and rubbing his eyes. He had been on his best behaviour at first, apart from his difficult question about men taking over again for the Land Girls. But he seemed oddly distracted now. She hoped he wasn't sickening for something.

'Didn't you sleep well, Peter?' Selina asked, passing him the milk jug. 'You look a bit peaky.'

Peter yawned extravagantly before shaking his head. 'I'm fine, Aunt Selly,' he insisted. 'The thing is, I didn't put the light out until gone midnight.'

Violet, who had been washing up the breakfast dishes

now that Joe and the girls had gone off about their duties, turned to stare at him in amazement. 'Gone midnight?' she repeated, looking shocked. 'Goodness me, no wonder you keep yawning.' Her gaze moved to Selina in silent reproof, but she didn't say anything more, merely returned to her task. Her small daughter Sarah Jane glanced up from her crayoning, as though aware of an atmosphere, and giggled when Peter winked at her.

Feeling judged, Selina said testily, 'From now on, Peter, you must go to sleep earlier than that. It's not healthy to be up so late. I sent you up to bed at nine o'clock as usual. What on earth were you doing all that time?'

'Reading,' he said promptly.

Violet turned again, her eyes bulging, and tutted loudly before returning to the washing-up. 'Comics, I daresay. Or one of them Boy's Own Annuals?'

'Oh, I wasn't reading anything like that,' Peter declared, looking offended. 'I found a shelf of books in my room – novels and travel guides and so on – and guess what? Some of them are written in *German*. I learned a little German at that ghastly school, Aunt Selina,' he added, turning to her. 'Didn't get very far with it before I left, of course. But it was fun, flicking through the books and trying to pick out words I recognised. Next thing I knew, the clock on the landing was striking twelve.'

'Books in German?' Selina was baffled, but then recalled that he was sleeping in Ernest Fisher's old room. 'Of course, that was Mr Fisher's room. He's German, you know.'

'I say, I think you told us about him once. The man who was a spy?' Peter sat up enthusiastically.

'Do you mind?' Violet demanded, glaring round at them

with soap suds dripping from her hands. 'We don't talk about that sort of thing here, remember? *Loose lips sink ships.*'

'But that's daft . . . The war's over,' Peter exclaimed. 'What harm can it do?'

Selina sucked in her breath. 'Peter! Don't speak to Mrs Postbridge like that. Apologise at once.'

'But . . . Oh, very well.' Peter pulled a face, but said reluctantly, 'I'm sorry, Mrs Postbridge.'

Violet dried her hands on her apron, shaking her head. 'Well, I never . . . These young people!' Grabbing up a trug of cleaning materials, she stamped out of the kitchen in search of something to clean.

Once they were alone, Selina gave her nephew a furious stare. 'That was very rude of you, Peter. I know it seems like it's not important to keep secrets anymore. But Mr Fisher still works for the government, and so does his daughter Alice. We've all had it drummed into us that we're not to talk about work like theirs. And it could make a difference, you know. Just because the war's over, that doesn't mean there aren't bad people out there who'd like to see it start up again. Enemies of Britain and her allies. So take care what you say, understand?'

Peter toyed with his breakfast, not meeting her eyes. 'Yes, Aunt Selly.'

She finished her cup of tea, which was lukewarm, and sighed. This visit to the farm was not turning out to be as relaxing as she'd hoped. Quite the opposite, in fact.

'Perhaps you could show me these books,' she suggested, trying to lighten the mood. The last thing she wanted was for Peter to slip back into the sullens when he'd been so well-behaved these past few days at the farm. 'I don't know much German. But perhaps you could teach me a few words, since you're such an expert.'

'Rather,' Peter said, his grin returning, and he jumped up, scraping his chair back so violently that it fell over. 'Oops. Mum used to say that I don't know my own strength.' He bent to pick up the chair, blushing fiercely. 'Sorry.'

'You've certainly got the fidgets today.' But Selina couldn't find it in her heart to be annoyed with the boy. He'd had a difficult year and was trying his best. She ruffled his hair, and then put an arm about his shoulder. 'Let's see these books, then.'

They spent an hour poring over Mr Fisher's books, and laughing as they tried to pronounce some of the impossibly long German words.

'I'm glad the war is over,' Peter confided at one point, flicking through the pages in search of more words that he recognised. 'I wanted to enlist when I was younger. I thought it would be smashing to be a soldier with a gun and a uniform. But I'm glad now that I don't have to. I think war is rather horrid, isn't it?'

'Yes, Peter, it is.'

He fidgeted unhappily. 'Some of the boys at school wished they hadn't missed out. Our housemaster served in the Great War; he was always banging on about guns and shooting. He ran a rifle club for the older boys, but I never joined. I'm not a coward but I'd rather not shoot anyone if I don't have to do so.' He looked up at her, uncertain. 'You don't think I'm a coward, do you? When I told the other boys at school how I felt, one of them knocked me down and the others took turns kicking me.'

Selina wished she could have words with those vile boys.

Yes, and their schoolmasters too. But she did her best to unclench her fists and smile. 'Of course you're not a coward, Peter,' she assured him. 'Besides, most soldiers don't want to shoot anyone either. They just want to do their duty and protect their country.'

Peter began to say something, but was interrupted by Violet Postbridge yelling up the stairs for them both in a strained, high-pitched voice. Quickly, they put away Mr Fisher's books and hurried down into the kitchen.

'Is everything all right, Mrs Postbridge?' Selina asked, for Violet was looking quite cross and flushed, and her husband Joe was there too, leaning on his stick and glaring at Peter, of all people.

'You went up to the top field yesterday afternoon, didn't you, lad?' Joe asked, without answering her question.

Peter blinked. 'Yes, sir.'

'You left the gate open and the sheep got out. When we went up with the feed this morning, we found the blasted animals wandering free along the cliffs. It took me and the dogs an age to track them all down and get them back safely into the field.' Joe's voice was rough with temper. 'There's a sheer drop along that stretch. It's a miracle none of them fell to their deaths.'

'Oh, Peter!' Selina groaned. 'I told you not to leave any gates open.'

'Selina, did you go up there with the boy?' Violet demanded.

'No,' Selina admitted grimly, wishing she had. After years working on a farm, it was deeply ingrained in her to shut gates behind her. 'I . . . I got chatting with Tilly about the new piglets and let Peter go up there by himself. I'm so sorry, Mr and Mrs Postbridge.'

‘I’m only glad we brought the lambs and their mothers down to the little pasture here, and the pregnant ewes with them, when the snows started. Otherwise, we might have lost half the lambs to the sea,’ Joe pointed out tersely. ‘The young ’uns don’t have the good sense yet to steer clear of the cliffs.’

Peter started to stammer an apology, but Joe slammed his stick down on the kitchen floor so hard, it cracked the slate.

‘I don’t want your apologies, boy,’ he thundered. ‘I won’t have you wandering this farm unaccompanied, do you hear me? You’ll think me a tyrant, I daresay. But I can’t afford to lose a single lamb, not the way things are going. From now on, you’ll stay in your room or with your aunt, or you’ll *both* go home.’

Selina was shocked. She had never seen the ordinarily easy-going farmer lose his temper like this before.

Caroline came in that moment, clearly taken aback at the raised voices. ‘Sorry to interrupt,’ she stammered, ‘I . . . I came for the pigswill bucket.’

Violet pointed silently at the metal pail, which stood in the corner, ready for food scraps to be scraped into it.

Caroline grabbed it up, and then glanced round at Peter. ‘Would you like to help feed the pigs, Peter?’ she asked tentatively, her gaze meeting Selina’s. ‘You could tag along too, Selina. You haven’t seen much of the new litter of piglets yet, have you?’

‘Sounds jolly,’ Selina agreed, jumping at the chance to extricate her nephew from this awkward situation. She understood why the Postbridges were angry. Endangering livestock was the most serious transgression possible. But surely they could see that the boy hadn’t done it deliberately?

'Come along, Peter. I'm sure we can all sit down later, when things are less heated, and lay down some ground rules about proper behaviour on a farm.' And she steered Peter out of the kitchen.

Out in the chilly, sunlit yard, Caroline threw her a sympathetic look. 'Mr Postbridge was furious about those sheep getting loose . . . I suppose it was Peter who left the gate open. Is that what he was shouting about?'

Briefly, Selina explained what had happened. 'But Peter's very sorry about it, aren't you?' She put a comforting arm about his shoulders.

To her surprise, Peter shrugged off her arm. 'I thought I'd closed it,' he muttered. 'But I've never shut a farm gate on my own before. I wish someone had showed me how before I made such a mess of it.' His voice was sulky, his face turned away. 'And I wish you'd let me stay and make a proper apology to the farmer, before dragging me away like that.' He stuck out his chin. 'I'm not a child, Aunt Selly. I made a stupid mistake, and I'm not afraid to admit it.'

Selina studied him cautiously. 'I didn't mean to drag you away. You looked upset, that was all. Would you like to go back and apologise on your own, and then join us in feeding the pigs?'

Peter gave a rough nod and strode back to the farmhouse.

'Oh dear.' Selina fell into step beside Caroline, tilting her face to the wintry sunshine and wishing it was enough to warm her. 'I'm not doing a terribly good job of mothering my nephew, am I? The thing is, Peter thinks he's all grown up. The head of the family.' She smiled sadly. 'But he's still a boy at heart. And some days—'

But she was interrupted by Peter stamping back towards them, scowling and with a flush in his thin cheeks.

'Oh no . . .' Selina groaned. 'What's the matter now?'

They'd reached the pigsty, and the sturdy pigs had come over to the gate, grunting and snuffling, eager for slop. Caroline put down the bucket, consternation in her face. 'What's happened, Peter? You can tell us.'

His hands were bunched into fists, a martial light in his eyes. 'I was just going into the kitchen, to tell them how sorry I am, when I heard Mrs Postbridge say it was only what could be expected from a boy like me, given that I've been thrown out of school for bad behaviour. She said I'm obviously a . . . a thug and a troublemaker, and I shouldn't have been brought here in the first place.' He stopped, breathless. 'It won't matter what I say now, will it? I could apologise a thousand times, they'll still think I'm rotten through and through. No matter that I made a mistake. They've already made their stupid minds up.' And he lashed out with his foot and sent the bucket of slop flying across the cobbles.

'For goodness' sake!' Caroline cried, jumping back to avoid being splashed by the smelly mess.

Selina was horrified. 'Peter, what on earth do you think you're doing?' She tried to grab him by the arm, but he dashed away, running full pelt for the track that led up to the top field and the cliffs. 'Come back this instant,' she shouted after him, but it was useless.

'Gosh, what a mess.' Caroline righted the bucket, tutting. She set her fists on her hips, looking down, disgruntled, at the slop on the cobbles. 'I'll have to get the shovel and clear this up.'

'I'm so sorry.' Selina bit her lip. 'I don't know what's got into the boy. That damn school, I expect . . . I'll have to go after him. I can't let him wander the cliffs in that mood.' She gave her friend an apologetic look. 'If you can wait ten minutes, I'll bring him down to clean it up for you.'

'No, don't bother. It needs to be done now.' Caroline gave her a weary smile. 'I don't envy you, looking after Bella's kids. You must need the patience of a saint.'

'Yes, the one thing I *don't* possess!' Selina agreed with a broken laugh, and then hurried after her nephew before he could do himself a mischief in that dangerous mood.

She found Peter standing on the gate he'd failed to secure before, staring mournfully at the grazing sheep, who would soon need to be moved to a lower pasture, given the increasingly cold weather.

He turned his head as she approached, and she realised he'd been crying. 'I'm sorry about the slop bucket, Aunt Selly. I don't know what came over me.' His voice was bitter. 'Though maybe Mrs Postbridge was right. Maybe I *am* a born troublemaker.'

She perched on the gate beside him, her gaze on his averted profile. 'She only said that because she doesn't know you. You're a good boy, Peter. But something awful happened to you this year. You lost your mother.' Feeling tears prick at her eyes, she took a deep breath. 'Of course you're unhappy and confused. And instead of keeping you home until you felt more able to take on the world, I sent you off to that horrid boarding school. It's no wonder you're at sixes and sevens.' She sighed, looking across the frost-whitened field, and remembering happier days spent up there as a Land Girl, before Johnny had broken off their engagement, before her sister had died. 'We can stay up here awhile, if you like. But you do need to go back and apologise to Caroline, and then to the Postbridges again.' She came to a decision. 'And then you and I should take a drive out in the car.'

He looked at her, surprised. 'Where are we going?'

'You may have heard us mention Joan, who used to be a Land Girl here. She married a young man called Arthur Green, I think it must have been around September. I'd like to pay them a visit. It's a bit of a hike out of the village, though. Perhaps it's extravagant, given fuel rationing, but we can take the car to save our legs,' she added, grinning.

'I'd like that, thank you.' Peter swallowed. 'And thank you for not flying off the handle at me. I've behaved like an idiot, and probably deserve far worse than having my head bitten off by the farmer. But I'm going to be more careful from now on, I swear it.'

She laughed at his earnest expression, relieved that he seemed to be returning to his usual, more reasonable self. 'That's the ticket.'

After helping Caroline wash down the cobbles with a pail of hot soapy water, and then apologising profusely to the Postbridges, Peter jumped into the car with her, looking relieved to be escaping the farm.

'What are the names of your friends again?' he asked, winding down his window, the cold air blowing his hair about.

'Mr and Mrs Green,' Selina told him, driving carefully along the narrow, icy lanes. 'Joan was a friend of mine, a fellow Land Girl. She married Arthur, and they live in a ramshackle old cottage in his parents' grounds. When I last saw her, Joan was planning to redecorate the place and spruce up the garden. I can't wait to see how she's getting along with the project.'

Selina had some vague idea that Arthur Green, who'd come home from war in a terrible state, and had taken a long time to settle back into ordinary life again, might be able to advise her on how best to deal with Peter's mood swings. Not that Peter had been to war, of course, or seen dreadful things as poor Arthur must have done. But he seemed to have gone through a traumatic ordeal at that school.

But when she drove out to the little cottage, she found only Joan, homely as ever, clad in bulky overalls, a paintbrush in hand. 'Selina,' she cried. 'How marvellous to see you. I never seem to get any visitors out here. And I'm sorry, but Arthur's not here today. He and his parents have gone to an auction, hoping to pick up cheap furniture for the cottage. I spoke to Mrs Newton the other week, and she said you might be visiting while she was away in Penzance. But who's this?'

'This is my nephew, Peter,' Selina said proudly, and the two shook hands. 'I'm still hoping you and Arthur will come to visit us at Bodmin. Then you can meet his sisters too.' She eyed Joan's paintbrush thoughtfully. 'I take it you've been painting?'

'Just giving the hallway a lick of fresh paint. Do come in. I'll make tea, shall I? Oh, watch out for wet paint!'

As they chatted amiably in the kitchen, Peter spotted a small dog in the back garden and ran out to play with it.

'Joan,' Selina said quickly, 'do you think your husband might be able to speak to Peter before we go home?' She explained the situation, and Joan listened in concern, but then sadly shook her head.

'I don't think Arthur will have time. Not on this visit. He's taking a portfolio of sketches and paintings down to a gallery in Truro tomorrow and will be gone several days. You remember he's an artist? People have started taking an interest in his work, and there's a chance he may be invited to exhibit in the spring.' She bit her lip. 'I'm ever so sorry.'

'Perhaps if you were to come and visit us at Bodmin, then?' Selina asked, determined to find a solution.

'Well, erm . . .' Joan blushed. 'Thank you for the invitation, but the doctor thinks I shouldn't travel any long distances for a while. Not until a certain happy event has occurred.'

Selina gasped. 'You mean . . . You're *expecting*?'

'I know, it's not obvious yet.' Joan nodded, laughing at her shocked expression. 'My brother Graham joked at the time that Arthur and I would need to get married quickly, and he wasn't far wrong.' Her blush deepened. 'Though my mother-in-law insists we should call it a "honeymoon baby" and hope nobody works out the dates.'

'You dark horse!' Selina hugged her, adding her heartfelt congratulations. 'Goodness, everyone's falling pregnant at the moment. Violet thinks it's because of the war, and she's probably right. It's a shame, though, about Arthur not being here. Maybe he could speak to Peter another time?'

'I'll tell him about it, never fear.' Joan turned to make the tea, a healthy glow in her face. 'I'm sorry to hear about your nephew's troubles . . . But he's young, and I'm sure he'll bounce back in time.'

'Yes, I expect so.' Not wanting to admit how worried she was, Selina could only smile, hoping that Joan was right.

CHAPTER THIRTEEN

As Sheila was about to head into Penzance with her granddaughter, hoping to hear the former lady Member of Parliament speak on the topic of poverty, she was shocked to hear a telephone ring. 'Blimey,' she exclaimed, dropping the glove she'd been fumbling with. 'You got a telephone here, Lily?'

Lily grinned. 'You should tell Joe to have one installed at Postbridge Farm. Then we could telephone each other any time we liked. No need to wait for a letter to arrive.'

'Fancy that.' Sheila pulled on her gloves, checking her reflection in the hall mirror. 'We never had a telephone in Dagenham. But then, we never needed one. If we wanted to speak to someone, we put on a hat and coat and walked around to their house.'

The sound of ringing stopped. Demelza's husband Robert could be heard speaking in a booming voice.

'Robert paid to have it put in,' Lily whispered as they headed out to the car. 'He organises the local Quaker meetings, so it's been invaluable for him. But it's useful for us too, especially when livestock goes AWOL.'

They drove into Penzance, a growing seaside town with pretty shopfronts and a beautiful vista over the bay, where St Michael's Mount rose mistily out of the sea like a fairytale castle. But Sheila also noticed signs of deprivation: gaunt-faced women pushing filthy prams up and down the steep, cobbled lanes from the seafront, and gangs of kids roaming about in clogs and ragged clothing despite the cold weather. It seemed even bustling Penzance had a problem with poverty.

'I'm glad to see they've removed the beach defences,' Sheila remarked as Lily was parking down by the harbour. 'I couldn't stand all them ugly, brutish lumps of concrete littering the beach. And the mines just scared me silly. Now, come summertime, people will be able to swim and build sandcastles again.'

'We had to secure the coast against the enemy back then,' Lily reminded her. Having found a place to park the farm van they'd borrowed for the day, she got out and went around to the back to fetch her shopping basket. 'Better ugly lumps of concrete and a few mines than an invasion force,' she added cheerily.

'I daresay,' Sheila said, climbing laboriously out of the van. 'But it's still prettier without 'em.'

'True enough. Now, Gran, where's this talk being held?'

'Here's the address, love.' Sheila handed over the cutting she'd taken from the newspaper. 'The lady who's giving the talk is called Mrs Ethel Newbury-Holmes. Bit of a mouthful, ain't it? I expect she's posh. Used to be a Member of Parliament too, so maybe I won't understand a word she's saying. But I've heard good things about her. And I've got paper and a pencil, so I can take notes on what she says.'

'You're taking this very seriously, ain't you, Gran?' Lily gave her a sympathetic smile. 'You always were a kind soul. I was surprised, I admit, when I heard you were a councillor now. Tristan and I weren't sure at first whether it would suit.'

'You mean, you weren't sure I was up to the job? You thought grandmothers are only good for knitting, not turning up to the Parish Council every month and listening to men in suits droning on about this and that.' She joined in with Lily's laughter. 'Oh yes, I know what you was thinking, my girl. But Bernie said being on the council was the only way to get things done. And it turns out he was right. So, here I am, hoping to learn how to get things done from this Mrs Newbury-Holmes.'

'Sorry, I didn't mean to be rude. Look, I know where this address is, so I'll walk over there with you. But I can't promise to stay for the talk,' Lily admitted, settling her shopping basket on her arm. 'I've got a few errands to run while I'm in town. I hope you don't mind.'

'Of course I don't. Anyway, I'll be scribbling notes the whole time, so I wouldn't be good company. You do your shopping, love. Just don't forget to come back for your ol' gran, will you?'

They walked round to the hall together, where there was already a long queue of people waiting to hear the former MP speak. Lily stood with Sheila awhile, chatting about little Morris and his latest antics, and how he was coming on in leaps and bounds. As the queue shortened, though, people shuffling into the hall at last, her granddaughter excused herself and hurried away to do her shopping, promising to call back in an hour.

Feeling shy, Sheila followed the others into the hall, not

meeting anyone else's eye, and found a seat near the back where she wouldn't be in anyone's way. It was cold and draughty. She set her notebook on her knee and waited. After a while, a portly gentleman shuffled onto the raised platform and gave a rambling introduction to the former Member of Parliament. There was a polite round of applause, and a tall, hawkish-looking woman stood up, smiling at the audience. It was so cold in the hall, the lady was still wearing her fur coat and hat. She was in an old-fashioned pale blue twinset with pearls, her skinny legs clad in nylons, a pair of posh heels on her feet. She thanked the compère politely and then gave a speech which ran for some forty-five minutes, without notes and without once hesitating or losing her train of thought.

Sheila struggled to take it all down, since every few minutes the former MP would produce a statistic or suggest a solution to the issue of poverty that made her mutter, 'Oh blimey, yes,' under her breath and scribble these ideas down frantically.

Not everyone enjoyed her speech, though. One man got up and walked out halfway through. Another demanded to know how the lady had voted in some government bill during the war, which Sheila barely remembered. But then, she'd been too busy during the war to sit reading about Parliamentary Bills and so on. She'd had her caff to run, and her family to look after in the Blitz, and once in Cornwall, she and Arnie had been courting. She'd had no time for politics. Now though, it was all she could think about, even wary of accepting Bernie's proposal in case she'd have to give up her new-found interest and go back to being a housewife.

When the talk was over and everyone had left, Sheila

found herself still scribbling, trying to complete her notes. A shadow fell across her, and she glanced up. It was Mrs Newbury-Holmes, with another lady behind her.

'You've taken copious notes there, madam,' the former MP remarked, peering down at her with raised brows. 'Are you a journalist?'

Sheila jumped up, embarrassed. 'Gawd, no, bless you,' she exclaimed, fumbling to put away her notebook. She hesitated, then recalled what Bernie had said once about taking her work more seriously, and drew herself up, putting out a hand to the other lady quite as though they were equals. 'I'm Mrs Newton and I'm a parish councillor.'

'Are you indeed?' They shook hands in a friendly way, which put heart into Sheila.

'Yes, and I'm running a fund to help the poor and the needy in our area. It's very rural, and there's not enough work to go round. And some of the women – I mean, *ladies* – they're war widows, and they're struggling to make ends meet.' Sheila hesitated. 'I'm not saying the government's failed them. But, like you said, these are difficult times, and someone's got to help out. We can't walk by on the other side and watch people starving and kiddies running about barefoot.'

'Oh, quite,' Mrs Newbury-Holmes agreed, watching her.

'Only I've never done anything like this before, see? So I thought I'd come and hear your ideas, and take a few notes, so that I won't forget what you said by the time I get home,' she finished lamely, realising that she'd been rambling on, and the lady and her companion were both staring.

'Not at all,' the former MP said politely. 'Whereabouts are you a parish councillor? Here in Penzance?'

'Oh no,' Sheila said with a laugh, and fell in beside her as they walked towards the exit. 'I live in Porthcurno and run the village shop. It was my late husband's shop, but I took it on after he passed away. It's a tiny place, though, and it's coming on for winter, and some of them folk are in dire need. That's why I set up a fund to help them, and a donation centre for clothing and shoes, so nobody has to go without.'

Mrs Newbury-Holmes was listening with interest. 'Sounds to me as though you should run for Cornwall Council in the next elections.'

Sheila stopped dead, flabbergasted. 'Me? Run for election as a Cornwall councillor?'

'Why not? It's a good stepping stone if you're interested in politics. After all, once you're a councillor, you could run for parliament.'

'Now you're pulling my leg!' Sheila chuckled, and even went so far as to dig the former MP in the ribs. 'I ain't posh enough for that. Blimey, I wouldn't even know what fork to use at dinner. They'd throw me out soon as look at me.'

'You'd be surprised the kind of people who run for parliament, Mrs Newton. I can assure you that you've already done good work as a parish councillor and should be commended for your efforts. There are many members of Parliament who haven't done anything even remotely as useful as that, and yet there they sit, in the House of Commons, passing laws to line their own pockets.' The lady shook her head, her look disapproving. 'We need more people like yourself on those benches. Not more people like them.'

By then, they'd emerged into the gloom of the late November afternoon. 'I still think you're joking about me running for Cornwall Council,' Sheila stammered, shaken off balance. 'But thanks for talking to me. And for your speech. I can't wait to try some of these ideas out on the Parish Council.'

The former MP shook her hand again, smiling. 'It was lovely to meet you, Mrs Newton. And I'm happy to help. In fact, my assistant will give you my home address, so you can contact me with any questions you might still have. Now, if you'll excuse me, I have another appointment.' And with that she swept away, climbing into the back of a sleek black car that had pulled up at the kerb while they were talking.

Her assistant, a stout woman in early middle-age, handed Sheila a printed card without a word, before following Mrs Newbury-Holmes into the vehicle.

Just as the car was pulling away, Lily came dashing up breathlessly. 'Was that her?' she hissed, excitement in her eyes. 'Blimey, I bet that fur coat is worth a fortune . . . She must be very rich.'

'She might be rich, but she's ever such a nice lady. She talked to me for bloomin' ages.' Her head still reeling from everything they'd discussed, Sheila showed Lily the card. 'And she gave me this so I could write to her.'

Lily was astonished. '*Write* to her? Whatever for, Gran?'

'In case I have any questions she didn't cover in her talk.' She took a deep breath, adding proudly, 'Also, she said I should run for election to Cornwall Council. For parliament too one day. She said as how I've done more than most MPs do for the poor.'

'Sounds to me like she was having a laugh.' Lily was looking dubious.

Sheila was offended at this lack of confidence, but decided

not to scold her granddaughter, given that she was staying in her house. 'Anyway, I took ever so many notes. Now I just hope I can read my own handwriting!'

'Come here, love, and sit on your old great-gran's knee,' Sheila urged little Morris, who dropped his toy and scrambled onto her knee at once, beaming. Her great-grandson was happy, inquisitive and intelligent, and rapidly becoming her pride and joy. She cuddled him, and he squirmed, giggling noisily. 'Do you know any Christmas songs?'

He nodded, waiting in expectation.

'Christmas is coming,' she chanted, 'and the goose is getting fat . . .' Then paused to let him join in.

'Pwease put a penny in the old man's hat,' he responded, though getting a few of the words wrong, and then threw back his head with a roar of laughter that reminded her strongly of his father, Tristan, who also had a good sense of humour.

Tristan had not always been so prone to laughter, of course. Her young grandson-in-law had come back from wartime service with terrible burns, deeply depressed by what he'd considered to be his failures, and Lily had nursed him back to health. Eventually, he'd joined the fire service in St Ives where they'd been living and worked his way back to happier times. Like the birth of his son.

'If you haven't got a penny,' she went on with an encouraging nod. 'A ha'penny will do. If you haven't got a ha'penny . . . ?'

'God bwess you!' he cried.

'That's right,' Sheila chuckled, holding him tight. 'Aw, bless you too, little man.'

Lily bustled past with an armful of freshly laundered clothes. 'These are for you, Gran.'

'What's that?'

'We've been collecting hand-me-downs from folk hereabouts,' her granddaughter said, placing the stack on the table. 'These are all in good repair, and I've washed and ironed them, ready for your charitable fund.'

'Gawd, you didn't need to do that,' Sheila exclaimed, letting Morris wriggle free. 'You must be rushed off your feet already, what with the boy and this farm.'

'That's all right. Besides, Demelza helped me with the laundering,' Lily told her, smiling. 'And Mary too.'

Sheila's brow wrinkled. 'Mary?'

'I think you met her once. She was a trainee nurse like me, one of my closest friends at the Convalescent Home for Wounded Servicemen in St Ives. She's Mrs Jeffries now, though.' Lily knelt with a hanky to clean Morris's face. 'She married a teacher and they moved to Penzance this summer so Dick could take up a new position here at the school. Anyway, he put up a poster at the school last week, asking for clothing donations for your fund, and these came in from parents, so they're mostly children's clothes. I'll pop them in a bag to take back to Porthcurno.'

Sheila was touched by such a kind gesture. 'Thank you for taking the trouble . . . And Demelza too, especially given her condition.'

She hadn't seen much of Lily's sister-in-law during her stay. The poor thing had been 'indisposed' with morning sickness, despite having already produced an infant less than a year ago – a baby girl called Teresa with plump cheeks and strawberry-blonde wisps of hair, whom she'd heard bawling for a feed occasionally.

‘If you give me their address,’ she added, ‘I’ll write Mary and Dick Jeffries a thank-you note too.’

‘You can thank them in person.’ Lily grinned at her. ‘They’re coming to dinner tonight.’

‘Blimey.’ Sheila, who had invited Bernie to supper that evening too, was surprised. ‘I hope that won’t be too much hard work for you. It’ll be a full house.’

‘We can manage,’ her granddaughter assured her cheerfully. ‘Besides, Mary always brings a large pudding with her, and her husband will help with the dishes afterwards, along with Tris and Rob.’ She laughed merrily, carrying Morris off for his nap. ‘We all muck in here, you’ll see.’

Sure enough, dinner that evening in Penzance was a lively affair, the small farmhouse dining room packed with folk. It was dark and snowy outside, but Tristan and Robert had herded their large flock of sheep into fields nearer the house to keep a closer eye on them, while the newborns and the lambing ewes were under shelter in a large, covered enclosure. The two sheep farmers stamped in from the bitter weather, snow on their boots and coats, just in time to sit down with their guests. Mary and Dick were good-natured and friendly, and it was soon clear that Mary was expecting, revealing a rounded tummy as soon as her coat came off.

‘Only two months to go,’ the curly-haired young woman told Sheila with a smile, easing wearily onto the sofa. Mary and her husband Dick both had strong Cornish accents like Tristan and Demelza, Sheila had noted when they were first introduced. ‘But we’re all prepared. I’ve been knitting booties by the dozen, my parents bought us a second-hand crib at their last visit, and Dick's painted the nursery a glorious bright yellow. I can't wait for Baby to arrive!'

'Enjoy those broken nights,' Demelza muttered.

'Well, it looks like you must enjoy them,' Mary quipped, accepting a cup of tea from Sheila, who'd insisted on making herself useful while the two women cooked. 'Thank you, Mrs Newton.' She nodded to Demelza's increasing tummy. 'Given that you've decided it's time for round two.'

'That was more of an accident than a decision,' Demelza admitted, chewing on her lip, then flushed when everyone laughed.

'Accidents do have a tendency to 'appen, love.' Sheila chortled. 'Anyway, you might as well have two babies as one. That's what we thought when little Violet came along, after we'd grown used to the idea of only having Betsy, who was Lily's mum.' She sighed, wishing again her eldest daughter had survived the war. 'Ah, those were the good ol' days.'

Bernie, standing up to drink his tea, as there weren't quite enough seats in the cramped front room to go around, gave her a wink. 'Plenty of time for more good *new* days ahead, Sheila.'

'Amen to that,' Robert murmured.

They sat around one big table to eat a roast chicken meal with all the trimmings, and afterwards each enjoyed a portion of Mary's fruit pudding, heated up and served with lashings of condensed milk.

'You've outdone yourself, ladies,' Dick announced as he pushed aside his dessert bowl. 'Three cheers for the cooks!'

And they all cheered, while the young women grinned, looking bashful. Then the three men rose, with the exception of Bernie, who'd offered to help with the washing-up but been told to stay and entertain the ladies instead, and began clearing the table.

'Have you had a good holiday here, Mrs Newton?' Mary asked, producing wool and needles from her bag, and began to knit with a practised air.

'Oh, I've had such a wonderful time, thank you.'

Across the cosy room, Sheila caught Bernie's eye and smiled. They'd walked out together every other day during her stay, and she had indeed enjoyed herself being away from home and Violet's disapproving eye.

Only that morning they had strolled arm in arm along the seafront at Penzance, in an icy wind laced with snowflakes, where he'd braved the weather to take off his hat and once again proposed marriage to her. She had said no, of course. But she couldn't deny the man was good company. Indeed, she was beginning to feel so much affection for him, she could happily have agreed to marry him, if it hadn't been for her fears over what might happen once she was a wife again. Bernie might claim that he wouldn't interfere with her running the village shop or sitting on the council once they were wed, and she believed he meant it, but she also knew that men had a funny way of changing their minds once they'd achieved the thing they were after. So, although Sheila liked him a great deal, she was not yet ready to say yes.

On her last day in Penzance, Sheila had a comfortable chat with her other granddaughter Alice, who'd had a telephone installed in her flat in London, and got all their news too. She and Patrick were still working for the government and had high hopes of being able to afford their own house soon, with a garden too, out in the growing suburbs. She also spoke briefly to Ernest, who was still staying with Alice and her husband.

'How's the weather been in Porthcurno, Sheila?' her son-in-law asked down the crackly line.

'We've been having a nasty, cold snap,' Sheila admitted, pulling her cardigan closer in the draughty hall, 'but I'm sure it won't last.'

'I wouldn't be so sure,' Ernest told her. 'The government expects heavy snowfall this winter, and not just up north. I hope Joe and Violet are prepared for this "cold snap" to get worse before it gets better.'

Sure enough, when Bernie drove her home from Penzance, snow lay thicker than ever along the verges, the sky glowering with dark clouds.

Sheila mentioned Ernest's warning. 'He says we could have blizzards, even down here in Cornwall.'

'I'll believe it when I see it,' Bernie told her easily, and whistled between his teeth. 'You warm enough, my darling? Or would you like that blanket from the back seat?'

Shivering in the chilly car, Sheila reached through for the tartan blanket to wrap about her knees and caught his quick grin. 'Don't you tell Violet. She already thinks I'm as old as the hills and that I need looking after.'

'Ah, but to me, you're still the fresh-faced girl I fell in love with at school,' he told her softly, and she chuckled, torn between wanting to tell him off for such ridiculous flattery and a growing curiosity to know how it would feel to be Mrs Bernard Bailey.

CHAPTER FOURTEEN

Caroline hugged Selina in the snowy farmyard, while they waited for Peter to return from visiting the pigs with Grace and Tilly for the last time. 'I wish you didn't have to go,' she admitted, 'but Mrs Newton's due back from Penzance today. And I doubt you'd be comfy squeezing into the attic rooms with us Land Girls. Not now you're so posh,' she added with a wink, hoping her friend wouldn't mind her teasing.

'*Posh*?' Selina laughed and shook her head. 'Hardly. But I do need to get back to Bodmin. Jemima and Faith will be missing us madly by now, and although their cousin Nancy is good with the girls, she's still quite young and I don't like the idea of leaving her in charge for so long.' She was smiling, though. 'It's been lovely seeing you again, Caro. We must keep in touch.'

'Of course.' Caroline carried Peter's abandoned bags to the boot of her car, placing them beside Selina's case. 'So,' she added shyly, 'you've had plenty of time to meet our new Land Girl. What do you think of her?'

Selina's lips twitched. 'It might be more pertinent to ask

what she thinks of *you*,' she murmured, glancing about as though to check nobody was listening. But they'd left Joe and Violet deep in conversation in the farmhouse kitchen, and there was still no sign of the others returning from the pigsty. 'Grace is a lively girl, for sure, with a strong sense of humour. But I've seen the way you look at her . . .' She hesitated, her smile lopsided. 'You will be careful, Caro, won't you?'

Caroline chewed on her lip, not sure how to respond to that. 'What . . . What do you mean?'

'Oh, come on.' Selina took her by the hands. 'I know you like her, so there's no point pretending.' Her look was compassionate. 'I remember how upset you got when I had to leave the farm this summer. I haven't forgotten what you said that day.'

'Please, don't,' Caroline mumbled, pulling her hands free. She felt horribly embarrassed, recalling how badly she'd behaved when Selina left, the emotional way she'd declared her feelings, the tears she'd shed as they parted. She'd been half hoping that Selina had forgotten, or would at least pretend to have done so, for both their sakes. But clearly not.

'Look, it's all right,' her friend assured her. 'I didn't mind then, and I don't mind now. But I don't want to see you hurt by being too . . . let's say, *friendly*?'

Caroline swallowed. It was on the tip of her tongue to defend the other girl and insist that Grace would never do anything to hurt or upset her. But she knew that wouldn't be entirely true. Grace had joined Tilly in mocking her for being an 'old lady', even saying something about getting her a walking stick for Christmas, hadn't she? They'd been joking, of course; there were only three years' difference between her and Grace. But it had hurt at the time, and made her wonder if Grace, with her lively ways and sparkling humour, did in fact feel closer to nineteen-year-old Tilly than her. Also, Caroline had deliberately held back from being too open about her feelings this time, fearful of saying the wrong thing and landing herself in hot water. It would be disastrous if Grace were to take offence and make a complaint about her to the farmer and his wife. She could lose her position at Postbridge Farm and be forced to return to her parents in disgrace, a horrible thought.

'Nothing's happened,' she whispered, for Peter was already striding back across the yard, Tilly and Grace following in his wake. 'But I'll be careful. I promise.'

'Good.' Selina embraced Tilly and shook Grace's hand, and then turned to give Caroline one last hug. 'I'm going to miss you all. I hope you have a marvellous Christmas. Think of me from time to time, won't you?'

'Always,' Caroline choked.

'Well, better jump in, Peter,' Selina told her nephew cheerfully. 'It's time to go.'

Within a few minutes, Caroline found herself waving a tearful goodbye as her best friend disappeared down the hill into Porthcurno village, knowing it might be months, maybe even years, before they saw each other again.

Grace bumped her from behind. 'Eh, don't cry,' she told her. 'It's bread and butter pudding tonight. And I helped make it.' She was smiling when Caroline turned to go back inside. 'Though maybe that's enough to put you off. You know I can't cook for toffee.'

'No, it . . . it sounds delicious.'

Grace hesitated, glancing up at the gloomy skies. 'Want to nip out for a walk along the cliffs before the snow starts falling again?'

'I shouldn't, sorry,' Caroline told her cautiously, not meeting her eyes. She would have liked nothing better than to say yes to an hour spent walking out alone with Grace, but she recalled Selina's warning about being too friendly. It was better to avoid dangerous situations like that, at least until she knew the girl well enough to trust her. 'Now Selina and Peter have gone home, I need to strip their beds and put fresh linen on. Mrs Newton's due back from Penzance soon and she'll play merry hell if it's not been done.'

And she hurried back inside the farmhouse before the other girl could protest.

Mrs Newton came home late afternoon, accompanied by Mr Bailey in his swanky car and bursting with news about Lily and Tristan and the others at the farm in Penzance. 'Oh Joe, they've got a telephone,' was almost the first thing she could be heard telling Mr Postbridge, her voice high and breathless with excitement. 'I spoke to Alice for nearly half an hour on it, and to Ernest too. They've been working ever so hard in London, he says. Patrick's in fine form and had a promotion recently too, so he and Alice are thinking of moving from their flat to a house with a garden. Only think, Vi, our little Alice *buying* her own home, and her still so young. She's done bloomin' well for herself, ain't she?'

Caroline, seated at the kitchen table with Tilly, both girls sponging mud off their green Land Army jerseys to save them being washed again, glanced across at the other girl with a grin. Mrs Postbridge and her mother were always going on about Alice and how well she'd done for herself. That young woman could do no wrong in their eyes, it seemed.

'Of course she has, Mum, and a house with a garden does sound lovely,' Violet agreed, 'but I'm not sure about having a telephone here. Sounds expensive to me.'

'Lily says all the farmers have telephones in Penzance,' Mrs Newton dropped in, with a cunning glance at Joe. 'Makes it easier to call the vet in an emergency, she told me, and to keep in touch with other farmers when livestock goes missing.'

'Eh?' Joe, still struggling with his boots in the porch, stopped to stare round curiously at his mother-in-law.

'And Bernie here has a telephone himself and knows all about how to go about getting one rigged up, even all the way out here.' Mrs Newton winked at Mr Bailey, who gave a supportive nod. It was obvious she was keen to have a telephone installed at Postbridge Farm. 'Besides, just imagine being able to speak to Alice any time you like, Violet. On Christmas Day, say, or your birthday.'

'Hmm.' Violet looked unconvinced.

'I'd be interested to look into that,' Joe rumbled, and began a low-voiced conversation with Mr Bailey.

Her mission accomplished, Mrs Newton smiled and bustled over to the range to keep warm, holding out her hands to the iron hotplate. 'It's bloomin' perishing out there, Vi,' she told her daughter, glancing out the window with a dramatic shudder. 'Snow everywhere, nasty bitter wind, going right through to my bones . . . I stopped to speak to Margaret at the shop on our way through the village, and she says they've barely seen a soul these past few days. People must be staying home to keep warm. I swear, we ain't had such a cold winter in decades.'

Caroline finished sponging her jersey and got up to hang the green monstrosity over the range rail to dry. It would only take an hour or two, she estimated.

'The fire's lit in the snug. You go through, Mum, and take Bernie with you,' Violet told her mother, setting a tray with teapot and cups. 'I'll be right behind you.'

Once they'd gone into the snug, Joe whistled for the dogs and limped after them, only pausing to give the girls a friendly nod. 'Good work today, you two. It's not easy, being out in these freezing temperatures all day. Make sure to keep warm and not catch a chill, won't you?' And with that, he followed the others into the cosy back room and shut the door.

Tilly also hung her jersey over the range rail, smoothing out the damp creases. 'Caro, if the weather improves next weekend, would you like to make up a foursome with me and Benny?' Benny was the name of the village lad she'd been dating. 'We're taking the bus to Penzance for the Saturday matinee, so long as Joe doesn't need us, and always assuming we're not snowed in by then.'

Taken aback, Caroline stared at her. 'M-Make up a foursome?' she stammered. 'You mean, a double date?'

'That's right.' Tilly laughed, seeing her expression. 'Sorry, I meant to say . . . Benny's got an older brother, Trevor. He's seen you about the village a few times and wanted to ask you out himself, but he's shy.'

'I'm not sure . . . How much older is he?' Caroline asked, not knowing what to say for the best. The last thing she wanted was to start dating a boy. But she could hardly say so outright to Tilly.

Tilly pulled a face. 'I knew you wouldn't be interested. And you're right. Trevor's only just turned twenty. Benny's younger than me, you see. He's seventeen.' She shrugged. 'Ah well, it was worth a try.'

'Grace might go,' Caroline said slowly, though she felt uncomfortable even suggesting it.

'*Grace*?' Tilly raised her eyebrows. 'I . . . I'll ask Benny, of course. But you were the one Trevor had his eye on.'

Just as she was struggling to formulate a response to that, a loud knock came at the back door, then the door to the porch creaked open and someone poked a head round.

'Hello?' It was a telegram boy, easily recognisable by his navy-blue uniform with smart red piping, topped by his matching pillbox hat with a GPO crown. 'No dogs about, are there?' Many visitors to the farm had a lively fear of Joe's newest dog, young Pip, who tended to chase after them when Joe wasn't about to call him to heel.

Caroline and Tilly stared at each other in astonished silence.

'No, the dogs are in the other room.' Tilly bounded to the door. 'Goodness, a telegram?'

'Just came in over the wires at Eastern House,' the boy told her proudly. 'Mr Cotterill wrote it up himself and asked me to cycle straight over before it got too dark to see.'

In the snug, Joe's farm dogs started to bark, no doubt hearing a stranger's voice in the kitchen. The boy glanced towards the door, startled, and gulped.

'But who's it for?' Tilly took it from his gloved hands. 'Oh my . . .' Her voice died away.

'It's a telegram for Miss Ponsby.' The boy, who looked about sixteen, peered at Tilly's face. 'Is that you, Miss?'

Tilly shook her head silently.

'What?' Caroline gave a gasp. 'For . . . For *me*?' Her voice was a squeak. 'No, that can't be right. I . . . I never get telegrams.'

'It's your name on the envelope, Caro.' Slowly, Tilly turned, holding out the telegram in its thin buff envelope. Sure enough, it was addressed to her, with the official 'GPO Telegram' heading.

'Sorry, Miss.' The telegram boy gave her an apologetic smile and hurried away, pulling the door shut behind him.

Violet Postbridge came out of the snug at that moment, Joe at her shoulder. The dogs ran out ahead of them, barking frantically now and pawing at the door to the farmyard. 'What on earth . . . ?'

'Heel!' Joe told the dogs, who fell back at his stern voice, their tails wagging furiously.

Mrs Newton had also appeared in the doorway, staring out of the snug. 'Blimey, I never heard such a bloomin' racket . . . Girls? What's happened?'

'Caro got a telegram,' Tilly told them breathlessly. 'It came in through Eastern House. The boy's just gone.'

Everyone looked at Caroline, who swallowed and bent her gaze to the sinister envelope in her hand.

'Must be urgent, or whoever it's from would have sent a letter,' Joe remarked unnecessarily, and whistled sharply to young Pip, who had gone back to the farmhouse door. Pip returned to his side at once but with his tail still thumping excitedly, peering up at his master. 'Calm down now, boy. Blow me, this new dog's a handful.'

'Open it then,' Violet urged her.

But Caroline stood frozen, holding her breath. The

telegram had to be from her family back home in West London. Who else would have sent her an urgent message? Her heart began to thump violently as her brain whirled, going through all the possibilities . . . Had somebody died?

'Best leave the girl alone, eh?' Mrs Newton nudged her daughter meaningfully. 'Ain't none of our business. Come on, you two . . . I hadn't finished telling you about that Mrs Newbury-Holmes.' And she pulled Violet back into the snug.

But Joe, no doubt eager to escape his mother-in-law's tales of her Penzance trip, mumbled something about needing to check on the pigs and headed into the porch to pull on his boots and coat. The dogs milled about him eagerly, young Pip starting to bark again, much to the farmer's irritation. 'Give over barking, Pip!' he grumbled before hurrying outside, both dogs slinking at his heel.

They were alone again in the kitchen. Tilly looked at Caroline sympathetically. 'Do you want me to stay while you open it?'

Caroline shook her head, unable to say a word.

'In that case, I'll be upstairs if you need me,' Tilly murmured, and disappeared, discreetly leaving her alone with the telegram.

Caroline turned it over in her hands, her heart thumping, still trying to guess the contents. It had been some weeks since her last letter from her parents, and they'd given no indication that anything might be wrong at home. So only something truly awful and unexpected could have merited a telegram, of all things . . .

As she reluctantly began to tear open the envelope, she heard footsteps on the stairs. Grace appeared in the kitchen, breathless and with her hair arranged in plump, soft braids drawn into a bun at the nape of her neck.

'Tilly says you've got a telegram?' When Caroline nodded, showing her the envelope, she went on impatiently, 'All right, who's it from? What's it about?' Grace tutted at her helpless look. 'You haven't read it yet, have you? But it must be urgent . . . What are you waiting for?'

Instead of replying, Caroline dragged out the single sheet and read the message over several times to herself without taking it in.

'Well?' Her friend came closer, her eyes wide. 'What does it say? Please, Caro, you're worrying me now.'

Swallowing, Caroline read the telegram out loud in a faltering voice. '*Grandmother at death's door. Come home at once. Father.*'

There was a short silence, broken by Caroline's sob as the words finally made sense to her.

'Oh, Caro, I'm so sorry.' Grace pulled her into her a fierce hug and Caroline wept into her shoulder.

When she pulled back, Caroline reached for her hanky. 'I . . . I can't believe it. Gran's always been a picture of health. I wish I knew what was wrong.'

Grace had taken the telegram and was reading it herself. 'Nine words exactly,' she pointed out, and pulled a face. Telegrams were charged at ninepence for the first nine words only, further words being more expensive. 'Cheaper not to go into detail.'

Caroline couldn't reply, still weeping into her hanky. Her head was reeling . . . Could Gran have been involved in a terrible accident? Or had she caught that particularly bad strain of influenza that was going around? Even previously healthy people had been knocked sideways by the flu before now.

She wasn't sure what to do for the best. Home was so far away, a long day's journey. The awful truth was the old lady's health might have worsened in the time it had taken the telegram to arrive. She could even have died. Again, she wished she knew the exact situation. If only they'd already had a telephone installed at the farm . . .

'I have to go,' she blurted out, stumbling to the porch in search of coat and boots. 'I need to catch the next train home.'

But Grace followed her. 'Look, I know you're upset,' she said gently. 'I would be too. But you can't leave until tomorrow. You've already missed the last bus to Penzance train station today.'

Caroline groaned, feeling caught in a nightmare. Tomorrow might be too late. But what choice did she have?

'Besides, you need to get some food down you before rushing off. And to pack a bag. You don't know how long you'll be gone, remember.' Grace hesitated. 'Listen, do you want me to come with you tomorrow, if Joe can spare us both?'

'Take you back to London with me? Oh no, I . . .' Caroline gave a stuttering, nonsensical reply, struck dumb by the idea of Grace travelling home with her on the bus and train, then being introduced to her parents.

The thought was unspeakably wonderful, a cosy hug at a moment of dreadful unhappiness. Yet it was also terrifying. For she wouldn't be able to hide her feelings for such a long period, would she? And her sharp-eyed mother would be bound to spot her partiality for Grace, and there would be embarrassing questions and recriminations, and then her overprotective father would probably put his foot down and try to stop Caroline ever leaving home again . . .

Besides, what would Grace say if she gave herself away like that? Would her friend ever speak to her again once she knew that Caroline liked her far, far too much?

'No, you're right. It would only complicate everything,' Grace answered for her at once, practical and understanding. 'Look, maybe Joe will run you down to the bus first thing tomorrow to save time. You go ask him; I'll start packing a bag for you.' And with that, she hurried away, leaving Caroline alone and in tears, that awful telegram staring back at her like an accusation of wrongdoing.

Grandmother at death's door. Come home at once. Father.

CHAPTER FIFTEEN

It was still dark when Selina was awoken early by the sound of hurrying feet and voices along the upstairs landing. *Who on earth . . . ?*

Pushing aside her troubled dreams, she swung her legs reluctantly out of bed, but winced at the cold air, thankful for her thick woollen bedsocks. Snow had lain deep around Thornton Hall ever since her return from visiting Postbridge Farm, blanketing much of Bodmin Moor and its surrounds in crisp thick whiteness. The hall's open fires and electric heaters had kept the cold at bay so far, but the night before had brought another of those interminable power cuts, so her small two-bar heater had not managed to warm the room before bedtime.

Thrusting her feet into slippers, Selina pulled back her bedroom curtains to reveal white lawns and shrubberies slowly glimmering in the dawn half-light and shivered reluctantly.

Her cosy bed still beckoned, but the sound of whispering urged her to the door instead, frowning with concern. It was the second morning in a row that she'd been woken by some faint commotion, but yesterday she'd been too exhausted to move and had drifted back to sleep without rising to investigate. The unseasonal cold had taken its toll on everyone that winter, and even the promise of Christmas just ahead was not enough to keep their spirits up.

She crept along the landing, belting up her dressing gown. 'Hello?'

No answer.

The doors to the children's rooms were closed, she saw thankfully. But Nancy's door was partly ajar, and she stopped on the threshold, alarmed by the sound of someone choking inside, as though being sick.

Had one of the children fallen ill and run to their cousin for help instead of their aunt? It was possible, she supposed, though a little disheartening. Still, if the girls saw their new nanny as a confidante, that was not a bad thing.

Selina had harboured a few doubts about the young woman at first. But Nancy had been an attentive nanny so far, it could not be denied, and on her return from Porthcurno she'd heard nothing but good reports from Mrs Hawley about her cousin's hard work and sweet, bubbly nature.

Worried, she gently pushed the door wide to Nancy's room, peering inside. 'Hello? Can I help?'

But it was not a child being sick. To her shock, Nancy herself was kneeling on the floor, the new maid crouched beside her, holding out a bucket.

Nancy vomited once more, then turned an ashen face in her direction, her eyes wide with fright. 'Oh,' she groaned unhappily, 'Cousin Selly . . . I'm so sorry.'

'Sorry?' Selina came inside, swiftly closing the door so the children would not hear them. 'What is there to be sorry about? If you're unwell, that's hardly your fault . . .' Then she gasped. Nancy had straightened to accept a damp facecloth from the helpful maid, and her thin nightdress was straining in a tell-tale manner across a gently rounded belly. 'Good God . . . !' Restraining herself, she dismissed the maid with a word of thanks, asking her to take the bucket with her, and waited until the girl had scurried away before saying with difficulty, 'Nancy, forgive me, but . . . Please tell me you're not *pregnant*?'

Nancy sat heavily on the edge of the bed, hugging herself. 'Not much point trying to deny it, is there?' she muttered.

Selina exhaled slowly. 'I see. And the child's father? Are you and he going to be married?'

Nancy shook her head miserably. 'I told him about the baby, and he . . . he said it was my problem. That I should either try to get rid of it or give it up for adoption.'

Horrified, Selina exclaimed, 'What a beast . . . Then he must be made to marry you, that's all there is for it.'

'He won't do it. He's gone overseas with the navy. Says he may never come home.' Nancy blenched, holding her belly as though feeling queasy again.

'Then we must write to his commanding officer. I'll do it if you don't want to. As your cousin and employer, I can insist that he returns home and—'

'I don't even know his surname,' Nancy blurted out.

'Oh Lord.' Selina closed her eyes, feeling a little queasy herself. But after a moment's thought, she said crisply, 'Well, I'd better have the whole story. But not now. You can get the children up as usual and leave them with their tutor after breakfast. Then you and I will go for a walk,' she added warily, 'away from prying eyes and ears. The fewer people who know about this, the better.' She hesitated. 'Does the maid know you're pregnant or does she simply think you're sick?'

'Peggy knows,' Nancy admitted unhappily. 'She caught me throwing up last week and knew at once. Her sister's expecting a baby too, so she knows the symptoms.'

Selina wanted to scream. A scandal was the last thing she needed. But perhaps the maid would be discreet enough to keep her mouth shut. 'I'd better have a word with Peggy myself, make sure she doesn't talk out of turn. Meanwhile, you should get dressed. Unless you're too unwell to deal with the children today?'

Nancy shook her head, not meeting her gaze. 'I . . . I'll be fine now. The sickness is only when I first get up.'

Although not feeling terribly sympathetic, Selina gave Nancy a hug. She might have behaved foolishly, even recklessly, but she was still her cousin-in-law. 'Never mind,' she said, aware that the young woman must be feeling scared and in need of comforting right now rather than disapproval. 'You've got yourself into a pickle here, but we'll try to find a way through together.'

Once the children were safely installed in the schoolroom with their tutor, and she and Nancy had breakfasted, Selina pulled on her wellington boots and coat and collected a wicker basket from the porch. 'We'll walk the dogs and gather any wood we see for kindling,' she told Nancy, and whistled for the dogs, who came running.

They crunched across the snowy lawn and into the woodland that adjoined the grounds, the dogs running eagerly ahead. Selina, who hoped to drive into town later, studied the skies with concern. But it was barely snowing now, and Mr Underhill, the groundsman, had cleared the drive all the way to the main road, where she could hear an occasional vehicle passing by.

'Now nobody can overhear us, perhaps you could tell me about this young man.' Selina stooped for a few twigs that would make useful kindling once dried, shaking off the snow before nestling them into her basket. 'I take it you didn't know him very long, given that you don't even know his surname.' She tried not to sound unsympathetic, understanding only too well how quickly one could fancy oneself in love. 'How did you two meet?'

'At a dance,' Nancy admitted. 'Reginald was rather dashing in his uniform. Tall, dark, handsome, and ever so charming.' Her smile faltered. 'I had no idea what kind of man he was deep down. I believed what I saw. You must think me a complete idiot.'

Selina shook her head. She had blindly adored Johnny, her own soldier beau who'd made a girl pregnant while serving in France and broken off their engagement to marry her. Although she'd tried hard to put that betrayal behind her, she suspected it might never be possible.

'No, it usually takes a while to know someone well enough to judge their character. This sounds more like a whirlwind romance. Besides, men feel things differently to us.' She bent to collect another snow-covered twig. 'We may fancy ourselves in love, and imagine it to be reciprocated too, while a man's only saying what he thinks we want to hear.' She saw Nancy blench and could have kicked herself. 'Sorry, that's probably not helpful.'

'No, you're right. Reggie was so warm and friendly; I fell head over heels in no time. He took me to the pub once, and to the cinema a few times. But looking back, he couldn't have meant all those sweet things he said, could he? He only wanted one thing, and afterwards . . .' Nancy blushed, pushing gloved hands into her coat pocket. 'P-Please don't think b-badly of me,' she stuttered, 'but Reggie came to the house one night when my parents were asleep and threw a stone up at my window. I let him in through the back door, just to see what he wanted. We started kissing and . . . Well, one thing led to another.'

Embarrassed by this candid revelation, Selina looked away. Carefully, she tugged a fallen branch free of the undergrowth. 'And after that?'

'I saw him about town, but he always said he was too busy to stop and talk. I didn't know what to think. Then I heard he was dating another girl.' Nancy's voice choked with tears. 'I confronted him and he told me it was all over between us. I was almost glad at first, because I knew I'd been a fool, falling for his smooth talk. But then . . .' She closed her eyes.

'Then you discovered you were pregnant.'

'Yes,' Nancy said in a small voice. 'It was awful. He'd been officially demobbed by then, but had joined the Royal Navy instead – he wanted to see the world, he claimed – and was set to go overseas. So I knew I had to be quick. I didn't know who his parents were or where he'd been living, but I saw one of his friends in the street and told him I needed to speak to Reginald urgently. He came to the house the next day, but only when my parents weren't there. I think he was afraid my father knew about us and would punch him.'

Selina looked at her sympathetically, hearing the hurt in

her voice. 'And what did Reginald say when you told him you were expecting?'

'He called me a little idiot. He was so angry.' Nancy wiped away another tear. 'He said he wasn't the m-marrying kind, and didn't care about being a father. Well, you know the rest . . . Reggie left town that week and I've not seen or heard from him since.'

Having reached the long ride of oak and beech trees that marked the boundary of her late sister's large estate, they stopped walking. The dogs played in the undergrowth nearby, sniffing and rustling about in the snowy bushes, no doubt catching the scent of a rabbit.

'Please don't cry. Honestly, he's not worth it.' Yet Selina's protest was half-hearted. She herself had cried for weeks over Johnny's betrayal, and later shed tears of pure fury over her neighbour Cameron Bourne when she discovered that he too had been playing her for a fool. Sometimes it was better to get the grief out and not let it fester. Selina gave Nancy a quick hug, seeing how cold and pale she had become. 'What I don't understand,' she added with a frown, 'is why you came here, asking for work as a nanny. By your own admission, you already knew by then that you were pregnant.'

Nancy's weeping intensified. 'It . . . It wasn't my idea,' she sobbed, burying her face in her hands.

'Here, take my hanky. It's clean.' Selina was perplexed. 'But whose idea was it, then?'

'I was so scared, I tried to pretend it wasn't happening at first. But when my clothes started to get tight, I knew it couldn't be long before people started to guess. So I told my parents.'

'I take it they weren't particularly supportive?'

Nancy sniffed into the hanky. 'They threw me out.'

Even though she had half suspected this, Selina was still shocked to hear it confirmed. 'My goodness. In your condition?'

'My father was furious,' Nancy said, barely coherent. 'He called me horrid names . . . Told me to pack a bag and never come back. Behind his back, my mother gave me money for the train and suggested I should come here. She urged me to be honest with you about the baby and pray you'd take me in, since Sebastian and I were cousins.'

Selina felt a flurry of frustration. 'I wish you had been honest.'

'I know it was wrong to lie to you, but I was so frightened.' Nancy raised a tear-stained face, her eyes fixed on Selina's. 'Please say you won't throw me out . . . I've nowhere else to go.'

Faced with that pleading look, Selina knew she had no choice. Besides, her real fury lay with Nancy's parents, who had thrown their pregnant daughter out into the streets with nothing but a suitcase of clothes and the train fare to Bodmin. 'Of course I won't turn you away. You made a very silly mistake. But it isn't the end of the world.' She was thinking hard, still unsure how to deal with the situation. 'I mean, it's a bit tricky. I'm not sure what we should tell people once you begin to show, or even if Thornton Hall is the best place for you to have a baby.' At Nancy's apprehensive look, she shook her head. 'But clearly you must stay here for the time being. So please don't worry.'

'Oh, thank you so much. And I can still look after the girls,' Nancy insisted, her face brightening. 'Nobody need know the truth yet. I've been wearing my baggiest clothes, trying to hide my tummy. Though I know that won't work forever.'

'No,' Selina agreed. 'But I see no reason why you shouldn't keep working for the time being. Peter doesn't need a nanny, of course. But the girls have grown very fond of you.' She stamped her feet; they were turning to blocks of ice, despite her boots. 'Shall we walk back to the house? I don't think there's much more wood out here for the gathering,' she said, picking up the basket. 'This will have to do for kindling. But there are plenty of logs up at the house. And surely this cold weather must ease off soon, don't you think?'

Nancy agreed with a happier smile, and they walked briskly back to the house, the dogs bounding around them, tails wagging.

She had spoken optimistically, trying to keep her cousin's spirits up, but, in truth, Selina was not at all comfortable with the situation. She now had a young unmarried woman in the house who was expecting a child, and while she wasn't particularly bothered that Nancy had behaved recklessly with this young man, she knew most of their neighbours would think otherwise. With the help of important local figures like the doctor and William MacGregor, she had worked hard to be accepted as part of this tight-knit community after her sister's tragic death. But this unexpected pregnancy was likely to cause one hell of a stink.

The longer she could keep Nancy's condition quiet, the better. But she would need to take William MacGregor into her confidence, at least. He managed the estate and had a right to know.

* * *

As soon as Selina had parked her car in a snowy side street in Bodmin town centre, Peter jumped out of the passenger seat, buttoned up his overcoat and said brusquely, 'Thanks for the lift into town, Aunt Selly. I'll meet you back here later.'

Selina stared at her nephew, bemused. 'I thought you were coming to lunch with me and Mr MacGregor.'

'Sorry, not hungry.' Peter turned up the collar of his coat, looking up and down the street. 'Will you be long?'

'About an hour,' she said reluctantly. The boy had been behaving awkwardly since coming home from school, and William had agreed to discuss his behaviour today, man to man, in the hope of settling him down, since it was clear he would never confide in his aunt. 'The thing is, Peter, I was rather hoping you and Mr MacGregor might have a chat—'

'Later, maybe.' Peter trudged away, hands in his pockets, leaving Selina frustrated.

William was waiting for her at a corner table. He stood up at her approach, looking surprised. 'Hello, where's Peter?' The solicitor pulled out a chair for her and she sat down, feeling flustered.

Briefly, she explained what had happened. 'I don't know what to do about him,' she admitted with a sigh. 'He's not rude as such. I just feel we can't talk anymore.'

'I wouldn't worry too much. Boys his age can be difficult.' His eyes twinkled at her as he summoned the waiter. 'I'll walk back with you after lunch and have a word with him if you like.'

'Thank you.'

The restaurant was draughty, and the menu limited, many

items crossed off due to food shortages. But the off-ration food was as delicious as ever, and while they ate, they discussed how the household was coping with the constant blackouts and the possibility of installing a generator at the hall for emergency use.

Selina, tucking eagerly into her meal, could not help contrasting her life now with her days as a Land Girl in Porthcurno. Then, they had gulped down sausages in gravy or rabbit stew for their main meals, with bread and butter pudding afterwards or tinned fruit with a dash of condensed cream. Tasty enough after a long day's work in the fields, but she couldn't ever remember being presented with slivers of duck cooked with orange for her lunch. Some days she felt like pinching herself.

But while these posh lunches with William were marvellous, they also served to remind her that she didn't truly belong in this world. It was only through caring for her late sister's children that she was even living at Thornton Hall, and if the solicitor didn't always insist on paying for these meals, she could not have afforded to walk through the door. Such thoughts kept her feet firmly on the ground . . .

Guiltily, Selina recalled her other reason for lunching with William today. 'There's something else I need to discuss with you,' she began, patting her mouth with a napkin. 'It's rather delicate, I'm afraid.'

William looked at her gravely. 'Whatever it is, I hope I can help.'

Lowering her voice, Selina explained about Nancy and her unfortunate situation. William's eyes widened, but he said nothing, merely listened in silence until she'd finished.

'I wondered if you had any advice for me,' she added,

searching his face hopefully. 'I've told Miss Furniss she can stay for now. But it can't be long until her condition becomes obvious, and I'm worried what people may say. Not worried for myself,' she added hurriedly, in case he misunderstood her concern, 'but for the children. I don't want them to hear any nasty gossip about their nanny. Though if she stays until after the birth, I'll have to explain her pregnancy to them . . . Peter might understand, but the girls?'

'Well, quite,' he agreed sombrely.

Selina bit her lip, wishing she could read his expression. 'Do . . . Do you think I should have told Nancy to leave?' she asked falteringly. 'She did come to the hall under false pretences, and now she's put us in the most dreadful fix. Only I didn't feel I had a choice. She's not been well, poor girl, and she has nowhere else to go, and with all this snow . . .'

He was shaking his head. 'No, of course she must stay. You did the right thing.'

'Oh, thank goodness.' Selina sagged with relief. She would have hated to argue with him if he'd told her to send Nancy away. 'So what now?'

'I'm not sure. But at least nobody else knows yet. For now, I suggest you do nothing.'

She felt soothed by this common-sense advice, and agreed heartily, but her good mood didn't last. Waiting for Peter beside the car after lunch, chatting to William, she turned at the sound of her name and saw her nearest neighbours on the moors, Helen and Cameron Bourne, crossing the road towards them. The Bournes, brother and sister, were dressed alike, both wrapped up against the cold in funereal black.

Selina stiffened. She hadn't forgiven Cameron for trying to worm his way into her affections after Bella's death, perhaps thinking he could influence Peter's financial decisions if he became the boy's uncle. And she disliked his sister too since discovering Helen and Peter's father had once had a fling behind Bella's back. Both siblings had proved themselves untrustworthy, even treacherous, and she shuddered as they approached. But since they were well known and respected in Bodmin, she kept a polite smile on her face.

'Hello,' she said coolly as they all shook hands. 'The snow's been bad on the moors, hasn't it? How have you been coping?'

'Oh, we're used to the snow. I suppose you must find it difficult as a newcomer.' With a dismissive smile, Helen glanced with sly interest at William. 'You two been lunching together? How cosy.'

'We meet regularly to discuss estate business,' William told her brusquely, and it was clear he had little time for the Bournes either.

'And there's plenty to discuss, I hear,' Cameron said, looking away as he adjusted his gloves. 'Ah, there's Peter . . .' Her nephew, who'd just emerged from a bookshop along the street, waved cheerfully. 'We heard about his expulsion, of course.' Cameron lowered his voice. 'The lad needs a firm hand. Something I daresay he hasn't had since his father died.'

Selina's lips tightened. 'We must go, I'm afraid. The girls will be waiting—'

'But don't they have a nanny now?' Helen interrupted sweetly, her eyes alight with malice. 'A cousin of theirs, I believe? And rather, erm, tubby.' She laughed behind her hand. 'Or she will be soon, from what I hear.'

Selina felt abruptly sick, her chest tight, and did not know what to say. She barely registered William saying goodbye to the Bournes and then helping her into the passenger seat, saying, 'Let me drive you home. You really shouldn't have come out in this snowy weather, not as a new driver.' Looking surprised, Peter bounded into the back seat, and William set off back to Thornton Hall. 'I'll have a word with Peter another day,' he muttered, glancing at her sideways. 'You look done in. It's the weather, I expect.'

She agreed, her whole body cold and icy. But they both knew it wasn't the weather that had left her standing numb and speechless in the street back there.

Selina had no idea who had spoken out of turn. The maid, perhaps, or a visiting tradesman could have noticed Nancy's growing waistline and drawn his own conclusions. They might never find out. But if the Bournes knew about the pregnancy, then it was likely the whole town did too. Helen and Cameron Bourne, eager for this opportunity to get back at her, would have made sure of that.

Nancy would soon find every face set against her in this Cornish backwater where unmarried mothers were still shocking and unacceptable. And the girls and Peter would suffer for it too as their family became the source of cruel local gossip.

Whatever was she going to do?

CHAPTER SIXTEEN

Sheila was pink-cheeked with triumph as the last of the villagers trooped out of the parish hall after her soup-and-sandwiches social. She had shaken so many hands, and patted children's heads, and listened to folk and their unhappy stories of need and neglect since the end of the war, that she felt quite dizzy. But the event had been a roaring success, and she and Mrs Treedy now had a list of likely candidates for the parish fund, all of them equally in need of financial help.

She mentally thanked Mrs Newbury-Holmes for her useful suggestion of a social event like this. It had indeed been just the thing to bring their small community together.

'Have a wonderful Christmas!' she called after the last couple and their gaggle of children, all looking happy and full after their hot soup and plate of sandwiches.

Sheila turned back to Mrs Treedy, who'd helped her organise the event, only to find her talking to Hazel Cotterill. Her baby boy nestled comfortably on her hip, Hazel was holding young Lily by the hand – the child she'd named after Sheila's own granddaughter, who'd delivered the baby single-handed after Hazel had gone into labour prematurely during an air raid.

'Oh, Hazel,' she said, her voice hoarse after all the chatting she'd done over lunch. 'Thanks for helping us out today. It was very kind of you.' Hazel had been slaving away behind the scenes, keeping the soup hot and making extra sandwiches to order. 'I didn't think you'd have time, what with Dickie and Lily to care for. You must be run off your feet.'

'I've always got time for a charitable cause,' Hazel insisted, 'and I was happy to do it.' She was wearing her glossy brown hair longer than in the summer, when she'd still been expecting, and looked curvier than ever and contented with it.

'How's Charlie? Still working as an apprentice?'

'He's well, thank you, and yes, he's in his final year. I wanted him to come home for Christmas.' Hazel's face fell. 'But he says it's too difficult, what with the cold weather and money being so tight. So we won't be seeing him until spring now, most likely.'

'Oh, bless him, poor thing . . . That must be hard on the boy, as well as you and your husband. How's George doing these days?'

Sheila had a soft spot for George Cotterill. He'd been kind enough to employ Violet and Lily as cleaners at Eastern House when they'd first come to Cornwall, allowing them to live in a cottage in Porthcurno more usually set aside for military personnel. There hadn't been much space in the tiny cottage, especially once they'd taken on three evacuee kids as well, but it had provided them with a cosy home for a spell, and they'd been grateful for it.

'He's in good health,' his wife said fondly, and nodded to Mrs Treedy. 'We were just discussing George, in fact.'

'Gossiping, eh?' Sheila laughed, winking at Mrs Treedy. 'He's your boss, ain't he?' When Mrs Treedy had first approached her for work in the spring, she'd twisted George's arm to give the lady a job at Eastern House, since she herself couldn't afford to employ her. 'How are you getting on with that, by the way?'

'Eastern House is a lovely place to work.' Mrs Treedy was enthusiastic. 'And Mr Cotterill is such a kind boss, always letting me go home early if one of the kids is feeling poorly. Though it's been hard work recently, what with all the shortages and the power cuts. I'm working in the kitchens now, and it's near impossible to come up with tasty meals for the staff with next to nothing in the pantry and the electricity going off every five minutes.'

'We're all in the same boat,' Hazel agreed sadly.

Sheila touched her arm. 'You wouldn't fancy coming onboard with the parish fund, would you, love?' she begged. 'I still need a few more bodies on the committee, and you've a good head for figures, ain't you?'

'Not too bad,' Hazel agreed, but glanced uncertainly at Dickie on her hip. The baby boy seemed to be falling asleep, his lids closing drowsily. Lily, by contrast, was shifting restlessly from foot to foot and dragging on her mother's hand. 'The thing is . . .'

'You're too busy. Of course you are. I'm sorry, I shouldn't have asked.'

'No, I'd love to join you.' Hazel smiled shyly. 'But would it be possible to bring the children with me to committee meetings if George isn't home to keep an eye on them? He works late some evenings, you see.'

'I won't mind if you bring the kiddies, love. Goodness, we can all take turns looking after them.' Sheila winked. 'The more the merrier, eh?'

A few days later, Sheila was washing up breakfast dishes when she heard raised voices in the snug. She tried not to listen, for it was only Joe and Violet arguing again, and what went on between a man and wife was their own business. But as the row grew more heated, she caught a note of distress in her daughter's voice and frowned, stopping to listen with her hands sunk in warm soapy water.

What on earth was the matter with those two? They'd been snapping at each other for months now. She'd tried asking Violet about the situation, but her daughter was as closed as an oyster when it came to Joe.

Sheila had often lost her temper with Arnie over some nonsense, and it had always blown over quickly. Whatever was going on between her daughter and son-in-law, it didn't sound like nonsense.

Joe came stamping out of the snug with a furious expression. Seeing her there, he muttered, 'I'd best check on them new lambs,' and whistled for his dogs to follow. Before she even had time to dry her hands, Joe was in his coat and boots, and striding across the yard towards the lower field where they kept ailing and vulnerable animals during winter months, such as pregnant ewes.

Violet came out of the snug, dabbing at her eyes with a hanky. Spotting Sheila, she stopped dead, flushing. 'Mum? Oh . . . I thought you'd gone down to the shop.' She checked the wall clock. 'Running a bit late, ain't you?'

'Yes, but Maggie will be holding the fort. I thought I'd

wait a bit before going down today. It was so cold and dark this morning, I couldn't face trudging down the lane before it was properly light.'

Without comment, Violet took up a tea towel and began drying the breakfast bowls, gazing out of the window.

Sheila hesitated, then returned to the washing-up, also in silence. They'd had porridge again that morning, which was still mercifully plentiful, but Sheila was having the devil of a job scraping gluey, stuck-on porridge off the bottom of the pan.

At last, she could stand it no longer.

'Vi, whatever's going on between you and Joe these days?' Sheila burst out. 'And don't tell me to mind my own business, my girl. When the two of you are going at it hammer and tongs every day, it *is* my business. I live in this house too, you know. As do them poor Land Girls. It's not nice, being made to listen to people constantly sniping at each other. Fair sets my teeth on edge, it does.'

Violet said nothing, drying a bowl with her fair head bent. But her shoulders shook.

Feeling guilty at having made her cry again, Sheila dropped the porridge pot into the sink and put a comforting arm around her daughter. 'Oh, you silly thing. Tell your old mum what the problem is. You never know, I might be able to help.' She drew out a chair at the kitchen table and pushed her daughter down onto it, then sat beside her, holding Violet's hand. 'Come on, out with it.'

Violet pulled a face, not meeting her eyes, then said reluctantly, 'Oh, you might as well know . . . I've been nagging at Joe for us to have another child.'

Sheila breathed more easily. She had feared something

more serious was amiss. Perhaps even an affair, though Gawd knew Joe had no time to be messing about behind his wife's back. 'Is that all? Of course you want another baby, what's wrong with that?'

'Nothing,' Violet agreed, her tone aggrieved. 'The war's over and we should be looking to the future. Only, Joe refuses to see it like that. He says we can't afford to feed another mouth, especially not with food shortages. I told him that's rubbish. It would be a good two years before a baby was born and weaned from the breast . . . Surely we won't still have shortages by then?'

'He'll come around soon enough, love. Once we're into the spring and things are looking up, you'll see.'

'No, he won't.' Violet became tearful again. 'Do you remember how sick I got when I was carrying Sarah Jane?'

Sheila grimaced. 'How could anyone forget? You were laid up for days, and I ended up doing most of your chores.' She saw her daughter's face stiffen, and added hurriedly, 'Not that I begrudged doing it. I was happy to help out, love.'

'Well, Joe's worried it'll happen again if I fall pregnant. He says there'll be no one to look after Sarah Jane when I'm sick, and besides, who would do the cooking and cleaning for me now you're at the shop most days? I've told him straight, I'll look after Sarah Jane and get all the housework done when I'm expecting again, even if I have to do it on my bloomin' hands and knees. But he won't listen,' she finished bitterly.

Sheila considered this. 'You should tell him, if it's a boy next time, you might not get so sick. It's girls that make you queasy. When you're carrying a boy, they say it ain't so bad.'

She hesitated. 'I only had you and Betsy though, so I can't know for sure.'

'Sounds like an old wives' tale to me.'

'But you can be sure those old wives knew a thing or two about having a baby.' Sheila gave her a wink. 'Anyway, don't give up hope. Babies have a way of coming along regardless.'

'What does that mean?'

'Only that you catch more flies with honey than vinegar.' She patted her daughter's hand. 'Make up with Joe, love. Be a bit nicer and stop snapping the poor man's head off. And maybe buy yourself one of them lacy new nighties we saw in that magazine the other day.' She grinned. 'After a while, you might find he's more open to the idea of another child.'

'Seduce him, you mean?' Violet blushed.

'Well, why not? You still love him, don't you? And Joe loves you, that's obvious. Besides, what's wrong with a bit o' hanky-panky between a married couple? Oh, don't look like that . . . It's not just for newly-weds, you know.' Sheila chuckled. 'Why do you think you were born so long after Betsy? Sometimes a man just needs a little gentle persuasion.'

Violet jumped to her feet, clearly flustered by this intimate turn in the conversation. 'I'd best go and check on Sarah Jane. I left her playing upstairs nearly an hour ago and she'll be up to all sorts by now.' Lips pursed, she glanced at the wall clock again. 'And you need to get down to the shop, Mum, before Aunty Margaret thinks you've got yourself in trouble.' Her sharp blue eyes flashed a warning to let it go before she turned away.

With a shrug, Sheila gave up and said no more on the topic. But she was determined to grab a quiet word with her son-in-law as soon as possible. Because it seemed to her that

Joe would have to choose between a few extra chores around the house and a wife giving him daggers for the rest of their marriage. Assuming it lasted much longer, that was . . .

Down at the village shop later that week, Sheila found her sister Maggie deep in conversation with Jack's mum, Mrs Treedy. On her return from visiting Lily in Penzance, her sister had given her a glowing account of Jack Treedy as a helper, saying, 'He was ever so useful, and such a hard worker too. I don't think he's as wild as folk have made out.' Impressed with this, Sheila had taken Jack on as a Saturday boy to help with jobs Maggie usually undertook, like sweeping out the shop, taking inventory, and stocking the vegetable crates. The lad had thanked her most politely. But she'd seen his unhappy expression and knew he'd been hankering after longer hours, if only to help out his widowed mum with the household bills.

She couldn't afford to take Jack on full-time, though, and could only hope he'd find better-paid employment in early spring when farms began taking on labourers. Now the war was over, most farmers were beginning to look to men again to take over from the Women's Land Army. Even Joe had mentioned the idea, much to their own Land Girls' disappointment.

'Morning Maggie, Mrs Treedy,' she called out cheerfully, unwinding her scarf. 'Has the shop been busy this morning?'

'Not too bad,' her sister said and handed her a buff envelope. 'This came for you. Postie couldn't be bothered to bicycle up the hill to the farm, so left it here.'

Sheila glanced at the London address on the back and eagerly tore open the envelope, not even bothering to remove her hat and coat first. ''Ere, it's from that ex-MP . . . Mrs Newbury-Holmes. The lady I met in Penzance. I wrote to let her know about that soup and sandwiches social event that went off so well for us.' She spread out the folded sheet and read it. 'Blimey,' she gasped, 'she says it sounds like I done a good job, and she's even written down a few other ideas for me. Ways to bring the community together and raise money for good causes. What a smashin' lady, eh? To go to all the trouble of writing to me . . . I never thought for a minute that someone posh like her would remember my name, let alone write back.'

'You can be quite memorable on occasion, Shee,' her sister remarked.

Mrs Treedy said nothing but merely stared.

Gawd, she was acting as giddy as a schoolgirl, Sheila realised with a start of embarrassment. Hurriedly, she put away the prized letter in her handbag and took off her coat at last. She would read it through again later when she was alone.

'Anyway,' she said, clearing her throat, 'how's your Jack, Mrs Treedy? He did a bang-up job of helping my sister while I was away in Penzance. You must be very proud of the lad.'

'Good morning, Mrs Newton,' Mrs Treedy replied, sounding far from happy. 'In fact, it's Jack we've been talking of.'

Removing her hat, Sheila hung it up behind the counter and donned her work apron. 'Oh yes, how's that?'

Mrs Treedy bit her lip, looking pale and wan, and said nothing.

With a sad shake of her head, Maggie answered for her. 'It seems Jack's been saying "strange things" lately,' her sister explained carefully. 'Poor Mrs Treedy's beside herself. She doesn't know what to do for the best.'

Sheila, who had begun to check the takings for the week, stopped and looked round at her sister in bewilderment. 'Strange things? What on earth do you mean?'

'Jack's got an odd idea in his head,' Mrs Treedy said unhappily. 'And I don't know where it came from. No doubt all them newspapers he's been reading, ever since you taught him his letters.' She gave a muffled sob. 'He talks of nothing but politics and the government. It fair drives me up the wall. Only now he's started going on about *Australia*.'

'Eh?' Sheila was baffled.

Maggie put a hand on her arm. 'He's thinking of emigrating, Sheila,' she said plainly. 'To Australia, of all places.'

'No . . . You're pulling my leg.' Sheila looked at them dubiously. She recalled spelling out a few newspaper articles with the lad about British citizens making the decision to move to Australia for a better life now the war was over. Remembering how hard life had been in London's bombed-out city streets, she could understand an urge to start again. But she'd never imagined that someone in a lovely spot like Porthcurno would contemplate a new life down under. It left her feeling a little guilty too, worried that her reading lessons might have been what had put such an idea in his head in the first place.

'It's true,' her sister insisted. 'Jack told me himself. I meant to mention it to you, but I didn't think he was serious. Only here's his mum now, saying he's looked into the cost of a passage.'

'Well,' Sheila said slowly, 'the boat fare can't be cheap. I doubt he could even scrape the fare together.'

'I hope you're right, Mrs Newton.' Mrs Treedy picked up her shopping basket. 'I'd best get on.'

A thought struck Sheila. 'Hang on a minute, love. I've a favour to ask.'

Mrs Treedy looked wary. 'Oh aye?'

'You know I've been organising this, erm, fund for the parish.' Sheila was as tactful as possible; she didn't want to offend the woman by using the words 'poor' or 'needy', given she was on the list to receive money. 'The thing is, we're keen to run more events like that soup-and-sandwiches social you were kind enough to help out with. It was so successful at bringing certain folk together, you see.' She hesitated. 'Folk who need a helping hand.'

Mrs Treedy's lips had tightened. 'Folk like me, you mean?'

'Well . . .' Sheila dithered, and then said frankly, 'Yes, exactly. You're a hard worker, and a good mum to your kids. But you still can't make ends meet, and that's a fact. Now, you know this village better than I do, and I bet you know more people who might benefit from our fund.'

'I might,' Mrs Treedy agreed cautiously.

'I know you're busy, bless you, and I don't want to make your life harder. But if you could give up an hour every few weeks to come to one of our meetings, I'd be ever so grateful.'

Mrs Treedy blinked. 'To do what, sorry?'

'I'd like you to sit on the Parish Fund Committee, if you're interested.'

'Me? Be on a committee?' Mrs Treedy's eyes widened and her mouth fell open. Her grip tightened on her shopping basket. 'Well, I don't know . . . I've never been on one of them.'

'I'd never been on a committee either before I joined the council. Now I'm on several of the bloomin' things.' Sheila gave her a reassuring smile. 'To be honest, it's just half a dozen people sitting around nattering until it's time to wet your whistle with a nice cuppa and a biscuit.'

'But won't the other committee members mind me coming along?' Mrs Treedy was once again wary. 'I don't know nothing about organising and such . . . They won't want someone like me sitting down with them.'

'Honestly, it was the Chair of the Council who asked me specially to find other villagers for the committee. People like you.'

'Oh . . . But what good can I do?'

'Well, the soup-and-sandwiches event went swimmingly, didn't it? And you were ever so good at helping me make out a list of folks who could benefit from the fund,' Sheila reminded her with an encouraging smile. 'But you could do so much more if you were on the committee, love. We need someone who knows firsthand what the problems are. Will you join us once or twice a month to help us come up with fresh ideas?'

Mrs Treedy smiled. 'I'd be glad to, Mrs Newton.'

'Call me Sheila, love,' she said with a wink, and held the shop door open for her. 'I'll let you know when the next committee meeting's due. And if you need a lift to the parish hall, Mr Bailey will be glad to pick you up in his car.'

Mrs Treedy looked stunned. 'In that posh Daimler of his? Oh, I say . . . My Jack's always going on about that car. Goodness me.' Mrs Treedy seemed overcome, wandering out of the shop in a daze and almost turning the wrong way before correcting herself and heading home.

'Another satisfied customer,' Maggie murmured, watching her go, and they both chuckled.

Sheila went back to the ledger and picked up her pencil. 'You don't think Jack's serious about emigrating, do you?'

'I don't know. But you remember what it was like back when we were his age, Shee . . . Everything had to happen at once. No waiting.'

'True enough. That don't make it right, though. A young man like Jack Treedy shouldn't have to go abroad just to get work.' Sheila shook her head, deeply troubled. 'It'll break his mother's heart if he goes, that's for sure.'

Joe Postbridge managed to evade Sheila for the next few days, perhaps guessing that his mother-in-law wanted to speak to him. But eventually, at dinner, Sheila told him, 'You and I need to have a chat, Joe,' while passing him the peas. 'How about tonight?'

'Ah, erm . . . One of the ewes has gone into labour,' he rumbled, helping himself to peas and handing the dish to Grace. 'I've put her in the barn and might be out there with her all night. Sorry.'

Before Sheila could reply to that, Tilly burst out, 'Oh, I forgot . . . We had a workman turn up while you were out today, Mr Postbridge, asking to look about the place. He said he was from the General Post Office and would come back in a few days, weather permitting.'

'The GPO?' Violet was staring at Joe. 'Have you gone and signed us up for a telephone?'

'I have,' Joe agreed, and hurriedly stuffed his mouth with food before any more explanation could be demanded of him.

Sheila beamed approvingly. 'Well, I never . . . Now we'll be able to speak to Alice and Lily at Christmas.'

'I wish you'd said,' Violet told her husband, frowning. 'What must he have thought? Look at the state of this kitchen. I've been so busy getting ready for Christmas, I'm behind with my cleaning.'

'I'd be happy to help you with the housework, Mrs Postbridge,' Grace told her. 'Any time you need a hand, just holler.'

Violet looked surprised. 'That's kind of you, Grace. But it's not right to ask you to take on extra chores.'

'I don't mind.' Grace winked at Tilly across the table. 'You'll muck in too, won't you, Tilly?'

Tilly swallowed her mouthful. 'Of course.'

As they were clearing the table though, Sheila noticed how Tilly slipped away upstairs to avoid pitching in, while Grace stayed to scrape food remnants into the metal pigswill pail. Violet had followed Joe into the porch, muttering at him as he pulled on his boots, so Sheila took the scraped plates off the girl instead.

'Thank you, Grace, that's very helpful. No, I can do the rest. You've done enough for today.'

But Grace lingered at the table instead of following the other girl upstairs.

Sheila, filling the sink with soapy water, studied her discreetly. 'You all right, love?'

Grace looked up at her quickly. 'Just a bit tired, Mrs Newton.'

Sheila left the pots and pans to soak and came back to the table, drying her hands. She thought the girl looked a little lonely. 'Are you missing Caroline? Poor lamb . . . I hope her gran's a bit better.'

'Yes, she's very fond of her.'

'But I'm sure she'll be back here with us soon. She's become part of this family . . . and I know she has a soft spot for you in particular. And why not? You're a kind soul, Grace, and I bet your family's very proud of you.' She hesitated as the young woman fell silent and turned her head away. What had she said wrong? 'What's up, love? I suppose you wish you were going home for Christmas too, is that it?'

Grace shook her head. 'I'm happy staying here, Mrs Newton, honest. I love my folks. The thing is, whenever I go home . . .' She got up to rinse out her tea mug. 'Well, sometimes me mum and dad . . . I think they'd like to cocoon me in cotton wool. Stop me ever leaving again.'

'Bless 'em, of course they do. They're your folks. Well, we'll have a cosy enough Christmas here at the farm, eh?'

Grace smiled, then murmured something about having a library book to finish reading and disappeared upstairs. Sheila was left uncomfortable, aware that she'd somehow upset the girl without meaning to. But as she was trying to puzzle it out, Violet came back, looking flustered.

'Thanks, Mum. I'd better do the washing-up before that water gets cold.' Violet stood at the sink, her face pinched and unhappy. 'Joe's gone out to the barn. So it's just you and me in the snug tonight, Mum.'

'Righty-ho. I'll fetch us some sloe gin. That'll warm our cockles. Poor Joe though . . . It's perishing out there.' Sheila hesitated. 'Shall I take him out a nice hot cup of tea?'

'Suit yourself,' Violet muttered.

Sheila shrugged into her coat and carried a tray across the snowy yard to the barn. Joe's hurricane lamp lit up a soft bed of straw where the mother ewe was struggling to give birth, while Joe crouched beside her with troubled eyes.

'I've brought you something to keep out the cold,' Sheila told him, and pulled a hip flask from her pocket with a wink. 'Violet didn't see me take this. Tea's all very well. But I thought you might like something a mite stronger, given the snow.'

Joe took the flask with a rueful grin. 'Thanks, Sheila.' Helping himself to a swig of brandy, he turned back to the ewe. 'Wish I'd got that telephone line set up last month. I may need to drive over to fetch the vet later, if this one gets into difficulties.'

'I can sit with her while you're gone, if you like. So long as I can bring me knitting.' Sheila hesitated. 'Joe,' she added tentatively, 'I hope you won't mind me sticking my oar in, but Vi told me about you not wanting another child.'

'Yes, she said.' His tone was curt.

'Oh, love, I know you're worried about her.' Sheila put a hand on his arm. 'But you've no need. The first baby's always the hardest. Violet knows what to expect now, she won't be so sick with a second one.'

'It's not only the morning sickness,' he muttered.

'What, then?'

The ewe was bleating unhappily and rolling her eyes. He crouched again to the animal, putting a hand on her heaving belly. 'Don't you remember how hard the birth was with Sarah Jane? I was afraid we'd lose both of them . . . I can't go through that again. And what if the worst happens and Sarah Jane's left without a mother?' He shook his head. 'I won't do it and I've told Violet why, and that's an end to it.'

Sheila exhaled slowly, understanding at last. 'It's true things didn't go well last time,' she told him gently. 'But every baby's different, love. And it's drivin' Violet up the wall, wanting another one.'

He grimaced. 'I know that.'

'You're right . . . It's a risky old business, having a baby. Anything could go wrong. But we just lived through a war, didn't we? You lost a leg, for Gawd's sake. But you didn't give up living, did you? You came home and met my Violet, and yes, things went wrong between you, but you persevered. And in the end, you married her, and Sarah Jane came along.'

Her son-in-law looked round at her, tears in his eyes.

'Oh, love . . .' Sheila gripped his shoulder, trying to be reassuring, though she was crying too. 'I know you're scared of losing her. I'm scared too, to be honest. I already lost one daughter; I don't want to lose my Violet as well. But if we won't take a risk when it matters . . . Well, there ain't much bloomin' point being alive, is there?'

CHAPTER SEVENTEEN

Wearily, Caroline walked the half-mile from the train station to her parents' home through snowy streets, a cold wind biting at her bones. Reaching the cosy terraced house where she'd grown up, in an area that had thankfully escaped damage in the Blitz, she knocked, peering at the curtained windows lit against the encroaching dusk. All the way from Cornwall, sitting for hours in draughty rail carriages, or waiting on icy platforms, she had tried not to think about her grandmother, fearing she might arrive to find the old lady had died.

The door opened and her mother stood there, blinking in amazement. 'Caroline?' She seemed flustered at first, then exclaimed, 'Goodness, you look different. I almost didn't recognise you. Come in, love. It's perishing out there.'

Caroline stamped the snow off her shoes and stepped into the narrow hall. It was like stepping back in time. One of her old coats was still hanging on the stand, beside a framed photograph of her in her school uniform, smiling toothily into the camera, blonde pigtails resting on her shoulder. She grimaced, studying it. No wonder her mother hadn't recognised her.

'I came as soon as I could, Mum. How's Gran?' Her voice shook on those last words, and she stood stiffly, braced for bad news.

'Gran?' Her mother looked blank-faced before saying slowly, 'Oh yes, she's been very unwell, poor old thing. But she'll be better now you're home. Oh love, you look frozen . . . Take off that hat and coat.' Snapping on the hall light to dispel the gloom, she shook snow off Caroline's hat and coat and hung them on the hall stand. 'Stanley?' she called over her shoulder cheerily, as though there was nothing wrong. 'Our little girl has come home at last.'

'What?' Her father strode out of the back room, newspaper in hand, and stopped dead at the sight of his daughter. He gave a deep sigh. 'At last . . .'

Her mother had put on weight since she'd left home early in the war and was now rounder than ever, her pink cheeks flushed from exertion, or maybe cooking, her hair in disarray. Her father, on the other hand, seemed to be thinner. A tall, gangling man, silvery hair receding from a high forehead, he thrust aside his newspaper and came to embrace her.

'It's wonderful to see you, Caroline,' he told her. 'Your grandmother will be overjoyed. You got my telegram, then? But of course you did . . . Otherwise, you wouldn't be here.' There was a stern significance in his voice, which instantly had her defensive.

'Where's Gran?' Caroline demanded.

'She's resting in her room,' her mother began, but Caroline didn't wait to hear the rest.

Running lightly up the stairs, she knocked at the door

and went inside without waiting for an answer. Her grandmother was sitting up in bed against the pillows, her face lit by a lamp on her bedside table. Under her bushy white hair, Gran looked pale and drawn, and definitely unwell. But not dying, surely?

Gran was blowing her nose as Caroline burst in. Lowering the hanky, she stared at her in astonishment. ''Ello, love,' she said huskily, clearly suffering with a sore throat. 'What on earth are you doing home? I wish I'd known you were coming . . . I'd have made an effort to get up today.'

'Dad said you were at death's door and I was to come home at once.' Caroline's voice shook with emotion.

'*Death's door*?' Her grandmother laughed merrily. 'Bless you, I'm full of a cold, that's all. Oh, I had a chesty cough last week, that's true enough. But the doctor prescribed a strong linctus, and I've taken a few steam baths to clear out my lungs, which seems to be doing the trick.' She shook her head. 'You'll have to put up with me for a few years yet.'

'Oh, Gran . . .' Caroline surged forward and hugged her grandmother. She found herself weeping as she explained in a muffled voice, 'I've been out of my mind with worry. When that telegram arrived . . . I thought the worst. Thank God you're all right.'

Her grandmother patted her on the back. 'There, there, love. What's my naughty son been telling you? Sending you a telegram, eh? Whatever next?'

Caroline became aware that her parents were standing in the doorway. She turned to glare at them. 'How could you do such a thing? You must know I've been worried sick all the way here. And they need me back on the farm . . . I'm not on holiday in Cornwall, Dad,' she exclaimed, and saw him look away, guilt in his face. 'I'm working there. In case you hadn't noticed, food stores are running low and this country still needs Land Girls out in the fields. You had no right to call me back under false pretences.'

'*False pretences*?' Her mother folded her arms, frowning. 'Your gran gave us a right scare last week. At one stage, we weren't sure if she would ever recover.'

'Eh?' Her grandmother looked up, startled. 'I never knew that.'

'Hush, Mother.' Caroline's father waved a silencing hand. 'I'm sorry if you were upset by the message, Caroline,' her father told her grudgingly. 'But your grandmother *was* in a bad state, and if my telegram was an exaggeration, it was at least a well-intentioned one.' He hesitated. 'Now you're here though, we can have a wonderful family Christmas, all of us back together again. And maybe after a taste of home life, you won't want to go back to being a Land Girl,' he added suggestively. 'I know times are still tough, but I'm sure the farmer can spare you. The war's long over.'

Flushed and angry, Caroline struggled to stay polite. They had dragged her all the way from Cornwall for nothing more than a head cold, and at a time when travelling anywhere was difficult and expensive. But she reined in her temper . . . These were still her parents. 'I'll stay for a few days, Dad,' she said with restraint, 'but then I'm going back to the farm. It was very wrong of you to lie to me.'

'I didn't exactly lie,' her father began, but fell silent when she flashed him a look.

'Only a few days?' Her mother sounded aggrieved. 'You know how much we love you, Caroline, and how badly we've missed you. Letters just aren't enough . . . Besides, like your father said, the war is over. It's time to stop playing at being a farmgirl and settle down.'

Caroline's hands clenched into fists by her side. 'I'm not a *girl* anymore, Mum. And it's not up to you what I do with my life. You can't stop me leaving.'

'Of course we can't,' her dad said. 'But would it be so very dreadful to come home again?' His brows knit together, his eyes perplexed. 'We've only ever wanted you to be happy, love. I don't understand why you need to keep living at the other end of the country from us.'

Caroline felt awful, but didn't know how best to respond. How could she explain without causing an even worse scene?

Her grandmother gave an unhappy sob. 'Caroline, love . . . I've missed you too. Please stay a little longer, if only for my sake. And don't blame your mum and dad. It's true what they said, I have been ill. Maybe I'm better now, but I'm still not meself.' She gave her a pleading smile. 'Besides, it does me good to see your face again.'

Caroline groaned inwardly. She had no wish to hurt her family, especially not her grandmother, who was clearly still unwell.

'Well,' she said gruffly, 'I could stay for a week or two, I suppose.'

'If you stay that long, you might as well stay until Christmas,' her father said in a practical way, and winked at her mother. 'Deirdre, I've put Caroline's bag in her bedroom. Why don't you show her what you've done in there, while I go down and put the kettle on? While my mother's resting, the three of us could have a cosy chat downstairs.'

Caroline kissed her grandmother on the cheek, who was indeed looking exhausted, and allowed her mother to show her into her old bedroom. Like the downstairs of the house, her bedroom was just as she'd left it when she had gone to join the Women's Land Army. She'd half expected to walk into a dusty tomb, everything covered in cobwebs. But her mother must have been dusting and cleaning; the place was spick and span. Even the books on her bookcase, some girls' annuals from her childhood and a few favourite hardbacks, had been dusted. There was a new bedspread on the bed though, and her old china dolls had been neatly arranged on an upper shelf.

'It does look nice, Mum,' Caroline admitted, walking around the room and reacquainting herself with her old possessions. How small everything seemed though, she thought with a pang, feeling like a stranger in her own home. 'Thank you for taking the trouble to get it ready.'

Her mother was standing by the window, looking out towards the allotments that sprawled at the back of the house. 'It was no trouble, love. It's marvellous to have you home again. I've baked a jam sponge as it happens. If you're peckish, we can have a slice of that now, with a cup of tea.'

'Yes, please, that sounds lovely. And I'm sure it will be good to sleep in my own bed again.' Caroline joined her at the window and looked out at the snowy muddle of allotments. It was almost dark, yet she could see someone digging out there, wrapped up against the cold. 'Goodness, it's a bit late for working on the allotments, isn't it? Who on earth's that?'

'That's next-door's youngest boy, Albert,' her mother told her, with a curious sidelong glance. 'You and he were friends, weren't you?'

'Of course. He enlisted early on in the war. So Albert

made it through?' She felt relieved and thankful, recalling the smiling young man who'd often walked to and from school with her over the years.

Her mother nodded. 'He came back from Germany a few months ago. His older brother Jimmy was killed in '43, you know.'

'Yes, you wrote to tell me.'

'So terribly sad. His mother was beside herself when Albert was sent out to Germany, scared stiff they might lose him too. Even after the war was over too, for there's still a few Jerries out there willing to take a potshot at our boys. They've got to be ever so careful on patrol. Pat was thrilled when he came home at last. And he's such a good son, helping out around the house and working on the allotment. Pat's not been well lately, and Kenneth's got a dodgy knee, so neither of them can do much digging these days . . .' She nudged her daughter. 'I could ask Albert over to dinner tomorrow, if you'd like?'

Caroline stared at her. 'Whatever for?'

'Why, so you two can have a nice chat, of course,' her mother said vaguely, bending to smooth out an imaginary wrinkle in her bedcovers, 'and catch up with what you've been up to during the war. After all, you young people won't want to spend all your time with your parents now you're home.' She hesitated. 'Maybe Albert could take you to the pictures one evening? I could suggest it to his mum.'

'You'll do no such thing,' Caroline exclaimed, her cheeks flooding with warmth. 'Goodness, Mum! I didn't come home to start dating the boy next door. I came home to see Gran.' Her eyes narrowed on her mother's guilty face. 'I hope you didn't ask me back here just to start matchmaking. Because if so . . .' She stopped, forcing herself to swallow the angry words on the tip of her tongue. She'd barely been home five minutes. It would be awful to start arguing with her parents straight after walking through the front door.

'Stuff and nonsense, of course we didn't. It was just a passing thought. I'll leave you to unpack.' Her mother dragged the curtains shut and hurried out. 'We're glad to have you home, love.'

Now she was back in her parents' home, it seemed Caroline was to be given an endless string of jobs that needed doing before she could possibly return to Cornwall. After a few days spent sitting with her grandmother, reading to her from magazines, playing cards or chatting about her days as a Land Girl, her mother began to drag out projects to occupy Caroline's time. 'These tatty old curtains need restitching,' she told her daughter, uncovering the sewing machine for her, 'and maybe you could help your dad repaint the kitchen this weekend?' Once those tasks were done, she encouraged Caroline to turn the frozen soil in the allotment. 'There's a sack of early seed potatoes that are nicely chitted and ready to be planted up,' her mother said, handing her a spade. 'You've been working on a farm for years. You must know all about growing vegetables.'

Out in the allotment, she soon bumped into Albert. 'Hullo, Caroline,' he said with a grin, resting on his garden fork. 'The prodigal daughter returns!'

She laughed, her breath steaming on the chilly air. 'How are you, Albert?'

'Bert, please.' He grimaced. 'Albert makes me sound like I'm a hundred years old. And I'm fine. Made it through the war unscathed, as you see. Now I'm back and wondering what to do next.'

'Strange, isn't it? You get used to being on your own, making your own decisions, and then you come home to live with your parents and . . . Well, get bossed around again.' They smiled at each other in quick understanding. 'By the way, I was sorry to hear about your brother Jimmy.'

His face fell. 'Thank you.'

'He was so sporty . . . I remember him winning all the athletics cups at school.' There was an awkward silence. 'And your mum's not been well recently, is that right?'

'She's had a bad chest, yes. But the doctor thinks she'll be better come the spring.' He looked her up and down with interest. 'You've sprouted at least a foot since I last saw you. Been in Cornwall, your dad told us. Working as a Land Girl? Sounds like hard work.'

'Sometimes, yes.'

Happier to chat than struggle to turn the icy soil, Caroline perched on an upturned bucket and told him about Postbridge Farm and some of their near misses from bombing raids during the war. He seemed fascinated by the proximity of Eastern House, with its secret communications tunnels dug into the cliff, and laughed out loud on hearing about her antics with the other Land Girls.

A few nights later, Albert turned up on the doorstep in a clean new shirt and jacket and ate dinner with the family. Caroline glared at her mother on seeing him but politely said nothing. It wasn't his fault, after all. Still, she resented such an unsubtle attempt at matchmaking, especially after she'd asked her mother not to interfere.

Gran, recovering nicely from what she'd now decided was

'a touch of bronchitis', came down to sit with them, while Caroline's father beamed approvingly at Albert, and even cracked open a prized bottle of French red wine he'd been keeping in a cupboard since before the war, saying, 'Since this is a celebration . . .'

'Of what?' Caroline had a sinking feeling, as she watched him uncork the bottle.

'Why, of our young people coming home safely after that awful war, of course,' Gran supplied for him, and pushed forward her glass. 'Just a little for me, please, Stan.'

Caroline had exchanged glances with Bert, who'd grinned but said nothing.

The next day, he invited her out to the picture house, and although she suspected her mother of having suggested the outing behind her back, Caroline decided to say yes. She had always enjoyed her weekly outings to the cinema in Penzance with the other Land Girls, and thought it might take her out of herself. She had been in the doldrums lately . . .

The truth was, she was missing Grace. She knew she ought not to have feelings for another girl. Not after all the trouble it had caused when she'd stupidly blurted out to Selina that she 'loved' her, never thinking of the possible consequences, only following her heart. That disastrous admission had almost wrecked her friendship with Selina and had put her in peril of being gossiped about by the others at Postbridge Farm. Thankfully, though, Selina had kept the whole thing quiet.

As hard as it was to be away from Grace, their enforced separation might be a good thing if it prevented her from making a fool of herself again, Caroline decided.

After Christmas, she would return to the farm with smiling indifference on her face, determined to keep her distance . . .

With that in mind, she'd written to Mr and Mrs Postbridge to say she wouldn't be returning until the end of the year, and hoped they wouldn't mind, given that December was often a quiet period at the farm. Violet had written a terse note back to say she would be missed, but if her grandmother was still unwell, they would allow it.

Unfortunately, her parents seemed to believe she was back for good.

When Bert turned up one day to take her to a matinee at the cinema, their first visit to the pictures having been a success, her mother caught them on their way out. 'Come the spring,' she said cheerfully, 'you two should go for a picnic in the park. The pavilion was hit during the Blitz, but they're rebuilding it. They've even got plans to turn that old duck pond into a proper lake.'

Caroline was taken aback but kept quiet. There was no point upsetting her mother by reminding her that she wouldn't be there in the spring.

But when they passed the local park on their way back from the pictures, Bert stopped to point out the snow-covered rubble where the old pavilion had been hit. 'That wasn't a bad idea of your mum's, you know. I haven't been on a picnic in years. Not since before the war.'

'I won't be here in the spring, I'm afraid,' Caroline admitted. 'I'll be going back to Cornwall after Christmas.'

'What?' He looked shocked.

'I'm still a Land Girl,' she pointed out. 'I haven't turned in my uniform. Besides, the farmer's been talking about hiring new workers – demobbed soldiers like you – and I don't want to risk losing my job by not being there.'

'But you don't need to be a Land Girl anymore,' he stammered. 'You could get work here in a shop.'

'In a shop?' Caroline laughed. 'I like the fresh country air down in Cornwall, and being near the sea . . . I don't want to lose that.'

'But I don't understand.' His brows tugged together. 'I thought you liked me.'

'I do.'

Bert stared at her. 'Like this, though?' He pulled her close and kissed her. She stood frozen in shock, then struggled to get free. Bert refused to let her go at first, his kiss only growing fiercer, his hands pulling her tighter. She squealed and kicked him in the shin. He swore and released her. 'Ow, what the hell did you do that for?'

'Oh, I don't know,' Caroline exclaimed, breathless and flushed, and feeling both furious and apprehensive. It was dark and the street was deserted. Although her time on the farm had given her muscles, Bert was still bigger and stronger than her. 'Maybe because you were kissing me against my will?'

'It was only a bloody kiss . . . I thought you wouldn't mind,' he grumbled, then took a step back, looking her up and down with a sneer. 'My mother always said there was something off about you. Maybe she was right.'

'I beg your pardon?'

'Oh, forget it.' Bert stamped away, leaving her to walk home alone.

Back at the house, rather tearful, Caroline told her parents what had happened, but they merely shrugged.

'Why shouldn't the lad give you a kiss?' her father asked. 'I'm only surprised he hasn't tried before.'

Her mother peered at her. 'Do you not like Albert?' When Caroline said nothing, she asked tentatively, 'Or is it that you aren't ready for a boyfriend yet?'

'Deirdre, for goodness' sake,' her father exclaimed, 'the girl's twenty-six. If she's not ready now, she never will be.'

'Then I never will be,' Caroline agreed, and saw the shock in their faces. Blushing at what she'd revealed, she hurried upstairs before they could ask any more unwelcome questions.

The next day, she wrote to tell the Postbridges she'd be coming home earlier than planned, probably on Christmas Eve itself. She felt guilty to be leaving her family at this special time of year, yet also thankful and relieved to be contemplating a peaceful Christmas at the farm, where nobody would rag at her and make her downright miserable.

After walking out to post her letter, she sat through a painful dinner. Her mother was silent and withdrawn, her dad frowning at her in disappointment, while her gran cheerily tried to persuade her to 'give Albert a second chance', as though his inexpert kisses had been the only stumbling block. By bedtime, she felt dejected and desperate to get back to the farm. There, at least, she was accepted as part of the 'family' and not judged for the way she dressed and behaved, or chided for not having landed a boyfriend. In Cornwall, she was just Caro, one of the Land Girls. No questions asked.

Early on the morning of Christmas Eve, she packed her case and left home for the second time in her life, hugging her gran.

'I'm sorry, Gran,' she whispered.

'You'll be back in no time, love. They won't want you Land Girls working on farms much longer,' the old lady said confidently, 'not now our boys are starting to come home.'

'Please don't go,' her mother begged her in tears at the station. 'You have to stay for Christmas lunch at least. Stanley, tell her.'

But her dad said nothing, just looked at her miserably.

Caroline hugged her parents. 'I love you both,' she told them, choking with tears herself, 'but I must go back to the farm. Have a wonderful Christmas! Think of me . . .' She trailed off, and hurried away through whirling snow to board her train, numb with cold and grief.

At Penzance Station, Caroline climbed wearily out of the carriage, dragging her heavy case after her, and found herself looking into Grace's smiling face.

'What on earth . . .?'

'Mrs Postbridge got your letter, so I decided to come and meet you at the station,' Grace explained, laughing at her expression. 'Only, I've been waiting for hours, as I wasn't sure which train.'

'Oh, Grace . . .' Overjoyed, Caroline gave her a tight hug, her voice thick with emotion. 'Thank you, thank you.'

'There's only one problem.' Grace gave her a lopsided smile. 'They've cancelled the bus back to Porthcurno, haven't they? So it looks like we'll be stuck in Penzance for Christmas.' She bit her lip, her eyes twinkling. 'Do you think Violet's daughter might put us up for a day or two?'

CHAPTER EIGHTEEN

Selina had given Mrs Hawley a few days off over Christmas to spend with her own family, and so found herself helping Nancy prepare the large Christmas lunch. The two women worked side by side to produce an excellent meal. The main event was a real turkey – at last, after years of making do with meat substitutes – served along with fresh, albeit mushy, vegetables dug out of the snow from their own garden, and a vast jug of delicious gravy. At least, William pronounced their efforts to be 'excellent', pushing aside his plate afterwards with a contented sigh.

Selina had rather daringly asked the solicitor to join her and the children for Christmas lunch, half expecting him to refuse. But he'd accepted with pleasure, and indeed she was very glad now. It was a joy to have an intelligent, personable man about the house at Christmas. They had Peter, of course. But at fourteen he was still a boy, and his conversation was hardly in the same league as Mr MacGregor's, especially in his current surly state.

Having a male guest had also given her an excuse to bring

up an expensive bottle of champagne from her sister's cellar for the occasion. It would have been a waste to open a bottle just for herself, as Nancy was not drinking alcohol and Peter disliked wine.

'Yes, excellent,' William repeated, and leant back in his chair to smile down the table at Selina. Behind him, the fragrant Christmas tree glittered with wreaths of tinsel and bright, tiny ornaments, the snowy lawns outside the window creating a perfect festive backdrop. 'Thank you for inviting me to share Christmas with you and your charming family, Miss Tiptree.'

Finishing her own meal, she shook her head at his formality. 'I told you, you should call me Selina,' she insisted, and saw Nancy look down with a secret smile, while Peter glanced wonderingly at them both. Embarrassed, she got up, plate in hand. 'Christmas pudding, anyone? Our marvellous Mrs Hawley made it weeks ago with the help of Jemima and Faith, so it should be ripe for eating now. Just don't swallow the sixpence!'

Peter said nothing, playing with his cutlery in a despondent way.

'I'll help you with the pudding,' Jemima declared, and jumped up happily to collect the plates.

Nancy turned to help Faith with her party hat, which had slipped over one eye, and Selina threw William a meaningful look, glancing towards Peter.

It had been at the back of her mind that he might be able to speak to the boy during this visit, and now was as good a time as any.

'I say, Peter,' William remarked, touching his linen napkin to his lips, 'I seem to recall you were interested in learning how to drive a car, is that right?'

'Yes, sir.'

'Since your aunt's going to be busy in the kitchen for a spell, how about you and I nip out to my Wolseley for a quick first lesson?' When Peter sat up, surprised, he added swiftly, 'I'm not saying you can drive her, of course. But we can turn the engine over, and I'll show you what the pedals are for and even how to change gear, if there's time. What do you say?'

Peter brightened. 'I'd like that, sir.'

Selina took her time in the kitchen, wanting to give William a lengthy opportunity to speak to her nephew. Eventually, though, there were no more plates to scrape and wash, and the pudding had been thoroughly steamed and was ready to be doused with brandy and set alight.

Having recalled everyone to the dining room, she carried in the Christmas pudding, brandy flaming fiercely atop, and everyone cheered and applauded.

'I'll tell Mrs Hawley how much you appreciated the spectacle,' she told them, placing the pudding in the centre of the table, its dark gleaming dome still licked with a ribbon of flame.

Faith, her eyes wide with astonishment, asked if the Christmas pudding was 'perfickly' safe to eat.

'Of course,' Selina told her fondly. 'And don't worry about the brandy . . . It will have burned away by now.'

'More's the pity,' William murmured, and everyone laughed.

After lunch, they played a noisy, energetic game of charades around the table, reminiscent of her days at Postbridge Farm. At last, the game over, Selina rose to put on the light, as the room was growing gloomy and the fire in the hearth had burned low.

‘Oh, fiddle!’ she exclaimed, flicking the light switch back and forth without response. ‘Not another power cut? What a nuisance. I’d better fetch some candles.’

‘Let me help,’ William said at once, waving Nancy to stay seated. ‘No, please, I insist.’ And he followed Selina out to the kitchen.

‘What did Peter say?’ Selina asked eagerly as soon as they were alone.

‘I couldn’t get the boy to talk to me,’ William admitted heavily. ‘As soon as I asked why he was looking so glum, he clammed up, wouldn’t say a blasted word.’ He grimaced. ‘I’m sorry.’

Disappointed, she rummaged for three fresh candles in the cupboard. ‘Never mind. Perhaps I could—’

‘Selina,’ he interrupted her huskily, and she turned to find William close, his gaze intent on her face.

‘Yes?’ At the look in his eyes, her voice died away and she stood very still, gazing back at him with her heart thumping. *Too much champagne*, she thought dizzily.

‘Merry Christmas.’ William brushed a stray lock of hair from her cheek, leaning forward, and she guessed he was planning to kiss her.

But the moment was swept away as Faith lurched into the room, holding up her empty pudding bowl and asking if she could stand on a chair and wash it up for herself. ‘Pwease,’ she added conscientiously.

Jerked out of the spell, Selina took the bowl from her niece and shook her head. ‘N-not today, dearest,’ she stammered and led the little girl back to the dining room, carefully not looking at William. There, she dispelled the gloom by lighting the fresh candles with a book of matches she now kept permanently in her pocket, blackouts becoming more frequent by the day.

'Ah now,' she said with a laugh, 'isn't that festive? Let's just hope the electricity comes back on before bedtime, else we'll be going to bed by candlelight too.'

Having returned to his place at the head of the table, William sat down and poured himself another drink without looking at her.

Flustered, Selina watched him secretly, wondering what the man was thinking and whether he would indeed have kissed her, given the chance. To her relief, Nancy didn't seem to have noticed that anything was amiss, too busy asking Faith not to keep blowing the shrill tin whistle she'd found inside her Christmas cracker along with a party hat and joke. Fortunately, Faith was soon distracted by the substitute of a Scotty dog brooch, while Nancy surreptitiously pocketed the whistle.

'Aunt Selly, why do the lights keep going out?' Jemima demanded.

Peter told his sister authoritatively, 'Because the power stations that supply the electricity haven't got enough coal to go round, silly.'

'But why not?'

Peter floundered at this, glancing instinctively to William for guidance. It was a look that gave Selina hope he might yet open up to the older man over whatever was troubling him.

'Because the Coal Board is in chaos,' William explained, 'and severely underfunded by the government. The war's left this country in a terrible mess, I'm afraid, and it's likely to get worse before it gets better.' Seeing the children's unhappy expressions, he said bracingly, 'But never mind . . . It will all be sorted out in time. Meanwhile, we'll just have to get used to doing everything by candlelight again, like they did in the last century. Now, look what I've found . . .' He reached for the final cracker from the box, still lying unpulled on the table. 'Who fancies pulling this last Christmas cracker with me? Peter? Jemima?' He smiled at Selina. 'Or maybe the head chef herself?'

Selina blushed at that look, shaking her head. 'The children . . .' she murmured.

'Me, me!' Jemima cried, and pulled the cracker with him, laughing gleefully as it banged.

By the time William eventually left, it was pitch-black and chilly outside, and the electricity still wasn't back on.

Shyly, Selina stood on the step to wave him off, torch in hand. 'Thank you for coming.'

'Thank you for inviting me.' He studied her face, his expression turning serious as he added, 'I meant to say earlier, I haven't heard anything on the Bodmin grapevine about Nancy and her unfortunate condition.'

She was surprised. 'You think Helen and Cameron Bourne are keeping it to themselves?'

'For now, perhaps.'

'Perhaps I should walk over and see them tomorrow,' she mused. 'Maybe take Helen some Christmas cake as an excuse.'

He hesitated. 'Look, I'm aware that you and Cameron have become good friends since Bella passed away. But I should probably warn you—'

'It's all right,' she interrupted. 'I know what kind of man he is.'

William looked taken aback, but nodded. 'Well, thank you again for a wonderful Christmas Day. The children are delightful, aren't they?' He turned his coat collar up against the cold. 'I'm only sorry I couldn't get Peter to tell me what's wrong.'

Selina was just closing the front door when the electricity came back on, followed by a faint cheer from Nancy and the children, whom she'd left playing a game by candlelight in the sitting room.

'Better late than never,' she muttered.

Frankly, she didn't want to see either of the Bournes again. Her sister's journals had described how each of the Bournes had betrayed her trust in their own way, and it was hard not to feel contempt for the brother and sister. But she also didn't want to see her innocent nephew and nieces the focal point of local gossip through no fault of their own, which must happen if their nanny's condition was more widely known.

Sweet-natured Bella had somehow found it in her heart to forgive the Bournes and remain friends with them, right to the end. Now it seemed she had little choice but to follow her sister's saintly example.

Selina was nothing like Bella, though, and she knew it would not be easy to look that scheming pair in the eyes and smile . . .

Wrapped up in hat and scarf, Selina set off early next morning across the moor. Boxing Day had dawned cold but bright, and the snow had partially melted along the moorland track between their properties, making it a pleasant walk after so many days spent cooped up inside.

She caught sight of wild ponies in the distance, and more than once stopped to watch rabbits hopping about among the icy bracken.

Helen Bourne opened the front door, blinking in surprise at this unexpected visit. 'Selina?' Her nearest neighbour was not as neatly dressed and coiffured as usual, but clad in a scruffy old sweater and skirt, her hair quite wild. 'What are you doing here?'

'Have I come at a bad time?' Selina was taken aback.

But Helen shook her head, and stood aside. 'Please, come in.'

In the chilly hall, Selina pulled off her gloves. 'It's a bit late, but I wanted to wish you a Merry Christmas,' she said awkwardly, and held out the tin containing a prettily decorated Christmas cake. 'This is for you.'

Helen took the tin. 'That's very kind,' she said stiffly.

'Is your brother at home too?'

'Sorry, no.' Helen led the way to a small sitting room. Her escritoire stood open, with pen and paper on the leather desktop, so it was obvious that she'd been interrupted in the act of writing a letter. 'Please, sit down.' Helen nodded to the armchair beside the smouldering fire, and then sat opposite, nursing the cake tin on her lap. 'Cameron has gone away,' she said, not meeting Selina's gaze. 'I spent Christmas Day alone.'

'Oh no, how awful.' Selina didn't like Helen, whose brief fling with her brother-in-law had caused such terrible heartache for Bella. And she *loathed* Cameron. But she felt guilty, knowing Helen had passed Christmas alone in this cold, empty house, only a short walk from Thornton Hall. 'I wish I'd known; I would have invited you to lunch with us.' She frowned. 'But surely he's not away on business again? Over Christmas?'

Shaking her head, Helen shrank back into the armchair. All the old malice was gone from her face. Glancing up at a silver-framed photograph on the mantel of her and Cameron in their youth, she whispered, 'He left me to get married.'

Selina stared. 'He did *what*?'

'We took a fortnight's holiday in Paignton this summer,' Helen explained miserably. 'One of the large hotels on the esplanade. It was wonderfully civilised. Tea dances and a tennis pro. I had a marvellous time. But while we were there, Cameron met someone . . .' Her mouth tightened. 'Mrs Fiona Hamilton. No children, no relatives to speak of, and bored out of her mind since her husband died last year, leaving her a widow at barely forty.'

'I see.'

Helen bent her head, picking at a loose thread on the armchair cover. 'You know how charming Cameron can be when he puts his mind to it. He swept Fiona off her feet, and they kept in touch after the holiday ended. He started going away for a few days at a time, claiming he was off on business or visiting friends from his university days.' There was a terrible bitterness in her voice as she finished, 'But I knew where he was going. To see *her*.'

Selina bit her lip, feeling almost sorry for her, something she'd never thought would be possible. But Helen had been so very attached to her brother . . .

'And are they married now?'

Helen nodded. 'Last week. I was invited to the wedding. But I refused. I couldn't have stood there and watched while . . .' A spasm of pain crossed her face as she glanced towards the writing desk. 'When you rang the bell, I was writing to an old friend who's just lost her husband. I thought she might like to come and live here with me. Two old spinsters together.'

'You're hardly old, Helen.' Selina managed a sympathetic smile. 'But where are Cameron and his wife going to live? Not here, presumably.'

'No, she has a vast country house in Paignton overlooking the sea. They're on a Mediterranean cruise for their honeymoon, then he'll move in with her there.' Helen got up to prod the fire with the poker, her movements restless and almost violent. 'So, you might as well go home again. Prince Charming's not here.'

Selina got to her feet. 'I didn't only come here to see Cameron.' Belatedly, she recalled her true mission. 'The thing is . . . When I saw you in town recently, we were discussing my cousin, if you remember.'

Helen barely seemed to be listening. 'Your cousin?'

'I had the impression you know a few things about Nancy that are . . . private.' Selina didn't want to give away any further information, but also couldn't risk not speaking plainly. 'I was hoping you might keep those things to yourself.'

'Not gossip about the baby, you mean?' Ushering her into the hall, Helen gave a wild laugh. 'Well, you don't need to worry about me talking to anyone in town. Cameron took the car when he left. And I can't drive anyway. So I'm stranded here. It's unbelievably tedious.'

Pulling on her gloves again, Selina frowned. 'But what about your maid?'

'We lost our maid weeks ago, even before Cameron ran

away to get married. He had no money left to pay her, you see.' Helen smiled, nodding grimly at her surprised look. 'That's why he had to marry the wealthy widow. To get out of debt.'

'I'm so sorry.' Selina hesitated at the front door, genuinely concerned. 'Hasn't Cameron provided for you at all?'

'I have a monthly allowance. But this place belongs to Cameron. He could turn me out of doors any time he likes.'

'I'm sure he would never do that.' Though Selina knew it was more than possible. She recalled a dinner party at the hall soon after she'd arrived there, attended by the Bournes, and wracked her brain for the names of some of the other guests. 'Look, why don't you go and stay with the Knowleses in Bodmin? I'm sure John and Deirdre would be delighted to have you as a guest.' Seeing Helen's lip curl at this suggestion, she stammered, 'Or . . . Or those two elderly sisters who were friends of Bella's? What were their names?'

'I'm happy here,' Helen said flatly.

Selina didn't know what else to say. She felt perhaps she ought to invite the woman to stay with them at the hall. But the thought filled her with horror.

'Well, do walk over to us if you need anything. Even just a chat.' She smiled awkwardly. 'I could do with some advice about Peter. He's been rather difficult lately.'

'Hardly surprising. This is his first Christmas without his mother,' Helen pointed out.

Selina was taken aback by this crisp appraisal. Could she be right? Was Peter's bad behaviour purely down to grief? 'Come to dinner tonight, at least,' she said guiltily, before she could change her mind. 'Or lunch tomorrow? You can hardly survive out here on your own.'

With a shrug, Helen showed her out. 'I'll be fine. The butcher and greengrocer vans still call occasionally. And I've lived here all my life, remember? This is my home.' A flicker of malice returned as she added cattily, 'Besides, you've got your hands full at the hall, haven't you? All Bella's noisy brats underfoot, and now an illegitimate one on the way . . .'

And she shut the door in Selina's face.

CHAPTER NINETEEN

Sheila thoroughly enjoyed Christmas Day at Postbridge Farm, which was as raucous as ever, despite Grace and Caroline being 'missing in action', as Joe insisted on putting it, his face dour as he and poor Tilly were forced to undertake all the usual jobs on their own, and in such bitter weather too.

Given the cold, the family decided not to venture down into the village for the Christmas Day service, which was a disappointment, as Sheila had grown to enjoy singing hymns and rather missed it. She would have liked Bernie to come calling, as she'd knitted a soft red scarf for him. But Violet pulled a face at this suggestion, so Sheila arranged for them to have lunch together on Boxing Day instead, weather permitting.

Christmas Day lunch went well, and the four of them played cards together in the snug afterwards, gambling with dried beans instead of coins, just for fun. Since they'd already had a glass of wine with their lunch, Sheila brought out her home-made sloe gin, and after they'd all enjoyed a tipple, she fell into a light doze beside the fire.

When she woke up, it was nearly dusk and the fire in the snug had burned low. Tilly was reading a magazine with Sarah Jane cuddled on her lap, but Joe and Violet had disappeared.

'You been stuck with the kiddy?' Sheila asked the girl, surprised.

'Mr and Mrs Postbridge asked me to look after her while they had a nap,' Tilly told her innocently. 'They were both feeling tired.'

Having carried the bottle of gin and the dirty glasses out to the kitchen, Sheila had just begun scraping dirty dishes into the pigswill pail when she heard a creak from upstairs. Violet and Joe in their bedroom, presumably.

Gone for a nap?

With a chuckle, she ran the tap and began to wash up the pots and pans as noisily as she could, singing an old Christmas carol at the top of her voice for good measure.

It seemed the Postbridges were having a very merry Christmas, and good luck to them, she thought with a grin.

On Boxing Day, Sheila persuaded Joe to take her to Bernie's house on the tractor, since it was too icy to drive an ordinary vehicle down the steep track from the farm. Her son-in-law agreed, saying he needed to speak to the vet about the shire horse, who'd developed what Joe felt might be equine influenza. 'Most likely not serious,' Joe insisted, pulling on his gloves, 'but I'd prefer to have the vet's advice, all the same. Pity the GPO haven't installed that telephone line yet . . . That would have saved me the trip. But I suppose the snow's held them up.'

Sheila felt a tug of concern for the old shire horse, but Joe had already assured Tilly that most horses pulled through flu unscathed, so she tried not to worry. 'I'm sure the GPO will be up here as soon as the roads are clear again,' she told him reassuringly.

'Merry Christmas!' Bernie greeted her on the doorstep, smart in a suit and tie, as though they were going out for lunch somewhere posh, not staying in. 'Am I allowed to say that on Boxing Day? It's past Christmas now.'

'I don't think there are any rules, and even if there are, stuff 'em,' Sheila said. 'Merry Christmas, Bernie.'

He raised a hand to Joe, who was turning his tractor in the narrow lane. 'Good of Joe to drop you off, but I could have driven up to fetch you.'

'Don't be daft,' Sheila told him affectionately, taking off her hat and coat in his hallway. 'You'd only have got that lovely car of yours stranded in a ditch.'

'I hope my driving's a little better than that,' he said mildly, closing the front door. Then he turned and kissed her on the lips, which left her a little breathless.

'Cheeky!'

Bernie chuckled. 'A chap needs to take his chances where he can. Besides, I've no time to waste on asking permission. Lunch is ready.'

The dining table was set with gleaming silver and glassware, the white linen cloth topped with a red runner, a Christmas log as its centrepiece, bristling with holly and red berries.

Sheila was impressed. 'Oh, I say . . .'

He pulled out her chair. 'If Madam would care to park herself here, I'll fetch the first course.'

'Silver service, no less,' she murmured.

'Of course.' Bernie inclined his head. 'To match my hair,' he replied, and they grinned at each other.

The meal was delicious, a dish of cold partridge with stewed veg, and a pudding of rich, sweet lemon meringue pie, and she savoured every mouthful.

'You certainly know the way to a woman's heart, my lad,' Sheila told him as they sat relaxing after lunch with a small glass of sherry each. 'That was sumptuous.'

'I had a little help from my housekeeper's brother in obtaining the partridge,' he admitted sheepishly. 'But the lemon meringue pie was my own creation.'

'And very tasty it was too.' Sheila raised her glass in a salute.

They talked of weather and politics for a while, and the parish fund. Then he asked how Christmas Day had gone at Postbridge Farm, and she gladly told him, leaning back on the sofa with a smile as she regaled him with tales of Sarah Jane's excitement on Christmas Eve, waiting up to listen for Santa Claus until she fell asleep on the stairs . . .

'Christmas is for the kiddies, I always say. But we grown-ups are allowed a little fun too. Talking of which, I nearly forgot . . .' Sheila fished his present out of her bag. 'Merry Christmas, Bernie.'

Bernie unwrapped the scarf and smiled down at it. 'Thank you. Very handsome. And knitted by your own industrious hands, I daresay.'

'You're getting to recognise my handiwork, I see. But do you like the colour?'

'Absolutely.' He draped the berry-red scarf about his neck. 'It'll be perfect for when I become a socialist.'

Sheila choked. 'You? A socialist?' She saw his grin and

tutted under her breath. 'You teaser . . . I'm never sure when you're jokin',' she complained.

'That's because I like to keep you on your toes, Mrs Newton.' Getting up, he fetched a slender jewellery box from the sideboard repetition. 'This is for you, my dear. I hope you like it.'

A little flustered by his affectionate tone, Sheila bit her lip. 'I'm sure I will, whatever it is.' But she gasped on opening the box to find a gleaming pearl necklace inside, nestled on a bed of silk. 'Oh, Bernie . . . Oh no . . . This is too much.'

'Nonsense.' He perched on the edge of his chair opposite, watching her with a light in his eyes. 'I saw it in a jeweller's window in Penzance and knew at once it was the perfect gift.'

Sheila's mouth trembled. She'd never worn a pearl necklace in her life. To her mind, it was the kind of jewellery only posh women wore, like the well-heeled, middle-class women on the Parish Council who looked down their noses at her. It wasn't a necklace for someone like her, Mrs Sheila Newton, who spent her days in an apron behind the counter of the village shop.

'I don't know what to say,' she muttered, closing the box.

Bernie's smile faded and he sat back. 'You don't like it?' He seemed perplexed. 'I . . . I'm sorry, Sheila. I thought you would like pearls. I seem to have made rather a stupid gaff. Offended you, perhaps.'

She reached for him in quick reassurance, shaking her head. 'No, bless your heart. Of course I ain't offended. Nobody's ever give me such a lovely gift before, that's all.' Moved to the verge of tears, Sheila choked as she added, 'They're beautiful, Bernie. Thank you.'

'I thought they were a match for *your* beauty, Sheila.'

Tears spilled from her eyes. 'Don't.'

'You *are* beautiful, Sheila,' he insisted, and took her hand. 'I love you, and I know you said I wasn't to ask you to marry me again. But I want you to know that if you change your mind, I'll happily ask you again whenever you say the word.'

He lifted her hand to his lips, his eyes intent on her face. She thought she'd never seen something so romantic, and it fair took her breath away. 'You deserve those pearls, Sheila. Merry Christmas, my darling.'

Sheila gulped, unable to say a blessed word.

He leant forward and kissed her on the lips again. Only it wasn't a cheeky kiss like out in the hallway earlier, but it wasn't demanding either. It was a lovely kiss, just right for Christmastime, and she wished it could go on forever. But that would be asking for trouble.

Pulling back, Sheila wiped away her tears. 'I don't know why I'm blubbing . . . Making a fool of meself.'

But she did know why. She was more vulnerable than she cared to admit. And she was beginning to feel something suspiciously close to love for this polite, well-dressed gent, even if at times he seemed very different to the boy she'd known when they were growing up together. Could she be mistaking loneliness for love, though? She didn't want to give up her new-found independence just because he was good company . . .

No more was said about the pearls, and after another glass of sherry, Bernie checked the time and conscientiously insisted on driving her back to the farm, despite the poor weather.

'Goodnight,' he said deeply as she got out in the darkness,

and it felt like a significant moment, especially when she found herself unable to reply.

As he headed off again, Sheila turned away into the farmhouse, trying to decide what to do for the best.

Violet was making a suet pudding at the table, and Joe was standing beside her, his arm looped about her waist. The couple were giggling and whispering but jumped hurriedly apart when she came in out of the cold.

'Evening, Sheila.' Joe thrust his hands into his pockets, his ears turning pink. 'You're back early. Bernie gave you a lift up the hill, did he?'

'Well, I wasn't going to walk. Not in this weather.' Primly, her gaze shot to Violet, who instantly bent her head, focused on the suet. 'Making a pudding, love?'

Violet's eyes flashed but she said calmly enough, 'I fancied something stodgy for a change. How was Mr Bailey's cooking? Or did his fancy housekeeper do everything for him?'

'She weren't there, and besides, it don't matter who cooked what, it was delicious,' Sheila told her loftily, and drew out the box containing her gift. 'Bernie gave me this for Christmas.' Opening the lid, she displayed the gleaming pearl necklace. 'Beautiful, ain't it? Though not as beautiful as me, according to Bernie.' And she couldn't help beaming, still bowled over by his compliments.

'Well, I never . . .' Violet gasped, staring at the pearls.

Joe's bushy brows soared. 'He'll be asking you to marry him next.'

'He already did ask, thank you very much, and I said no.' Sheila winked as the couple gaped at her in silence. 'For now, at any rate. But I might change my mind one day. It's a woman's prerogative, after all.'

After Joe had gone outside to close up the pigsty for the night, Violet set the suet pudding aside in a mixing bowl with a clean damp cloth over the top. She washed her hands, looking round at Sheila thoughtfully. 'So, you think you might accept him one day?'

Sheila poured herself a cup of tea from the pot, mulling it over. 'I do like him, Vi. There's something about the man that . . .' She stopped, not sure what she wanted to say, and shook her head. 'Oh, I don't know. I'm no spring chicken, let's face it, and neither is Bernie. If I'm going to marry for a third time, I should probably quit faffing about and get on with it.' She chewed on her lip. 'Only I need more time to think about it, and maybe get to know him better. Does that sound daft?'

Violet put an arm about her shoulders. 'Of course not, Mum. You should do whatever you feel is right.' She hesitated, releasing her. 'Though, if you're interested in our opinion, Joe and I think he's a nice chap, too. I certainly wouldn't mind him for a stepdad.'

Sheila was surprised. Violet had always been opposed to the idea of her remarrying, even back when she and Arnie had been courting. 'You like him, then?' She frowned. 'He ain't nothing like Arnie. Nor your dad neither.'

'That's for bloomin' sure. I loved Dad to bits, but he wouldn't have known what to say to your Mr Bailey. Though the likes of them two would never have met, would they? Different worlds . . .' Violet pulled a face, and checked the pot with the back of her hand before also pouring herself another cuppa. 'But if you like him, none of that matters. Besides, you could do worse. He's a proper gent. And life's too short, ain't it? We need to grab all the happiness we can before it's too late.'

‘Talking of happiness, you and Joe seem to be getting on rather better these days.’ When Violet bit her lip, looking embarrassed, Sheila nodded wisely. ‘I’m glad to see it, love. You and Joe had me worried for a while. It’s not right for husband and wife to be forever backbiting. And it weren’t good for Sarah Jane, bless her. Oh, I know she don’t say much, but that little girl sees more than you think . . . She’s got sharp eyes, that one.’

‘Gawd, don’t I know it?’ To her surprise, Violet didn’t appear offended by this frank discussion of her marriage. Making up with Joe had clearly left her in a mellow mood. ‘She’s quiet on account of being an only child, that’s what I think. But maybe she won’t always be so lonely.’ She flashed Sheila a mischievous smile that reminded her of a younger, more carefree Violet, long before their wartime evacuation to Cornwall. ‘And that’s all I’m prepared to say on the subject.’

Sheila’s heart lightened. ‘Mum’s the word,’ she murmured, and hid her own smile, adding more briskly, ‘You know, we ain’t had suet puddin’ in ages. But it’s just right for this nasty cold snap.’

‘Exactly what I was thinking.’ Violet glanced towards the kitchen window, where a few solitary snowflakes could be seen whirling about in the dark. Outside, they could hear the clank of the pigswill bucket and the muffled tread of Joe’s boots across the snowy yard. ‘All this frost and snow, though . . . It makes me nervous.’

‘Me too, love.’ Sheila shivered, wondering what the coming new year would bring, and if 1947 would be any better or worse than 1946. Though it would have to work bloomin’ hard to be worse, she thought, cradling her tea to warm her chilly fingers. ‘Me too.’

CHAPTER TWENTY

After asking for directions, Caroline and Grace tramped up through the snow to Lily and Tristan's sheep farm, perched on a steep hill above Penzance, since there was no chance of getting a bus back to Porthcurno during the cold snap. The young couple lived there with Tristan's lively, ginger-haired sister Demelza and his huge brother-in-law, Robert. Caroline only knew Lily well, but the company was so relaxed and undemanding, they were all soon on good terms with each other.

Staying there was rather like being back at Postbridge Farm, with sheep huddled on the icy lower slopes, and a hectic, boisterous family atmosphere. Little Morris was constantly toddling about the place, baby Teresa yelling lustily for milk. Lily Minear was also strikingly similar to her aunt Violet in looks, being tall, slender and fair-haired, and of course she shared the same Dagenham accent, so that Caroline found herself accidentally addressing her several times as Mrs Postbridge, which made Lily glare but had everyone else in stitches.

When the two girls had first turned up on the doorstep, they were ushered in by Lily with a surprised smile of welcome.

Demelza too had looked taken aback to find strangers in their cosy front room, but had thawed when Grace offered to look after her little girl Teresa while Demelza finished wrapping some Christmas presents. And her husband Robert had swiftly readied a spare room for them, and produced Christmas cake and ginger snaps, with a small glass of brandy each to warm them up.

'Stay as long as you need,' Lily insisted. 'I'm not surprised the bus was cancelled. The coast road must be a nightmare in this weather. And I'm sure my aunt and uncle won't miss you, not for a few days at least.'

'It's very kind of you,' Grace told her, cuddling Teresa on her knee and making gurgling noises, which the baby seemed to find highly amusing.

'Is Tristan out with the sheep?' Caroline asked. 'Joe's lost a few because of this cold snap. Has it been bad here too?'

Robert was pulling on his coat. 'We've lost a couple of lambs.' He kissed his wife on the cheek. 'Sorry, darling, I need to help Tristan. He's on the hunt for some stragglers. I'm very glad you'll be joining us for Christmas,' he added to the girls, a twinkle in his blue eyes.

'I like him,' Grace whispered to Caroline once he'd gone, as they sat listening to Lily and Demelza banging pots and pans in the kitchen. 'Is he the Quaker?'

'That's right. He was a conchie in the war.'

'A conscientious objector? Oh, of course . . . Quakers are pacifists. Did they put him in prison?'

'Gracious, no. Robert got a medal for bravery. Battlefield

ambulance driver. He and Demelza shipped out to France together after they were married,' she added in a low voice, 'and both drove ambulances under fire, even crossing into Germany with the front line. They only came back when they discovered that Demelza was expecting Teresa.' Caroline smiled at the memory of their triumphant return from war, pitching up at the farm late one winter's night. 'Robert drove his battered old ambulance all the way home from Germany to Cornwall. Can you imagine?'

'No,' Grace admitted frankly.

'My big brave Viking,' Demelza called through from the kitchen, clearly having ears like a bat. 'He's a man in a million.'

'Sounds like it, love,' Grace called back, and winked at Caroline. 'This is fun, isn't it?'

'Yes, but I hope we're not putting them out. You know how short food is at the moment. If we stay longer than Boxing Day, I'll give Lily my ration book, in case she can use it for extra food.' Caroline sipped her brandy and shuddered. 'Goodness, that's strong.'

'Get it down your neck, girl.' Grace nudged her in the ribs, grinning. 'It'll put hairs on your chest.'

'That's what I'm afraid of.'

The two men came back in from the fields eventually, stamping their feet and clapping their hands, declaring it to be 'perishing' out there. Tristan's aunt Sarah emerged from a side room, leaning on a stick, and was helped to the dinner table. A hot meal was served for the grown-ups, the two children having gone to bed, and they tucked in, the conversation a rapid, constant back and forth. The men largely talked politics, while their wives discussed what they would be serving for Christmas lunch, and how to make it stretch for two unexpected guests, which embarrassed Caroline. Aunt Sarah, whose mouth was drawn down after a stroke, fell into conversation with Grace about Liverpool, a city she'd apparently visited in her youth.

After the meal, Aunt Sarah retired to bed early. Demelza fetched down a wailing Teresa and put her to the breast. Lily served everyone a cup of tea, and sat knitting by the hearth, more like Violet Postbridge than ever, her needles clacking as the fire burned steadily, the room growing so warm that Caroline soon felt drowsy and ready for bed.

At last, the mantel clock chimed eleven.

'Gosh, it's almost Christmas Day.' Yawning, Caroline caught Grace's eye. 'I wonder what they're up to at Postbridge Farm right now.'

'Sloe gin,' Tristan muttered.

Robert grinned. 'Mince pies with brandy.'

'Sarah Jane will be so excited . . . Her first proper Christmas Eve.' Demelza smiled indulgently as she shifted her sleeping baby into the crook of her arm. She glanced towards the hearth where young Morris had hung up his stocking earlier with his father's help. 'I can't wait for Teresa to be old enough to hang up a stocking.'

'I remember one Christmas Eve,' Lily said contemplatively, unpicking an errant stitch in her knitting, 'tiptoeing downstairs after midnight to see if I could spot Santa coming down the chimney. Only, I met Gran on the stairs instead, still supping from a bottle of stout, three sheets to the wind.'

Demelza bit her lip, while her husband roared with laughter.

'I'd have paid good money to see that,' Tristan said, lifting a glass of brandy to his lips.

Brow wrinkling, Caroline turned a mystified face to Grace, repeating, 'Three sheets to the wind?'

'Drunk,' Grace supplied.

Caroline snorted.

Robert drained his cup of tea and got wearily to his feet. 'Time for bed. I'll carry Teresa. You on your way up too, love?' he asked his wife.

'Right behind you,' Demelza agreed, handing him the baby. 'I'll help Lily clear the tea things away first.'

'No, let us do that,' Grace said promptly, jumping to her feet. 'We owe you.' Winking, she plucked the tray from Demelza's unresisting hands and headed out to the kitchen with it. 'Merry Christmas.'

'Merry Christmas,' Demelza called after her, surprised, but followed her husband and child, also yawning extravagantly. 'Busy day tomorrow.'

'Every day's busy,' Lily muttered, but had put away her knitting. As Grace came back into the room, Lily glanced at Tristan. 'Bed?'

'Bed,' her husband agreed. 'Though I'll need to pop an orange and a tin whistle into Morris's stocking before locking up. You'd best show our guests to their room.'

The tiny spare room was cluttered with old packing crates and various odds and ends, but it had a corner sink with a mirror and the bed looked comfortable.

Lily checked they had enough pillows, and apologised that it was only a single bed. 'One of you can sleep on the floor with blankets and cushions if it's too much of a squeeze,' she said, grimacing on her way out. 'And you'll be pleased to hear we have an indoor lavatory, just along the landing. Saves a cold bottom in this weather!'

Left alone with Grace in the small, chilly room, Caroline unpacked her nightie and washbag, and glanced nervously at the bed. 'I'll use the sink first, shall I?'

Grace headed out to the loo, while Caroline splashed her face and cleaned her teeth. Then she tiptoed down the freezing cold passage to the loo while Grace washed herself. Luckily, Lily had been able to find her a spare toothbrush and nightdress.

There was not much room in the single bed, and it sagged in the middle. Caroline pulled the blanket up to her chin, leaving her bare toes uncovered and chilly. She wanted to turn on her side and pull her knees up, but didn't dare bump into Grace.

'Shove up!' Grace hissed, making the springs creak as she shifted position.

'You shove up,' Caroline whispered back. 'I'm right on the edge.'

Grace gave a groan. 'Blast . . .'

'Oh, what now?'

'We only forgot to turn the bleedin' light out, didn't we?'

They both looked up at the bare bulb hanging over the bed.

Caroline grimaced. 'Oops.'

'You got in last,' Grace told her in a lofty tone. 'That means you should be the one to get out and turn off the light.'

'Why, you . . .' Caroline dug her in the ribs.

Bafflingly, the light went out on its own. Somewhere along the landing, they heard a man shout, 'Blackout!' followed by a curse from Demelza as the baby started crying.

Seconds later, Morris' piping voice began chanting, 'Santa! Santa! Santa!' and had to be hushed by his fond parents.

Caroline couldn't help herself. She fell back on the pillows, struggling with hysterical laughter, and heard Grace chuckle too beside her. 'Santa! Santa!' she repeated, imitating the child's high voice. They began to giggle helplessly, the bed shaking under them. 'Santa!'

'Stop it, shut up . . . They'll hear us,' Grace spluttered.

'I . . . I'm trying . . . but I can't help it,' Caroline choked, tears in her eyes. 'Anyway, it's not a blackout. It's a power cut.'

Grace turned to face her, warm and close in the dark. 'Hush now, will you?' she insisted.

But however hard Caroline bit her lip, she only laughed harder, caught in hysteria.

'I can see there's nothing for it, Miss Ponsby, but to shut you up myself,' Grace told her in mock-stern tones, and leant forward in the glimmering dark.

Caroline froze in shock as their lips met. Grace was kissing her!

Kissing her!

Caroline lay perfectly still, hands balled into fists by her sides, eyes shut tight, flushed with excitement and not quite able to believe what was happening.

Afterwards, Grace found her hand and squeezed it gently. The two girls lay side by side in the darkness, breathing hard.

'There now,' Grace murmured. 'That's torn it.'

Caroline sat up with a jolt on Christmas Day morning, alone in bed, opening her eyes on an unfamiliar room, but remembering everything instantly. 'Oh goodness,' she whispered to herself, her cheeks flaring with heat.

She found her friend downstairs, staring out of the window at icy fields. Robert and Tristan were standing beside a tractor some distance away in greatcoats and caps, farm dogs running about them. Robert was cradling a wriggling lamb in his arms, its fleecy white body held firmly against his broad chest while the two men examined it.

'Hello there,' Caroline whispered, and Grace turned, looking round at her with wide dark eyes, her head a crown of tight luscious curls. She looked beautiful.

Daringly, Caroline reached for her friend's hand. But as soon as their fingers tangled, Grace jerked away and hurried from the room, muttering, 'Sorry, I left the kettle on the stove . . . It'll be boiling itself dry by now.'

Speechless, Caroline stayed where she was, suddenly cold inside.

Had she done something wrong?

It was Grace who'd initiated that unexpected kiss last night, not her. Yet now she was behaving as though she blamed Caroline for it. Hated her, even. Her eyes filling with tears, Caroline bent her head. It hurt to breathe and everything inside was aching. She didn't know how she could possibly bear to go on . . .

Hearing Lily and Morris on their way downstairs, she wiped a quick hand across her eyes. There would only be awkward questions if anyone saw her crying.

Unhappily, she trailed into the kitchen. Lily, who'd come downstairs with an armful of Christmas presents, was chatting to Grace about the weather, while Morris played excitedly with his Christmas stocking.

Lily turned with a smile on seeing Caroline. 'Merry Christmas,' she said. 'I was just telling Grace, I spoke to one of our neighbours earlier. She came by with a jar of home-made chutney for Christmas lunch while I was out feeding the chickens. Anyway, her brother's a driver on the buses, and he says they should be running again from the day after Boxing Day. They're not expecting much more snow this week, and the road to Porthcurno will likely be passable by then.'

'That's excellent news.' Caroline heard a tell-tale tremor in her voice and could have kicked herself. She added swiftly, 'I wanted to thank you again for taking us in. It was very kind of you.'

'Nonsense, we were glad to have you.' Lily studied her thoughtfully. 'You look tired . . . I hope the bed was comfortable and not too much of a squeeze.'

'Oh, we didn't notice, honestly. Too exhausted.' Grace came forward to help Morris retrieve his Christmas orange, which had rolled under the kitchen table. 'It *was* a tight squeeze, though. Last time I slept in a bed that small, I was a baby.' But she was grinning as she straightened. 'No, I'm only pulling your leg. It was cosy, wasn't it, Caroline?'

Her cheeks burning, Caroline managed to stutter, 'Very c-cosy, yes.'

Thankfully, Lily had bent over her son and so didn't see her embarrassment. 'It's called an orange, Morris,' she was saying. 'It came on a ship across the ocean, just in time for Santa to pop it in your Christmas stocking. Mmm, delicious! I haven't smelt an orange in years.'

That night, Grace slept on the floor in a makeshift heap of blankets. Caroline climbed into bed without comment and lay there shivering, her thoughts whirling until she fell into a troubled sleep. Grace had never once mentioned their kiss or shown her any special attention, leaving Caroline miserable and racking her brains to understand what had gone wrong. And Boxing Day was no better, with Grace still determinedly sleeping on the floor. They might as well have been polite strangers sharing the same room.

Returning by bus to Porthcurno a few days after Christmas, they found a GPO van in the yard and a man in uniform halfway up a newly sunk telegraph pole, who gave them a wink and made a cheeky remark as the girls passed underneath, which they quite rightly ignored.

Hearing the dogs bark, Tilly ran out to greet them with the exciting news that a telephone was being installed at the farm. 'Isn't it a smashing idea? This means I'll be able to telephone home, as my father had a telephone line put in last year to help with his business.'

When Mrs Newton came back from the shop that evening, she and Violet tried the telephone for the first time, ringing first Lily and then Alice, with much laughter and festive greetings, until Joe grumbled about call costs. Then Alice's father, Mr Fisher, rang them back while everyone crowded curiously into the snug, where the receiver had been installed . . . but only so they could hear what it would sound like to have the telephone ring.

'Goodness, that's loud,' Mrs Postbridge exclaimed, clapping her hands over her ears.

Over dinner, Mrs Newton told Caroline about her soup-and-sandwiches social, which had gone down very well in the village. In return, Caroline had felt driven to explain why she'd left her family without even spending Christmas with them, stammering and blushing throughout the difficult story, and had been reassured by hugs and exclamations of support from both Tilly and Mrs Postbridge. Mrs Newton had even called her 'a very brave girl', for standing up to her father.

Caroline didn't feel particularly brave. In fact, she felt more like a coward, too scared to ask Grace why she was acting as though nothing had happened between them. But she was terrified Grace might declare that what they'd done was disgusting and unnatural, and that she wanted nothing more to do with her.

That fear left her silent, unable even to meet Grace's eyes across the dinner table. But she kept remembering the kiss they'd shared, convinced that she would never again in her life experience such a breathtaking moment.

But over the following weeks, it seemed like Grace's sudden chill spread outwards, as heavy snow blocked the roads and plummeting temperatures left everything under a deep freeze. Slowly, the rations dwindled, while the livestock began to perish in the cold, and still Grace would not speak to her beyond clipped, stilted exchanges about tasks that needed doing on the farm.

Everything was so miserable, Caroline thought one night with a groan, throwing herself down on the bed and burying her face in the covers. There was no promise of light on the horizon. Only the relentless darkness of a winter that refused to end.

CHAPTER TWENTY-ONE

Sheila was blissfully deep in the Land of Nod when someone banged on her bedroom door, and she heard Violet call, 'Mum! Get up, quick! There's someone on the telephone, asking for you.'

Befuddled, Sheila lay blinking at the darkness for a few seconds, still surfacing from a strange dream where she'd been chasing a chicken around and around the kitchen table . . . A telephone call? For her?

'You'd better not be pulling my leg, Violet Postbridge,' she muttered, throwing back the bedcovers and stumbling into her slippers and dressing gown, the room still dark. 'Gawd, it ain't even light yet. What's the blessed time?'

'It's nearly eight o'clock in the morning, Mum. We let you sleep late because you looked so worn out last night after spending all evening on the yearly accounts.' Violet looked at her with a worried frown when she emerged. 'You'd best hurry, though. It's a posh-sounding man on the phone, and he won't wait forever.'

'A posh-sounding man?' Sheila stared at her. 'Do you mean Bernie?'

'No, a Mr Chilcott. And he sounds young. I don't have a clue who he is or what he wants. He said it was urgent, but he'd only speak to you.'

'*Urgent*, my . . . my foot,' Sheila exclaimed, gripping the banister as she made her slow way downstairs, her joints always a little stiff after she'd been sleeping. 'I don't think I like telephones. And I don't appreciate being hurried when I've just woken up. So if you wouldn't mind not badgering me . . .'

Violet tutted but said nothing more, following in silence.

Downstairs, Sheila found Joe in the snug, standing next to the telephone table. He held out the receiver to her with a baffled look. 'It's someone from the government for you,' he hissed. 'Says he's in Whitehall.'

'*Whitehall*?' Now Sheila was sure they must be pulling her leg. 'Hello? Mrs Newton here,' she said gruffly into the speaker and waited, listening to the loud crackle on the line. 'Who's this?'

A young man with a plummy voice introduced himself as Mr Chilcott, working with a new government department in London's Whitehall, dealing with communities in crisis during the cold snap. 'You're listed as current proprietor of the Porthcurno village shop, Mrs Newton. Is that correct?'

Bemused, Sheila agreed. 'When I last looked, yes. What's all this about?'

'There's a supply drop coming your way at about noon, and we'll need you to be on hand to receive and distribute the contents.'

'Eh?' Sheila almost dropped the telephone in shock.

'The drop zone should be just off the main street, somewhere in the vicinity of Eastern House. There's a large open space there. Do you know it?'

'We call it the village green,' she agreed, stammering, 'though it's just a field, to be honest. Common land, you know.'

'Yes, yes,' the man said impatiently. 'Be there at noon to collect the supplies, and distribute them to those most in need in Porthcurno and the surrounding hamlets. We felt the village shop would make the best distribution centre. Further instructions will be attached to one of the parcels dropped by the pilot.'

'*Pilot*? You mean these supplies are coming from . . . *an aeroplane*?'

'That's correct.' He paused. 'Now, I have a great many more calls to make today, as you can imagine. Thank you for your cooperation, Mrs Newton. Good day.' And the line went dead.

Staggered, Sheila handed the telephone back to Joe.

Behind them, Violet fidgeted. 'Who was it, Mum? And what was that about an aeroplane?'

Still unsure she wasn't dreaming, Sheila repeated what she'd been told. 'It's all to be distributed through the village shop, according to that bloke,' she added. 'Though how he knew to ring me here, I've no idea.'

'We do have several family members who work for the government,' Joe pointed out.

'It sounds like a good idea . . . Only I dunno how you'll ever get down the hill, Mum.' Violet was staring glumly out of the window. 'That snow's three or four foot in places, maybe higher.'

'I daresay the tractor could clear it,' Joe pondered, joining her at the window. 'But it'll take time, and we'll need people with spades walking behind the tractor to make sure the path stays clear.'

'I'll tell the Land Girls to get ready,' Violet said, and dashed away.

'Aye, and you'd better get yourself dressed, Sheila,' Joe pointed out, discreetly averting his eyes from her night attire. 'It's mighty cold out there.'

Sheila was soon dressed and outside in her thick winter togs, supervising the preparations for Operation Sweep, as Tilly was calling it. Thankfully, it had stopped snowing at last. But the drifts were still waist-high all the way down to the village, the track completely blocked, and the adjacent fields not much better.

The three Land Girls, armed with spades and woolly hats, lined up behind the tractor, while Violet called the dogs back inside, who'd run out into the snow after them, barking excitedly.

Joe, cloth cap pulled down low, collar turned up high, started the tractor, with the big scoop lowered all the way to ground level. Then he sent it forward at a slow walking pace, lumbering into the snowdrift that was blocking the track and scooping snow as he went.

Both Joe and the tractor were soon lost in a mess of wet snow, the three girls briskly shovelling the road behind him to clear the debris. Just watching them made Sheila shiver and draw her coat closer. It was going to be a very cold walk down.

'Will you and Sally be coming down to see the food drop,

love?' Sheila asked her daughter on the doorstep, using their affectionate name for Sarah Jane without thinking, though she knew Violet didn't much like it.

But Violet didn't even seem to have noticed her slip, shaking her head as she watched the tractor disappear down the snowy hill. 'She's got a sniffle, poor lamb. I told her to stay in bed this morning, just to be on the safe side.'

'Very wise,' Sheila agreed, adjusting her thick woollen scarf. 'Bless her heart, I hope she gets well soon. And that she don't give it to me,' she added darkly. 'I've just shaken off one bloomin' head cold, and I'd rather not have another, thank you very much.'

With a chuckle at Violet's pursed lips, she set off in the wake of the Land Girls, taking it slowly down the steep track, so she didn't slip and break her leg.

Down in the village, Joe and his tractor cleared a narrow tunnel of sorts along the main street, while the Land Girls hurried about, shovelling paths and knocking on doors where they could reach them, telling the occupants about the food parcel drop.

Sheila unlocked the shop and called up to her sister in the flat.

Margaret came downstairs wrapped in a house coat and cardigan, asking in bewilderment, 'What on earth's going on?'

It didn't take long to explain, and Margaret soon began clearing a space to accommodate the food drop, looking cheerful to have the shop open again.

Meanwhile, Jack Treedy had come along with his mum and the eldest of his younger sisters. The three of them stood on the edge of the snowy green, staring up into grey skies as they watched for any sign of an approaching aeroplane.

Sheila went to join them, stamping her feet and banging her gloved hands together to keep warm. 'Brr,' she moaned, 'it's bloomin' perishing out here. When will this snow ever stop?'

Mrs Treedy shivered. 'I thought it was ever so romantic at first, watching the snow come down at Christmas,' she admitted. 'Now it's miserable. Feels like we're living at the North Pole.'

'How are the kiddies?' Sheila couldn't help wondering how on earth Mrs Treedy had coped for the past few weeks with so many mouths to feed and the village shop closed due to the snow.

Not that she'd closed the shop lightly. The shelves had stood empty day after day, with no supplies getting through from beyond the village, and almost no local fresh produce worth selling, thanks to the low temperatures.

Her sister had insisted on staying in the little flat above the shop though, much to Sheila's concern, insisting she would be safe enough on her own.

'Cold and hungry, mostly,' the widow said, a little sharply, and then caught Sheila's eye. 'Not that I'm complaining,' she added. 'We're all in the same boat, aren't we? But it's hard to explain to the young'uns why they keep having to miss out on a hot meal, especially in such cold weather, and with the house so damp . . . I'll be glad of this food drop, I can tell you. My soups are getting a bit thin, and we've had no flour for bread in weeks.'

'Oh, love.' Sheila gave the woman a hug, her heart squeezed in pain. 'You should have told me, I would have brought something down for you.' Though they'd not been in much better shape at the farm, apart from having fresh eggs, thanks to the chickens being housed in the kitchen porch now and making a fine old mess in there too.

'There it is!' Jack shouted, pointing up into the grey skies, where a small black dot could be seen steadily approaching.

'Gawd . . . I never thought I'd live to see the day when I was glad to have a plane drop something on me, I can tell you.' Sheila glanced around for Joe. 'We think this is the plane coming now,' she called to him. 'Though I daresay we'll need a hand carrying everything back to the shop.'

'I'll organise a line,' Joe told her.

Sure enough, the aeroplane dropped lower as it approached, and moments later, a large, bulky package strapped together with cords was ejected and came floating down towards them on a parachute. Many villagers had come out to see this astonishing spectacle, some applauding with relief, others shaking their head in amazement. Despite the parachute, the gigantic package landed with one heck of a thump and was dragged a few feet through the snow before stopping.

The men ran forward with spades, digging out a clear path to the package, and soon cut the ties that bound it together, boxes spilling out at once. Under Joe's guidance, the villagers formed a straggling human chain between the green and the village shop, and Sheila and Margaret found themselves directing people where to place each food parcel in the shop.

Soon, the tiny premises was crowded with boxes and crates, most labelled, but some not. Jack Treedy found a crowbar and began opening the unmarked crates, shouting out the contents to Margaret, who kept a careful note of them.

There were dried goods, flour and sugar, tea and coffee, large pallets of tinned meat, fruit and condensed milk, plus oils for cooking, dried herbs and spices, a few sacks of animal feed, and an impressive pack of medical supplies to cover most eventualities. There were also lengthy instructions on contents and distribution protocols, thankfully, that were passed to Sheila for her perusal.

During all this commotion, Bernie turned up, riding a horse through the gleaming tunnel of snow dug out in front of the shop by Joe's tractor. Everyone stared as he dismounted outside the shop, looped the reins over a protruding post, and sauntered into the shop in the manner of a cowboy from a Western, complete with a wide-brimmed leather hat.

'Blimey, what in the name of . . .' Sheila gawped. 'I didn't know you had a horse, Bernie. Where on earth did he come from?'

'It's a she. And I borrowed her from my neighbour. Heard about the food drop and saw the plane coming in. Thought you might need a hand.' Removing his hat, he nodded to everyone else. 'Good afternoon, folks. Right, Sheila, where can I be useful?'

Gradually, the parcels were distributed to those in need, with some set aside for collection for outlying homes as soon as the road through Porthcurno could be cleared. One of the villagers mentioned an elderly widow living half a mile outside the village, who'd told a neighbour a few days before that she was running low on fuel as well as food. Joe took the tractor and used the scoop to push his way through the snow, carrying a supply of logs as well as emergency food supplies for the old lady. While this was going on, Sheila turned on the wireless she'd installed in the back room of the shop and turned it up so they could all listen. It cheered up the villagers no end to hear a few popular tunes on the radio while they were working.

Eventually, it grew dark, and the crowds began to disperse. Even Bernie had finally ridden home on his horse, cradling supplies for himself and his neighbours, and wishing them all a pleasant evening.

Mrs Treedy pulled Sheila aside. 'I wanted a word, if you can spare a moment,' she said, looking worried. 'Do you remember I told you about Jack wanting to go to Australia?'

'How could I forget? Silly boy, I hope he's put that nonsense out of his head.'

But the widow pulled a face. 'No, he's more serious than ever. I think it's this snow . . . He says Britain's more like Siberia now. He's been reading about all the sunshine and lovely beaches down under. He's applied for a passport too, and he's been working a few days a week on a farm, saving up for his boat ticket as soon as he's old enough to move there. Oh, I don't know what I'll do if our Jack leaves us. It's the other side of the world. I'd never see him again.' There were tears in her eyes.

Sheila didn't know what to say. If the young man was intent on emigrating to Australia, there wasn't much anyone could do about it. But she could hardly say that to Mrs Treedy, who was beside herself. 'Would it help if I asked Joe to have a word with him?' she asked uncertainly. 'He might listen to a man, where he ignores us ladies.'

Mrs Treedy also looked doubtful. 'I don't know. If you ask me, I think Jack's bewitched. He barely even mentioned Australia a year ago . . . Now it's all he can talk about.' She wiped away a tear. 'He acts tough. But he's still just a boy at heart. And I'm scared what might happen to him out there. It's an awfully big country.'

The Land Girls came trooping into the shop, spades on their shoulders, looking cold and exhausted, as well they might after all their hard work. Caroline said bleakly, 'We'd like to head back to the farm, if that's all right, Mrs Newton? We're bushed. Do you think we'll be needed again?'

'No, love, but leave one of them spades with me, just in case it comes in handy later.' She watched the girls traipse off into the gathering dusk. 'They're such good girls,' she told Mrs Treedy and Margaret, who was sorting out supplies for Violet up at the farm. 'We were bloomin' lucky to get a crew like that. Oh, we've lost a few girls over the years, changing jobs or leaving to get married. But Caroline . . . She's a nice, hard-working girl. And she don't chatter on all the time like some of them.'

Mrs Treedy didn't appear to be listening, peering out of the window as her son ran after the three girls trudging up the snowy hill. 'My Jack quite likes that new girl. Jamaican, isn't she?'

'No, from Liverpool. But her mother comes from Trinidad, if that's what you mean.'

Mrs Treedy looked uncomfortable. 'I haven't spoken to her much. But Jack's got a crush on the girl, if you ask me.'

'Are you hoping he might stay in Porthcurno if she gives him any encouragement?'

'The thought had crossed my mind.'

Sheila made a face but said nothing. She rather thought that Grace was too thick with Caroline to look twice at Jack Treedy. That wasn't any of her business, though. 'Well, it's getting dark. I'll start tidying away and when Joe gets back, I'll close up the shop until tomorrow. There are still plenty of canned goods here. Anyone still needing food can come by in the morning.' She turned to her sister. 'Maggie, are you sure you don't want to come up the farm? It's awfully cold down here.'

She had asked Margaret up to stay with them during the worst of the snow and been rebuffed. Her sister valued her independence too much, she supposed. Besides, she and Violet had never got on, so keeping them apart was probably for the best.

To her surprise though, Margaret nodded. 'I will come with you tonight, Sheila. I'm sick of the electric heater cutting out when the electric goes off . . . Anyway, I can help carry some of this. Don't forget you need to take your own rations up to the farm for Violet. And a bag of animal feed for Joe's livestock.'

Mrs Treedy made an unhappy noise, and they turned to see Jack waiting outside the shop for his mother, shoulders hunched and his hands in his pockets. No doubt Grace had sent him packing yet again.

It was a shame for the poor boy. But a good lesson too. Some things in life were simply impossible and you had to learn to let them go, Sheila thought, glancing at his flushed face. She kept this nugget of wisdom to herself though, having also learned that people didn't always want to hear the truth. Not when a little white lie made them feel better. Or even a great big whopper.

CHAPTER TWENTY-TWO

'Finally!' Selina threw aside her lap blanket and rushed into the hall at the sight of the postie doggedly battling the sludge of thawing snow to reach the steps of Thornton Hall. Only the day before, the groundsman and his boy Walter had finally been able to dig out a path for vehicles to reach the hall from the main road, which had apparently been gritted by the local council, though snow still lay in thick drifts on the verges.

Looking half-frozen, the postie thrust a bunch of envelopes into her hand, touched his cap with a muttered word of greeting, and turned back to his van.

'Can I offer you a hot drink before you go, John?' she called after him.

'Very kind, Miss, but no thank you. I've a dozen properties yet to reach before dark.' He grinned. 'Thaw's setting in though, thank goodness.'

'Yes, a blessing.'

She watched until he'd successfully turned his van in the wet snow, then hurried inside to pull off her wellies again, her gloved hands already numb with cold.

She imagined that Mrs Hawley, who had not been able to reach the hall since early in the new year, when snow had begun to fall in earnest, would soon be back at work. Since the first week of the year, Bodmin Moor had been blanketed in white – a beautiful sight but chilling too. Thankfully, the housekeeper had struggled to the telephone at the village stores and called to apologise, and also to direct Selina towards stores of food in their various pantries and larder, to keep them going through the cold snap.

'Don't worry, Aunt Selly . . . I can always take Father's hunting gun out and shoot some rabbits for the pot,' Peter had told her on hearing they would need to be frugal with their meals. 'And Jemima can skin them, if I show her how.'

'I'll do no such thing,' his sister had exclaimed with a shudder, while little Faith copied her, both girls pulling disgusted faces.

Selina had chuckled. 'Thank you, Peter, and I'll bear that in mind,' she'd told the boy fondly. She knew he was trying his best to be the man of the house.

The groundsman and his son lived in a cottage on the estate, of course, and had soon made themselves useful, dragging a cart of logs and kindling up to the great house to keep the range lit and at least one downstairs fire burning all day, earning them Selina's heartfelt gratitude and a hot mince pie apiece. She thought their own stores must be quite low, although she had seen young Walter heading out with a dog and rifle before, and rather suspected the boy to be a dab hand at rabbiting himself.

Most of the post bundle turned out to be Christmas cards, held back due to the snow and only now being delivered. But among these she found a letter from Caroline, and retreated to her cosy fireside seat, blanket over her knees, to catch up on gossip from the farm.

Having spent several winters working as a Land Girl at Postbridge Farm, Selina knew how grim it could get at this time of year . . . Pitch-black mornings, water frozen solid in the animal troughs, the windows and attic skylights frosted over. But there would also be beautiful, ice-frilled cobwebs on gates and fences, dazzling white fields begging for someone to sink their boots deep into them, and a chance to slip and slide over frozen puddles on the lane down to the village.

Caroline's letter made her sit up though, concerned. Among her anecdotes about Tilly finding a rat frozen to a drainpipe, and Joe losing his pipe when it fell into a snow drift, was news that dear old Barney, the farm's loveable shire horse, had died, and Caro was having 'a wretched time of it'. It also seemed that Caro and Grace had been forced to spend Christmas in Penzance, and from the letter's despondent tone she guessed something had happened there to cause an upset between the two young women. She only wished she could be on hand to give her friend comfort.

The final paragraph made her smile, at least. There'd been a food drop to the snowbound village, apparently coordinated by Violet Postbridge's mum, Mrs Newton. It all sounded rather dramatic and she was sorry to have missed it. But Caroline's description of the eccentric old shopkeeper stomping about in wellies, organising a human chain and the distribution of food parcels, left her chuckling.

One of the other envelopes was more official-looking. Tearing it open, Selina discovered that her driving test had been cancelled and would need to be rearranged for spring.

‘Good news,’ she muttered. She’d been worried about the prospect of her test, having had little opportunity so far to drive on a regular basis.

There was a knock at the door, and Peter stuck his head around. ‘Aunt Selly, may I help Mr Underhill and his son dig out the coal bunker? We gave up at the last attempt. But now the snow’s thawing, Walter says we should easily reach it this time.’

‘Of course, but stay warm. The last thing we need is for you to catch pneumonia.’

Already winding a thick brown scarf about his neck, her nephew nodded, unsmiling, and took himself off to help the groundsman and his boy.

Selina sat listening to his footsteps dwindle, and wished she knew how to get the boy out of his doldrums. Like Caroline, her nephew was struggling with this wintry weather, but also some deeper issue . . . Could Helen Bourne be right when she’d said his misery was down to this having been his first Christmas without his mother? In which case, perhaps it was simply a matter of waiting. This thaw and the brighter weather might give Peter a fresh zest for life, better suited to a boy his age than constant low spirits.

On impulse, Selina drew out a sheet of writing paper, and found pen and ink. Sitting at the desk, still wrapped in a blanket, she penned a reply to Caroline’s letter, commiserating over the horse’s death, laughing at Tilly and Joe, but also touching tentatively on her own problems over Christmas. She couldn’t help Caroline get through this bad patch, being miles away on Bodmin Moor, but she could perhaps reassure her friend that she wasn’t alone in having a complicated life . . .

'Aunt Selly, Aunt Selly . . .' Faith came dashing into the room just as she finished writing her letter. The little girl's face was pink with excitement. 'Can we go outside too? Pwease say yes.'

Jemima had followed her, her look one of entreaty. 'I've learned all my French and Faith has finished tracing her alphabet. Please may we put on our coats and watch Peter dig out the coal bunker?'

Selina smiled indulgently at the two girls. 'All right,' she agreed, 'but only if you wrap up in coats and scarves. Understand?'

The two girls dashed away, giggling and hugging each other. Putting away her letter, Selina went after them. Somebody would need to supervise their outdoor activities, and that somebody could hardly be Nancy, who was looking wan and weary these days, her pregnancy now quite advanced.

She found the girls by the back door, pulling on their coats and boots. Nancy was there too, helping Faith with her woollen mittens.

'I'll walk with them, Nancy,' Selina assured her with a smile. 'You shouldn't be going outside in this cold weather. Not in your condition.'

Adjusting her woolly hat, Jemima looked round at them curiously. 'What condition?'

Selina bit her lip, throwing a look of chagrin at Nancy, who blenched.

'I haven't been well lately, that's all your aunt means,' Nancy explained, reaching for a scarf. She gave Selina a smile. 'We won't stay outside too long.'

As quickly as she could, Selina dragged on her own coat

and boots, making sure to grab gloves on her way out too. 'Would you like to make a snowman?' she asked Faith, tucking the little girl's hand into hers.

Faith nodded enthusiastically. 'Yes, please!'

But they'd barely crossed the lawn when a snowball struck Jemima in the chest. She glared at her brother, who was leaning on his spade beside the coal bunker. 'You meanie!' Bending to the thawing snow, she seized great fistfuls of slush and patted them into a large wet snowball, which she threw at her brother.

Luckily for Peter, her aim was not particularly accurate. It missed him by several feet. But she was already bending to make another snowball as he stood laughing . . .

Nancy grinned, a pink tinge to her cheeks. 'Time for a snowball battle?' she asked Selina shyly.

Selina chuckled. 'Why not? At the rate the weather's warming up, I doubt there'll be much snow left soon.'

Despite her growing tummy, Nancy stooped for a handful of slushy snow too. Sometimes, it was easy to forget that Nancy was still very young. Only a few years ago, she would have been a schoolgirl. Perhaps it was simply boredom and a lack of friends her own age that was making the young woman so miserable, rather than fear for the future. As for Peter . . . Well, a snowball fight might be just the thing to cheer him up. At least for today.

A snowball thudded into the side of her head, cold and icy, and she shrieked.

'Sorry, Aunt Selly . . . I was aiming for Jemima.' Peter grinned, his look mischievous.

'Now, why don't I believe you?' Selina demanded, breathless and laughing as she scraped wet snow off the side of her face. 'Wretched boy . . . But you'll soon be sorry.' And she too bent to make a snowball.

As Selina had predicted, the snow continued to melt as the days slid into February, but slowly on the high moors. She and Nancy sat glued to the wireless as though it were still wartime, listening for the latest bulletins. Food supplies had become critical. The usual winter vegetables had rotted in the soil and later plantings were still not ready for harvest. Mr Underhill lopped down the occasional tree and chopped it up for firewood in the absence of coal. But the winter wonderland was gradually receding, and the postie soon came up the drive again with another clutch of letters, including a swift reply from Caroline to her own letter.

Things at Postbridge Farm had become desperate during the worst of the January snows, Caroline wrote. Joe had lost over two-thirds of the flock and all but one of his three dairy cows. They'd even taken to keeping the chickens in the kitchen porch overnight to avoid any more birds freezing to their perches in the coop. Meanwhile, the soil had been too cold and wet for tilling and sowing until early February, when the Land Girls had been forced to do almost an entire month's work in a single week to get the spring crops into the ground.

'Poor things,' Selina muttered, showing the letter to Nancy. 'I wish I could be there to lend a hand . . . Though, to be honest, I'm glad I'm not a Land Girl anymore. It sounds awful.'

William MacGregor telephoned at regular intervals to check on her and the children, and to make sure they had everything they needed. Once or twice, he even managed to reach the house by car, bringing much-needed provisions, though she always begged him not to make the attempt again whenever he left.

Twice during February she sent a note and some food over to Helen Bourne with the groundsman, to ask if she needed help or would like to stay at Thornton Hall with them, acutely aware of her neighbour's remote location.

The first time, she received a polite note from Helen in return, rejecting both the food and the offer of company as unnecessary, but thanking her for the kind thought. The second time, Mr Underhill returned to say the house was in darkness and nobody had answered the door. No doubt Helen had gone to stay with friends, Selina thought, which seemed eminently sensible, given the tough conditions out there on the moor.

One morning in early March, the day dawned with a cold, bright sunshine that heralded spring, and indeed she'd seen snowdrops peeking out of the icy ground outside her window for several days now, a sure sign that the world would soon emerge from its long, hard winter. Sitting with the children after breakfast, she heard a car engine chugging up the high-sided, narrow track, and hurried outside in her coat to see who it was.

Her heart leapt when she recognised William's black Wolseley, and she bit her lip, surprised by her own elation.

'Hullo, how are you?' William asked, coming up the steps. He stripped off his driving gloves before shaking her hand. 'This sunshine is very welcome, isn't it? I'm sorry I haven't telephoned for a while. It's been a hellish week.'

She assured him that it didn't matter and that she was

very well, but noticed how he avoided her gaze as he shrugged out of his coat too.

'How are the girls?' he asked, peering down the hall. 'And young Peter?'

She didn't need to answer that: the three children came dashing down the hall to greet him, also excited to have a visitor at last. With a smile, Selina slipped away to pour their guest a small brandy, for he was looking chilled.

Once the girls had been scooped up by Nancy and taken away to the kitchen, while Peter went outside to admire the Wolseley, Selina and William sat warming themselves by the fire.

'Those are fine logs,' he remarked, glancing at the hearthside basket. 'I'm glad you've not been suffering during this shortage of coal. I was worried.'

'We heard on the wireless a few days ago that the shortage is over and fresh deliveries should soon be on their way.'

'Yes, the government finally found a way to dig all the frozen coal out of the snow and distribute it,' he said, almost savagely, and knocked back the last drop of brandy. 'About bloody time too.'

'I imagine they tried their best,' she said mildly, surprised by his grim mood.

William made an angry noise under his breath. 'Yes, of course . . . And I wonder how many people died while they were *trying their best*?'

Selina swallowed, knitting her hands together in her lap, unsure what to say. William had always been such a cheerful, polite soul, barely a harsh word to say about anyone. She had never seen him like this.

He caught her wary expression and grimaced. 'I'm sorry,'

he muttered. 'It's just . . . Oh, damn it, I can't keep the truth from you any longer. The fact is, Helen Bourne is dead.'

Selina sucked in her breath, horrified. '*What*?' She shook her head, instinctively denying it. 'No, that's not possible. I was only in touch with her recently. I sent a note over with Mr Underhill and . . . He said the house was empty. I thought she must have given up and gone to stay with friends in Bodmin. Maybe John and Deirdre Knowles . . .' She searched his face. 'Please don't tell me that . . .' She couldn't finish, the words dying in her throat.

He reached across and took her hand. 'She never left Bourne Cottage. I'm sorry.'

Selina felt awful. She'd disliked the woman, not just for the hurt she'd inflicted on Bella but for her spitefulness and cold way of speaking. But she had still been a human being.

'When . . . When did she die?' she whispered, worrying that Peter might overhear. She could hear him in the porch, knocking snow off his shoes.

'Maybe ten days ago.'

She was aghast. '*Ten days*?'

'The doctor's not sure of the exact timing. There'll be an inquest, of course. But not for a while.' He looked wretched. 'So many people have died this winter, there's a backlog.'

'Was it the cold? Did she . . . freeze to death?' Selina felt guilt gnaw at her, wishing she'd insisted on Helen coming to them at the hall.

He hesitated, then said reluctantly, 'I suppose it will come out at the inquest. The thing is, Helen had been on medication since her brother left. Low mood, couldn't sleep, aches and pains all over . . .'

'I wish I'd known,' Selina groaned.

'Doctor Ford hadn't heard from her in a while, so he drove out there.' His face was grim. 'The house was dark, but the kitchen door was unlocked. He found Helen upstairs in bed. Been dead for days, he said. It wasn't the cold, though. She'd taken an overdose.'

'Oh God!' She jumped up, pacing the room, consumed by guilt. 'When she sent back that note with Mr Underhill the first time, insisting she was fine, I ought to have walked over there myself, *forced her* to come back with me.'

'And risked your life in the snow?' He shook his head. 'Besides, she would have refused to leave the cottage, and you know it. Helen Bourne was a damn prickly woman who never got on with anyone except her brother, and even he deserted her in the end.'

'Does Cameron know?'

William nodded, also getting to his feet. 'He'll attend the inquest, I'm told.' He hesitated. 'I could be doing the fellow an injustice, but it doesn't sound like he's grief-stricken over his sister's death. In fact, I believe he's already asked how soon the house can be put on the market. I'm sorry,' he finished roughly. 'I know you and Cameron were close once—'

'I was never close to Cameron,' she insisted, the two of them standing close, looking into each other's eyes. 'I thought he was someone different, that's all. Once I realised the truth, I never wanted to speak to him again. He's a dreadful, dreadful man.' Her voice shook. 'And I didn't much like Helen. She only seemed to wish ill on me and my family. I walked over to see her on Boxing Day, you know, and she more or less threw me out of the house.' She grimaced, recalling that last unpleasant meeting with Helen. 'But I'm sorry for her. To die alone like that . . .' She choked, unable to go on.

William pulled her towards him with gentle hands. Selina didn't resist, and when he kissed her, she closed her eyes almost gratefully, pushing aside the horror of Helen's death.

But the kiss soon deepened, becoming passionate, and her head began to swim . . .

'William, I can't. The children . . .' She shook her head and he drew back at once, a strange intensity in his face. 'I'm sorry.'

'No, it was my fault. To tell you such a hard thing and then expect—' He headed brusquely out of the room, buttoning his jacket. 'Look, I brought a food hamper and a case of lemonade for the kids. I'll fetch them from the car. I initially thought maybe a spring picnic . . . But I doubt you'll be in the mood now. And it's probably still too cold.'

'A food hamper? How marvellous you are . . . We're nearly out of everything.' She shook off the desire in her veins, struggling to come back to earth as quickly as he'd done. 'And a spring picnic would be wonderful. The children have been stuck indoors for weeks and this is the first sunny day we've had since . . . Oh, I can't even remember. Thank you so much, William.'

'You're welcome, my dear.' And his smile seemed to say he understood why she kept drawing back from intimacy, and didn't mind a jot.

Selina was glad, but only wished she could understand it too.

CHAPTER TWENTY-THREE

'Oh, this blasted rain . . . I thought spring was supposed to bring nicer weather?' Washing up her lunch plate, Caroline peered out of the kitchen window at leaden skies. She and the other two Land Girls had come back sodden and miserable, after a long, dreary morning spent digging out the remains of mushy potatoes that had rotted in the snows, and were facing more of the same that afternoon.

The telephone rang in the snug, answered promptly by Mrs Postbridge, and Caroline glanced round at Tilly and Grace in surprise. 'Who on earth can that be?'

Mrs Postbridge came hurrying in a moment later, followed by Joe, both looking shocked. 'That was my mum ringing from the village,' she told the girls breathlessly. 'She says the river's burst its banks and poor Mr Carstairs' cottage is already flooded.'

Joe was shrugging into his raincoat again. 'I knew this would happen,' he rumbled, slapping his wet cap back on too. 'All that snow . . . It had to go somewhere after it melted. I'd best get straight down there, see what I can do to help.'

'Mum says to take the tractor,' his wife told him anxiously. 'And any spare sacking you've got. They're making sandbags.'

He nodded to the three Land Girls. 'Follow me down to the village, quick as you can. We'll need all hands on deck to shore up them old cottages along the riverbank.'

And with that, he hurried out of the farmhouse.

Caroline dragged her sodden wellies back on, uneasiness in the pit of her stomach. 'That little stream? It's hardly *a river*. How can it possibly flood the village?'

'You heard Joe,' Tilly muttered. 'The snow must have melted, higher up the valley . . . I did notice it was looking swollen the other day. And it's been raining hard for several days.'

Grace pulled on her coat and hat. 'First all that snow, then rain, now floods . . . What's next, eh?' she demanded, shaking her head. 'A plague of locusts?'

'I'm sure it's not as bad as it sounds.' Caroline reached out to reassure her friend, but Grace flinched away before she could make contact. Bitter hurt flashed through her. What had gone wrong between them? She wished she understood Grace's bewildering change of heart.

Joe and his tractor were already out of sight by the time they started off down the steep hill together, the track slippery and running with water, much of it still icy and laced with mud.

Down in the village, they found Mrs Newton bustling about outside the village shop in the rain, organising the filling of sacks with sandy grit. A small group of village men were already engaged in this task when the Land Girls joined them. Joe stopped to shake hands with a few of the villagers, former soldiers recently returned from Germany. From what

Caroline overheard, the farmer had employed them as labourers before the war, and was asking if they were in work yet. Joe had once or twice mentioned intending to employ men about the farm. But everything had stopped during the winter snows. Now spring had come, he would soon swing back into tilling and planting again, with a thousand other jobs needing to be done about the farm before summer.

Caroline had been worrying that all three Land Girls would be ousted, replaced by male farmhands, and her eavesdropping did nothing to allay those fears. It was a grim thought, and not least because so much remained unresolved between her and Grace. She would hate to leave Postbridge Farm without ever discovering why her friend had turned cold after their one and only night together. It was hard not to worry that, in her inexperience, Caroline had somehow done something dreadfully wrong . . .

'Thank you for coming, girls,' Mrs Newton called out huskily. 'Now grab a spade and start shovelling!'

Using the spades Joe had brought down from the farm, the girls dutifully bent to the back-breaking work of shovelling sandy grit into sacks to act as a barrier against the floods.

'Natural leader, isn't she?' Tilly remarked admiringly.

'Who? Mrs Newton?' Grace raised her brows. 'You mean she's a born bossyboots.' But she was smiling.

'No, she *likes* helping people, and sometimes the best way to achieve that is to take charge,' Tilly insisted. 'Don't forget, Mrs Newton lost her eldest daughter in the Blitz, and probably still blames herself for not being there to help her. If you ask me, that's why she's always first to muck in when there's an emergency. Not just to be helpful, but to . . . to make up for not being able to save her daughter,' she ended in a rush.

Caroline glanced at Tilly, impressed by the younger girl's logic. 'I'd never thought of it like that,' she admitted, leaning on her spade for a breather. 'But you're right, Mrs Newton is always first to help out. And she does often mention having lost her daughter in the war. Betsy, wasn't it? Lily and Alice's mum.' She bent to her work again. 'How did you figure that out?'

With a shy smile, Tilly whispered, 'I've been reading a library book on psychology, about why people choose to do things a certain way . . . I can't say I understand all of it. But it's awfully fascinating.'

As though to prove a point, Mrs Newton came stomping towards them through the deep puddles and driving rain, her hat soggy and bedraggled. 'Girls, you're doing a grand job, but the men can finish them sandbags quicker. Joe needs a hand near the river, where the flooding's worse. He's taking planks down there on the tractor, and you're to shore up the cottage doors with them. Can you manage that?'

'Yes, Mrs Newton,' the three girls chorused, wiping rain from their faces as they handed their spades to waiting village lads and trudged after Joe in his tractor.

Caroline grimaced, peering ahead as they waded through dirty water almost up to the tops of their wellies. 'I wonder how much deeper it's going to get.'

Tilly gave a little shriek. 'Oh, crikey . . . The water's gone in my boot.'

Grace said nothing, trudging along with her head bent, hands in her coat pockets. Of course, the heavy rain was enough to make anyone miserable, Caroline thought, but watched her in concern, hoping she was okay. Surely nothing could be so bad that they couldn't even discuss it? If only Grace would open up and talk to her . . .

Joe had deposited the planks on a wall beside the last few cottages. 'Not sure how much good this will do,' he shouted above the noise of rain drumming on the rooftops. 'But maybe we can stop more water getting in.'

Briefly, he directed them to wedge the planks across the front doors of the cottages, using heavy stones and plant pots to hold them in place. It was clear that some water had already entered the properties, but given how quickly the water seemed to be rising, Caroline agreed that it was worth trying to save them from worse flooding.

An old gent came hobbling out of his cottage, bent double over a walking stick. The bottoms of his trousers had been tied up with twine and tucked into wellies, but he still looked sodden. 'My kitchen's flooded,' he told them unhappily.

Joe checked he was unhurt, and then helped him up onto the tractor. 'I'm taking Mr Faragher back to the shop,' he told Caroline. 'He's wet through and Mrs Newton has a good supply of dry clothes. You'd all best head back as soon as you're done. I don't like the look of this.'

Tilly and Grace were further down the lane, struggling to secure a plank across a doorway. 'I'll tell the others,' Caroline promised him as he left, and then waded through muddy water to the last cottage. 'Joe says we need to leave,' she told the girls urgently. But they were both staring in the opposite direction. 'What is it?'

'That's Mrs Dymock's dog!' Tilly exclaimed, and now Caroline could see the familiar golden Labrador in the swollen river, swimming laboriously against the current. 'Oh no, poor thing . . .'

Miraculously, the dog struggled to the bank and clambered out of the river on his own. Seeing the girls, he barked and splashed towards them, causing ripples in the knee-high flood.

'There, there, soggy old dog. You're safe now.' Grace bent to pat the dog's head, and squinted across the river to Mrs Dymock's thatched, whitewashed cottage. 'I don't believe she would have left her dog behind to drown. Do you think she could still be in there?'

Anxiously, Caroline repeated what Joe had told her about them getting straight back to the shop.

'Yes, but I bet he didn't know Mrs Dymock might not have got out.' Grace shook her head. 'If there's even a chance the old lady is still in that cottage, we have to rescue her.'

Tilly looked unenthusiastic but nodded. 'We ought to check, at least.'

There was a footbridge further along the river. But, to their dismay, the water was already in full flow over it. The Labrador dug his heels, refusing to follow them any further. Scrambling up onto a grassy bank instead, the dog stood there, merely wagging his tail apologetically when Caroline called him down.

'Oh, leave him,' Tilly said, shivering.

Thankfully, the water flooding the bridge wasn't more than knee-high. But the current was forceful. Tilly stumbled several times, getting thoroughly soaked, and Caroline was almost knocked off her feet too. 'Honestly, we should go back and get Joe,' she gasped, clutching Grace for support. 'This isn't safe.'

'I know, but look!' Grace nodded to the cottage, where Caroline could now see a face at an upstairs window. 'I knew it . . . That's Mrs Dymock. She must be cut off by the water. We haven't got time to go back, Caro. Let's get her out first.'

Caroline was anxious for the old lady. 'Yes, all right. But how can we get her back across the bridge? She's eighty, at least. We can't ask her to wade through all this icy water.'

'I'll carry her,' Grace told her, grinning. 'Piggyback-style.'

But when they reached the cottage, Mrs Dymock flatly refused to ride piggyback on Grace's back. 'I'm staying here, thank you,' she said with dignity, leaning out of the upstairs window. 'You girls should go back while you still can. The ground floor may be flooded, but I doubt the water will reach me up here.'

Tilly was shaking violently, her teeth chattering. 'Gosh, this water is so cold. I . . . I wish I could get warm. Can't we go inside?'

'We can't risk opening the front door of the cottage,' Caroline pointed out unhappily, 'it would only make the water inside rise higher.' She rubbed Tilly's arms to warm her up, and then gave her a quick hug. 'Maybe Mrs Dymock's right and we should go back.' She turned her gaze to Grace, silently urging her to agree. But Grace was deep in thought.

'There's a flat roof over the kitchen, with a window into my spare room,' Mrs Dymock called down helpfully. 'You can climb up there if you want to get out of the water. I'll go and open the window for you.'

'Oh, yes please,' Tilly moaned, very pale now.

Grace looked up into the driving rain, frustrated. 'We

need to get the old lady out of here,' she whispered to Caroline. 'If this water rises any further . . .' She left the words unspoken.

'But you heard her.' Caroline's nerves were at full strain. 'She won't budge, and I don't think Tilly's strong enough to go back across that blasted bridge. What else can we do?'

'You stay here and look after Tilly and Mrs Dymock,' Grace said decisively. 'I'm going back to get help. Though not by the road. I bet it's quicker cross-country.' She pointed across the wet fields to where a few village roofs could be seen through the rain mist. 'That way.'

Before Caroline could stop her, Grace had already set off, splashing briskly through the knee-high water. 'Oh, do be careful!' she called after her, but her voice was drowned out by the rushing river.

It was almost an hour later when Caroline, sitting with Tilly and Mrs Dymock, finally heard the tractor engine and leapt up. 'Thank goodness,' she gasped. She'd begun to fear Grace had lost her way and come to grief in the waterlogged fields. But when she poked her head out of the window, seeing Joe jump down from his tractor on the other side of the footbridge, there was no sign of Grace with him. No doubt she'd sensibly stayed at the village shop to dry off.

'The water's gone down a little,' she told the farmer, 'so I think you can risk carrying Mrs Dymock out of the front door.'

Joe took Mrs Dymock safely across to the tractor and returned for Tilly, who was still too cold and shaky to walk. 'Where's Grace?' he asked, frowning.

'Didn't she send you to find us?' Caroline asked, her heart stuttering with fear. 'She set off for the village over an hour ago.'

Joe shook his head, looking grave. 'That old dog of Mrs Dymock's turned up at the shop without her, so Mrs Newton sent me to check on her.' He carried Tilly across the flooded bridge with difficulty, wading through the strong current, with Caroline following close behind. 'I've not seen hide nor hair of Grace.'

'But where can she be? Oh God, she must have lost her way crossing the fields, or . . . or . . .' Unable to finish such an impossible thought, Caroline pointed out the way Grace had taken across the fields. 'It'll be dark in a few hours. We have to look for her.'

'And we shall. First, hop into the trailer, and we'll take these two back to the shop to get warm and dry,' Joe told her. 'Once they're safe, I'll bring men and dogs back to search for Grace.'

'I want to help,' Caroline pleaded.

'No, you should stay with Tilly and Mrs Dymock at the shop,' Joe said stubbornly, helping her climb into the trailer. 'No point you getting cold and wet too. Don't fret now . . . We'll find Grace.'

Caroline felt sick with fear. She wanted to go with him, convinced they wouldn't find Grace without her help. Yet she was so terrified of stumbling across Grace's lifeless body, drowned in the icy waters, it was almost a relief to accept his decision and wait with the others at the shop. Besides, Tilly needed her support. The poor girl looked quite exhausted.

* * *

Back at the village shop, Caroline saw Tilly and Mrs Dymock comfortably installed in the upstairs flat. Looking rather woebegone, they sat huddled together on the sofa in front of a two-bar heater, wrapped in blankets and warming themselves with hot cocoa prepared by Margaret. Caroline couldn't bring herself to sit down even for a minute though, pacing back and forth under an old coat that Mrs Newton had flung about her shoulders, her ears straining for the sound of the tractor returning. At last, she heard a muffled shout and dashed back downstairs, throwing open the shop door. A dark figure emerged from the rain, cradling something in his arms.

'Grace,' she choked, tears running down her cheek. 'Oh, Mr Postbridge . . . Please say she's still alive.'

'Of course she's alive, love,' he reassured her, but with concern etched on his features. 'And she'll be fine, mark my words, so long as we get her up to the farm as quick as possible, and into a warm bed with a hot toddy. But first, some blankets to dry her off would be a good idea.'

Grace lay huddled in his arms, limp and wet, her eyes closed. She'd lost her hat and her clothes were dripping, her beautiful hair bedraggled.

'I'm here, Grace. Please try to . . . to hang on,' Caroline gasped, fearful and broken-hearted as she draped her own blanket over Grace. 'What can I do to help?' she begged as Mrs Newton hurried forward with more blankets and a thick towel to dry her face and hair.

'Run up to the farm,' Mrs Newton told her firmly. 'Tell Violet to run the girl a hot bath and warm some brandy for her. Hurry now!'

Caroline thudded up the muddy track to the farm,

slipping in her haste, terrified that her friend would die before they could get her back to safety, that she would never have a chance to tell Grace how much she cared . . .

How much she loved her, in fact.

Tilly peeked around the door of the attic bedroom and shook her head. 'Caro, you look exhausted,' she whispered, since Grace was still sleeping. 'It's gone midnight, why don't you get to bed? The doctor said she'd be fine, so you really don't need to sit with her.'

But Caroline refused, still too emotional to leave Grace's side. 'I'm fine here, honestly.' She usually shared with Tilly but had decided to move into Grace's room for the night. 'How are you?'

'Much better, thanks. That hot brandy tasted awful, but it worked wonders.' Tilly eyed her, concerned. 'I say, have you been crying?'

Caroline drew herself up, instantly wary. 'Of course not.'

But Tilly wasn't so easily deterred. She sat on the end of Grace's bed, peering into Caroline's averted face. 'What's the matter? Come on . . . I know I'm miles younger than you, but I can keep a secret.'

After such a terrible day, Caroline was tempted to pour out her feelings. But it was time she grew up and stopped wearing her heart on her sleeve. 'You're a sweet girl, Tilly, but this is private.'

'I'm not blind, you know.' Tilly gave her a lopsided smile. 'You and Grace are . . .' She pulled a face. '*Good friends*, isn't that the common phrase?'

Caroline froze, hardly daring to breathe.

'Look, if it makes you feel better, I'm dating Benny now,

but . . .' Tilly blushed. 'I once had a secret pash for a girl at school.'

'This isn't a schoolgirl *passion*,' Caroline choked, abruptly losing her stiffness. 'I love her.'

'Of course you do,' Tilly agreed, stealing a hurried look at the sleeping girl between them. 'But does Grace feel the same?' she whispered. 'Does she love you too, I mean?'

'I thought she did. But I was wrong.' She knew a moment of panic. 'Tilly, you won't repeat any of this, will you? Because it's top secret.'

'I understand . . . Mum's the word.' Tilly yawned behind her hand, getting up again. 'Gosh, I'm bushed. What a day! Time for bed for me. I think it's jolly romantic, though.' She started humming a popular tune from the wireless. 'You and Grace, two hearts beating as one . . . Like Cathy and Heathcliff.'

'Tilly, please!' Caroline hissed. 'Someone will hear you.'

'Sorry.' Tilly went away with an irrepressible chuckle, and Caroline rose to make up the spare bed, moving quiet as a mouse, not wanting to disturb her friend. All the same, when she tiptoed back to turn out the lamp, she saw that Grace had opened her eyes and was watching her.

'Oh, thank goodness, you're awake. No, don't try to get up. Do you want some water?' Caroline helped Grace sit up against the pillows. 'How are you feeling?'

'Like I could sleep for a week.' Grace was blinking at her surroundings. 'What . . . What happened? I don't remember coming to bed.'

'Joe carried you up here.' Caroline drew a chair to the bed, explaining briefly how she'd been found in a waterlogged field and brought back up to the farm. 'You were unconscious when they found you. Half-drowned, in fact. Mrs Postbridge gave you hot brandy with honey, and rang the doctor. He said to let you sleep, and he'll give you a proper check-over tomorrow.' She offered Grace a few sips of water, and gently brushed the hair back from her forehead. 'Do you remember what happened?'

'Yes . . .' Grace closed her eyes, frowning. 'I tried cutting through the field to the village. Only, the water was even deeper there. It got so cold, I couldn't go on. I tried to turn back, but I must have fallen, because I don't remember much after that.'

Caroline struggled against fresh tears. 'We nearly lost you,' she whispered, holding on to her self-control with difficulty. 'I thought I *had* lost you.'

'I'm sorry. It was stupid of me. I wanted to prove myself, I suppose . . . I didn't want to let you down.'

'Oh, Grace . . .' Caroline gave a broken laugh. 'You could never let me down.'

'But I did, didn't I? And I let Tilly and Mrs Dymock down too. You must have been waiting for ages . . .' Grace's lip trembled as she too fought tears. 'I caused everyone so much trouble.'

'Nobody's upset with you.'

'And I was so horrible to you after Penzance too . . . I could see you were hurting. But I couldn't stop.'

'We can talk about this later.'

'No, this is important.' Grace gulped. 'I nearly drowned today, acting like an idiot, and I know why. Because I've been so . . . so *miserable*.' She sought Caroline's gaze, her face intense. 'I love you,' she blurted out. 'I wanted to tell you that night at Lily's. Only I didn't dare.'

Caroline's eyes widened, fixing on her beloved's face. Her

heart thumped wildly. Grace *loved her*? Then the rest of what she'd said filtered through to her whirling brain . . .

'Didn't dare? I don't understand.'

'That's because I haven't told you everything,' Grace whispered. 'You see, you're not my first girlfriend. I met someone at the last farm where I was working and we fell in love. Head over heels, we were. There was a boy at the farm who fancied me too. I told him I wasn't interested, but he still followed me everywhere. One day, he . . . he caught us together and told everyone what he'd seen.' A tear trickled down her cheek. 'For weeks, nobody would speak to us. It was so awful.'

'Oh, darling.' Caroline's heart clenched in pain.

'In the end, the farmer told us to leave. My girlfriend went home to her family, said she never wanted to see me again, and I . . . I came to Cornwall, somewhere nobody knew about me.' Grace touched her cheek. 'I promised myself I'd never let myself have feelings for another girl again. But I couldn't stop looking at you . . . And then, in Penzance, I knew it was too late. I was already in love with you.' Her voice shook and she began to tremble. 'Will you hold me, Caroline? I know I don't deserve it, but just for tonight?'

'Of course I will.' Turning off the light, Caroline climbed under the blankets with her, and they held each other tight. Now that she understood why Grace had been so stand-offish after Penzance, her heart was full to bursting. There were no words for what she was feeling, she thought. Or maybe four words, at least.

'I love you too,' she whispered, and closed her eyes.

CHAPTER TWENTY-FOUR

Watching shoppers hurry past in the bright spring sunshine, Selina finished her toasted scone and pushed aside her now empty cup of tea. Her glance flicked back to the large wall clock. There was a hollow feeling in the pit of her stomach, but she couldn't delay things any longer. 'We'd better pay the bill and leave,' she told William, who was sitting opposite, regarding her with an indulgent smile. 'And you can stop looking like that. I'm not being silly. It's perfectly possible that I'll fail my driving test, and where shall I be then?'

'Grounded,' William said bluntly, but shook his head. 'It's not going to happen. You've had plenty of practice and you're a wonderfully confident driver. All you need do is answer the questions put to you, and show the examiner what you can do on the road. In fact, the only way you could possibly fail your test would be through nerves.' He touched her hand. 'So *don't* be nervous.'

'Easy for you to say,' she retorted. 'You don't even need to take a test.'

He grinned. 'Yes, rather a stroke of luck, the new Road

Traffic Act only applying to those who started driving from April '34 onwards. I'd been driving over a year by then, so I'm well in the clear. Whereas you . . .'

'Have to undergo the rigour of a proper examination. Yes, I know how *unlucky* I am, trust me.' Selina opened her purse, but he shook his head, taking out his wallet and summoning the waitress. 'You're not paying again, are you, William? It's really too bad.'

'Estate business,' he insisted.

She laughed. 'How can having tea and cake with me before my driving test be considered *estate business*?'

'You need a full driving licence,' he said carefully, as though making an argument in court, 'in order to take proper care of your nieces and nephew, and I am here solely to support you in that worthy endeavour. Thus far, we are speaking of estate business, and no fair-minded person could suggest otherwise.'

'Oh, very well. When you put it like that . . .' Pulling on her driving gloves, Selina realised that her hands were trembling, and caught his ironic look. 'Honestly, I'll be fine once I'm behind the wheel,' she snapped. 'It's the questions on the Highway Code that worry me. I read that damn booklet from cover to cover last night, and yet this morning I swear I could barely remember a thing.'

'Pure nerves.' Steering her out of the tea rooms on Fore Street, William walked up the hill with her towards the test station. 'The information will come back to you when you need it,' he said reassuringly.

She hoped he was right. But the sunshine was lifting her spirits, at least. It was a gorgeous spring day, the sort of bright dancing weather that made Selina doubt whether it had ever snowed at all. Yet it was only a fortnight since the last grey vestiges of winter had finally melted away, leaving a fresh spring landscape bathed in sunshine, spring flowers everywhere and lambs in the field.

She was grimly thankful she had not been required to take her driving test during the snow. Even on a sunny day like this, though, she would need to focus hard on not making foolish mistakes during the examination. She had been known, after all, to take the odd corner rather too fast, and once had nearly struck an oncoming vehicle in her attempt to avoid a wavering old lady on a bicycle. Thankfully, she'd been alone in the car that day, so nobody had seen the incident, except the other driver, who had shaken his fist furiously. She had told William about it, who had laughed, shrugging it off as unimportant. But she knew the examiner would not be so relaxed.

The examiner, a wiry gentleman in a grey suit and trilby hat, was waiting at the top of the hill where she'd left her car parked, ready for her test.

'There he is,' she muttered, blenching.

'Selina, I want you to listen to me.' When she turned, William gave her a mock-stern look. 'You're going to pass your test with flying colours, I promise. So chin up and keep smiling, yes? Just don't knock any more old ladies on bicycles into the gutter,' he added with a wink. 'Examiners tend to draw the line at attempted murder, I believe.'

She laughed reluctantly and left him.

The examiner shook hands with her, looking her up and down from under the brim of his hat. He walked around her car, checked the L plate was in the correct position, and then demanded to see her provisional licence and insurance certificate. Once she had produced these and they had been checked, he asked whether she could read a sign on the wall opposite, which she did without hesitation.

'Well, Miss Tiptree,' the examiner said in a kindly manner, opening the driver's side door for her, 'your papers are in order and your eyesight is excellent, so let's get on with the test. You said you've been driving without supervision for about six months now, so this should be a formality. But let's see, shall we?'

The next hour passed in a terrifying blur. First, the examiner asked a series of taxing questions on the Highway Code, and also asked her to demonstrate various hand signals out of the window for him, including the correct procedure for indicating a right-hand turn. She was relieved when the examination on theory came to an end and he finally asked her to start the engine.

There were a few hairy moments driving about Bodmin's busy town centre, with pedestrians seeming to leap into the road at every turn, but she felt that she acquitted herself adequately. When he asked her to drive out into the surrounding countryside, she stopped in good time to avoid a stray dog, and remembered not to drive at her usual breakneck pace. To her secret pleasure, there was no backsliding or slipping of the clutch on the dreaded hill start, and her reversing proved acceptable too, despite her taking two tries to get the angle right. The emergency stop had been a little shaky, she had to admit. But after giving her a dreary lecture on not hogging the middle of the road and making sure she took blind corners more cautiously, the examiner at last filled out a Certificate of Competence to Drive with her name and address on it, and handed it over with a smile. She had passed her test!

'Drive safely now, Miss,' he told her in an avuncular fashion, and touched the brim of his hat as he got out of the car. 'It was nice meeting you. Good luck.'

She left the car where it was and hurried down to tell William, who was waiting for her outside the butcher's shop, reading a newspaper. As she came skipping towards him, he looked up with a smile. 'There, I told you, didn't I? There was nothing to be worried about.'

Selina stared at him in wonder. She had not even shown him the certificate yet. 'But . . . how did you know I'd passed?'

'My dear, nobody who'd just failed their driving test would be smiling like that.' He bent his head to kiss her on the lips. It was the merest peck, as they were in public and not even courting, but it was enough to make Selina catch her breath. He hesitated, frowning as he straightened. 'I'm sorry, I shouldn't have done that. It was damned impertinent of me and I apologise. But I couldn't help it . . . You just looked so adorable.'

Laughter bubbled out of her throat at this admission, causing several sombre-faced passers-by to turn and stare at her. 'Oh, William!' she choked, a hand to her mouth.

His brows rose. 'What on earth have I done to amuse you now?'

But Selina couldn't find the right words, so only shook her head, smiling at him shyly. 'Let me go and park the car somewhere less awkward, then we'll meet for lunch, shall we? Nancy should be fine looking after the children a little while longer and I feel like celebrating.' She halted, biting her lip. 'Unless you need to get back to work, that is.' William was always so ready to spend time with her, often at a moment's notice, that she sometimes struggled to remember that he was a busy and important man, with better things to do than go gallivanting about the town with a young woman like her all day.

'I do need to work, but I shall stay late instead.' William tucked the newspaper under his arm. 'I'll call into the office briefly, and meet you in half an hour at our usual nosebag. How's that?'

'Perfect.'

Having parked the car in a quiet side street, Selina bought some pretty spring flowers from a street seller and hurried to the church on the corner, wandering through the graveyard until she came to Helen Bourne's final resting place, adorned now with a handsome marble headstone. She lay the flowers on Helen's grave and stood back, not sure what impulse had driven her to visit the graveyard today, and lost for words now she was there.

The headstone had not been ready in time for her funeral. Selina studied it now, remembering that dismal day, the mourners standing in thick snow, everyone shivering in the chill air, snowflakes whirling about. Helen had been her nearest neighbour, and she had felt it important to pay her last respects but had left the children at home, not wanting to upset them with another funeral so soon after their own dear mother's. To her surprise, only a handful of townsfolk had shown up, mostly close acquaintances of the Bournes, but she had put that down to the bad weather. William had been there too, of course, along with Cameron and his new bride.

After her name and dates came the carved inscription, *Missed by her loving brother, Cameron Bourne.*

Selina wondered if that was true. Did Cameron really miss his sister? They had been so close for years, and yet Cameron had not stayed above an hour after the funeral, only showing his face briefly at the wake he himself had arranged at a local hotel. He had attended the inquest and given evidence of his sister's mental health around the time of her death, which he'd deceptively described as 'robust'. Even though his testimony directly contradicted the doctor's belief that Helen had been depressed and struggling with her nerves, the coroner ruled Miss Bourne's death 'accidental' and gave permission for the funeral to take place. To Selina's astonishment, there had been no suggestion in the official verdict that Helen might have deliberately taken an overdose.

'I expect it was done to spare the family's feelings, and also allow any insurance policies to be paid out without question,' William had said grimly when she queried this oversight. 'And given there was no note . . .'

'Yes, I see what you mean.'

She had studied Cameron throughout the inquest, however, and could not help wondering if he felt guilty, knowing his sister's death might have been averted if he had not abandoned her so cruelly.

It seemed unlikely. Leaving the inquest, he had been pale but composed. A grieving brother, but not a man who might be blaming himself.

At the funeral, though, Cameron had wept as his sister was laid to rest. His new wife, Fiona, a heavy-set woman of about forty with rouged cheeks and scarlet lipstick, had produced a handkerchief from her bag and passed it to him without comment.

Later, at the wake, a sleek fox fur draped about her shoulders, she had shaken hands with Selina in a casual manner that suggested Cameron had told her little about his nearest neighbours on the moors. Avoiding Selina's searching gaze, he'd slipped away with his wife as soon as possible, excusing them both on account of Fiona's 'condition', a remark which had left the poor woman pink with embarrassment. So she was pregnant already, Selina had thought, glancing covertly at his wife. It was hard not to wonder if that had been the reason for their precipitous wedding last year. Since it was none of her business, though, she soon put it out of her mind.

She herself had been so busy since Helen's funeral that she'd not given much more thought to the Bournes, except to note one day in the local gazette that Bourne Cottage was up for sale. The happiness and well-being of her sister's children, her blossoming friendship with William MacGregor, and her care of cousin Nancy as her pregnancy progressed had occupied her every waking moment, leaving little time for idle speculation.

Now, here she was, bringing Helen Bourne flowers. A woman who had slept with her sister's husband and done her best to make Selina unhappy too.

'I'm sorry,' she addressed the headstone self-consciously. 'Sorry about everything. Not noticing that Cameron had left, not going over more often during the heavy snows to see if you needed help, and not remembering to call again once the weather began to ease. If I had . . . Well, perhaps you wouldn't be in the ground, and I wouldn't be here speaking to your headstone.' She glanced about the ancient churchyard, but thankfully there was no one else in sight. 'I don't know if you can hear me, or even care that I'm here. You were never very pleasant, let's be honest. But some of that may have been Cameron's fault, and you led quite a miserable existence out there at Bourne Cottage. So I hope you've found peace, Helen, and that you're happy at last. Goodbye.'

Over lunch, Selina told William about her impromptu visit to the grave, and he gave her a solemn look. 'Laying ghosts?'

'Making myself feel less guilty for not visiting her more after Cameron left,' she muttered, choosing a granary bread roll from the waitress's proffered basket. When the woman had gone, she said quietly, 'The truth is, I'm not as kind as Bella was. Try as I might, I was never quite able to forgive Helen for seducing Sebastian behind my sister's back.'

She had finally told William in detail what she'd discovered about the Bournes in her sister's journals. He had been as shocked as her by the revelations, and angry too when he learned how Cameron had kissed her out at Dead Man's Bluff, and agreed that he'd most likely been hoping for a position of influence with Peter once he came of age and inherited his father's wealth.

'You are a clever, level-headed young woman, Selina, and being a realist rather than "kind" is nothing to be ashamed of.' William raised a glass and drank her health, smiling. 'And now we come to my share of today's conversation.'

She raised her brows. 'Go on.'

William set down the glass, staring down into his wine with sudden hesitancy. 'Selina, I know I'm not worthy of the honour, and that I'm far older than you, though only by a dozen or so years,' he said, stumbling over the words, his gaze lifting shyly to hers at last, 'and you should feel free to throw your drink in my face even for daring to suggest it, but I wonder . . . That is, I would be the happiest man in the world if you would consent to be my wife, Selina Tiptress . . . I mean, Tiptree.' He blushed rosily. '*Tiptree*,' he repeated with careful emphasis, shaking his head. 'Forgive me, I swear I practised that. Perhaps I ought to have gone over it again before making a fool of myself.'

Selina sat dazed, an odd buzzing in her ears. 'I . . . I beg your pardon?' She stared at him blankly. 'You want to m-marry me?'

'Is it so surprising?'

'Yes,' she said bluntly.

'But all these months . . .' He shook his head, looking bemused. 'Visiting you at the hall, teaching you to drive, spending most of Christmas Day with you and the children . . . Not to mention all the kisses I've given you . . .'

'You've only kissed me two or three times,' she protested.

'That's two or three times more often than I kiss most women with whom I'm on first-name terms. And all the lunches and driving lessons? What did you think I was doing it for?' His gaze clashed with hers, half-humorous, half-confused.

'The estate . . .' Her voice tailed off, and she blushed.

'No,' he said ironically.

'No, I suppose not.' She took a deep gulp of wine. 'Golly.'

'I take it that's a no, then.'

She opened her mouth to say no, and then stopped herself.

His eyes narrowed. 'I have a chance?'

'I . . . I'm not sure.'

'Good God, I have a chance.' William leant back in his chair, drew a fat cigar from an inner pocket, caught her astonished eye, and hurriedly returned it to his pocket. 'Quite right. You're still thinking. The cigar will have to wait.'

'You expected me to say yes?'

'I was prepared for either yes or no. Yes, the cigar. No, continuing with our pleasant conversation,' he said, grimacing, 'before going home to lick my wounds as soon as decently possible.'

'But me saying maybe threw you.'

'As you say.' But he was looking more cheerful. 'So it's a maybe.'

'Perhaps.'

'Oh, you . . .' He laughed, but looked shaken. 'May I ask what the chief stumbling block is? Then I could at least try to stack the odds in my favour.'

'It's not a stumbling block, as such.' Selina met his gaze, feeling unexpectedly vulnerable. Right up until he'd asked her, she'd been sure she would not want to marry him. But the word *no* had refused to come, and she'd been surprised. She'd remembered how much she'd enjoyed their fleeting kisses, and felt a desire to have him kiss her again. Which could only mean one thing . . . She had feelings for this man. Feelings that refused to be suppressed. And there was no reason to suppress them, was there? She knew him to be a man of integrity, unlike her previous crushes, Johnny and Cameron – both weak-willed men, out to use her for whatever they could get. Yet there was still a nagging worry as she considered the possibility of a future with him. 'It's the children.'

William studied her intently. 'What about them?'

'If we married, you would still have your work here in town,' she pointed out, 'and as your wife, I would be expected to move in with you.'

'True.'

'Yet I'm still guardian to my sister's children until they all come of age, and I take that responsibility seriously.'

'So bring them to Bodmin.' He smiled. 'They're smashing kids. I'd be happy to bring them up as my own, if that's what worries you.'

Smiling at his generosity, she reached across briefly to touch his hand. 'But Thornton Hall is their home, William. They lost their father in the war, and their mother last summer. I can't drag them away from the hall, it's all they have left of their parents.'

His smile faded. 'Yes, I see what you mean. The fact is, you need to keep the children with you, yet it wouldn't be fair to bring them to live with me in Bodmin. Not after everything they've been through. Peter, in particular. The boy's just starting to come around . . .' He sighed.

'I'm sorry,' she whispered. 'Plus, there's Nancy now. Her baby's due next month. She can't be left to face the music alone.'

'Of course not.' He shook his head, fiddling with his glass. 'But there's no need to apologise. I would probably say no in your position.'

Selina bit her lip. 'You're forgetting something.'

'What's that?'

'I didn't say no,' she reminded him, and then took a deep breath, forcing herself to be brave. 'In fact, saying "maybe" was a bit of a fudge, given my . . . my feelings.'

William locked gazes with her, his own colour returning swiftly when she smiled. 'Oh, Selina . . . You mean . . . ? You have feelings for me?' When she nodded, her smile turning shy, he loosened his collar with one finger. 'Good Lord.'

'If I'm honest, it really ought to be a yes.' Her heart beat faster on admitting this out loud, but no half-expected sense of fear or apprehension accompanied the words, so perhaps this was the real thing. After so many false starts, was this true love at last? Well, why not? The dark years of the war were behind them, and it felt like time for something new, something better. 'All right, it's a yes . . . Yes, I would love to be your wife.' Seeing his eyes widen, a new emotion dawning in his face, she touched his hand again. 'But let's keep our engagement informal for now. Just between the two of us, if that's okay with you? Until we've worked out what to do for the best.'

He grinned, holding her hand. 'Here's to the best, then,' he agreed softly, and raised his glass to her.

That spring, things went on very much as they had for the past year, except that William visited the hall more often, and Selina spent more time with Faith now that Nancy was heavily pregnant.

Her cousin's baby was born at home in April, weighing a healthy six pounds, five ounces, a darling little girl whom Nancy called Isabella, in memory of the children's mother.

Faith, Jemima and Peter gathered about her crib the day after Isabella had been born, staring down in hushed awe at the new arrival.

'She looks like a doll,' Jemima whispered.

‘Can I see?’ Faith piped up, not quite tall enough to see over the padded side of the crib, so that Selina had to lift her.

‘What are those awful red bumps on her head?’ Peter demanded, his hands thrust carelessly in his pockets as though to indicate a lack of interest in babies, though it was clear he was as fascinated as his sisters.

‘Forceps,’ Mrs Hawley told him shortly, busy plumping Nancy’s pillows so she could sit up.

‘Four *what*?’ he repeated, mystified.

‘Right, enough admiration of the baby. Time to give Nancy and Isabella some peace and quiet,’ Selina announced, guiding the children out of the room. Faith hung back, begging to be allowed to kiss her newborn cousin, but she shook her head. ‘No, sweetheart, because you might have germs. When she’s a bit older you can kiss her.’

‘Germs?’ Faith wrinkled her nose.

Authoritatively, Peter began to hold forth on the topic of germs, while Faith stared at him, open-mouthed, and Jemima dashed off, muttering something about crocheting a pink hat for Isabella. Mrs Hawley bustled away with a laundry basket full of washing, seeming cheerful to have a new baby in the house despite all the extra work involved.

Selina paused in the doorway. ‘Congratulations,’ she told Nancy softly, who was looking tired but happier than she had been in months. ‘She’s lovely.’

‘Thank you.’ Nancy beamed. ‘Will you pass her to me, please? She’ll need feeding soon.’

‘Me?’ Selina swallowed, taken aback. She’d never handled a baby before, let alone a newborn. But, with Nancy’s encouragement, she bent over the crib, gathered up the tightly swaddled infant, and lifted her gently. One hand came up instinctively to support the baby's head, and she made a soft cooing noise, murmuring, 'Hello, Isabella. Aren't you a beautiful baby? Yes, you are,' while passing her carefully to her mother.

Nancy grinned, cradling the baby in her arms. 'See? You're a natural.'

With an embarrassed laugh, Selina handed her cousin a cup of tea and hurried away, closing the bedroom door to give her some privacy just as Isabella began to cry lustily.

You're a natural.

She'd never really thought much about babies before. Being a wife and mother had never been an ambition of hers. That was doubtless why she'd enjoyed being a Land Girl for years, happier with the rough and tumble of work on a farm than dolling herself up for a party. But she'd always been interested in *men*. And, since saying yes to William's unexpected proposal, she'd become more curious about the possibility, wondering what her own baby would look like, and if she could ever be as loving and protective a mother as her sister Bella had been.

Now, still breathing in the sweet, alluring scent of a newborn baby, Selina thought she finally knew the answer . . .

CHAPTER TWENTY-FIVE

Sheila put her arm around Mrs Treedy, who was weeping silently. 'Now, don't take on so . . . Your Jack will be coming home to Porthcurno soon enough. You mark my words. There ain't no call to fret over the boy. He just wants to see the world. And once he's seen it, he'll come back again.'

Outside the shop, a heavy pack on his back and sturdy boots on his feet, Jack Treedy stood in bright spring sunshine, surrounded by all his younger brothers and sisters, who were skipping about him in the dusty street and chattering. There was barely a cloud in the sky, and the young man looked excited to be heading off into the wide blue yonder.

Sheila couldn't blame him for wanting to broaden his horizons. Life in Britain was improving. But not quickly enough for Jack, who was leaving his family behind, possibly forever, now he had saved up enough for his passage to Australia.

As a child, she'd secretly craved a life of adventure herself, exploring far-flung lands, the exotic places she'd seen on the silver screen. Not that she regretted a moment of her life, or her lovely Betsy and Violet, and all their children and grandchildren now. But she did sometimes wonder if there was still time left for a little adventuring . . .

'How are you doing these days, love?' Sheila asked the widow quietly. 'Pardon me for asking, but I know the fund paid out at last.'

Mrs Treedy wiped away her tears. 'Yes, bless you. That money was a lifesaver. I couldn't have coped without it.' She sighed, watching her eldest son kick his brother's football along the street, their siblings cheering. 'I only wish Jack would change his mind.'

Maggie, who'd been listening, came out from behind the counter to hug the distraught widow. 'There, there, love . . . You'll have the other kids to comfort you.'

They hurried outside as the bus pulled up further along the village street, the driver watching the commotion curiously.

Sheila shook Jack's hand. 'Good luck to you, lad. Don't forget to write to your mum, eh?' She pressed a small envelope into his hand. 'Here's a few bob from me, for your travels.'

'Thank you, Mrs Newton,' Jack told her earnestly. 'I'm grateful, and not just for this. You offered me a job in your shop, even after I was such a twerp, stealing that pork pie.' He swallowed, adding, 'You made me see I didn't have to fall into bad ways, that I could do something different with my life . . . And I plan to.'

'Bravo.' Tears in her own eyes, Sheila reached for her hanky. 'Goodbye then, lad.'

'Goodbye.' He turned to hug his brothers and sisters, telling them exuberantly, 'Goodbye, goodbye . . . Yes, I love you all too. Look after Mum and each other for me, won't you?'

The bus driver sounded his horn impatiently.

Pale and suffering, Mrs Treedy walked with her son to the bus, hugged him tightly and watched him climb aboard. All the children ran after the old mud-flecked vehicle as it trundled out of the village again, whooping and shouting, 'Goodbye!' with Jack waving at them through the back window until the bus was out of sight.

'I'll never see him again,' Mrs Treedy moaned, lifting her apron to hide her face, which was streaming with tears. Her eldest daughter hugged her silently, and then the kids shuffled back home together, surrounding their mum in a protective pack.

Back in the shop, Maggie began tidying the magazine rack. 'Folk are saying it's going to be a glorious summer to make up for all that snow,' she mused, then added innocently, 'Where's Bernie these days? Didn't he used to take you for a drive when the weather was fine?'

Sheila, pricing up tinned goods, held on to her temper with difficulty. 'Maggie, just come straight out with whatever you want to know.'

Her sister turned, a knitting mag in hand. 'All right, I will. Bernie was in and out of the shop most of last year. I thought wedding bells were in the air for sure. But the old boy's not been around much since Christmas, and you've barely mentioned him in weeks.' Maggie peered at her. 'Have you and Bernie called it a day?'

Sheila counted to three in her head before replying, 'No.'

'Then why on earth—'

'He asked me to marry him, all right?' she snapped, exasperated. 'And I said no. Or rather, that I needed to think about it more. So this is me thinking.'

Maggie's mouth fell open. 'He *proposed*? You never told me.'

'I don't have to tell you everything, Maggie,' Sheila said loftily, returning to pricing up the tins. 'You're my sister, not my keeper. Anyway, it ain't worth shouting about until I make my mind up.'

'And have you?'

'Of course I haven't.' Sheila shook her head. 'Bernie's a lovely man. But he's a bit old-fashioned in his ways. I'm worried he'll try to persuade me to give up the shop once his ring's on my finger. And half of me thinks he might succeed . . .'

Maggie looked thoughtful. 'But why would you want to keep running this place once you're comfy in that posh house of his?'

'You think I done the wrong thing,' Sheila demanded, 'telling him I weren't ready to get married again?'

'That depends, doesn't it?'

'On what?'

Maggie smiled. 'On whether you love him or not.'

'*Love*?' Sheila gave a derisive snort. 'I ain't got time for love. I've got this bloomin' shop to run, and the charitable fund to administer, and council business to attend to.'

Maggie hesitated. 'Or maybe you *are* ready to get married again, Sheila, and you can't bring yourself to admit it. Because you've been different since Christmas. You had a light in your eyes when Bernie was courting you, and that light's gone out.'

'Oh, don't talk nonsense,' Sheila exclaimed, and spun around as the shop door jangled, never so happy to see a customer in her life. 'Good morning, Mrs Penhallow. How are things up at the Grange? They not sold that old place yet? That's a shame . . .' Rattling on like this, she hurried to fetch the lady's usual order of veg, piling early spuds into a paper bag for her and barely letting her get a word in edgeways. 'It's been on the market a fair few months, ain't it? But it's bound to sell now we're headed into summer, then I suppose you'll be looking for a new housekeeping job.'

The lady replied, but Sheila wasn't listening. Not really. Instead, she was trying to pretend she didn't give two hoots about Bernie's proposal, too busy keeping the village ticking over to bother with romance.

You had a light in your eyes when Bernie was courting you, and that light's gone out.

She wished people would leave her alone to make this important decision on her own. Because the more she thought about getting married again, the more she didn't have a blessed clue what to do.

Spring gave way to summer, and a lovely summer too, Sheila thought, happy to have abandoned her winter woollies at last for frocks and sandals. Violet's salad vegetables were growing nicely in the garden, and Joe had finally received a grant from the government to help him rebuild his stock, including a dozen young ewes in prime condition and a sturdy ram. The bank had also agreed to loan him money to replenish his stocks of seeds and tubers for planting out, since he'd lost these to rot during the dreadful winter weather. This had improved Joe's mood considerably, and he went about the farm whistling these days instead of frowning, while Violet too was forever smiling, albeit secretively.

One Saturday afternoon, putting on a hat as she prepared

to walk down to the village for a special summer event to which everyone in Porthcurno had been invited, Sheila remarked to Violet, 'Come on, spill the beans. You've had a smile on your face for weeks now. And don't bother telling your old mum there ain't nothing going on, because I know when my daughter's keeping secrets.' She tapped the side of her nose. 'Let's hear it, then.'

Violet blushed, glancing over her shoulder to where the Land Girls were washing their hands at the sink, ready to accompany them down to the village. Sheila didn't know what the big event was all about, since nobody had thought to inform her, despite her being a councillor, she thought caustically. But it seemed that everybody was going, including Joe, who surely had better things to do on a summer's afternoon.

Violet shook her head, smirking. 'As a kid, I thought you had eyes in the back of your head, Mum. You always knew what I was up to. But you're so busy these days, you can't see what's right in front of your nose.' And she dropped a protective hand to her belly.

'Gawd, Vi . . .' Sheila clapped a hand to her mouth. 'How long have you known?' she whispered.

'A few months now, but I wanted to keep it quiet until I was sure.'

'I'm so happy for you, love. When's it due?'

'October, most likely. It's been hard to keep the news to ourselves, I can tell you.'

'Joe must be as pleased as Punch.'

'Yes, bless him. He was worried when I first told him. But it's gone like a dream this time round. Barely a day's sickness.' She laughed at Sheila's expression. 'You never even noticed, did you?'

Sheila stared, thinking back. There had been a few mornings over late spring and early summer when Violet had struggled to get up in time for breakfast, but she'd put that down to weariness. They'd all been working so hard to get the farm back on its feet.

'I had no bloomin' idea,' she agreed. 'You're right, though, I should ha' guessed. You ain't been in such a good mood for years.'

Thankfully, Joe came into the kitchen before Violet could respond to that dig. He looked surprisingly smart for a trip down to the village, wearing his Sunday best. 'We ready for the off yet?'

'You're looking very handsome, Mr Postbridge,' Sheila remarked, and wished she could congratulate her son-in-law on being a prospective father again. But she knew Violet wouldn't welcome that in front of the Land Girls, not until the news was out.

'I told him to dress up today, just for a change,' Violet said hurriedly, and Sheila noticed she too was wearing a smart frock and had set her hair in a stylish manner. 'I'm glad you're wearing that new summer dress I ran up for you on the Singer last week. Fits nicely, does it?'

'Rather too snug,' Sheila admitted as they headed out of the door. 'I shouldn't have had that second bowl of puddin' last night. Though why we all have to be dressed up so smart for a village do, I can't imagine. What's it all about, anyway?'

Nobody answered, and Joe soon changed the subject, talking about the ewes that had arrived to replenish livestock lost in the deep snows. 'Those new farmhands I've taken on since the spring need training up, though. They know next to nothing about how to care for sheep,' he said grumpily.

'Even Caroline's an expert compared to them.' The Land Girls were walking ahead, just out of earshot, chatting merrily to each other. 'It's a pity,' he added quietly, 'but I'll need to let those three girls go after harvest time. I'd forgotten how much easier it is to do a job with four or five men about the place instead. Shearing was a doddle this year. These girls are great, but they just don't have the strength of a man, and now most of our boys are home from abroad, there's no longer any call for the Women's Land Army.'

Sheila sighed, shaking her head. 'Ah now, that's a crying shame. They've put their hearts and souls on the line for this country, them lovely girls have.' But she knew Joe was only doing what was best for the farm.

Down in the village, Sheila was amazed to find dozens gathered about the stretch of common land they called the village green. There was a refreshments table and a makeshift platform strung with bunting.

Bernie was there, also in his best suit and sporting a natty polka-dot tie with tiepin. He raised a hand in greeting. 'Sheila, could I have a quick word?'

Once he'd led her aside, Sheila asked bluntly, 'What's going on, Bernie?'

Bernie smiled. 'Sorry about the subterfuge. The truth is, everyone was under strict orders not to let on to you about this event.'

'Eh?' She stared at him, mystified.

'The villagers and the council want to give you an award,' he explained gently.

'Blimey.' Sheila couldn't breathe properly. 'An award?' She shook her head, rejecting the idea as nonsense. 'Oh, you're pulling my leg . . . Why on earth would anyone want to give *me* an award, of all people?'

'For your good works, Sheila,' Bernie told her. 'You've become something of a local celebrity, and the people of Porthcurno wanted to give something back in return for your kindness and generosity.'

For once, Sheila could not think of a single thing to say, staring dumbly as Bernie steered her up the wooden steps onto the raised platform.

'Ladies and gentlemen,' he began, addressing the villagers as they crowded closer to hear him, 'I'm Bernard Bailey, Chair of Porthcurno Parish Council, and I'd like to thank you for coming to this historic event. You will all know Mrs Newton as Arnie Newton's widow, a lady who bravely took on the job of reopening the village shop after Arnie sadly left us . . . I'm sure we can all agree that she's done a sterling job. Indeed, few would deny it's the best village shop for miles around.'

'That's because it's the *only* village shop for miles around,' Sheila muttered under her breath.

'Following her co-option to the Parish Council, Mrs Newton has given up her precious time to support this village during the difficult times we've suffered since the war. Not least in administering the food drop that kept us going during the big freeze, plus all her hard work supporting those who lost so much during the floods.' Applause broke out again and he inclined his head, waiting for it to die down before continuing, 'But Mrs Newton's biggest contribution to our community has been the parish fund she set up for those in need of special help since the war. It's changed lives and brought a new spirit of community to this village. In light of her many achievements, the council and village together would like to ask a very special guest to step up here and present Mrs Sheila Newton with a small token of our appreciation.'

Sheila gawped at him, mystified. *Special guest*? Whoever could he mean?

Beaming, Bernie went on, 'Today, we're greatly honoured to have a former Member of Parliament and well-known philanthropist in our village.' He turned to help a smart lady in a large floppy hat up the steps onto the platform. 'Please, let's have a big round of applause for our special guest, all the way from London . . . Mrs Newbury-Holmes.'

Sheila clapped a hand to her mouth, finally recognising the lady's distinctive profile as she turned smiling towards the crowd. She could scarcely believe her eyes, blinking in astonishment. *Mrs Newbury-Holmes*? Here in Porthcurno? Surely the busy former MP had not only come to see her, though? This had to be a mistake . . .

'Thank you so much for that kind introduction, Mr Bailey. But I can assure you, it is I who am honoured,' Mrs Newbury-Holmes was telling everyone, her posh BBC accent curiously out of place in the tiny Cornish village. 'Honoured to have been invited and to be awarding this token of the Parish Council's appreciation to a highly industrious and committed soul, a lady who is not only a pillar of her community, but is providing a vital service in these times of need to everyone in and around this most charming village of Porthcurno.' She paused, turning slightly as Bernie handed her something wrapped in crepe paper. 'Now, if you would come forward, Mrs Newton?'

Sheila stepped forward in a daze, the applause and cheers

from the crowd deafening. Tears had blurred her vision, but she blinked them away and saw Mrs Newbury-Holmes smiling broadly and holding something out to her. 'F-for me?'

There was a moment of silence as she unwrapped the award and stared down at it in shock. It was a handsome carriage clock, with a gold plaque beneath, which read in beautiful copperplate, *To Mrs Sheila Newton, with grateful thanks for all her good works, from the people of Porthcurno, June 1947*.

'Oh my Gawd . . .' She gulped, barely able to find her voice. 'Thank you,' was all she could manage in broken tones, tears rolling down her cheeks. 'Thank you so much.'

Down in the crowd, she saw Violet applauding, a proud smile on her face, and Joe at his wife's side, grinning as he balanced Sarah Jane on his shoulders so the little girl could witness her grandmother clutching a gold clock and bawling her silly eyes out. Grace put her fingers to her lips and gave a shrill navvy's whistle, while Caroline and Tilly cheered. Beyond them, she saw her sister Margaret in a pretty frock, beaming and clapping for all she was worth. All her regular customers were there as well, plus Mrs Treedy and her children, the vicar and his wife, and young Joan and Arthur Green too, so many people she knew, she couldn't count them all.

'It's good to see you again,' Mrs Newbury-Holmes was saying as she shook Sheila's hand. 'Congratulations, Mrs Newton. A well-deserved award, if I may say so.'

'That's very kind of you, Mrs Newbury-Holmes. Though I'm sure you shouldn't have come all this way just for me.'

'It's been a pleasure.' The lady beamed. 'I hope you haven't forgotten my suggestion of standing for election to Cornwall Council.'

'Oh, you . . . !' Sheila was half laughing, half crying. 'Well, maybe once I've got me breath back.' She cradled the clock happily. 'I'll treasure this, Mrs Newbury-Holmes. Thank you again for *everything*.'

Bernie had stepped back to let her and Mrs Newbury-Holmes take centre stage. But he smiled when she turned her head, seeking him out. 'This is your day, Sheila,' he told her, and she saw tears in his eyes too. 'Congratulations.'

Soppy old fool, she thought, weeping along with him. But he did look a little sadder than she remembered. What could be making him unhappy? she wondered. And why had she let too many weeks slip past without meeting him for lunch, or a bracing walk and a chat, like they'd done so often last year?

'Well, if nobody needs me anymore, I shall go and sample some of those delicious-looking scones,' Mrs Newbury-Holmes murmured, heading down the steps with her gaze fixed on the refreshment table. 'Perhaps with a little strawberry jam and cream too.'

'Cream first,' Sheila called after her quickly, 'not jam,' and then spun as she spotted Bernie trying to slip away too. 'Oh no you don't, Bernard Bailey . . . I'd like a word with you.'

Across the green, others were also beginning to head for the white-clothed tables set out with summer refreshments. Already, some of their fellow councillors had gathered about Mrs Newbury-Holmes, others staring curiously from a distance. It wasn't often the village had a celebrity visitor, and Sheila guessed they intended to put a few political questions to the former Member of Parliament.

Bernie looked round at her warily. 'Oh yes?'

'How did you get hold of Mrs Newbury-Holmes?'

'Your daughter,' he said, holding her gaze. 'Violet still had the envelope to hand from one of her letters to you. Her London address was printed on the back.'

'I see.' Sheila made a mental note to take her daughter to task for sneaking around behind her back to arrange this . . . But then shook that thought away. It had been a lovely gesture, after all, and she was pleased as Punch. 'Well, all right . . . You asked me a question a while back, and I said no. Or at least, no for now. Do you remember?'

'How could I forget?' He gave a rueful grin.

'Well, having given it some more thought,' she said carefully, wrapping up the beautiful clock again in crepe paper, 'I've decided it's a yes.'

He stared. 'I beg your pardon?'

'But I ain't giving up the village shop, not for love nor money, and that's my final word on the matter.'

Bernie took a deep breath, then threw back his head and laughed. 'Sheila Newton, you are the most amazing woman . . . Are you serious?'

'I can say no again if you prefer.'

'No,' he said quickly, and seized the clock from her, handing it to Maggie, who'd come up to congratulate her. 'Would you hold this for a moment, Margaret? I rather urgently need to kiss your sister. I hope you don't mind.'

Maggie, who had been a fervent admirer of Bernie's ever since he and Ernest had evicted her ex-husband from the Harvest Supper, took the clock, wide-eyed and smiling. 'Be my guest.'

'Maggie, no! Bernard . . . We can't do that in front of all

these people,' Sheila hissed, but Bernie can't have heard her, as he took her in his arms and delivered a firm kiss straight to her lips.

Much to her embarrassment, the villagers started cheering and applauding again, witnessing this very improper behaviour by the esteemed Chair of their Parish Council, and she even heard a deep, familiar rumble of laughter from Joe, somewhere in the crowd below. Heat rose in her cheeks, and she was quite breathless by the time Bernie released her. She only hoped Mrs Newbury-Holmes had been too busy adding a handsome dollop of cream first to her scone to have noticed all the palaver.

'I'm afraid I'll *have* to marry you now, Sheila,' Bernie pointed out, grinning down at her. 'Or folk will talk.'

CHAPTER TWENTY-SIX

'Oh, I say,' Caroline gasped, nudging Grace in the ribs. 'Will you look at that?'

Grace, who along with everyone else had been fascinated by the spectacle of Mrs Newton and Mr Bailey embracing passionately in full view of the whole village, chuckled behind her hand. 'I know . . . Hilarious, isn't it? You don't expect people that age to go around kissing in public, do you?'

Perplexed, Caroline wrinkled her nose. 'Sorry? Oh, not those two . . . I meant Tilly and her boyfriend, Benny.' She pointed across the green to where Tilly was once again holding hands with a sturdy-looking, dark-haired boy about her own age. 'They've been going steady a while now. She's awfully young to be getting serious over a boy.'

'What are you, her mum?' Smiling, Grace turned her face to the sun. 'Anyway, they're only holding hands.'

'I suppose you're right.' But Caroline wished secretly that *she* was allowed to hold Grace's hand in public, just as Tilly was allowed to hold Benny's.

It was a beautiful June day and there was barely a breath

of wind stirring the trees about the green. The distant church bell rang the half-hour as a gang of small children dashed past, giggling madly, no doubt for the same reason that had left Grace grinning.

Caroline admired Grace's profile. 'I wish I was good at drawing like Joan.'

'Joan?' Grace's brows tugged together.

'One of our former Land Girls. You've met her, remember? She left to marry Arthur Green and they've just had a baby. Look, they're over there.' Caroline nodded to the young couple, chatting animatedly to the Reverend Clewson and his wife. Joan had a summer glow, cradling her baby in her arms, while Arthur looked happier than she'd ever seen him. Married life clearly suited them, though the two rarely left their cosy cottage these days to venture into the village, and hadn't called at the farm in ages. 'Joan loves drawing, and Arthur's an artist. They used to go out sketching together on the cliffs. I've never been terribly good at drawing, but looking at you . . .'

'Hush, will you?' Grace was frowning. 'Here comes Joe.'

Caroline felt a stab of frustration, but didn't have time to say anything as Joe ambled towards them, his daughter riding on his shoulders.

'I'm taking Sarah Jane back home,' the farmer told them cheerfully. 'There are still a few jobs to do before supper time, only I've given the other farmhands the afternoon off. If you don't mind, could you round up Tilly and get yourselves back up the hill? I'd like you two girls to check on the new sheep up in the top pasture, to see how they're settling in. And Tilly can feed the pigs and chickens, as usual.'

'Yes, Mr Postbridge,' Grace said without expression, and

waited until he'd set off across the green again before turning to Caroline with a worried expression. 'I hope he didn't overhear us. I wish you'd be more discreet, and pay attention. Folk don't like it when girls get too close to each other. Not like we are.'

Caroline felt a flicker of rebellion but decided not to get into a row over it. Grace was right to be cautious when they were out in public, after all.

She beckoned Tilly, who abandoned Benny with a quick smile and came hurrying across to them instead. 'Are we heading back now?' the younger girl asked.

'What do you think? Can't have us Land Girls enjoying ourselves for long, can we?' Grace pulled a face. 'Mr P says you're to feed the pigs and chickens, and we have to check on the ewes.'

'Looks like you were having a good time over there,' Caroline said with a wink. 'When's the engagement?'

Tilly flushed almost as red as her hair. 'Don't be silly,' she chuckled. 'It's only Benny. We're just messing about, that's all.'

'Don't mess about too much with boys,' Grace reminded her. 'You know what they say . . . If you can't be good, be careful.'

'And if you can't be careful, find a vicar!' all three girls chanted together, and then burst out laughing, for it was a saying much favoured by Mrs Newton.

Tilly sobered up quickly, though. 'Honestly though, we were only holding hands.'

'Yes, and as Mrs Newton's always saying, we all know where *that* leads,' Grace told her loftily, and strode away with her hands in the pockets of her mustard breeches.

Tilly glanced at Caroline as they hurried after her. 'Are you and Grace getting along better these days?' she whispered.

'Let's just say, we're not being good, but we are being careful,' Caroline whispered back, though rather wishing they didn't have to be quite so careful.

At the farm, Tilly peeled off to collect the pigswill bucket, and the other two continued up the track to the top field.

They paused at the final bend in the track, where they could hear the sea breaking against the cliffs ahead, and Caroline spotted a skylark high above in the bright blue sky. At least, she thought it must be a skylark. They could only see a dark dot against the sun. But the bird's song was breathtaking.

'Beautiful,' Grace murmured as they stopped to listen. Warily, she checked the track towards the farmhouse, nestled in the distance, and then the empty fields around them, before her hand crept out and took Caroline's. 'Should be safe enough now. It's just you and me out here.'

'I don't know why you get so worried,' Caroline told her. 'I'm sure Joe wouldn't throw us out if he knew.'

'But Violet might. She's got a conservative mind, that one. Besides, she won't be in a mood to put up with anything that feels dangerous right now,' Grace said wisely.

They walked in silence for a while, holding hands, their shoulders brushing. 'What do you mean?' Caroline asked.

'Well, she's preggers.'

Caroline stopped dead, staring. 'I beg your pardon?'

'Mrs P . . . She's expecting another baby.'

'How can you know?'

Grace gave one of her rich, earthy laughs. 'Bless you, Caro, you're such an innocent. Why do you think she's been filling out lately? Have you ever seen her eating more than her ration?'

'That's hardly proof.'

'All right, then.' Grace considered for a moment. 'When I first came to the farm, I thought Violet didn't know how to smile. She was always frowning and snapping at everyone. Now she's all sweetness and light. She even offered me a second helping of pudding the other day, without me even asking for it. And poured cream on top as well. Love does that to people.'

'Love makes you give people extra pudding and cream?' Caroline demanded, incredulous.

'Yes, because it puts you in a good mood. Makes you want to be generous and kind.' Grace pulled Caroline close. Her smile was infectious. 'It makes you want to do this . . .' And she kissed Caroline on the lips.

Caroline closed her eyes, and listened to Grace's heart beating against hers. Up above, the skylark sang divinely. Sheep baaed in the distance. A slight breeze off the sea stirred her hair.

'See what I mean?' Grace pulled back, smiling into her eyes.

Caroline sighed. 'Yes, maybe I do.'

There was a slight noise in the distance, and Grace released her at once, striding on up the track without looking back.

Glancing over her shoulder, Caroline could see Joe in one of the lower fields, starting the tractor. Swiftly, she followed Grace uphill. 'He won't have seen us. He's too far away.'

'I know,' Grace admitted. 'But that was stupid of me. We need to be more careful.'

Reaching the top field, they climbed over the five-bar gate. The sheep that had arrived to replace livestock lost during the snows were grazing quietly in the sunshine. They seemed to have adjusted well to their new surroundings, despite having come all the way from South Devon where the winter had not been as devastating to farm stocks.

'They seem happy enough up here,' Grace muttered, studying the sheep. But she looked tense, hands once again in her pockets.

'It's not right,' Caroline complained bitterly. 'Why should old Mrs Newton get away with kissing her boyfriend in front of everyone, but we can't even hold hands in the middle of nowhere?'

'That's just the way of the world,' Grace said, though her eyes were miserable.

'Well, it shouldn't be. We should fight it.'

Grace turned, saying urgently, 'You can't fight this, Caroline. It's bigger than us. If you try, people will just tear into you and destroy your life. Believe me, I've seen it.'

'I remember what you told me about that other girl,' Caroline said awkwardly. 'But this isn't the same. There's no one on this farm who would treat you badly. Not even Violet. She's got a good heart, for all her sharp ways.'

'What about the boys in the village who gave me a hard time? Have you forgotten about them? All it would take is one word in the wrong place, and we wouldn't be able to walk down the village street without folk staring at us.'

'Let them stare!' Caroline cried passionately.

'You're only saying that because you don't know how awful it feels.' Grace shook her head grimly. 'No, you'd leave, and I'd never see you again. Is that what you want?'

Caroline blenched. 'Of course not. But I love you, and you love me. Why shouldn't we be together? It's nobody's business but ours.'

Grace laced her fingers with Caroline's. 'Maybe one day, yes. But not right now. Not while we're still working as Land Girls. After we leave here, we could get a flat together. Maybe in a big city where people don't look too closely at young women living together.'

Caroline flushed. 'I would love that.'

'But we'd still need to be careful. Wherever we live, there'll always be people pointing fingers, saying nasty things, getting us sacked from our jobs. It's a hard road to follow. Are you sure you wouldn't rather settle down with some nice fella and have half a dozen kids?' Grace met her eyes. 'I wouldn't blame you.'

'But I'd blame myself.' Caroline bit her lip. 'I can't believe you're willing for that to happen rather than stand up and fight.'

Grace groaned. A tear squeezed out from under her eyelid, running down one dark cheek. 'You don't understand . . . My whole world fell apart last time. But it's not just about me, love. It's about you too. I couldn't protect my girlfriend, and I had to watch while she was hounded, while she had stones thrown at her, and there was nothing I could do about it. I don't want to see you hurt like that.'

'Did you love her as much as you love me?' Caroline whispered.

Grace sighed. 'I thought I did. But I love you to bits, Caroline, and it feels more powerful than it was before.'

Caroline nodded, understanding. 'Yes, Selina was everything to me. It broke my heart when she left. But then

I met you . . .' She smiled. 'I love you more than I ever loved Selina, I see that now. Only, you say we can't even act on it.'

Grace's lips twitched. 'Oh, we can act on it,' she whispered. 'We just can't be caught, all right?'

After a last kiss, they headed back down to the farmhouse, strolling hand in hand until the first bend. Then, by mutual silent agreement, they let go and walked the rest of the way without touching.

Caroline hated the necessity for hiding their love. But Grace was right. She had declared her love to Selina and somehow escaped intact, never punished for the things she'd said so openly. Next time, she might not be so lucky.

A fortnight after Mrs Newton had been so thoroughly kissed in front of everybody in the village, she announced to the household that she and Bernard Bailey would be getting married in August, and invited them to toast their happiness with a glass of her home-made sloe wine. It ended up being more than one glass, of course, and the evening turned raucous, and Grace jumped up and gave them a few songs. 'A proper little songbird,' Mrs Newton said admiringly, and Caroline couldn't help feeling proud of her girlfriend, even if she had to keep it hidden.

Late the next day, her head hurting from too much sloe wine, Caroline was weeding tender young plants with the other girls when she heard a car horn. 'Hello, someone's pulled up in the farmyard,' she said, frowning as she straightened up. 'I didn't know Violet was expecting visitors.' But as she shielded her eyes against the late-afternoon sunshine, squinting at the car, she froze in horror. 'Oh no!'

Grace was beside her in an instant. 'What's the matter?'

‘My parents . . .’ Caroline’s stomach churned with fear. She’d boldly walked out at Christmas after her parents had tried to tell her how to live her life. But much of that had been bravado. Deep down, she was still apprehensive about defying them. And now they’d driven all the way from London to Cornwall to see her. But whatever for?

Her father opened the back door of the car, and she was relieved to see her grandmother climb out, leaning on a stick and studying the farmyard with an interested eye. So Gran was well, at least.

‘I’d better find out what they want.’ Caroline took a deep breath, determined not to let them bully her into going home again. Though she doubted they’d be impressed by her unfeminine appearance. The sun had been beating down on her all day in the fields, and she was hot and sweaty, and probably covered in dirt too.

‘I’ll stay here and keep working.’ Grace took up her hoe again, a grim expression on her face that Caroline recognised. Grace was keen not to do anything that might jeopardise Caroline’s reputation, even if it meant saying nothing while she was dragged away. ‘It’ll be safer that way.’

‘Oh no, you don’t.’ Seizing the hoe from Grace’s hand, Caroline threw it unceremoniously to the dirt, then pulled her towards the farmhouse.

‘What are you doing? They’ll see us holding hands,’ Grace hissed, trying to pull free. But Caroline only tightened her grip, walking more quickly. ‘Have you lost your marbles? Look, it’s your dad . . . He’s coming this way. Please, Caroline, let me go.’

Caroline paid no attention. ‘Hello, Dad,’ she said coolly, and dragged Grace forward. Her mother and grandmother stared across the car bonnet at them both, eyes wide. 'Hello, Mum. It's good to see you looking so well again, Gran.'

'It's good to see you too, love,' Gran said, smiling, though her curious gaze was on Grace. 'And who's this?'

'This is my girlfriend,' Caroline said firmly. 'Grace Morgan from Liverpool. Grace, this is my mum and dad, and my gran.'

'Your *what*?' her mother said blankly.

Swallowing hard, Grace stuck her chin in the air. 'How do you do, Mr Ponsby, Mrs Ponsby?' Her voice wavered a little, but she kept smiling, her perfect teeth showing. 'How do you do, Caroline's gran? Very nice to meet you all. It's a hot day, isn't it? Have you driven all the way here from London? That's hundreds of miles . . . You must be bleedin' exhausted.'

'Caroline,' her father began, frowning thunderously, 'I don't know if this is some sort of practical joke, but I'm not interested in speaking to you in front of this person.'

'Then you won't be speaking to me at all,' Caroline told him.

He stiffened. 'Now listen here—'

'Just say whatever you've come to say, Dad, or go away again. Your choice. But she's not leaving.' Caroline folded her arms, while Grace stood uncertain, eyeing her family with trepidation.

'Very well.' Her father cleared his throat, his chin jutting. 'Your mother and I have been discussing your future for some months now, and we've decided the only way forward is to take you back home where you belong. Young Albert is willing to give things another go, and if you don't like him, there are some very nice young men whose mothers attend our church. You wouldn't lack for invitations to parties or the cinema, and you certainly wouldn't need a . . . a *girlfriend*.' He flicked a disgusted glance at Grace, then looked back at Caroline in direct entreaty. 'Your mother and I just want to see you happy and settled now the war's over, not still living halfway across the country from us, buried here in . . . Well, the back of beyond.' And he gazed about the mucky farmyard with disdain, frowning at the dusty hens pecking ever nearer his car.

Albert.

Caroline's jaw clenched and she struggled not to be rude. These were her parents, after all. But she felt quite incensed at their interference. Had they learned nothing from her visit at Christmas? Besides, she doubted that groper would ever be interested in another date with her. Not after she'd kicked him in the shin.

Grace made an odd choking noise, and everyone looked round at her in surprise, including Caroline.

'Grace?' she asked, staring. 'Are you all right?'

'Sorry,' Grace muttered, a hand to her mouth, and then dissolved into helpless giggles. 'Sorry, sorry. But it's so funny, isn't it?'

'What exactly is funny about this situation, young lady?' Caroline's father demanded sternly.

'Well, you, for starters, Mr Ponsby.' Grace chuckled again. 'Thinking you can turn up here and drag your daughter off by the hair like a bleedin' Neanderthal.'

Caroline's mum gasped. '*Language*, please!'

'What, are you worried about my language, love?' Grace addressed her directly, and Caroline's mother shrank back, looking shocked. 'To be honest, you should be worrying about your daughter. She's your only child, is that right? I'd be a bit more careful if I were you, unless you don't mind never seeing her again. Because that's the next move in this little game, isn't it? Threaten to cut her off, make her scared to lose you . . . Only she isn't scared. Are you, Caroline?'

'No, I'm not scared,' Caroline agreed defiantly. It felt good to have Grace backing her up.

'So, the only question you really need to be asking is, do you want Caroline in your life? And if you do, you should stop badgering her. Because she's a grown woman and it's not your business who she dates. It's *hers*.' Grace reached for her hand, entwining her fingers with Caroline's. 'And right now she wants to date me, not *Albert*,' she ended in a mock-whisper.

Her dad said nothing but bent his head. Meanwhile, her mother gave a tiny sob, and knuckled a fist to her mouth, staring at them both.

Caroline bit her lip, not sure whether to laugh or cry. She peered at her gran, who was regarding Grace with approval. 'Gran? What do you think?'

'I think I wouldn't mind a little sit-down in that nice farmhouse, if nobody minds,' her grandmother murmured, and began to wander that way, leaning on her cane. 'And maybe a cup of tea? It was an awful long journey, as your friend rightly says, and I'm . . . what was the phrase she used? *Bleedin' exhausted*.'

After an awkward pause, Caroline's parents trailed after her gran, disappearing inside the farmhouse, where no doubt a bewildered but polite Violet Postbridge would soon sort them out with a cuppa and maybe a slice of cake too.

Grace blurted out, 'Sorry, Caroline, I couldn't help myself.

Just listening to your dad going on and on . . .' She threw an unhappy glance over her shoulder. 'Tilly must be wondering why on earth we've left her to do all the weeding on her own. Shall I go back and help her, poor thing?' Grace squeezed her hand. 'Have I made things worse for you?'

'Don't be daft,' Caroline told her, close to tears. 'You stood up for me, Grace. You took a risk . . . *for me*.' Her smile was tremulous. 'Nobody's ever done that before. It was wonderful. And terrifying.' They both laughed. 'I don't think my parents are going to give me any more trouble. But I really like Mr and Mrs Postbridge, and Mrs Newton, and I don't want to upset them by being too open about us.' She disentangled her hand from Grace's, but gently. 'Is that all right?'

'Oh, Caroline . . . It's more than all right.' Grace gave a slow smile that warmed her heart. 'It's love.'

CHAPTER TWENTY-SEVEN

It was a warm afternoon in August when Selina directed William down the narrow, bumpy track just past Porthcurno village to park outside Arthur and Joan Green's pretty, thatched cottage. Stretching wearily, she climbed out of the Wolseley, and peered into the back of the car. Faith was fast asleep, leaning against her big brother, and Jemima was engrossed in a paperback, none of them aware that they had arrived at their destination.

'We're here, sleepyheads!' she exclaimed. 'Wakey, wakey!'

Peter, who'd been daydreaming, looked round with a start. This woke Faith, who yawned and rubbed her eyes, while Jemima carefully checked her page number before closing the paperback and peering out of the window.

'This doesn't look much like a farm,' Jemima remarked.

'That's because this isn't Postbridge Farm, silly.' Peter jumped out of the car, and then turned to help Faith clamber out too. 'We're staying with Aunt Selly's friend tonight, remember? We won't go to the farm until after the old lady's wedding tomorrow.'

'*Old lady*? That's Mrs Newton to you,' Selina exclaimed, stifling a horrified laugh. 'Soon to be Mrs Bailey, of course.'

Jemima got out of the car, staring past Selina. 'Is that your friend, Aunt Selly? Look, she's got a baby!'

Selina turned hurriedly to greet her hostess, who was indeed cradling a baby in her arms. 'Joan!' she cried, kissing the curvy, dark-haired young woman on the cheek. 'Goodness, don't you look marvellous? Such a glow in your cheeks . . . And is this your little one? Caroline wrote to tell me you'd had your baby in June.'

'Yes, this is Felix.' Joan beamed, showing Selina the soft-cheeked young baby she was cuddling. 'He's nearly two months old now.'

'Congratulations!' Selina stroked the baby's tiny fist, feeling again that tug of longing to be a mother herself. 'And how's Arthur? Has he taken to parenthood or is he still wondering what hit him? All those broken nights . . .'

'Oh, we couldn't be happier,' Joan assured her, looking tired but ecstatic. 'Even with having to wake in the night to feed and change him . . . He's the most adorable little soul.'

Selina smiled, feeling thrilled for her. 'I'm sorry we're so late. Poor William doesn't know this part of Cornwall very well. I said I'd drive, but he insisted on taking the wheel.'

'Is that him?' Joan whispered, looking past her.

Selina turned, smiling. William was indeed coming around the Wolseley, rolling down his crumpled shirtsleeves that had been pushed to his elbows in the summer heat.

'Yes, this is my fiancé, William MacGregor,' Selina introduced him shyly. 'William, this is my good friend Joan, a former Land Girl from Postbridge Farm. We've shared many adventures together.'

'Very good to meet you,' William said, smiling.

They shook hands. Joan's eyes were twinkling. '*Fiancé*?' she repeated. 'I must be behind the times.'

'Not at all, we've hardly told a soul yet,' Selina reassured her, and glanced back at the children. 'In fact,' she added, lowering her voice, 'we haven't even told the children. So if you could keep it under your hat for the time being? I was planning to tell them before this visit, as it's going to mean some changes. Only, the household has been chaotic as usual, and I've barely had time to sit down with them for a proper discussion.'

'Of course.' Joan smiled down at Jemima, who was standing a little forlornly on the grassy track. 'You must be Jemima. Your aunt has told me all about you. I'm Mrs Green, but you can call me Joan.' She gazed about at the three children. 'Would you all like to see your rooms?'

As they all headed towards the house that belonged to Joan's in-laws, Mr and Mrs Green, Selina said quietly, 'By the way, thank you for agreeing to this. You're a brick. There was no room at the farm, and I'm trying to keep a tight rein on the budget. So this is a lifesaver.'

'It's my mother-in-law who's the brick, since we've no room in our little cottage. I'm only sorry I couldn't find a bed for your Mr MacGregor as well.'

Selina bit her lip. 'Oh, William's staying in a pub outside the village. We thought it best. You know how people gossip.'

Joan laughed. 'Don't I just?' She threw a glance back at William, who was retrieving their suitcases from the back of his car. 'I say, he's rather distinguished-looking. You've landed on your feet there. Something of a military bearing too?'

'He served in a local regiment in the war. Came out of it with a commendation. But he doesn't like to talk about it.'

'Arthur's the same. Though you can hardly blame him. Poor lamb, he had a dreadful time of it. But that's all in the past.' Joan smiled. 'Now we have Felix, we're both looking to the future.' She paused. 'By the way, I daresay you'll discover this tomorrow, but Violet Postbridge is also in the family way.'

'Again? Sounds as though the farm will be busier than ever soon.' Selina chuckled. 'You know, it seems only yesterday we were all scrambling about Postbridge Farm in those horrid mustard breeches, getting mucky and exhausted. Terrible times, I suppose. We were always worried about getting blown to bits or Hitler invading, and eating the most disgusting stuff just to stay alive. Yet it's strange . . . When I look back on those days, I only remember the good times, all the laughs we had together.'

'Me too,' Joan agreed, smiling softly.

'Though I was rather catty to everyone, I'm afraid,' Selina admitted guiltily. 'I hope you can forgive me.'

'I don't remember you ever being catty,' Joan assured her, with more tact than truth, Selina felt sure.

'Where is Arthur, by the way?' Selina hesitated. 'I was hoping he might have time for a proper chat with Peter while we're here. The boy likes cars, if that's any use as a starting place.' They were nearly at the Greens' comfortable-looking detached house, which stood in its own grounds with a neatly clipped, low privet hedge leading to the front door. 'You remember I wrote to you about his expulsion from school?'

'Yes, and I read your letter out to Arthur, who quite understood.' There was sympathy in Joan's kind face. 'Poor

Arthur, he's been staying out of my way today while I've been madly baking cakes.' She glanced at Peter, who was bringing up the rear, his hands in his pockets. 'I say, Peter . . . Your aunt tells me you know a thing or two about engines. My husband's messing about with a sidecar that won't start.' She pointed out their little cottage down the lane opposite. 'I don't suppose you'd mind giving him a hand?'

Peter's face brightened. 'Rather,' he agreed readily, and hurried off.

Joan and Selina shared a conspiratorial smile.

'I'll carry your bags upstairs, shall I?' William was peering through the open doorway of the house. 'Then I'll go and find that pub where I'm staying tonight.'

'Good idea, thank you.' Selina added with a shy smile, 'But you'll come back and join us for tea, won't you? Joan has baked us some cakes.'

'Sounds perfect.'

An hour later, Selina and Joan were sitting in the sunny cottage garden, catching up with all the latest gossip while baby Felix had a nap in his cot indoors. Jemima read her paperback on the grass and Faith played games with snapdragons, popping the bright flowers over her fingers to make little creatures that growled at each other. From the lane beside the cottage came the sound of male voices and spanners as Arthur and Peter tinkered with the sidecar. From the few words Selina caught, it was clear that Arthur was also talking to the boy about the nature of grief and how it could change people.

Her heart ached for her nephew, who was still coping with the early death of his beloved mother. But he'd improved in recent months, perhaps with William a more frequent visitor to the hall. She rather thought it was a father figure he lacked, but he would surely never admit it.

William returned to join them, and just as Joan was bringing out more tea and cake, Caroline and Tilly came bounding towards them, with Grace sauntering into the garden in a more dignified manner. Selina jumped up to embrace her dear friend Caroline, and to kiss Tilly on the cheek. She shook hands with Grace, who didn't look like the hugging sort. Or not until one knew her better, at least.

'How are you all?' she demanded of the Land Girls with a grin, and was being regaled with their news when a car horn sounded outside in the lane, and more new arrivals soon crowded into the garden.

Selina gasped. 'Alice!' she cried, rushing over to greet Violet's youngest niece, who was wearing a smart linen dress smoothed over a slightly rounded belly. 'Oh my goodness . . . Joan's just had a baby, and now I hear your aunt Violet is also expecting. Not you too?'

'Blame Patrick,' Alice grinned.

'Eh?' Her husband looked wide-eyed. 'I seem to recall, my darling, that it was six of one and half a dozen of the other.' He shook Selina's hand. 'Good to see you again. You're looking very smart.' His gaze flicked to William, hovering nearby, and he added in a murmur, 'And that must be the solicitor. Alice has been gossiping on the telephone to Caroline, you understand.'

Blushing, Selina shook her head at them both. 'Stop it . . . Anyway, congratulations. Everyone, *but everyone*, seems to be producing babies at the moment. What on earth is going on?'

'Britain's repopulation programme, of course,' William said calmly, leaning in to shake Alice's and Patrick's hands. 'It's not unexpected, only nature redressing a balance. Hello, I'm William MacGregor, pleased to meet you both.'

Selina turned gratefully to accept a fresh cup of tea from Joan, and saw that Lily had followed her sister into the garden, tall and smart in a green frock with matching heels. Her husband Tristan was on her arm, young Morris toddling after them excitedly, his wild ginger curls catching the sunlight brilliantly. Though Selina realised he could hardly be a toddler anymore, especially when he made a beeline for Faith. The two young children stared at each other for a moment before Faith handed him one of her snapdragons and pulled him down onto the grass to play with her, chattering in a lively fashion.

'How do you do?' William was saying in a friendly manner, introducing himself to Lily and Tristan. No, Selina thought, watching her prospective husband with secret amusement, he would have no trouble fitting in with her friends . . .

'No Demelza and Robert?' she asked Lily after they'd hugged.

'Robert was needed to mind the farm, and Demelza's got baby Petunia to care for now, as well as little Teresa . . . Oh yes,' she added, laughing as Selina's eyes widened, 'Dem had her second back in May, didn't you hear? The number of nappies and baby clothes we've been washing . . . The farmhouse has been like a veritable laundry all summer!' She turned to make a quip to Alice about how her own hands would soon be pruny from washing nappies too, and the two sisters were soon joking and giggling as though they'd never been apart.

Selina stood drinking tea and smiling while she listened to everyone chattering at once. It was as though a flock of noisy starlings had descended on Joan and Arthur's idyllic cottage garden. She caught Caroline's eye, who rose discreetly to join her. 'I meant to say I got your letter,' Selina whispered in her ear. 'I perfectly understand why you didn't want to say any of that on the telephone. So your parents turned up at the farm to take you home? How dreadful of them . . . But at least they went away empty-handed.'

'Yes, Grace terrified them into giving up. Gran quite liked the farm. I told her I'd stay in touch. But only Christmas cards for the foreseeable future.'

'That's a shame. Family is so important. But in your case . . .' Selina studied Caroline's girlfriend with interest. 'Grace seems awfully brave. And a good friend to have on your side.' She paused, spotting a secret smile on Caroline's face. Something had changed since her last visit, she felt sure. 'In your letter, you also said Joe had told you he couldn't keep any Land Girls on after harvest time. That made me rather furious. After all our hard work too . . . But I suppose it was inevitable. Things are gradually getting back to the way they were before the war.'

'Women back in the kitchen, men back in the workplace, you mean?' Caroline sounded bitter.

'Awful, isn't it?' Finishing her tea, Selina put the cup and saucer aside. 'You know, we badly need skilled groundsmen at Thornton Hall, but it's so isolated, it's hard to recruit them. Our current man is planning to retire next year and move upcountry with his son. It strikes me that if you and maybe Grace are both looking for work on the land . . . Well, *groundswomen* are as good as groundsmen in my book, and there'd be a cottage you could share that goes with the job.'

'Oh, Selina . . .' Tears sprang to Caroline's eyes as she realised what Selina was proposing. 'I don't know what to say.'

'Discuss it with Grace and let me know. Though it was William who suggested it in the first place, so all thanks should go to him.'

Caroline's eyes widened. 'William? Does . . . Does he know that . . . ?'

'That you and Grace are *a couple*?' Selina mouthed the last words rather than speaking them out loud. 'Yes, of course. I hope you don't mind me telling him. But he and I . . . We're going to be married this autumn and will live at Thornton Hall with the children.'

'Oh, congratulations!' To her relief, Caroline seemed genuinely pleased.

'We're just waiting until they can rig up a suitable office at the hall, so William doesn't need to drive into Bodmin every day. He'll be taking on a lower caseload too, to make life easier, given that we'll have Bella's children to care for together.' She blushed rosily. 'And maybe one or two of our own.'

'Goodness. Kids too?' Caroline hugged her. 'I wish you both very happy.'

'Thank you.' Selina grinned, adding with a rush, 'He's even bringing his mother to live with us too, as she's partially invalided these days and he doesn't want her to be alone. She's a lovely woman and I've been madly busy adapting a downstairs room for her. I hope she likes what I've done with it.'

'I'm sure she'll be thrilled, Selly. But listen, do you really want me and Grace on your doorstep every day? Two young women living together? Won't people talk?'

'Frankly, I don't give a stuff.' Selina was feeling defiant. 'I'm sick of people telling women how to behave. Women did men's work all through that blasted war . . . Yes, and often better than the men themselves. We deserve to live our lives however we damn well choose!'

'Hear, hear,' William murmured, bringing them a bowl of gleaming strawberries. 'Maybe you can begin by choosing whether you'd prefer strawberries with sugar or cream.' And they all laughed.

The next day, they all set off on foot together, walking to church for Sheila Newton's marriage to Bernard Bailey. Selina had taken the children aside after breakfast and told them that she and William would be getting married later that year. She had half expected them to be unhappy; children often disliked changes to their routines. But, to her relief, Peter took the news with surprising maturity, shaking William's hand and wishing them both happy. Jemima hugged her and beamed. Faith simply ran in circles, giggling happily.

'There you go,' William murmured, taking her arm as they set off for church. 'Piece of cake.'

'I was terrified they wouldn't like the idea.' Selina heaved a sigh. 'Once again, I underestimated them.' She found herself smiling though, her steps a little lighter as she realised that everything was going to work out. 'I've got to stop doing that.'

It was a marvellously sunny day, the green Cornish hills bathed in brilliant sunshine, a light sea breeze snapping at dresses and locks of hair. She smelt salt and heard the whisper of the tide washing in over the pure white sands of the bay. Soon, Selina thought with a delicious shiver, she would be going to church as a bride, with William waiting for her before the altar. Faith would make a wonderful flower girl, and Jemima a charming bridesmaid. Peter was rather too old to be a pageboy. But perhaps he could be best man. She suggested this to William, who thought about it and then nodded. 'I'd like that,' he told her with a smile. 'An inspired suggestion, if I may say so.'

Behind them came Lily and Tristan, holding little Morris's hand. And just ahead, pushing Felix in his pram, walked Joan and Arthur.

Arthur had enjoyed a lengthy heart-to-heart with Peter yesterday, Joan had told her in the evening. Tears had been shed, and not just by Peter. But apparently Arthur had every confidence in the boy's ability to work through his grief and return to being happy and contented, even if he would never quite lose the pain of Bella's death. Selina had spoken to Peter herself earlier that morning, and been relieved by his level mood. She had done the right thing, arranging to stay with Joan and Arthur over the wedding weekend. Now at least she felt more confident that her nephew was well on the road to recovery, and might yet be able to return to formal education, perhaps at a local school where she could keep an eye on his progress.

At the church, they found a crowd of well-wishers, friends and family, all chatting as they waited for the bride to arrive. The groom was already in the church, according to Reverend Clewson, who was floating about in his white clerical robes with his usual air of panic, trying to herd everyone into their seats in good time. But nobody was willing to move, not in this fine weather, with the sun beating down and the scent of flowers everywhere. Besides, they were all too busy catching up on gossip . . .

Alice and Patrick were standing with Alice's dad, Ernest Fisher. He turned to shake hands with William, looking him up and down with interest. 'Ah, Selina's intended . . . You're a solicitor in Bodmin, I understand? Tell me, what do you think of this Michael Foot fellow? His father Isaac was MP there for years . . .' And the two men stood talking about politics while Selina chatted to Alice and her husband.

'Hello, stranger,' a familiar voice came from behind, and Selina turned in astonishment to see her old friend Penny standing there, her husband John by her side.

'Penny!' she exclaimed, and hugged the former Land Girl. 'It's been ages, I swear . . .'

'Another year, another wedding,' Penny said flippantly. 'We always seem to meet in a churchyard. Don't you remember last time? I had the most horrid hairstyle. Better now, though, don't you think?' She patted her brown curls, which sat neatly on her shoulders. 'John wants me to grow it long. Easy for him to say, though. He doesn't have to wash it over a sink in a fisherman's cottage.'

Selina shook hands with John, who was grinning. The burly fisherman gave her a wink, glancing towards William.

'That your new fancy man?' John drawled in his thick Cornish accent.

'Fiancé, thank you. William MacGregor.' William turned his head and Selina hurriedly introduced them, saying, 'Penny and I were Land Girls at the farm long before Joan came along. In fact, Penny, Caroline and I were the original three at Postbridge Farm. Though it all seems so long ago now.'

'Well, I remember it like it was yesterday,' Penny retorted, her bright gaze narrowed on Selina's face. 'If you recall, you and I fell out over a boy. That's why I left. You thought I was making eyes at someone you fancied, so you and Caroline browbeat me for days over it. Not that I'm complaining . . . After all, if I hadn't moved to Bude, I would never have met John. And he's the love of my life, so I suppose I should be grateful to you for being so . . .' She paused, her chest heaving.

'Careful now, Pen.' John took his wife's hand.

'I was only going to say *forthright*,' Penny finished in a burst, but Selina didn't believe her. 'Oh, and did you hear about Eva and Max? She's expecting again. This will be her second child.' Eva had been a glamorous friend of Violet and Hazel Cotterill back in the day, who'd kept in touch with them all in Porthcurno after moving to London with her husband Max, a handsome American pilot. 'I bet she's still a smashing dancer, though,' Penny added enviously.

'Everyone is pregnant,' Selina complained, throwing up her hands.

'Well, I'm not.' Penny looked dissatisfied.

'Not for want of trying,' her loving husband pointed out.

'Early days yet,' Selina said into the silence that followed, trying to sound encouraging. 'One day, I'm sure . . .'

William, sensing a change in the conversation was required, cleared his throat. 'I believe that's the bride arriving. Shall we go inside?'

They turned to find Mrs Newton marching sturdily along the path to the church, resplendent in a pink linen dress with a plunge bodice and a vast corsage of white satin appliqué flowers sewn to one shoulder, a bouquet clutched in her hand, Joe Postbridge by her side. Her heels clacked on the path as she came to a halt beside them. 'Why aren't you lot in church yet?' Alice's gran demanded, puffing a little as she adjusted her bodice. 'I'm not taking my vows to Bernard Bailey with a load of scrapin' and shufflin' going on behind me. Go on, get inside.' She smiled at Penny as an afterthought. 'Hello, love, nice to see you again.'

'Nice to see you too, Mrs Newton. Congratulations! Is Mr Postbridge giving you away? I think that's a lovely idea,' Penny replied breathlessly while being dragged away by her husband. 'And so sorry. We'll be in our seats in a jiffy, honest.'

Selina and William dashed after them into the church, thankful to see that Peter had already had the presence of mind to usher his sisters inside. Bernard Bailey stood in readiness at the altar, lean and upright in a grey pinstriped suit, his profile austere but handsome, waves of silvery hair at his temple. The bridegroom looked nervous, which Selina thought was rather sweet.

In the front pews, wedding guests in suits and hats and fancy dresses had turned, craning their necks to see who had just come in.

Caroline wagged a finger at the latecomers, looking amused. Grace was seated to one side of her, Tilly on the other, with a dark-haired lad Selina didn't recognise squeezed in rather close beside the youngest Land Girl. That must be the infamous Benny, she realised, mentioned in Caroline's letters. It seemed love was in the air for all of them that summer, she thought happily . . .

Violet too was peering around at them, Sarah Jane

fidgeting and kneeling up mischievously beside her. Ernest Fisher sat bolt upright on her other side, holding a squirming Morris on his knee, with his two fair-haired daughters Lily and Alice, along with their husbands, sitting in a row beside him.

In the pews opposite, Penny and John were hurriedly shuffling into place beside Joan and Arthur and baby Felix. Beyond them, she could see Mrs Newton's sister Margaret blubbing into a hanky, a wiry lady in a floppy hat keeping her company. Half a dozen ginger-haired cherubs also sat crowded into the pew, giggling and whispering incessantly, while the Reverend Clewson frowned down on them to no avail.

Selina suspected these must be the Treedy children; she'd heard from Caroline that the oldest boy, Jack, had already grown bored with Australia and was sailing home again, much to his mother's delight. Apparently though, the intrepid lad had his sights set on America next.

Nearby sat Hazel and George Cotterill with their pretty young daughter Lily, a rosy-cheeked baby Dickie gurgling and bouncing on Hazel's knee. The church was absolutely *crammed* full of children, Selina realised, and felt again that strange urge to be bouncing one of her own offspring on her knee . . .

'Ladies first,' William murmured in her ear as she hesitated. 'And top gear, please. Mrs Newton is at the church door.'

Embarrassed, Selina fairly sped down the aisle until she reached the pew where Peter, Jemima and Faith sat eagerly awaiting them.

'Phew, we made it,' Selina gasped as she slid into the pew.

'Yes, we certainly did,' William agreed, sliding in beside

her, a little breathless too. With a smile meant only for her, he raised her hand to his lips and kissed it, just as the organ began to play and the congregation shuffled to their feet to welcome the bride.

EPILOGUE

August 1947, Dagenham, East London

'Where in Gawd's name are you taking me, Bernard Bailey?' Sheila demanded for about the tenth time since they'd left the hotel. He'd only told her as the train pulled out of Penzance in a cloud of steam that he'd decided on a London honeymoon, and it was no use complaining that she didn't want to go back to the Big Smoke because the whole trip was booked and paid for.

After they'd checked into their posh hotel and left the bags there, her new husband had hailed a passing taxicab. Then he'd insisted on blindfolding her, for goodness' sake, giving the cabbie directions in such a low voice that she hadn't caught a word . . . Though the journey had taken so long, she'd begun to think he was kidnapping her.

'What must I look like, eh?' Sheila complained, reluctantly allowing Bernie to steer her around, only able to see a strip of light under her nose and a flash of dirty pavement below that. 'Wandering the streets with a blindfold on? Blimey . . .

Some joker'll come up and play "pin the tail on the donkey" if you're not careful!'

'Patience,' Bernie told her, also for about the tenth time. 'We're nearly there.'

'Well, you could have got the cabbie to stop a little closer.' She clung on to him, almost missing the kerb as he steered her across a busy street. 'Bless me, I nearly fell there . . . Barely married five minutes, already you're trying to bump me off. I thought we'd have at least a few happy years of marriage before you got that bloomin' desperate.'

Chuckling, Bernie guided her around a street corner. The sound of traffic was more muted now. In the distance, she heard the whistle of a factory shift ending. A clink of bottles from a delivery van. A front door slammed shut. Voices passed them by, some laughter, people muttering . . .

Under the blindfold, Sheila tensed, catching her breath. There was something familiar about the acrid smell of the air, and the sounds of everyday life all around them . . .

'Bernie,' she whispered as he came to a halt, 'where are we?'

At last, his hands came up to release the blindfold, and she blinked, adjusting to the sharp light of summer, before gazing about herself in wonder.

'Gawd blimey,' she moaned, and began to cry. 'Oh my saints . . .'

'Hush, it's all right.'

'What have you done? Why have you brought me here?'

'What's the matter, Sheila?' Bernie cupped her shaking cheek, wiping away a tear. 'I thought you'd be pleased. Since we're staying in London a full week . . . I know we're visiting Alice and Patrick tomorrow, but I couldn't not bring you back to your old haunts first.'

Your old haunts . . .

Sheila turned on her heel, slowly taking in the dusty brick houses in their narrow rows, the spaces where a building or two had taken a direct hit, like a gaping hole in a row of teeth. There was still rubble blocking some gates, or pushed aside for workmen to go in and out. Bits of the insides of houses hanging out for all the world to see. Wallpaper, someone's ruined sofa, a tattered curtain flapping where a window used to be . . .

It felt as though someone had hollowed her out. She stood speechless, trembling. Then somehow found her voice.

'Gladys lived there . . .' She lifted a shaking hand to point at one of the houses, where a young woman stood briskly sweeping the step, her hair tied up in a scarf. 'Her dad's name was Norman. He worked as a butcher. Oh, he was a proper gent. Used to give us special cuts of meat on the cheap. Always let you put it on the slate if you didn't have the cash.' She smiled sadly. 'When the war kicked off, he was the man you went to when you needed something on the black market, no questions asked. He knew everybody, Norman did.'

'Maybe that's Gladys grown up,' Bernie said helpfully.

'No,' she said emphatically, shaking her head. 'Norman was killed in a direct strike on their Anderson shelter. Him, and his wife, and poor little Gladys too. She was only sixteen. Lily was at school with her. Gawd, she cried for days when she heard the news . . .' Sheila rummaged for her hanky, adding hoarsely, 'Oh, what did you bring me back here for, Bernie? I don't want these memories . . . They hurt too much.' She jabbed herself in the chest. 'Right 'ere.'

'Darling, I'm so sorry.' Chastened, Bernie pulled her close, and they stood together for a long time. People walked around them, looking curiously at Sheila while she averted her face. 'I'm an idiot. It was a mistake to bring you here. Please forgive me.'

But she shook her head. 'No, it's not your fault. It was the war, that's all. People got killed. And those of us who didn't . . .' With a loud sniff, she dried her tears. 'Well, you know as well as I do . . . You had to keep going somehow. Put it out of your mind. But coming back here now, looking at what we lost in the war, our old lives, everything we loved, my daughter Betsy . . .' She stopped, unable to go on.

'I take it you wouldn't rather come back to live in Dagenham, then?' he asked, peering at her. 'I thought perhaps . . . Now the war's over?'

'No, love.' Sheila managed a smile. 'Cornwall's my home now. That's where my family is and that's where I'm staying.'

Gently, Bernie took her arm, and she stumbled on, haunted by the ghosts of her past. But then she saw it and came to an abrupt halt.

'Oh Gawd . . . It's still standing.'

'What is?'

'Number 27.' Sheila gave a cracked laugh. 'Wait till I tell Vi and the girls. Oh, and will you look at that front door? Someone's painted it bright yellow. Well, I never.' She walked past her old house, shaking her head in disbelief. 'Looks like a bloomin' banana.'

Bernie put his arm about her, seeming relieved that she'd stopped crying. 'Listen, let's go back to the hotel, have a slap-up dinner and start our honeymoon in style. We can forget we ever came here.'

'Oh no, you don't,' Sheila told him, steering her husband

the other way. 'I don't want a slap-up meal, love. There used to be a little caff just around this corner, if it survived the bombs, and I fancy a nice cuppa tea, don't you?'

And Bernie laughed, going with her willingly.

ACKNOWLEDGEMENTS

Thank you once again to my wonderful agent Alison Bonomi for everything. Knowing you're always there for me makes all the difference and is much appreciated! Also, thanks as ever to everyone at LBA for your unstinting support and hard work.

My thanks also to the amazing team at Avon Books. Now we're at Book 8 of the Cornish Girls series, I'd like to give a big shout-out to everyone who's been involved in putting this marvellous saga series out there. For Brighter Days, on the editorial side, my grateful thanks once again to my brilliant editor Emma Grundy Haigh, and to Jess Zahra, also Maddie Wilson, Jade Craddock, and Tania Charles. Across other departments, I'm grateful to Megan Smith, Emily Hall, Jessie Whitehead, Hannah Lismore, Angela Thomson, Emily Gerbner, Jean-Marie Kelly, Sophia Wilhelm, Francesca Tuzzeo, Melissa Okusanya, Hannah Stamp, Katie Buckley, Emily Scorer, and Aisling Smyth. Thank you all for your hard work, attention to detail, and inspired contributions!

A massive thank you to my five lovely grown-up kids – for

being there, and for the cuppas that keep me going when on a deadline – and to my long-suffering husband Steve for not minding that he married a novelist with her head always stuck in her latest novel while burning his dinner.

I must also thank my characters for having been such fun to write these past five years, especially perhaps Gran (Sheila Newton). If any of these characters is based even loosely on me, it would be Gran. Except for all the home-made sloe gin, honest!

Finally, a huge thank you to my readers, whose affection for the Cornish Girls and their courageous exploits during the forties continues to amaze and humble me. Thank you all from the bottom of my heart. I couldn't do any of this without you, and that's a fact. I hope you enjoy reading *Brighter Days for the Cornish Girls* as much as I enjoyed writing it.

Betty x

Go back to where it all began – don't miss the first book in the glorious Cornish Girls series …

Available now in paperback, eBook and audiobook.

Follow up with some festive fun for the Cornish Girls …

Available now in paperback,
eBook and audiobook.

Can the bonds of motherhood give them the strength they'll need to get through the war? …

Available now in paperback, eBook and audiobook.

Can love still thrive in the uncertainty of war?

Available now in paperback, eBook and audiobook.